"The Other Wor
lost science oper
in the very heart

"There's A Wol
Niven—In a land of clean air and fusion bombs, of
werewolves and trolls, how long can a man of industry
survive?

"Many Mansions" *by Robert Silverberg*—Is murder by
time travel the only way to a fulfilling marriage?

From the best-selling author of the HORSECLANS AND
CASTAWAYS IN TIME series comes this amazing
collection—a tour of the Earth the day after tomorrow or
a moment before yesterday, when one person's tamper-
ing with time can create whole new worlds. . . .

ROBERT ADAMS'
BOOK OF
ALTERNATE
WORLDS

ROBERT ADAMS'
BOOK OF
ALTERNATE
WORLDS

Edited by
ROBERT ADAMS
MARTIN H. GREENBERG
& PAMELA CRIPPEN ADAMS

A SIGNET BOOK

NEW AMERICAN LIBRARY

NAL BOOKS ARE AVAILABLE AT QUANTITY DISCOUNTS
WHEN USED TO PROMOTE PRODUCTS OR SERVICES. FOR
INFORMATION PLEASE WRITE TO PREMIUM MARKETING
DIVISION. NEW AMERCIAN LIBRARY. 1633 BROADWAY.
NEW YORK. NEW YORK 10019.

Acknowledgments

"The Other World" by Murray Leinster. Copyright © 1949 by Standard
Publications, Inc. Reprinted by permission of the agents for the au-
thor's Estate, the Scott Meredith Literary Agency, Inc., 845 Third
Avenue, New York, NY 10022.

"Target: Berlin" by George Alec Effinger. Copyright © 1976 by Robert
Silverberg. Reprinted by permission of the author.

"Adept's Gambit" by Fritz Leiber. Copyright © 1968 by Fritz Leiber.
Reprinted by permission of Richard Curtis Associates, Inc.

"Last Enemy" by H. Beam Piper. Copyright © 1950 by Street and Smith
Publications, Inc. Reprinted by permission of the agents for the au-
thor's Estate, the Scott Meredith Literary Agency, Inc., 845 Third
Avenue, New York, NY 10022.

"Aristotle and the Gun" by L. Sprague de Camp. Copyright © 1958 by
Street and Smith Publications, Inc.; renewed © 1986 by L. Sprague de
Camp. Reprinted by permission of the author.

"There's a Wolf in My Time Machine" by Larry Niven. Copyright ©
1971 by Mercury Press, Inc. From The Magazine of Fantasy and Science
Fiction. Reprinted by permission of Kirby McCauley, Ltd.

"Many Mansions" by Robert Silverberg. Copyright © 1973 by Agberg,
Ltd. Reprinted by permission of the author and Agberg, Ltd.

"Remember the Alamo!" by T. R. Fehrenbach. Copyright © 1961 by
Condé Nast Publications, Inc. Reprinted by permission of the author.

"One Way Street" by Jerome Bixby. Copyright © 1954 by Ziff-Davis
Publishing Co., Inc.; renewed © 1982 by Jerome Bixby. Reprinted by
permission of the author.

SIGNET, SIGNET CLASSIC, MENTOR, ONYX, PLUME, MERIDIAN
and NAL BOOKS are published by NAL PENGUIN INC.,
1633 Broadway, New York, New York 10019

First Printing, July, 1987

1 2 3 4 5 6 7 8 9

PRINTED IN THE UNITED STATES OF AMERICA

CONTENTS

INTRODUCTION

What if . . . ?

How would our world be today if . . . ?

Alternate-world stories are, especially for the history buff, among the most exciting and entertaining of the many subgenres of science fiction/fantasy literature. Although I am certain that I must have read stories of this type between the time that I was eight years old—when I first discovered pulp magazines and the wonders they held for a kid who did not need funnybook pictures to aid him in fantasizing—and my twentieth birthday, the first one that made a distinct and lasting impression upon me was *Lest Darkness Fall*, by L. Sprague de Camp. That was in an army hospital in the fifties, and the book came off a Red Cross cart, having been donated by some patriotic soul.

To a guy who loved history, this was meat and potatoes, so as soon as they would let me out of bed, I began actively searching for more of the same, and found some. I have found more and more of the precious, enthralling stuff over the years, have even written some myself, in my CAST-AWAYS IN TIME series for Signet Books.

Fortunately for the reader but most unfortunately for the harried anthologist, the majority of the better alternate-world stories run to at least novella if not to actual novel length and are, therefore, not easily included in a work of the following sort. However, despite this obstacle, I think that my collaborators and I have herein given the reader a fair sampling of alternate-world tales by some of the true masters of the genre.

THE OTHER WORLD

by Murray Leinster

Murray Leinster was the name used by the late (1896–1975) Will F. Jenkins, one of the great pioneer writers of American magazine science fiction. Known for decades as the "Dean of Science Fiction," Leinster earned his living as a freelance writer from 1918 until his death. Although he wrote in many genres, including the mystery and the Western, he is best known for his work in sf, where he published well over fifty novels and short story collections. He won the Hugo Award for his story "Exploration Team" in 1956 and was Guest of Honor at the 1963 World Science Fiction Convention. His finest short stories can be found in The Best of Murray Leinster *(1978).*

Dick Blair dug up a Fifth Dynasty tomb in Lower Egypt and found that one object, and one only, had been spoiled by dampness in a climate which preserved all the other objects in the tomb to perfection. Almost simultaneously, in New York, a plumber carrying a kit of tools turned into a doorway on Eighth Avenue and was never seen again, living or dead. Shortly after, a half-ton of dried figs vanished inexplicably from a locked warehouse in Smyrna, and—in New York—a covered barge complete with a load of bricks and building materials evaporated into thin air while a night watchman gazed goggled-eyed. His account of the event was not believed.

There were other pertinent events even before these. One year in New York's history, the number of missing persons who had no reason to vanish went up to four times normal. Most missing persons have their reasons for disappearing, but there are always a few who seem neither to have been murdered nor to have absconded. This year the number of such cases was unprecedented, and there was no explanation for it at all.

There was the time seventy-five years before when the four

prettiest members of a theatrical chorus went upstairs to doff their winter wraps in the home of a rich man who was giving a party, and never came down again. Then there was that indubitable werewolf which was killed in Avino province in Italy, in the 1850s. It was classed only tentatively as wolf because it had some oddities of conformation, but it had intelligence at least equal to that of the peasants on whom it had preyed for two weeks before its destruction. It had killed and partly or wholly devoured twenty-two human beings in two weeks. The scientists of the time were very much annoyed when enraged peasants stormed the place where it was held for examination and burned the carcass to ashes.

Before that, there was the well-attested disappearance of the carriage of a semiroyal princeling in the Tyrol. It went around a curve in the carriage road, and riding-foot-men a hundred yards behind found it utterly gone when they rounded the curve in their turn. Six horses, a coachman and footman, and two of the princeling's mistresses—one of whom was said to be the most beautiful woman in Europe at the time—vanished in the twinkling of an eye and no trace was ever found of any of them. And still earlier there was that shipload of immigrants to the United States which was sighted only forty miles off Sandy Hook, pressing forward with all sail set on a perfectly fair day, which never reached harbor and from which not one particle of wreckage was ever found.

When these items are put together, they add up convincingly to mere nonsense. The farther back into history one delves, the less credible the affairs become.

*But Dick Blair dug up a Fifth Dynasty tomb in Egypt and found that exactly one object had been ruined by dampness in a rock-hewn vault in which every other object had remained absolutely dry from the time of its entombment. That object meant the second discovery of the Other World and an explanation—*an* explanation—for very many mysteries which date back to the time of the Fifth Dynasty, five thousand years ago.

When he got back to New York, Dick Blair was very busy for a while, but at last, one night, he took a mass of greenish clay

*What follows has been cast in the form of fiction for obvious reasons. For one thing, it is extremely unlikely to be quoted in any newspaper. For another, it is extremely undesirable that any considerable group of people should take it for fact while any sizable residue of unexplained disappearances occur. —**Murray Leinster**

to his friend Tom Maltby. Dick was then only partly bleached out from the Egyptian sun, where he had dug out a previously untouched Fifth Dynasty tomb. But civilization already bored him. He was inclined to mourn the humdrumness of life in New York.

"This," he told Maltby, "is a hunk of dirt. It's colored with oxides, and once upon a time it contained something made by a worthy Egyptian at least five thousand years ago. At the Museum we're pretty good at re-forming objects that have been corroded past recognition, but we have to have at least a sliver of metal to work on. The X-rays say this is absolutely gone."

He handed over the X-ray negatives. They showed the distribution of the denser metallic oxides in the lump of clay. Maltby looked at them interestedly.

"With a sliver of the original metal left," Dick observed, "we run a contact down to it, use it as a cathode, run about a quarter-ampere to it for six months or so, and the oxides break down and the metal goes back to the shape it was originally in. It's amazing how detailed the things get sometimes. We even find the original decorations. But this one beats us."*

Maltby nodded.

"That's what I want. I said I'd try to work out an improvement on your system. It's in my line."

Maltby was a consulting engineer specializing in the prevention of electrolytic damage by earth currents. Every public utility has at least one engineer whose specialty is the prevention of damage of this type. Maltby was tops in the field. He'd checked the destruction of a very famous bridge, he had doctored a very modern skyscraper whose foundation piles were being corroded even in their concrete sheaths, and his process for restoring rusted objects underground was not unlike museum methods for rebuilding prehistoric relics.

He put down the dried clay and mixed two drinks. Dick Blair settled down comfortably.

"That hunk of dirt is now officially your property," he observed, "which is my doing. It may be a copper pot or pan or anything at all. I can't figure out how it rusted. The place was absolute, stony, desiccated desert without a drop of water for miles. The tomb was bone-dry and nothing else showed any trace of damage by moisture. Where'd the moisture come from?"

This is literally true, and standard museum practice. Provided that the corroded metal in the clay has not been disturbed, excellent reversals of rusting processes are obtained and artifacts which would have been unrecognizable are regularly restored to a condition suitable for exhibition and study. —**Murray Leinster.**

Maltby sipped at his drink. Dick went on:

"More oddities about that tomb—it's occupant wasn't a king, but he was fitted out for the afterlife in royal style! There were more imported objects in that tomb than you could shake a stick at. There was stuff from Cyprus, from Phœnicia, from Ethiopia, from Mycenæ, and slathers of regular Egyptian stuff. The writings in the tomb are weird. He was a sort of royal physician and miracle-worker, who happened to be cousin to the Pharaoh. There was a papyrus on medicine which is going to raise the devil! You simply can't translate it except as a description of the circulation of the blood—forty-seven hundred years before modern men knew of it. Another scroll is crazier. It describes animals which simply don't exist. The prize is a description of a small horse with three toes. I may add that the eohippus did not survive until his time. How'd he get such an idea?"

Maltby shrugged.

"Fairy tales can't always be wrong," he said. "Make enough fantastic statements, and some are bound to be right. You'd have trouble showing me there was modern knowledge fifty centuries ago, papyri or no papyri."

Dick Blair grinned. "The old chap in the tomb had modern ideas. I don't know whether you know it, but there were Pharaohs who never had even civil wars, much less foreign ones. He claimed he handled that for his cousin. Anybody who even thought evil of the king died mysteriously. And he boasted of the dirt he did to the King of Cyprus of his time. Magic, but modern."

Maltby raised his eyebrows. Dick went on zestfully:

"His funeral boasts say that a King of Cyprus had a pretty daughter and the then Pharaoh sent a message demanding her for his harem. The King of Cyprus refused. So before his whole court he vanished in a pool of quicksilver. My old gent declares he worked that. The King of Cyprus' son got ready to fight, but instead he and all his family—including the princess—died in a palace which poured out flames at every window. The next ruler was suitably abject and sent tribute. Nearly the same process happened in Phœnicia, Ethiopia and Mycenæ."

Maltby looked at the lump of clay. He said mildly, "Such a potent magician must have put a curse on his tomb in case anybody should rob it. Don't tell me he omitted that!"

Dick grinned again, and then said in sudden half-seriousness:
"Speaking of curses, an odd thing happened in Alexandria

while I was there. The very pretty daughter of one of the richest men in town vanished from her bed; with two maidservants watching her. She vanished in a pool of quicksilver. They screamed like all hell, and all her father did was throw dust on his head and die of a broken heart. That one made the newspapers, but the old *sheykhs* of Alexandria weren't surprised. They said it happens occasionally and has since time began. The funny thing is that the quicksilver business—"

He stopped and looked startled. Maltby said: "That King of Cyprus you mentioned?"

"Y-yes," said Dick blankly. "I never thought of the connection before. Odd, isn't it?"

Maltby said deliberately, "I know a chap who is digging into criminology. He's a queer duck. He has all the money in the world, but he's working like a beaver to set himself up as a consulting criminologist. And he says that he can't understand some records he's found. It seems there are several records of things disappearing in pools of quicksilver right here in New York. It doesn't make sense, and nobody's ever believed it. I must tell him about the King of Cyprus."

Dick blinked.

"That's crazy! In the Middle East quicksilver is considered more or less magical—"

"Mirages on a motor road look like quicksilver," observed Maltby. "I've seen a film of gas, formed in an electrolyte, look like it too. . . . Now I'm going to set up my apparatus for your hunk of clay."

He got out his gadgets. He had devised this particular setup to work out his corrosion-reversal process for buildings. It was laboratory-size only, but it would serve for the clay. There was a plastic box with electrodes at its sides. He packed the relic into the box, filling the unoccupied space with more clay. A high-frequency oscillator came into play.

"There's no metal in this stuff to serve as a cathode," he observed, "and it's just as well. I'm setting up a standing wave in the middle of this clay mess. There'll be a constant potential difference between the middle and the outer surface. When the clay's moistened there'll be a steady flow of plating-out current from every direction toward the center. Presently some particle of metal will establish itself. Maybe several. I may have a dozen centers of potential—they'll establish themselves wherever the oxide is densest. Then we'll see what happens. I think the result should be pretty good, but it'll take time."

"At the museum," said Dick, "we figure on six months."

"I estimate two weeks," said Maltby dryly. "My current flow depends on the ions present, not on power fed to it. I'm not feeding current in at all. It makes its own."

He arranged a moistening solution so that the clay would gradually acquire an even moisture content. He turned on the oscillator and brushed off his hands.

"Now we wait. Have another drink?"

"No-o," said Dick. "Just what did you mean by that quicksilver business? It's odd to hear a story like that in New York. I didn't believe the one in Alexandria, though the local inhabitants did. And it's absurd to link them with an ancient papyrus with the same yarn in it!"

"I didn't mean a thing," admitted Maltby. "You spoke of a girl vanishing, and quicksilver, and of a forgotten king vanishing, and quicksilver. So I remembered Sam Todd telling me about a safe that was opened only a month ago in a perfume factory, and the flasks of essential oils worth up to hundreds of dollars an ounce vanishing in as many tiny pools of quicksilver. It seemed odd, so I mentioned it. That's all."

"I'd like to talk to this Sam Todd," said Dick. "I hate to be silly, but that's too damned queer—"

Dick Blair went about his business, which was partly that of relaxation just now. He'd been through a grueling grind in Egypt, and probably had a few tropical germs in his system which it would be a good idea to get out. He gave a lecture or two, wrote a magazine article, and kept himself available for consultation if needed by the Museum staff. But mostly he rested.

He met Sam Todd and found him a kindred soul who was, at the moment, almost ready to achieve his great ambition—to become a consulting criminologist with something to offer his clients. His material on quicksilver-pool disappearances and thefts was fascinating. The list went back for over seventy-five years. The tales were so impossible that it was only rarely that they had ever reached print, and that made it the more remarkable that on at least a dozen occasions the same story was told by persons who could not have heard of the others. A famous stallion vanished and when a groom looked in his stall there were four little pools of quicksilver descending to the floor. The horse was gone. There were other quicksilver droplets scattered here and there about the straw bedding on the floor, but they vanished too. No quicksilver was found when the stall was searched afterward. The old Delmonico's was robbed of priceless wines. The wine bottles disappeared in round and oblong pools of quicksilver, which afterwards vanished too. Only one person saw them. There was the disappearance of an obscure dancer—by no means talented—who had been said to be the prettiest girl on the New York stage that season. Her dresser, and a stagehand called by the dresser's shrieks, claimed that they saw quicksilver as the girl vanished. That quicksilver could not be found, either.

The only common factor in all the tales was the absence of a sequel. Not one of the vanished things, whether persons or goods, had ever been found again. No corpus delicti. No underworld boastings. Nothing.

All of this brought Dick's curiosity to the point where it became almost an obsession. Then he met Nancy Holt. Sam Todd had employed her to do research for him; she would be part of his staff when he opened his office. He thought a great deal of her brains, but the only personal fact he had noted about her was that she used a strictly personal perfume, which she said was made from a recipe of her grandmother's.

But Dick Blair saw her as the one girl on earth whom he could not possibly let anybody else marry. He fell hard the first time he saw her. By the third time he was sunk so completely that she knew it too. And then he had an occupation which was at once relaxing and absorbing. He got busy trying to make her fall in love with him.

Meanwhile, the electrolytic reconstruction of the object in the plastic box went on. After four days, X-rays showed half a dozen small bits of solid metal in the clay. In six they had joined, three of them to form the beginning of a round flat disk, and the others still separated at odd angles to it. In eight days they were all joined. There was an irregular disk some four inches in diameter. It had a rod projecting from one side, and there were two branches from the rod. In ten days the object was recognizable. It was a ceremonial mirror with a cruciform handle, a *crux ansata*, part of an Egyptian Pharaoh's royal regalia through all the years down to Alexander the Great. Its significance was that the Pharaoh was monarch not only of this world, but of the Other World beyond.

The outlines of the one in the clay were still rough. It was still being re-formed by the current the standing waves induced. Two days later the X-rays showed an odd, disk-shaped shadow that Maltby could not understand. On the fourteenth day he had still made no sense of it at all, but the X-rays indicated that all metal in the clay had been returned to its original shape. The object was as completely restored as Maltby's apparatus could make it. He called Dick on the phone to come and uncover it, with the precautions an archæologist would take.

Dick arrived at Maltby's flat. "Dammit, I tried to get Nancy to come along, but Sam had some photographs he wants made in the Police Museum. She's busy listing the subjects for the photographer. Bludgeons and sashweights and icepicks and other objects used by various murderers to express their lethal impulses. Damn!"

"That clay mess," said Maltby mildly, "seems to have yielded a *crux ansata*. Interesting?"

"Rather early for such things," said Dick restlessly. "And that mummy shouldn't have had one in his tomb. He wasn't a king."

"I can't make out," said Maltby, "a disk that the X-rays show in the clay. It appeared quite suddenly at the very end of the process, and it's quite opaque to X-rays. Even copper lets a little hard radiation go through. Any ideas?"

Dick shook his head, still thinking of Nancy. When Maltby dumped the clay out of the plastic box, though, his interest rose. He spurned a proffered knife and briskly took a wooden spatula to carve the clay with. He looked at the X-ray negatives and placed the clay block just so. Then he made curiously surgeonlike incisions and laid the clay back cleanly. In only seconds he lifted out the golden-copper crux exactly as shown by the X-rays, and regarded it with astonishment.

"It's perfect," he said blankly, "—and there's glass!"

The four-inch disk had seemed a solid mass of metal. Now the center was plainly transparent. They could see through it. Dick put it to one side and probed for the other disk, supposedly six inches from it, which should still be buried in the clay.

It wasn't there.

He searched for minutes, until the clay lump was dissected into portions in which the imaged second disk could not be hidden.

"Queer," said Dick. "We'll use the X-ray again later. I want to look over this thing. Extraordinarily early for good glass! Really clear glass didn't turn up until late in Roman times. Maybe it's crystal."

He picked it up impatiently. He cleaned the transparent

surface from the front. He reached behind to clean the back, and his face went bewildered. He could feel the back of the mirror. It was metal. But he couldn't see his fingers. He saw through them. Beyond them.

"Now, what the devil—"

He held up the thing and looked through it. He could see Maltby and the other side of the room. He took a book and slid it past the back of the supposed glass. It did not impede the view at all. He still saw Maltby and the other side of the room. The book seemed to be perfectly transparent as it passed before the windowlike center of the disk. Then Maltby made an astounded exclamation.

"Here! Look at this!" he said sharply.

He took the *crux ansata* from Dick. He turned it over. He laid it on his desk glass side down. There was an extraordinary optical phenomenon. An infinitely thin layer of the desk's surface seemed to be lifted up six inches above the desk. Beneath it could be seen the copper back of the disk. There was empty space above it, and then a film of desktop. Which, of course, simply could not be.

"You see through it," said Maltby, rather pale, "but there's a space that the light seems to dodge around. It skips from the front side of the disk to a spot six inches this side of it. There's that much distance that the light doesn't have to pass through. Things look six inches nearer. See?"

He held the right side up and held it over the desktop. The desktop did look nearer. He pressed down—and gasped. He was looking at woodfibers inside the substance of the wood. Then his hand dropped, and he was looking inside the desk, through the top. He was examining the contents of the top desk drawer from a point above the desk's writing surface.

The two of them babbled at each other. For twenty minutes or more they made absurd experiments. The fact remained. You looked into the transparent surface of the disk, and your sight skipped the opaque metal of the other surface and started on from six inches out in midair. Nothing in that six-inch space was an impediment to vision. The mirror could be held against a six-inch wall and anything beyond the wall would be visible. It was as if the light received on a small, circular area in midair curved through some unknown dimensions and returned to its proper line at the surface of the disk.

They had agreed on so much when Dick Blair said:

"What happens if you push something through?"

He thrust his finger toward himself, staring at its end through the unbelievably ancient instrument. His finger seemed to approach to the observed six inches. Then the impossible happened. He had no sensation, but he saw inside his finger. He saw inside the flesh. He saw the bone. He saw nerve ends and capillaries—

He jerked his hand away and stared at Maltby. But Maltby was paler than Dick himself.

"I was—looking at your finger from the side," said Maltby with difficulty. "The end of it vanished. And where it vanished, the end of it—looked like quicksilver."

They doubted their own sanity, but there could be no doubt of the fact. They pushed a pencil into the impalpable place in midair. The pencil disappeared. Looked at from the side, the spot where it vanished seemed a blob of quicksilver, which moved when the pencil was moved. From the proper side of the device, they saw into the inside of the pencil.

They pushed a watch, running, into that space. Dick saw its machinery in busy movement—or half its machinery. When it was withdrawn it was unharmed.

It was Dick who without warning suddenly thrust his whole hand up to the wrist into the enigmatic space. He looked at the bones and cross section of the muscles and tendons of his wrist, while Maltby at one side saw a changing blob of quicksilver-like reflection the shape of the seemingly cut-off flesh. And then Dick said in a queer voice: "I feel something."

He stood rigid for an instant. Then he jerked his hand out. He had something in his fingers.

It was a living green leaf, freshly plucked from what must have been a tree. It was a perfectly plausible leaf. There were only two things in the least odd about it. One was that it had been plucked from nothingness in an apartment three floors above the street and remote from any vegetation at all. The other was that it wasn't the leaf of any species of plant known on earth.

It was Dick Blair who pointed out jerkily that the thing which looked into desks and through desktops and into flesh and bone had been used by its long-dead owner to study anatomy and accounted for the five-thousand-year-old description of the circulation of the blood. He could look directly into the inside of a living body. Then Maltby made incoherent noises about dimensions being at right angles to other dimensions and a field of force which made them interchangeable.

Then Dick said, stridently, that the significance of the *crux ansata* as a symbol of power over the other world had plainly once possessed a literal sense. There was another world somehow continuous to this one. It had been speculated upon since Plato was in diapers. This leaf had come from it. Which, he continued, might be an unjustified inference from inadequate data, but he was damned if he didn't believe it, and anyhow he was going to put his hand in that round space again and see what turned up—

He did. He sweated as he fumbled. He broke off a spray of leaves from an unseen source, and dragged them back. It was the eeriest of sensations to stand in a lighted, well-furnished room with all one's surroundings completely artificial, and to reach into vacancy in that well-lighted room and produce from nothingness a batch of fresh foliage completely unlike any earthly leaves.

This grab into the unseen brought back something else, too. Coiled about the branch as if feeding on a leaf, there was a tiny living thing. It was perhaps six inches long. It had enormous, inquisitive eyes, and filmy wings. At the impact of the bright lights it blinked wisely and uncoiled itself and launched itself into the air. They both saw it clearly. It hovered delicately, like a humming bird, and then darted to the window and out.

It was very small and quite harmless, but it was a serpent, a snake. It had wings. It flew. And winged serpents are not native to Earth.

The two men were quite literally babbling to each other when the bell rang and Sam Todd stumbled into the room. His face was ashen-white. He looked as if he had been drinking for weeks and had the horrors.

"Dick," he said thickly. "I—was looking for you. I had Nancy at the Police Museum. We snatched a bite to eat and I—called a cab for her. Just as it was pulling up I—smelled something queer. Not that—special perfume she used, but—something else. I looked around and—Nancy was vanishing. The top half of her was gone into thin air and there—was a big blob of—quicksilver where her waist was, and it dropped to the ground and—she was gone! Maybe I'm crazy but that's what happened . . ."

Dick Blair cried out furiously, because he knew as well as Sam that no thing and no person which had vanished in a pool of quicksilver had ever been seen again.

Then Sam lifted his head, twitching.

"Queer smell," he said thickly. "Like—lush green stuff. I smell it now! My God, I smell it now! This is what I smelled when Nancy vanished. . . ."

And then Dick and Maltby realized that their nostrils, too, were filled with an odor they had been too excited to notice before. Its origin was obvious enough. It came from *crux ansata*. And it was the smell of a jungle at night—in the heart of New York City.

For three days Maltby worked like a madman, while Dick Blair went practically insane. The worst of it was, of course, that Maltby could promise nothing. He did not dare to chip away any part of what might be called the transparent surface of the instrument from the past. He had to analyze without injuring the object he analyzed, for fear of destroying it altogether. He checked the light transmitted, and found it circularly polarized. He checked the specific gravity of the entire object to six decimal places, and checked that against the density of a morsel scraped from the end of the handle. The whole instrument was made of bismuth bronze—copper and bismuth together. Normal bronze contains zinc or tin. It became certain that only one substance was involved, and that it was the bismuth-copper alloy. There was no insert of other substance to give the instrument its properties.

In the end, microscopic examination showed that on the fine line of division where the transparent and opaque parts ran together, there was one irregularity. There was a place where for half a thousandth of an inch the metal was in an in-between state—not quite the material of the handle, and not quite the enigmatic surface through which one looked *around* normal space.

That was the clue. Maltby worked on it for twenty-four hours straight, and had a one-inch ring of transparency in a flat slab of quarter-inch copper-bismuth alloy. It was not a duplicate of the entire *crux ansata* effect, but only of a part. The *crux ansata* seemed to look into another world and then back again to Earth at a remove of six inches in space. The peephole Maltby made looked only into another world. But that was a lot.

Looking through it, Maltby saw at first only spreading tree branches and thick foliage, speckled with sunshine from an unseen source. He touched a pencil experimentally to the transparent surface and nothing happened. The transparency was not penetrable.

He called Sam Todd on the phone and commanded him to get hold of Dick and bring him there. He worked on.

When they burst into his apartment he wavered on his feet from pure weariness. But he had a second bit of copper-bismuth alloy. This one was quite opaque. But there was a spot where you could push a lead pencil into it, and it vanished and you could pull it out again if it was not allowed to go in all the way. Moreover, if you looked through the peephole into the other world, in the direction of this second opaque spot, in between the illogical foliage you could see the part of the pencil which disappeared from Earth. It enlarged and grew smaller as it was pushed or pulled from Earth, and if it was pushed all the way through it could be seen to go tumbling through the tree branches toward the ground below this jungle.

"I've got a beginning," said Maltby drearily. "I've gotten what is probably a sort of cockeyed alignment of copper crystals with bismuth, in a crazy allotropic state. Normally, light-bending seems to call for one arrangement and matter-bending calls for another. Just for simplicity I'm assuming that this—this Other World is occupying the same space as Earth, and that it's a matter of bending light to get it into that world, and to get it to come out again. It has to bend through an angle we normally can't conceive of. And I'm guessing that matter more or less bends in the same fashion. That's not clear, but I'm so tired I don't think very straight."

Dick said tensely, "What have you got ready for us?"

"I've got a one-inch peephole you can look into the other world with, and a space an inch across that you can push things through into the other world. I know how to make them, now. If I can stay awake, I can make a doorway somebody can go through."

"Get to work!" commanded Dick. "Nancy's there! You've got to get to work!"

"Agreed," grunted Maltby, "but I haven't slept for so long I can't remember it. You take this peephole and go somewhere high and look around. While I make a doorway for you, you'd better be stocking up on information."

Sam Todd said, "And guns. But I'll attend to that!"

"Since you may use a taxi," added Maltby, "you'd better carry only the peephole. If you took the thing that matter can go through, you might be driving down Fifth Avenue in our world and drive through the space a tree occupies in the other. And the tree trunk might try to come through into the cab."

"How long will it take to make the doorway?" demanded Dick.

"Maybe three hours, maybe four."

The three of them separated instantly. Dick went raging to the Empire State Building and rode to its top, where he quite insanely held a small slab of copper alloy to his eye, and looked into the Other World.

Below him there was terrain identical with Manhattan Island in form and size and shape. But it was covered with foliage of which not one leaf was recognizable. To the south there were marshes where on Earth he saw tall buildings; and flowing streams, in the Other World, coursed merrily across the paths of streets in this.

At first he saw but one sign of humanity. That was a great villa, apparently of brick, with wide and spacious lawns. But he saw no human figures about it. It was too far away, on the Brooklyn shore. Then, here and there on the twin of Manhattan Island, he saw trails winding apparently at random through the heavy woods. It was a sunny day in the Other World. Everything seemed utterly tranquil and utterly at peace. And Dick, staring with desperate intentness, made notes which identified this trail—meandering from side to side—roughly with Fifth Avenue almost beneath him, and that trail with Twenty-ninth Street. By sighting with both eyes open, one looking at Earth and the other into the Other World, he identified the position of the one vast villa as roughly south of the Navy Yard.

Then he saw movement on the trail a thousand feet below his eyrie. In the Other World a horse-drawn vehicle plodded slowly between giant tree trunks in the space otherwise occupied by Altman's. There were two human figures in the vehicle, and at first he thought them naked, before he saw loincloths about their middles. Behind the vehicle trotted a four-legged creature far too large to be a dog. But the equipage turned beneath overhanging branches and he lost sight of it.

He went uptown to Radio City. Again from a vast height he surveyed endless forests. From here, though, he saw plowed fields which before had been invisible. More, in the middle of a virgin wilderness, he saw the sunlight glinting on acres upon acres of glass. It looked extraordinarily as if hothouses sufficient to supply a small town with foodstuffs were in existence. And he thought, but he was not sure, that he saw horses pulling plows. There were two of them. If men guided them, they were too far away to be seen with the naked eye.

It seemed all peace and serenity there. But Dick, staring from a great height, knew such hatred and horror as made him tremble. This Other World lay beside the earth that men knew, in that greater cosmos men have not yet begun to visualize. And Dick had an idea of the perverted significance that had been given it. Eons since, other men had found a way to pass between the worlds. Men had moved to the Other World, with the power to return to Earth where and when they wished. And man is the most predatory of animals; his favorite prey is other men.

That first discovery had unquestionably taken place far back in the dim dawn of history, when all of civilization lay in Egypt. A scientist or a magician of that time had doubtless made the first crossing between the worlds. Perhaps he told his king and was duly slaughtered for reward, after the king had made the discovery his own. At first, perhaps, the Other World had seemed to the king merely a possible refuge from rebellious nobles or an unruly people. A fugitive king, driven from his throne by his own tyranny, could retire to the Other World and be in safety from all his enemies. He could take his women and his slaves and build a palace in which to live in perfect security. Perhaps some king did do this, fleeing from successful civil war. But in exile he would crave revenge. And what could be more obvious than to make a doorway back to Earth which would open into the bedroom of his former palace, where his successor on the throne lay asleep behind guarded doors?

Then Dick remembered a scrap of history almost lost in the mists of time. He himself had first translated an ancient papyrus which told of such a thing. There had been such a king who had gone into the afterworld and bided his time, and had come again to rule Egypt in terror and blood when all his enemies died in a single night.

That was unquestionably it. The later kings of the Fifth Dynasty had ruled more ruthlessly than any other kings of Egypt. Magic slew their enemies. Disasters overwhelmed their foes. There was no treasure they could not lay hands upon, nor any human being they could not seize or slaughter. All Earth was at their mercy, when they could walk at will into the most secret, most guarded, most hidden retreat of the normal Earth.

They would be the masters, then, those men of the Other World. They would not need to battle for loot, when loot could be taken without hindrance. They need not capture cities for

slaves, when slaves could be stolen in absolute safety from any
place where men lived.

Dick could only guess at the development of so purely parasitic a society. The robbery of gold would soon cease to have
meaning. Gold would have no more value than a clod of earth,
when it could be taken as easily. Jewels would have no more
value than so much glass. But fine fabrics and soft carpets, and
luxuries of food and drink, and horses and strong men for
slaves and pretty girls for playthings—those things would have
value. And there would be no great nation of the parasitic
Other World. It would be absurd for them to rob each other
with the Earth to loot, so they would not need to combine in
defense against each other. Their society would be anarchic.
They would set up villas, as time went on, wherever. Earth
cities promised easy supplies of luxuries and slaves. The master
of one villa would owe no allegiance to any other. Yet how
would they keep the loyalty of their guards?— because guards
against the slaves they must have.

There Dick's imagination failed him, but such faint imagin-
ings as he could contrive were enough to make him half-mad
when he got back to Maltby's place.

Sam Todd came in. He had brought guns. He began to divide
with Dick, but Dick said grimly:

"No division, Sam. I'm going through the doorway alone as
soon as Maltby has it done. You've got to stay behind. I may
need some help I can't anticipate. I need somebody cruising
about—watching through the peephole we already have—ready
to give me help if it's needed. And if both of us go through,
who's going to tell the authorities about this business and bring
help along?"

Sam laughed without amusement.

"Tell the authorities?" he asked sardonically. "How long
would they listen before they'd usher me into a padded call?
Oh, it could be done in time, but I'd need to spend weeks
convincing them that I wasn't crazy and the peephole wasn't a
trick, and then they'd refer to higher authority and they'd need
to be convinced, and then they'd decide that the democratic
procedure was to send an observer or an ambassador through.
We'll get Nancy back and then talk about such things!"

"But you'll stay behind to help me when I need it!" snapped
Dick. "You know damned well you can do that better than
Maltby! And you've more reason to do it as well as more
money to spend if it's needed. You stay behind! Look here!"

He spread out his notes on the correspondence of locations. Plowed fields near Seventieth Street, Manhattan. The great villa south of the Navy Yard on the Brooklyn shore. What looked like an enormous stretch of hothouses in the Sixties on the East Side. A road leading past the Empire State Building, curving through Altman's.

Sam accepted the memorandum. What Dick had said was true enough, but so was what he'd said himself. To wait for action by authority would be sheerest folly. There couldn't be any more delay. The two of them had to work as private adventurers to try to go to her help. There were plenty of others who needed help too, no doubt. But for speed there would have to be action without hindrance.

Presently Maltby brought in a sheet of copper foil, neatly rolled. He said wearily:

"Here it is. It's just a doorway. You can't look through it, but somebody can go through."

"I'll go through where Nancy did," said Dick grimly. "We'll get a cab and you show me the exact spot, Sam."

"All right, but we've got to arrange a way to communicate—"

"In the taxi," snapped Dick. "Come on!"

Maltby spoke like a sleepwalker, tonelessly, "We'll have to hold this thing sideways to the way we're going."

"Right! I'll carry it. Coming?"

Sam Todd picked up his burden of weapons in a bag and gun case. They went downstairs. The street seemed incredibly normal. Dick carried the rolled-up foil. They got into the cab, and it started downtown.

This was three days after the disappearance of Nancy Holt in the seeming of a pool of quicksilver. Dick Blair knew that if his guesses were right, the disappearances of humans were for their enslavement. Nancy had been a slave for three days. Sam spoke to him, and he nodded, but he hardly heard what Sam was saying.

At Thirtieth Street, Sam opened his bag and began to pass its contents to Dick. Two automatics, with ammunition. A riot-gun—a sawed-off shotgun with shells loaded with buckshot. Two small objects which were tear-gas bombs. Bars of chocolate. A canteen.

"There," said Sam to the taxi driver. "Draw up to the curb, right there."

It was a perfectly normal street in downtown New York. There was asphalt pavement, a concrete curb and sidewalk, and a streetlight. There was a hydrant. A barbershop and a small stationery store occupied the street-level shops in a building which rose skyward.

The taxi stopped. The driver turned.

"We're not getting out," said Sam smoothly. He pointed ahead. "Hasn't that car ahead got a flat?"

The taxi driver looked front. Sam unrolled the copper foil.

"Remember how to leave messages for me," he said crisply.

Dick Blair touched his pockets, where his weapons and ammunition were. He picked up the sawed-off shotgun. Without a word, he stepped into the two-foot-by-three-foot sheet of copper-bismuth foil. He stepped *down.*

Maltby was asleep, his face lined with exhaustion. He did not see what was happening.

Dick Blair vanished in a pool of quicksilver.

There was bright sunshine where he found himself. There were gigantic trees, rising apparently to the height of the buildings which had surrounded the taxicab only seconds before. He tumbled down three or four feet and fell on his hands and knees on the ground. There was sparse brushwood here, and when he straightened up he saw a crude wooden platform; built of hewn planks. It had a cagelike structure of beams upon it, with a door now open. The door had a clumsy but effective latch so that it could not possibly be opened from the inside, but could be opened from without by a mere tug on a leather thong. In any case the cage was empty and deserted, but it had been made by men.

There was music that seemed like birdsong everywhere. The brushwood was green. The particular bush on which he first cast his eyes was not only green, but leafless. It was a mass of slender, branching boughs, each one green as a grassblade as if its stems had adapted their bark to perform the function of leaves. There was a small, strange flower only inches tall which waved long cilia with remarkable energy, like those marine creatures which fumble endlessly for plankton. But this waved slime-coated threads to catch dust motes which actually had wings and were insects smaller than gnats.

Overhead, the sky was blue. Something flew, and it was small and nearby, but its outlines were not those of a bird. Something howled suddenly, making an enormous din, and a feathered creature scuttled into view with a ducklike gait, stopped, made that monstrous tumult fitted to a being many times its size, and waddled on again upon some unguessable errand.

It went across a wagontrail that meandered through this forest, curving erratically, avoiding the larger trees. He moved to it, grimly intent, and examined the wheeltracks. They were wide, as of wooden wheels without metal tires. The horse tracks were of unshod hoofs. And where whitish dust lay in the road, he saw other tracks. They looked like the tracks of dogs, except that no dog was ever so huge. Great Danes might have such monstrous pads, but surely no lesser breed.

Then a rhythmic squeaking sound came through the music of tiny vocalists. Dick whirled. It sounded like the noise of a squeaky wheel upon a wooden axle. There were thudding hoofbeats, and then a cart came along the trail. It was a wholly ordinary cart, with a wholly ordinary horse in frayed but ordinary harness. A half-naked man, in a loincloth only, with hair to his shoulders and an unkempt beard, drove the horse. Behind him a beast like a wolf—only bigger—paced leisurely.

Dick stepped out into the road with automatic leveled.

"Hold up, there!" he said coldly. "I want some information!"

The bearded man gasped.

"My Gawd! Where'd you come from?"

He wasn't afraid. He was amazed. His mouth dropped open and he stared blankly. The horse stopped.

The beast trotted around the cart and looked at Dick. It was very much like a wolf. It was hairy and sharp-nosed, with pricked-up ears. But no wolf ever had such eyes of such keen intelligence. It look at Dick estimatingly. It was thinking, in the way in which a man thinks when he comes upon a strange thing.

The man in the cart said quickly:

"The critter has savvy like us. Get me?"

The beast turned its head and looked at the man in the cart. It snarled a little. The sound was bloodcurdling. The man in the cart paled. He seemed to go all to pieces.

The beast trotted toward Dick without haste and without fear. Its eyes were intent. He swung the pistol upon it. It stopped dead, regarding him. No, not him, the pistol. It was looking at the pistol. It made noises which were partly growlings and partly whines. They sounded oddly like speech. The man in the cart said, shaking, "It—wants to know where you come from."

"Never mind," said Dick harshly. "I want to know where new-caught prisoners are taken! Where?"

The beast understood. Plainly, impossibly, it understood. It made more noises. The man said, in panic:

"No! Please! Y'don't understand—"

He was talking to the beast. The beast turned its head and looked at him. That was all. The man sobbed. He caught the reins around the corner of the cart. He prepared to descend.

"The devil!" snapped Dick. "I want an answer to my question! Where are new-caught prisoners taken?"

The man, shaking in every limb, crawled down to the ground. He moved slowly, abjectly, toward Dick.

"It—it ain't any use to kill me," he panted. "I—ain't done you any harm—"

Out of the corner of his eye as he watched the man, Dick saw a flashing movement. He whirled and the automatic went off. The beast was in midleap and the heavy bullet tore into its chest, checking it in midair. It fell, inches short of Dick. It struggled convulsively.

"Kill it!" panted the man shrilly. "Before it howls—"

The beast essayed to scream, dying as it was. Dick shot again. It stiffened and was still. The man from the cart wrung his hands. He seemed stunned by catastrophe.

"Migawd!" he said in a thin voice. "Oh, migawd! That finishes me! Killin' it didn't do no good—"

"Hold on!" raged Dick. "I tell you I want to know where new-caught prisoners are taken! Answer me!"

The gun muzzle bore savagely on the other man. Five minutes ago Dick had been in a taxicab on a street of the most civilized city in the world. But he was not in that city now, nor bound to its code of conduct or its laws.

"I came here from New York. A girl was brought here three days ago. Where is she?"

The other man turned to him in incredulous hope.

"You come from N'York? You weren't brought? Can you get back? Gawd! Can you get back?"

"Yes, when I take that girl with me," rasped Dick. "Where is she?"

The other man fawned upon him. He scrabled up into the cart. He drove it invitingly close to Dick. His eyes were pleading and hopeful and terrified by turns.

"Which way, fella? Which way to get back? W-we got to move fast before somebody comes!"

There was a movement. A second beast came loping around the nearest bend in the trail. Its legs and chest were wet. The man squealed and lashed the horse crazily. It bolted ahead. The beast stopped and regarded Dick with the same intent air of estimation without terror that the other beast had shown. The horse and cart jolted and bounced out of sight down the trail. The beast looked at its dead fellow, and suddenly darted for the underbrush beside the trail. Dick's pistol crashed. The thing made gurgling noises. It toppled to the ground, kicking in utter silence, then lay still.

These dead beasts made Dick's flesh crawl. They had looked at him as men would look. The first beast had given commands to the bearded man—who spoke of his own kind as slaves. The man was subject to the beast. It had commanded him to get out of the wagon and keep Dick's attention on him, and while Dick looked at the man the beast had sprung. The second beast had deduced from the body of the first that Dick had killed it, and was darting to cover when a bullet stopped it. It had acted exactly as a man would have acted if he heard a shot and raced to see what had caused it, and then found himself facing an armed and unexpected enemy.

Dick had thought earlier of making a prisoner of some inhabitant of this Outer World, and of forcing him to lead the way to where Nancy might be held captive. But if men were subject to beasts, and accompanied everywhere by the beasts their masters . . .

Then his mind clicked on the few things it had to work on. He'd seen a man and cart and beast from the top of the Empire State Building. He'd seen a man and cart and beast here. He'd killed the beast and another had come shortly after. That was now dead too. So there might be another man and cart—

He marched savagely along the trail in the direction from which the second beast had come. Cart tracks showed that it was a frequented highway. Beast tracks in occasional patches of dust showed plainly, as well as the hoofprints of horses. He saw tiny pellets of wetness. They would be drops from the wetted pelt of the second dead beast. Dick found himself hurrying a little.

Half a mile, between leaves of unknown species and genera, brushwood which had leaves and no leaves, and berries of very improbable color. Something with a preposterous number of legs slithered across the highway. It saw him and squeaked and insanely whirled and went back across the highway and vanished, having exposed itself twice to danger. A furry biped eight inches tall ran behind a tree trunk and peered at him through large blue eyes which were not in the least human. The bird notes which filled the air kept on in a constant tide of sound.

Then a stream. It was possibly twenty feet wide and swift-running. The trail led into it and out on the other side. Some thirty feet beyond the water there was a second horse and cart, and a second more than half naked man. This man sat apathetically in stillness. The horse was still. The man, red-haired and with a monstrous red beard which was utterly untended, waited dully as if in numbed obedience to orders. There was no beast in sight. Dick had killed the beast which should have been here.

He halted on the near side of the stream and lifted an automatic suggestively.

"You!" he said coldly. "I'm going to ask some questions! You'll answer them! Understand?"

The man raised his eyes. They fixed themselves dully upon Dick. It was seconds before surprise dawned in them. For a time, then, there was merely blank amazement. Then other emotions passed over his features in succession. Hope, and sudden recollected despair, and then a burning fury.

"Where'd you come from?" demanded the redbeard in a croaking voice. "The *ruhks* ain't stripped you. Did you—did you come from some'rs by yourself, or—" Then his voice dulled again. "No . . . you just busted outa a cage trap. . . ."

The fury died in him. He drooped.

"Go on some'rs else," he said dully. "I ain't seen you. The *ruhks*'ll track you down by smell, an' they'll kill you. That's best anyways. Go on!"

Dick said evenly:

"I've just killed two beasts that look like wolves. One was wet, as if he'd forded this stream. Are those beasts *ruhks?*"

The red-beard's eyes lighted again, this time in delight.

"Killed two of 'em? Good! Swell!" He suddenly cursed in a terrible, gleeful passion. "If only every one was dead there'd be some killin' around here! Fella! You got guns? I hope you kill plenty of 'em before they get you! I hope you kill thousan's of 'em—" Then he said eagerly, "Did y'break outa a trap cage, or—"

He trembled, unable to express a hope so remote that it could not be imagined.

"I came through a thing one of my friends made," said Dick.

"I was in New York half an hour ago. My friends can get through to here whenever they wish."

The redbeard blasphemed in fierce joy.

"How about other carts and *ruhks* coming along?" snapped Dick. "Is it safe to stand and talk?"

The redbeard suddenly grinned. He clucked to his horse. The horse moved forward and went into the stream. It halted in the middle.

"Wade out an' climb in," panted the redheaded man. "They'll track you by smell to this here stream. Then they'll hunt for where you come out. You ride with me an' I'll put you down miles away, an' you can get back to your friends. Tell 'em to fire the palace with gasoline an' kill them *ruhks*. We'll tend to the rest!"

When Dick waded out into the stream and then swung into the vehicle, he saw that the redbeard's back above his filthy breechclout was scarred in an intricate, crisscross pattern as if by long-healed sores which could only have been made by a lash. And there were other scars, which had been made by the teeth of beasts.

He clucked to the horse again. The animal pulled ahead to shore. Presently they were proceeding at a slow walk along the trail. And the redheaded man, in a hoarse and confidential whisper, spoke of destruction to be wrought upon a palace—which must be the villa on the Brooklyn shore—and then of tortures unspeakable to be inflicted upon overseers.

It was quite impossible, for the moment, to get from him anything but expressions of his hate.

After a time, the red-bearded man grew coherent. He was not actually mad. In the seven-mile ride between monster tree trunks, Dick came to understand that there are experiences one can have, after which self-control and a normal manner would be impossible. Yet too great a change from sane behavior would have a penalty on this Other World, where there were penalties for madness as for illness or crippling injuries or a rebellious spirit or anything which made a slave less than wholly useful.

The picture the redbeard painted was only partly like the pattern Dick had imagined. There were human masters, to be sure. They lived in the palace on the other side of the river. The red-bearded man had been a slave for years, but had never seen a member of the race or family he had been enslaved to serve. He had only rarely seen more than one overseer. Years

ago he'd been an electrician in New York, and on his way home
one night along Fourth Avenue, he suddenly felt himself falling, and all the world swirled about him and he was in a cage of
wooden bars, in a forest like this of monster trees and unfamiliar vegetation. Over his head an object rose, and drew back,
and minutes later another man fell into the cage with him. The
other man freakishly broke his arm in falling. They did not
know where they were, and they did not know what had happened to them. They shouted for help, and some beast snarled
horribly, nearby. Then they were silent in terror. And all that
night they thought themselves insane, and all night long the
beast prowled about outside the cage.

When dawn came, they saw it. It was one of the wolflike
creatures called *ruhks*. It regarded them with businesslike, icy,
intelligent eyes. Presently, in the dawn light, there came others
of the animals—a dozen or more. In their midst marched a man
with a spear, and with a pistol in a holster about his waist. He
wore a long, knee-length robe rather than garments they would
recognize. He looked at the two caged men without interest or
mercy. The *ruhks* made whining, barking noises to each other.
Their tone was unmistakably conversational. The robed man
stood back, and one of the creatures pulled on a leather thong
and the cage door opened. The two captives shivered in horror.
They pleaded with the man among the beasts, but he ignored
them. Now they shrank back in the cage and he gestured to
them to come out. When they did not, he prodded them out
with his spear.

Outside, the beasts pushed between them, separated them,
and then roughly flung them to the ground. Then, deliberatley—
and apparently under the orders of one of their own number,
who stood back and made noises at the rest—the animals ripped
off every article of their clothing. The red-bearded man was
numb with horror, but the other man screamed.

The thing that dazed the red-bearded man, then, was the
manner of the beasts. They showed no ferocity, though they
looked ferocious enough. They were businesslike and matter-of-
fact, like animals going through a well-rehearsed trick. They
released the stripped men.

Their leader looked at the other captive's broken arm and
turned its head to the man with the spear. The beast made
more specific sounds. The man with the broken arm was—
somehow it was clear—the subject of a comment or a question.
The man with the spear shrugged.

The beasts—the *ruhks*—tore the man with the broken arm to bits. It was hard for the red-bearded man, telling this to Dick, to convey the horror of their matter-of-factness. The beasts killed his fellow prisoner and devoured him without snarlings, without competition, as men would have divided a new-killed steer. Then, still matter-of-factly, they closed around the red-bearded man and herded him before them.

The red-bearded man had been marched for miles, with the beasts around him and the man with the spear ignoring him. Once the redbeard was sick, from sheer horror and fear. The beasts drove him on with bared fangs.

In the end he arrived at a slave pen, the crudest possible shed of logs within a palisade. He was turned into it. There were other humans there, men and women denned together on straw in a structure in all essentials a stable for domestic animals. They were themselves domestic animals, they told him. They had been of all possible walks of life originally. Each had been through the same experience—of falling into a cage trap, of being stripped by the *ruhks* who came to herd them to the slave pen, of being driven like captured wild animals, and of being treated thereafter as beasts of burden.

Dick interrupted here to demand if Nancy had been brought to that slave pen. The redbeard swore that she had not. No new prisoner had been brought to the slave pen for much longer than three days.

Because they had hands, the redbeard went on, they were driven by the *ruhks* to harness horses, to plow fields, to perform all the necessary tasks of the production of food and the gathering of fuel. The spear-armed man gave orders. The *ruhks* saw to it that the slaves carried them out. Some of the food and a little of the fuel they were allowed to keep and use. Most went to the river shore, to boats rowed by men in chains, which took them elsewhere. They were guarded in the slave pen by *ruhks*. When sent on errands, like the redbeard and the other man Dick had seen, a *ruhk* accompanied them. At such times they were subject to their four-footed guards. But the man with the spear was not their master. He was their overseer. Their master—or masters, they did not know which—lived in a palace on the other side of the river. What they knew of the palace they had learned from a slave sent to labor with them, brought to their pen across the river in one of the boats rowed by men in chains. What he told them, shivering, was not pleasant. And in a matter of days he was given to the *ruhks*.

The sun sank down among the giant trees on Manhattan Island as this tale unfolded. Sundown drew near. Then the redbeard drew rein.

"Here," he said bitterly. "You get out here. I'm a slave. I couldn't go back to livin' like a human again. I'll go on an' tell my story. I'll say my *ruhk* told me to wait an' went off, an' I waited till I got scared I'd be hunted as a runaway, so I started on an' I seen him an' another *ruhk* layin' in the road dead. That's all I'll tell 'em."

"That's right," said Dick grimly.

The red-bearded man drove on, chuckling to himself.

Dick ground his teeth as the horse and cart went out of sight in the gathering darkness. He had started wrong. It had seemed quite logical to plunge into the Other World after Nancy, and to force some inhabitant to lead him to her. The primitiveness of what he'd seen from the top of the Empire State Building had made him feel that the Other World would be all savagery. It was savagery, to be sure! But was not a kind he prepared for.

The *ruhks*, alone, made his original plan sheer suicide. They had obviously been the dominant species on this planet when some ancient Egyptian magician first stepped through a doorway of his own making to this world. Intelligence alone would have ensured their dominance, but they could not use tools to rise above the cultural grade of pure savagery. When the first Egyptians appeared, undoubtedly they strove to prey upon them. Undoubtedly they failed. And somehow—Dick could not imagine a process offhand—somehow an unholy compact had been arrived at. It continued until this day. With the master race to provide shelter and security and luxuries they could not contrive for themselves, it would be a mutually admirable compact which made them loyal slave guards. That such a compact would be kept was not wholly reasonable, but Dick had to accept the apparent fact. They would not be domesticated, like dogs. They would feel no reverence for humanity as such. But as slave guards they would have reasonable outlet for beastly instincts of cruelty. And the masters of this world would value them highly. While they were loyal, no slave revolt could possibly succeed nor any slave hope to run away.

They and their masters would surely apply every trick five thousand years had developed to track down and destroy the one man who had entered their world without being enslaved. As for Nancy—it was still true that no person or object which had disappeared with an accompanying tale of quicksilver had ever been seen again.

Dick tried not to think of what was Nancy's most probable fate. He fanned the sick hatred that had been growing all during the redbeard's tale. Among the things Sam Todd had provided him with was a compass with luminous dial. Dick set out doggedly to find his way through the night by its means.

A girl vanished in Paris. A prominent commissar disappeared in Prague. Two workmen, weaving their way home tipsily from a wineshop in Madrid, dropped utterly out of sight. There was a disappearance of cheeses in Belgium, of wine in Bordeaux and Athens and Málaga. A *dahabeah* lost half its cargo of dates in mid-Nile, and its crew saw quicksilver in the hold and dived howling overboard. In Damascus a shop in the Street of the Goldsmiths missed a bit of tapestry thicky interspersed with gold thread. In Baghdad a flask of attar of roses vanished into thin air. A sweetshop in London was robbed of its most expensive confections. A farmer lost two mules in Maryland. In Philadelphia a trusted employee seemed to evaporate under the most suspicious of circumstances; his accounts were correct to the last penny. In Denver a schoolboy did not come home from high school, in New Orleans the father of eight children disappeared, in Antofagasta a beautiful young girl vanished.

Over a very large part of the Earth, things which men had made and treasured, people whom others cared for and depended on, ceased to exist as far as the normal world was concerned. But nobody considered that anything requiring a new explanation had occurred; such things had been happening for five thousand years. Nobody thought to look for any common factor linking them. Nobody at all thought of the possibility of another world, beside this one in hyperspace and identical with it save in flora and fauna and population. Among all the two and a quarter billion humans on Earth, only Sam Todd and Maltby even guessed at such a thing.

Instantly after Dick Blair vanished in a pool of quicksilver, the taxi driver turned back his head and blinked. Three men had been in the cab. Now there were two.

"Hey!" said the taxi driver. "What happened to the other guy?"

"He got out," said Sam briefly. He rolled up the sheet of metal foil and looked at Maltby, sunk in sleep. "Now go back to where we came from."

The driver looked at him dubiously, and turned back to the wheel.

Sam reflected unhappily as the cab went uptown again. He reexamined the preparations that had been made for Dick's adventure. He was dissatisfied. The need for speed was great, of course, and of course since Nancy had gone into the Other World somebody had to go after her as quickly as possible. But still things were wrong.

He piled Maltby out of the cab at his house. He dragged him to his apartment and dumped him on his bed. Then he picked up the little copper-alloy window that Dick had used for his preliminary survey of the Other World. He remembered the location Dick had assigned to the villa, which must be in some sense the headquarters of the local interdimensional thieves. He went downstairs and got a taxicab and started for the Brooklyn Navy Yard.

Huddled back in the cab, he glued his eyes to the little peephole. As an experience, that ride was unique. The cab followed straight streets and traffic lanes in normal New York. But Sam Todd's eyesight traveled in a straight line through jungle, a jungle of giant trees through which his vision seemed to float eerily. He saw brushwood of unknown varieties, and deep, shadowed glades where there was no undergrowth but only a carpet of rotted leaves. Once he came out into a tiny natural clearing and saw a relatively small tree, barely forty feet high; with foliage which was not green at all, but heliotrope; the other trees seemed to shrink from it as if its vicinity were poisonous. There were occasional glimpses of trails cut through the forest, but they were rare, and once Sam saw a wooden cage, rotting away, which had no meaning to him.

But then the taxicab seemed to leave the earth and soar upward, and he jerked his eye away from the metal window and saw that it was actually sweeping up the ramp of the Brooklyn Bridge.

In the Other World there was, of course, no bridge at all, so that Sam looked down from the viewpoint of a bird in flight. He saw the river which was the counterpart of the East River flowing beneath him. He saw the great brick villa on the gently sloping farther shore. He saw a galley—propelled by many oars—pulling away from a small dock, and he saw a luxurious, old-fashioned carriage with four horses moving back toward the villa with trotting four-footed forms running beside it.

Then the taxi soared down from the crest of the bridge, and

trees rose to engulf it, and Sam winced as his eye at the peephole told him he was about to crash into great masses of foliage.

Presently the taxicab stopped by the Navy Yard. He paid the driver and got out. He was excited, now, because he'd seen signs of more than untouched wilderness. He stuffed the window in his pocket and walked a block. Then he put the peephole to his eye again. He saw a garden, plainly artificial and plainly watered and tended with the prodigal use of labor. He stood still, gazing. When he lowered the peephole, he saw three children and a fat woman staring at him suspiciously. He hastily put away the bit of metal and walked on.

He went into a tiny confectionery store and into the phone booth. He dropped in a coin and dialed at random. In the privacy of the booth he looked into the Other World while the voice of a telephone operator exasperatedly told him over and over that there was no such exchange and would he please hang up the receiver. But he was seeing walkways of smooth marble leading through fancifully trained foliage, and fountains, and statuary, and—

He saw a slave. The slave was utterly unkempt, with uncombed beard and hair, with no garment save a loincloth. But he wore gold-rimmed spectacles. He worked busily at the fertilization of a vine of climbing roses which was a veritable blanket of blooms. He finished that task and walked seemingly within a yard of Sam Todd in a telephone booth in the Navy Yard section of Brooklyn. As he passed, Sam saw ghastly scars upon his body. Some were the marks of lashes, and some were the marks of teeth.

There was somebody tapping on the glass of the phone booth door with a coin. Sam confusedly put the peephole in his pocket and went out. The woman who had tapped said acidly:

"When a person can't get their number, it's a pity they won't let somebody else use the phone!"

The street outside was incredible. Sam had just seen enough of the Other World to make his own seem unreal. As he looked at dingy storefronts, he seemed to see the wraiths of flowers and fountains and intricately trimmed shrubbery in the midst of shops and delicatessens. He had an idea of the location of the villa now, though. He oriented himself carefully and walked toward the place where the villa should be in the other cosmos.

A great, warehouselike building blocked his way. But there was an office building of sorts nearby. There was a phone booth in its untidy lobby. He took refuge in the booth and again surveyed the Other World.

He was within yards of the villa—which was gigantic—and within feet of a terrace where a little girl played with a kitten. She was a rather thin little girl, with delicate features, dressed in a healthily brief garment Sam could not identify. She treated the kitten with the extravagant affection normal in six-year-olds. But within two yards of her stood two giant, wolflike creatures, watching her. A little distance back stood six men in knee-length robes, with swords and shields in an antique style, and highly incongruous automatic pistols in holsters at their waists. Behind them again there was an elderly woman with a worried air, and behind her a row of young girls with bare feet and arms, each of them carrying a toy.

The six-year-old played absorbedly, but presently dropped the kitten with a sigh of quaintly adult weariness and then clapped her hands. The kitten darted away. Instantly there was movement all about. The two wolflike creatures moved nearer to the child. The worried-looking woman gave agitated, inaudible commands. The line of young girls moved forward. As each drew near to the child, the wolflike creatures regarded her coldly. Each slave, in turn, knelt and offered the toy she carried. The six-year-old contemplated them solemnly and waved them aside one by one. There was a girl with a swollen face, as if she had been struck a violent blow. She offered a squirming puppy. It was waved away. Extraordinarily elaborate dolls were offered. Every conceivable device for the amusement of a six-year-old girl was offered for approval by the row of slave girls who knelt abjectly, trembling, in their turns.

The child graciously accepted a mechanical toy of sheet tin, brightly colored. It was of the sort which is sold in five-and-ten-cent stores. The slave wound it and put it before the child. She backed away. The wolf creatures moved back to their former positions. The child solemnly watched the toy perform its jerky, mechanical antics.

Then one of the wolf creatures snarled suddenly. Its eyes were fixed upon Sam Todd's tiny copper-and-bismuth window. The beast flung itself before the child. There was swirling, rushing movement, and the child had been caught up swiftly and was being raced away.

Sam blinked and drew back. He assured himself of his safety and turned to stare in all directions through the peephole.

In the Other World more beasts were racing into view. There

must have been fifty of them who came boiling up from somewhere, fangs bared and snarling. Men appeared, racing, buckling on pistol belts over their robes.

Then there was stillness. Sam was bewildered. He turned the peephole in every direction. In the Other World, the spot from which he looked out was the exact center of a circle of snarling beasts and cold-eyed men, who held weapons ready.

Then he swallowed. The peephole was evidently visible in that other world. They didn't know that nothing could be shoved through it. They were prepared to fight—but he could not guess what they expected to happen next.

Then an extraordinary device came into view. It was thin and spidery and skeletonlike. It moved upon eight slender, shining wheels. A man in a robe ran panting beside it. He wore extraordinary goggles which should have blinded him. There was a curious, light, jointed girder at the forefront of the spidery device, and a large disk at its end. That disk could be set at any angle and moved in any direction by the girder. The man in the goggles shouted, but Sam could not hear him. The armed men, though, pointed. The spidery vehicle swerved straight at him.

For a moment he looked out of his phone booth. Everything about him seemed normal and commonplace and slightly dingy. But he felt hunted. Then he saw a tiny, a trivial oddity. The open door of the office building showed bright against the daylit street. Against that lighted background Sam Todd saw two small opaque specks in midair. They moved toward him, undulating up and down like the eyes or the goggles of a man running. In a flash of cold horror he understood everything.

The spidery vehicle carried a disk which was a portable doorway between worlds. The rest of the device was simply a carrier for that doorway, so that it could be pushed or pulled. The man in the goggles could see in both worlds as Sam could. And with the swinging, movable disk he could seize anything on Earth as a man may net a goldfish in a globe from which it cannot escape. He could take anything or anyone away from Earth into the Other World forever. And against this, Sam had no defense.

He flung open the phone booth and bolted. There was but one way to flee—to the open, blessed, asphalted street of Brooklyn, with its trucks and cars and hydrants and dusty shop windows. He had to plunge straight toward the space the goggled man occupied in the Other World. He probably had to run through the very substance of that man and his device. But, gasping, he rushed.

He reached the doorway. He thought he saw a momentary glow of light behind him as if the disk in the Other World had become a doorway, and light from the Other World sky shone for an instant into the lobby. But then he was outside.

At first he ran. But people stared, and he knew that if he ran on he would be stopped forcibly and questioned, and that while he panted out his utterly impossible story he would vanish before his captors' eyes in a pool of quicksilver, as Nancy had vanished.

He slowed to a fast walk. Sweat poured out of his skin. Once he turned and put the peephole to his eye and saw the spidery thing turning swiftly to pursue him over the clear lawn of the villa of the Other World.

It was nightmarish. It was worse. He felt stark panic. But there was a sure refuge if he could find it—

Twenty yards, and he dared to turn again. His actions were peculiar, and a demand for an explanation of his actions would be utterly fatal. But the device had to go around a massive plantation of shrubs on the villa lawn. He hurried, in an agony of haste, yet not daring to hasten too much.

Then he reached the subway entrance. As he swung to descend, someone coming up the stairs bumped into him. His hat fell off. He did not try to retrieve it. He plunged downward, but in spite of himself his head jerked around.

He saw his hat disappear in a curious coruscation, as of a pool of quicksilver.

As Sam rode back to New York underground, he felt cold all over and shivered violently, even while he sweated profusely. He sweated so much, indeed, that other passengers on the subway train looked at him oddly because he wiped his face so often.

In the Other World there was moonlight. It came down through the trees with a harsh bright radiance such as it seemed no mere moonlight could possess. But when Dick found an open space through which he could see the sky, the moon appeared wholly like the orb which circles Earth. The stars seemed the same, too. There was a Milky Way, and there were large bright heavenly objects which had the appearance of planets. It seemed unbelievable that the Other World could so completely resemble Earth in all its conformation and still not be the same.

The night noises were wholly unlike those of the world of men. The cries in this jungle darkness sounded strangely like bells, from tiny shrill nearby tinklings to single, deep-toned, far-away tollings as of illimitable grief.

But Dick had not gone far before he heard noises with which he felt almost familiar. They were beast-cries. But they were not the meaningless howlings of mere brutishness. Somehow he knew that they were the cries of *ruhks*. He had enough knowledge of this Other World now to guess at what would happen.

When the redbeard told his story—if the first man Dick had met hadn't babbled out his tale first—a coldly merciless hunt would begin for Dick. *Ruhks* would logically be entrusted with the night search. They would find his trail entering the stream. And when no trail appeared on the farther side, the *ruhks* would divide. They would hunt through the jungle on either bank of the stream, both upstream and down, for the spot where he had come out.

The one thing that could go wrong, of course, was that his scent might be detected in redbeard's cart. If that happened, redbeard would die, and Dick soon after.

But he heard the *ruhk* cries in the night. The compass direction was wrong for beasts actually on his trail. They had, then, gone on to the spot where Nancy had come into this cosmos. Dick heard them calling to one another from separated places. He'd guessed their tactics, and what he heard confirmed his guess. He headed for a point between the separating parties of those who sought his trail. This was a world of slaves and masters and there would be no system of swift communications. A man does not do skilled work under the lash. A slave telegrapher is unthinkable, and slave telephone maintainance crews are unimaginable. When human beings are classed as animals, only the labor of animals can be had from them.

So Dick went on through the darkness. The noises all about him compounded themselves into a sort of muted bedlam. There were the sounds as of bells, and at startling intervals something made a noise as of drums, and now and again the hunting *ruhks* howled their reports of futility. Dick reached the stream and waded it. A little beyond, he blundered into thick, squashy vegetation with a scent like that of garlic, only more pungent, and his feet crushed the pulpy leaves and he reeked of the smell as he went on. He was offensive to his own nostrils.

But even so he smelled the reek of a slave pen a good half mile downwind from it. He veered aside.

Presently he heard the lapping of waves through the darkness. He pressed forward cautiously. The glitter of moonlight on water warned him, and he went very tentatively down the last steep slope to the East River. The shore was wilderness. The water was completely tranquil. He waded into it and began a cautious march along the shoreline. Here there was little or no breeze. His scent would not be carried far, and that out over the river. He waded for a very long time, keeping from ten to thirty feet from the water's edge. Twice he disturbed private affairs of the inhabitants of the jungle. Once there was an ecstatic splashing in the water before him, and he advanced with care, and something sputtered alarmedly and flashed up the beach—he did not see it clearly, but it was very long and furry—and went crashing to safety among the trees. The other time was when he came on an animal fishing. It prowled upon the beach, staring absorbedly into the river, and as Dick came near it plunged from the beach and with a sweeping motion of an extraordinarily long paw sent a two-foot fish writhing through the air toward the land, with an accompanying shower of moonlit drops of spray. Then Dick loomed up and it fled. He heard the beached fish flapping convulsively as he went by.

Then, less than a quarter mile farther on, the moonlight showed him a small wharf going out into the water. His eyes were well used to the moonlight now. He saw a boat tethered to the wharf. Its thwarts were occupied by drooping, naked rowers. There were two *ruhks* on the wharf, squatted on their haunches like wolves or dogs.

Dick went quietly ashore. He made certain of his two tear-gas bombs and swung the sawed-off shotgun around and threw off the safety-catch. He had fired three shots from an automatic pistol and had been lucky. But one does not want to depend on luck when it is dark and animals may be charging. A sawed-off shotgun is better.

He went as silently as possible along the beach. But he touched a brushwood branch, and one of the *ruhks* turned its head. Dick was still. Presently the *ruhk* yawned and looked away. Dick went on. He did not really hope to reach the wharf undiscovered, of course—

He did not. A *ruhk* stared in his direction and stood up quickly while he was better than two hundred yards away. Dick broke into a run toward the wharf. Fortunately, the beach here was all of ten feet wide.

He was in full stride when both *ruhks* were up and staring keenly at him from their positions on the stem of the wharf. They could not see him quite clearly because of the background of brush behind him. One of them yelped questioningly. Since he was not another *ruhk* he should have been—to the creatures of this world—a fugitive. That he ran toward them instead of away was unsettling. He covered nearly fifty yards before the *ruhk* yelped again. Seventy-five before it snarled. A hundred before both animals trotted ashore to intercept him. And the *ruhks* were slave guards. They felt contempt for men. They stood poised and waiting while he plunged on still nearer. It was not possible for them to be afraid of him. It was unlikely that they would even feel the need for caution.

They stood on the wharf stem, snarling in indecision. Dick was actually within seventy yards before the first of them emitted a high howl and plunged at Dick.

He pulled the trigger of the sawed-off shotgun when it was twenty yards away, and practically tore it apart. The other leaped crazily aside into the brush. Dick ran on, leaping over the dying creature, and whirled as the second *ruhk* leaped from behind. The riotgun crashed again. At such short range, the heavy pellets hit in a compact mass of destruction and then caromed outward from each other with all the effect of an explosion.

Dick reached the planks of the wharf as a beastly howl came from the trail which led to this landing place. He saw four-footed figures rushing toward him, and tossed a tear-gas bomb, and ran out to the end of the wharf as the bomb created a cloud of mist around the shore end.

Human figures cringed below him in the boat. He saw dull, animal eyes and matted shocks of hair and naked bodies on which the moonlight shone. This was a galley. At one time it had been an oared cutter of a United States warship, and doubtless its disappearance from its proper place on Earth had caused some concern. Now a dozen chained men slumped over their oars upon its thwarts. They looked up at Dick and cringed. He heard scrabblings on the wharf planking, and fired furiously. A beast screamed. There were splashes. Dick fired again. *Ruhks*, plunging toward him, had run into the nearly stationary wall of tear gas, and were blinded. Some went overboard. A man in a white, knee-length robe came stumbling out of the tear-gas cloud. He carried a spear and there was a pistol slung about his waist, but he wiped streaming eyes and tried to see—if only so he could run away.

Dick moved savagely toward the tear gas and shot the gun's magazine empty. He came back carrying the spear and the overseer's pistol. With the sharp blade of the spear he sawed at the ropes which held the boat to the wharf. It floated free and he jumped down into its stern. None of the dozen chained men stirred. They simply looked at him in numb terror.

"Row, damn you!" raged Dick. "Get away from here!"

There was a splashing nearby. A blindly swimming *ruhk* snarled in the water. Dick killed it in cold ferocity. He turned back to the rowers. He opened his mouth to threaten them again. But suddenly the oars were beginning to dip, and suddenly they fell into cadence, and suddenly the boat swept away from the wharf and began to move out into the river. And Dick felt a dozen pairs of eyes staring at him incredulously.

"Look!" he snapped. "Somebody back on the real Earth has found a way to come through to this world, and how to get back. I came through to find a girl who's been kidnapped as I suppose you were! Play along with me and you'll get back too!"

There was silence. The rowers pulled automatically. They were living automatons. On the shore near the wharf there was a snarling, yelping tumult. *Ruhks* created a monstrous din. Then one of them seemed to silence the others and emitted high, keening cries which would carry a vast distance over the water on a night as still as this.

Then one of the rowers said dully:

"Telling 'em. They'll give us to the *ruhks*, now!"

A man near the bow cursed. The rowing kept on. Then another man said, marveling:

"He killed a *ruhk!*"

Dick said sharply:

"I'll kill some more!" He held up the overseer's pistol. "I've got an extra pistol. Who wants it?'

More silence. Then a voice said in a whisper:

"Could kill *ruhks* with that."

"Or overseers," said another in a hushed tone.

"Could kill anybody," said yet another, as if dazed. "With a pistol, a fella could kill 'em. . . ."

Babbling. Sudden, lustful babblings. The oars stroked irregularly. Dick barked at them as the babblings rose to uproar.

"Silence there!" Instant stillness. These men were cowed to where they were hardly men. The rowing took up its regular cadence once more. "There was a girl vanished from New York three days ago," said Dick harshly. "She wasn't taken to the slave pen back yonder. Where was she taken?"

A long pause, and then a voice said fumblingly:

"We didn't take her across the river. We ain't taken nobody across but *ruhks* an' overseers."

"Then she's still on Manhattan Island," rasped Dick. "How many other slave pens there?"

Another voice, heavily:

"One up by the hothouses. That's upriver. Across from Blackwell's Island—or what looks like Blackwell's."

The use of the name, alone, was an indication of the length of time the man who used it had been a slave here on the twin of Earth. Blackwell's became Welfare Island many years ago.

"We'll head for there, then," said Dick grimly.

The rowing went on. It was spiritless and dazed. Dick found a tiller and swung the boat about. A man said humbly:

"Give me that extra pistol, fella? There's an overseer I got to kill. He gave my girl to the *ruhks*. Lend it to me?"

"I'm getting some more," said Dick. "First—"

A man near the bow whimpered.

" 'Nother boat . . . it's got *ruhks* in it . . ."

Dick strained his eyes. He saw the boat, upstream, coming down, heading out on the wide, moonlit river. It came as if headed for the villa on the other shore, down where the Navy Yard should have been. It was impossible to see the size of the boat, but it could only have come from somewhere on Manhattan Island opposite Welfare. It could have come from that other slave pen. It could be carrying Nancy to the villa now. At least, its crew might know what had happened to her.

He swung the tiller over.

"Pull hard," he directed.

The two boats neared each other steadily. The other did not change its course. Its rowers—doubtless chained like these—rowed in the steady apathy Dick's own crew had shown. But now, slowly, a trace of spirit was coming to his crew. Presently a voice whispered:

"We goin' to take that boat?"

"Yes," said Dick. "I want to find out about that girl."

The voice said hungrily:

"Fella—let me have that spear anyway! I'm dead anyways, now, but maybe—"

Dick silently passed it to him, and he seized the haft of it without slackening his stroke on the oar.

The other boat was a hundred yards away. A voice called from it in a language Dick did not know. He did not answer. It was fifty yards away. Twenty-five. Its helmsman called again, this time obsequiously, as if the arrogance of a boat holding to a collision course implied that some mighty personage must be in it. Dick grimly shifted his own tiller as the other boat gave way, to keep collision inevitable. Under his breath he said:

"Pull hard!"

The helmsman of the other boat snapped agitated orders. There came animal noises from it. Sounds which were neither yelps nor snarlings, but something in between and somehow conversational. The *ruhks* in the other boat were calling to supposed fellow beasts in this.

Then, in panic, the other helmsman swung his boat clean around to avoid a head-on collision, and Dick swerved and crashed along the other craft's stern. So near, he could see a robed figure at the tiller and two uneasy *ruhks* balancing themselves as if to spring and regarding him and his craft with anxiety.

As the stern of his own boat scraped the other, Dick fired twice, point-blank. Then there was screaming, snarling uproar, and a man rose, grabbing at his pistol holster, and there was deadly battle in the waist of Dick's boat where a wounded *ruhk* had sprung on board. Dick fired again, and the thing was ended.

He called sharply to the other crew:

"Hold up, there! Back water! Try to get away and we'll sink you!"

The captured craft lay still, its chained rowers shivering and in dread.

Of course, Nancy wasn't in it. They'd never heard of her.

Dick had tried not to think of this possibility, but he could not help it. There were two slave pens on Manhattan Island, but Nancy had not been taken to either of them. She had not been carried to the palace of the masters on the Brooklyn shore in either of the now-captured cutters. Of the remaining possibilities, for her to have been devoured by *ruhks* because of an injury was most likely, and the bare suspicion drove all thoughts of humanity out of Dick's mind.

Certainly the slaves of this Other World knew nothing of her. There was but one way to learn definitely—no, two. If Dick could capture an overseer alive, he might force the man to tell him Nancy's fate if he knew it. And if that failed, then the palace itself—

Now, though, he had two dozen men to command. They were doomed, of course. No slave who had witnessed the killing of an overseer or a *ruhk* could be allowed to live, because his tale would inspire the others to wishful thinking. More, no slave who had seen an armed free man could be allowed to spread such tidings of hope.

So Dick acted with the ruthlessness that knowledge justified. He now had twenty-four followers, chained to their seats in the two cutters. He did not free them from their shackles. Instead, with the second boat following docilely because its crew could do nothing else, he made for a point on the Manhattan shore close to that small splinter of rock which lies southward of Welfare Island. As the boats headed for that spot, he took a notebook from his pocket and wrote grimly in its pages. It was a report to Sam Todd. It was a demand for arms. It told very curtly what had happened, but essentially, primarily, emphatically, it was a demand for arms to make a slave revolt not only possible but successful. Arms with which, by massacre, to make this Other World no longer a place from which thieves and slavers preyed on the world of men. Now that five thousand years of mysteries and crimes were solved, those mysteries and crimes must end. They must!

He landed on Manhattan opposite the little splinter islet. He tore out the pages on which he'd written his account and pinned them to the bark of the largest nearby tree with a thorn longer than his hand from a nearby bush. Sam would hunt the tree trunks hereabouts from Earth, looking through his peephole from the equivalent space—it was a park in New York—as early as tomorrow morning. He might even hunt them up tonight. When he saw a message at the arranged place, he would use the doorway Maltby had contrived, and retrieve it. He would obey it as nearly as he could.

Then Dick took his two boats up the river past all observation. He found a secure hiding place for both boats on a shore which should have been the Bronx. Then, and only then, he began to free his followers from their shackles. He had delayed that until he could tell them confidently that the means of fighting would soon be on the way.

It was late by the time they were well hidden and free. The slaves had among them now two spears and two automatic pistols, besides Dick's own. These were not arms enough. So Dick commanded them to cut saplings and make substitute spears. And if any could make bows or arrows—but that would take time.

Time was of the essence, of course. And arms were essential. At the moment they were probably safe. There would be no regular patrol of men or *ruhks* on the mainland, where no slave pen lay. But they could be found, and ultimately would be. If the freed slaves tried flight inland, of course they would be tracked down. That was a function of the *ruhks*.

So he asked grim questions of his followers. He began to outline the beginnings of his plans. The men were cowed, and they had been almost spiritless. But they were desperate beyond the desperation of mankind. Their hate was a burning flame. So Dick made plans to utilize their desperation and hate as substitutes for the spirit that had been driven out.

Back on Earth there was the barest beginning of a possibility of change. Sam Todd—still sweating when he thought of his experience in Brooklyn—went to the park which was the Manhattan shore oposite the splinter island south of Welfare. It was dark when he arrived, but he sat on a bench and put a copper-alloy peephole inconspicuously to his eye. He did not at first see the sheets of paper that Dick had pinned to the trunk of a tree for him to find. There was no light but moonlight in the forest where the big tree stood. But even so, Sam made a discovery which was disheartening. In the world of men there had been a fill-in at that spot. The park area had been raised in level by earth piled high, with grass and concrete walkways laid on top. Fifteen feet back from the shoreline of the Other World, the ground levels in the other world were completely different. Sam discovered, even before he saw the impaled sheets of paper, that any message Dick had left for him would be buried deep beneath publicly maintained park lawn. Actually, the scribbled sheets were stuck to a tree trunk under a drinking fountain on Earth. To get at them would have required an excavation besides an interdimensional door, and it could not be accomplished without either permission or discovery. In short, Sam simply could not pick up Dick's message at all.

But he had the twin to the metal peephole. It was a miniature interdimensional door. Maltby had made it to be sure he could. And sitting on the park bench, Sam wrote painfully in his turn:

"There's an earthfill covering up your papers. I can't get to them. But I have been looking around Maltby's place. Two miles northeast of here there is a pond in the world you're in. There is a cart trail past it. Just beyond the first bend in that trail to northward of the pond, there is an unusually large tree with mottled bark. That tree grows through the space Maltby's apartment occupies on Earth. Come there. I'll have something fixed up so you can come back—with Nancy, I hope. —Sam."

He fumbled in his pocket. The only suitable container was his wallet. He emptied that and put his message inside it. He put the end of his handkerchief between the zipper teeth and caught the cloth firmly. He rolled up the wallet into a cylinder and managed to squeeze it through the tiny round alloy doorway which corresponded to the alloy eye. Feigning to drink at the drinking fountain, he released the handkerchief by which the wallet dangled in the Other World. Then, through the peephole, he watched. The wallet fell at the foot of the very tree in the Other World to which Dick's report and demand for arms was fastened. Dick could not fail to find it when he came to make sure his message had been retrieved by Sam. The handkerchief showed up plainly.

As an emergency way to explain to Dick why his message hadn't been removed, and to arrange a better means of communication, it was an excellent idea. But it did not take into account certain facts.

The *ruhks* were slave guards. The slaves were cowed. But sometimes pure horror made them cunning. So the shoreline of Manhattan Island was trotted over, at least once in twenty-four hours, by a keen-nosed *ruhk* with the intelligence of a man. Being beasts with undiminished feral instincts, they made those rounds with all the satisfaction of hunting animals. They savored the smells of the jungle. Sometimes they snapped up an unwary wild thing and devoured it. But discovery of the scent of man on the shoreline was the purpose of the patrol.

Two hours after Sam dropped his message for Dick to find, a *ruhk* came padding through the darkness on that particular errand. He picked up instantly the scent of Dick's footprints where he had landed and selected a tree to hold his message. Slavering a little—because unaccompanied humans on unlawful errands were the lawful prey of *ruhks*—the beast followed the human trail. He did not find Dick. He did find two messages.

One was impaled on a thorn on a tree-trunk. One was the wallet on the ground.

The *ruhk* made sure that Dick had returned to the water. Then he picked up the wallet and set off at full speed to find the nearest overseer. The conversational noises of the *ruhk* were quite equal to an exact account of what he had found, so that an overseer and *ruhks* soon retrieved the other message. Both were sent across the river in a double-banked galley, specially summoned by light signals from the shore.

The master of all the slaves and *ruhks* of these parts, and the lord of all local overseers, had already had two frights that day. One was the unprecedented appearance of an armed free man in the Other World, a matter of great gravity. The other alarming event had been the appearance of a between-worlds peephole in his very palace, as if enemies capable of interdimensional travel spied upon him for purposes of their own.

He had the notes translated, because he had never bothered to learn any language but the language of his ancestors. He puzzled over the interpretation of the two. He was annoyed, and he was frightened. He gave orders for the finding of the place where—according to Sam Todd—a doorway for passage between worlds was to be opened by those who were not of his race and hence were enemies to him and all his kind. He gave explicit commands about that. Then he ordered an adequate ambush prepared about the place where the messages had been left.

Then the master of the villa relaxed again, as bustling preparations began for the execution of his commands. But he could not relax completely. He wondered if the disappearance of six *ruhks* with no explanation whatever—some three days before this most upsetting day—had any connection with today's events.

He was not aware that just before the six *ruhks* disappeared, Nancy Holt had vanished from the sidewalk where she waited for a taxicab. Nor was he aware that as she vanished Sam Todd had stared helplessly at a dwindling pool of quicksilver. But the master, in his palace on the Brooklyn shore, wouldn't have thought that matter significant even if he'd known about it.

Sam Todd was in the parkway beside the East River Drive at sunrise. He was unreasonably uneasy. He had been unable to sleep. He sat on a dew-wet park bench shivering a little with the morning chill. As the dawn-light strengthened, he put the peephole to his eye.

The sun came slowly up over the eastern edge of the Other World. Splendid sunrise colorings silhouetted the green forests of the Brooklyn hills, almost solid at the upper surface save where giant trees of a species unknown on earth threw up lacy fountains of foliage like spray. The surface of the East River was oily smooth, and reflected the reds and golds and violets of the fading night sky so that it looked like rainbows going into solution. Mists hung here and there over the treetops, and seeped out from the jungle's edge to make the shoreline mysterious.

Dick Blair's small squadron crept along the shore, barely out from the beaches. The rowers strove to be silent. Often they were hidden in the mists, and sometimes they were only vaguely visible, like ghosts. But now and again the sun's red rays smote fully on them. Then the crimson light made their bodies the color of blood.

Presently the two oared boats checked their motion. One turned in toward the land. Its bow touched, and Dick Blair stepped ashore. All was stillness and silence. Somewhere a fish leaped, and the "plop" of its splash was somehow shocking. The rowers seemed not to breathe. Dick looked, and listened, and then in the fathomless hush of morning his nostrils wrinkled suddenly. He smelled something. The hair rose by instinct at the back of his neck. He smelled beasts.

He stood still on the beach. He spoke in a low tone to the men behind him. They had been tense. Their bodies grew tenser still.

He stepped into the underbrush.

The silence held, save that somewhere in the forest far away a staccato bellowing noise set up and almost instantly thereafter ceased. Something stepped delicately into view on the shore of the island out in the river, spread long, angular wings, and suddenly soared out over the water barely two yards above it. A tiny twittering noise came from a treetop. One of the men in the boats shifted his position suddenly, and his oar splashed.

As if that small sound had been a signal, all hell broke loose where Dick had disappeared. There was the startling, thunderous crash of an explosion, which echoed and reechoed among the trees. A beast screamed. A second shot and a third, and then an automatic pistol roared itself empty and another took up the unholy task—and then there was a ghastly uproar of snarlings and screams and men shouting and more shots. Then the deeper bellowing of a sawed-off shotgun.

Dick came plunging from the brushwood, grinning savagely. Leaping forms came after him. He halted to fire twice, plunged on again, and splashed into the water and the bow of the beached boat.

The naked men shoved off in panic. He stepped along to the stern and sat down, saying composedly, "Don't get too far away! We've got a chance to kill some *ruhks*, now."

He began to reload his weapons. The brush erupted snarling forms. They howled their fury. Dick said:

"Act confused and scared. Make it convincing!"

The rowers of his own boat splashed and fumbled. Some of their awkwardness was confusion in reality, but not all. Neither cutter was more than ten yards from the shore, and both looked as if their crews were helpless from pure terror. Men bellowed from the brush, and the *ruhks* plunged into the water. Dick said hungrily:

"Out a little farther! Lure 'em! We'll kill 'em if we can get 'em swimming!"

The two cutters, splashing and clumsy and in seeming hysteria, went erratically out from the shore into the brightening dawn. Snarling beasts, intelligence forgotten in the instinct to kill, swam after them.

"Now!" roared Dick.

There were only two spears and two pistols besides his own weapons in the boats. But the men suddenly turned upon their pursuers. The *ruhks* could not yet believe that slaves would defy them. The slaves themselves almost failed of belief. One man in Dick's own boat screamed and fled blindly from the bow, trampling on his fellows, and in glassy-eyed fear went on over the stern. But there was an aching bloodlust in the others. As the beasts swam snarling closer, they yelled in triumph when they found their oar blades and sharpened saplings would reach. A man shrieked with joy when a sharp-pointed pole sank in a *ruhk's* furry body and the beast uttered raging cries and snapped at the thing which impaled it. Another man howled with glee as his flailing oar broke a *ruhk's* back and the thing screamed.

There were almost no shots. Dick held his own weapons in reserve. Once a *ruhk* got its paws over a gunwale and he raised a pistol, but a clubbed oar literally cracked its skull open. He almost relaxed, then. The other boat was close, and one *ruhk* did get on board it before three sharpened stakes impaled it simultaneously. No other came so near to close combat.

But the *ruhks* were intelligent. Devilishly, viciously intelligent. They had attacked in overconfidence, urged on by bloodlust and the shouts of men on shore. Overseers, those men would be. But Dick's own boat had killed six *ruhks* in a bare two minutes of tumultuous slaughter. A seventh paddled weakly toward shore. The other boat had done almost as well. The remaining beasts snarled horribly, but one among them yelped and growled meaningfully, and the rest obeyed. They did not retreat, but they did draw off, just beyond the reach of spears or oar blades. There they swam, raging.

The light grew momently stronger. The men in the boats now snarled and jeered in their turn at the animals they had feared so terribly. The *ruhks* made bloodcurdling sounds, their eyes blazing, just out of reach. One of them snapped at an oar blade. The men shouted and paddled fiercely to come to grips again. It was full dawn now, and though the sunshine was yet a deep orange there was brightness everywhere. The dew-wet trees looked golden-green and stark, sharp shadows played as the naked men derided the *ruhks* and strove with burning eyes to lure them within spear stroke or to overtake them.

But it was not right. The *ruhks* were brainy and they knew what they did. Dick realized it with a start. The overseers were not even shooting from the shore, and they had pistols and the range would not be much over fifty yards. There must be something else—

Dick jerked his head about and saw the answer. Around the southern tip of Welfare Island a large boat sped. It was a galley of two banks of oars, converted from a coasting schooner with clean, sharp lines. Its masts had been cut away, its deck removed and its bulwarks cut down. It floated lightly on the water. It was open to the sun save for decking at its bow and stern and a railed walkway in between, over the heads of the slaves at the oars. Overseers ran up and down that walkway now, their whips cracking mercilessly, and the long and clumsy oars bent as the slaves pulled the galley on. Sixty men pulled the oars—lash-scarred, chained, maniacs in despair. There were half a dozen robed men at the stern, besides one who handled a wholly modern small ship's wheel. There were others, with *ruhks*, at the galley's bow. A dozen men with firearms to four pistols and a shotgun—and one of the pistols was empty and another had only three bullets left. But the larger galley had no need to fight. It could merely ride down the smaller craft and spill their crews.

That was evidently its intention. When Dick shouted his

discovery, tumult broke out, alike on the shore and from the swiming beasts. The *ruhks* on the larger galley howled an answer. Dick leaped to his feet and shouted, and the two cutters struck out in flight.

But there was no escape. They might beach, to be sure. But on the Manhattan shore there were *ruhks* and overseers. In jungle fighting, the beasts would have it all their own way. If the boats beached on the long narrow East River island, the *ruhks* would even more surely have them in the end. They would be ferried there in monstrous numbers, and they had the grisly cunning of werewolves.

The sun shone brightly now. It was day, and the two small fleeing craft and the larger, vengeful one in pursuit made a strange picture against the shores which showed only jungle. And of all insane preoccupations, Dick Blair at this moment tore leaves out of his notebook and shredded them to confetti, and tossed them in the air.

Then Dick gave orders to his own crew. The other cutter drew nearer at his hail. Without slacking their straining effort to keep ahead, the cutters raced along with their oar tips almost touching, as if for mutual comfort. Then, when the bigger craft was barely fifty yards behind, they turned together for the farther Manhattan shore. The galley swung triumphantly. Closer. Forty yards. Thirty. Twenty. Ten. It would ride them down—

Dick flung the second of his tear-gas bombs. It was a perfect target and a perfect throw. The bomb landed on the bow deck of the galley, in the very thick of the men who waited so zestfully to do murder. It exploded with a totally inadequate "plop!" and dense white vapor spouted out. And Dick's tossing of paper fragments bore its fruit: for by it he had gauged the faint breeze exactly. The tear-gas cloud hung almost stationary. The galley rode through it. The mist rolled all along the length of the bigger boat, blinding overseer and slave and *ruhk*. When the galley came out of the quite inconsiderable cloud, its oars beat erratically and out of rhythm, its overseers' whips no longer flailed, it lost way and veered crazily. And then the two cutters plunged to its sides and the slaves swarmed over the low gunwale.

What followed was not pretty. The former slaves, armed with sharpened poles and two spears and clubbed oars, raged the length of the galley, killing. *Ruhks*, unable to see, died fighting blindly. Overseers fought hopelessly with no eyesight. The men with whips, who from the walk over the rowers' benches had lashed on the slaves to work, were so helpless in their blindness that the men of the cutters laughed at them, stripped their whips and weapons from them, and flung them down to their still-chained fellows. The eyes of the rowers streamed copiously, but with howls of joy they tore their tyrants to pieces.

It seemed a matter of no more than seconds. Certainly not more than two minutes elapsed between the time when the cutters were in full flight and the time when the revolted slaves had grown from two dozen men in small boats, freed by Dick, to more than eighty with the oared galley of the master of the villa in their possession. Sixty of them still wept uncontrollably from the tear gas they'd taken with their masters. But they grinned and howled and clanked their chains in glee, careless of possible retribution.

The men from the cutter were not blinded. The gas mist was gone before they boarded. But the eyes of some began to smart from traces of the stuff drifting up from the rowers' space. So Dick got the galley under way again to make a breeze to clear the last of it.

Sam Todd, white-faced, sitting on a bench in East Side Park in the New York City of Earth, put down the little metal peephole through which he had watched the battle in the dawnlight. Behind him, early-morning cars whirled past on the double highway. Around him innumerable buildings poured plumes of steam and sooty smoke toward the sky. A puffing tug towed coal barges over the very spot where, in the Other World, Dick Blair and a crew of freed slaves took account of their victory.

Sam Todd dazedly got up from the park bench. He knew that his message to Dick had not been picked up by Dick. The ready ambuscade told that somebody else had intercepted it, and made a trap for Dick and the naked scoundrels now obeying his orders.

Then cold chills went up and down Sam Todd's spine. Not one message, but both must have been intercepted. And his had told Dick how to find the tree which, in the Other World, grew through the space Maltby's flat occupied on Earth. And the folk who kidnapped slaves would had found it necessary to learn English.

Sam himself had risen before dawn to see if Dick had received his note. Now he knew somebody else had received it. He went white and sick, and suddenly he plunged blindly across the East River Drive without regard to the traffic. Brakes squealed about him, but he did not hear them. A car's bumper nudged his calf, but he did not feel it. Trembling and panting, he found a phone booth at the nearest corner, darted inside, and dialed Maltby's number with fingers that shook uncontrollably. He sweated as the phone buzzed, stopped, buzzed and stopped, in monotonous assurance that it was ringing. Presently Sam hung up and dialed the same number again.

There was no answer.

In a taxi on the way to Maltby's place, his teeth chattered. But he couldn't bring himself to use the peephole to look into the Other World. Only at the very last instant, when the cab turned into the last block, could he nerve himself to look. Then he had the cab stop short. He got out and put the peephole to his eye.

He saw the virgin jungle of the Other World. Nothing else. He moved slowly and timorously along the street, the early-morning sounds of New York seeming very loud indeed. He looked into the Other World, and then examined his surroundings in this so that he would not run into a blank wall.

Before the building in which Maltby lived, he stopped again. Shivering, he regarded the corresponding space in the Other World. He saw jungle, which here had little undergrowth and was merely a carpet of rotted leaves. He saw the mottled bole of the great tree he had described to Dick. Then he saw tracks in the dead leaves and wood mold on the ground. Something had come here on narrow, tired wheels like bicycle wheels. It was gone. It had accomplished what it came for.

Sam Todd went heavily into the apartment building and into Maltby's flat. It was quite empty. Maltby was gone. More, all of his experimental apparatus was gone, too. Everything that had been used to make the doorway between worlds was missing.

Sam knew that there had been many small pools of quicksilver glistening in this place recently. Maltby was now a slave in the Other World. The doorway he'd made for Dick to go through was taken. No more doorways could be made, because Maltby had been the only man who knew how to make them. Dick Blair was beyond help, Nancy—if she still lived—was beyond hoping for, Maltby would shortly be tortured to make him tell everything he knew, and Sam Todd was helpless.

The telephone rang in Maltby's apartment. It rang again. Sam swallowed, looking at it.

Then he turned and went tiptoeing out of the flat. He was

now the only man on Earth who knew that the Other World existed. He dared not talk about it, but he had to do something about it. His first impulse was to run away. He'd slept here last night. When Maltby was missed, he'd be asked about it. Naturally. As he was a man of ample means and a known student of criminology, the questioning would be very polite, of course. But he'd slept here. He'd gone out before dawn. He'd returned—and Maltby was missing. More: when Dick Blair was reported missing, Sam and Maltby had been the last two persons to see him. And Nancy Holt—

It would strike the police as a series of remarkable coincidences. They would expect him to explain them reasonably. When he couldn't, they would begin to get suspicious. And if he told the truth— There was nothing that could be more damning, in the eyes of the cops, than for Sam to tell the exact and literal truth. It would look like a very clumsy attempt to feign insanity.

His metal peephole would be considered a clever fake. It would be cut into to solve the mystery of its construction, and thereby be destroyed. The little door through which pencils and wallets could be thrust into the Other World would be considered also a device of modern prestidigitation. Sam Todd would be jailed until he explained the vanishing of his friends. In the Other World, Maltby would be subject to fiendish tortures, and Sam Todd's name would come out of his babblings. When newspapers were snatched into the Other World, they would presently reveal Sam Todd's exact whereabouts and that the police accused him of faking insanity. Shortly the newspapers would print the news of his inexplicable escape from a locked cell. Then there would be nobody at all on Earth who knew anything about the Other World, and things would go on as before—theft and blood and agony and murder for thousands of years to come.

Sam went to his hotel and up to his suite. He began to pack for hiding, and for combat. He had been studying weapons as a part of his work. He took what weapons he had ammunition for, and all their ammunition. And he took what money he could find. There wasn't enough. He was in the act of debating whether or not to cash a check at the hotel desk when his telephone rang.

He jumped. It rang again.

He swallowed, with some difficulty. His mind was in the Other World. He felt hunted. He tried not to think of Maltby, but Maltby would have to scream out every secret that he knew when the Other Worldlings began to work on him. He knew Sam's address and how to call him by phone.

The phone rang a third time.

Sam went quickly out of the door, sweating. He carried two bags. He left the telephone ringing.

Minutes later, he was at his bank. He cashed a large check. He cursed himself for knowing that he looked very pale. He cursed himself still more for being unable to devise a plan to save Maltby or even Dick.

He tried to close his mind and not think of such things. He went to Penn Station and paid off his taxi, then went by subway to Grand Central and left that with the passengers of an incoming train, apparently one of them. He took another taxi to a medium-priced hotel and registered as from out of town, asking for a room as high from the street as possible. Doggedly and bitterly, he meant to do what he could to fight the Other World. Within hours—days at most—the police would be hunting him. From the Other World he would be hunted, too. He had just two weapons—a one-inch peephole through which he could look into the Other World, and a one-inch space on a copper plate through which he could thrust things into the other cosmos. He had nothing else.

With the peephole he would learn the ways of the Other World. Slowly, carefully, he could find where doorways were placed and how they were made sometimes to be open and sometimes shut. In time he would be able to drop written word to some slave, guiding him to such a doorway and instructing him in its use. He might be able to drop small sharpened steel rods to serve as daggers. He should be able to pour down inflammable stuff and start incendiary fires to cover a break by such a slave. If once an interworld doorway fell into his hands, he would manage to get it underground where in the Other World it could not be found, or else to some upper floor of a skyscraper. And then he would act as the situation required. With one full-sized doorway opening into the other cosmos and freed slaves to tell what went on there, he could not fail to cause conviction and armed exploration.

From his eighth-floor room in the hotel he looked exhaustively out over jungle and placid waters. He saw only those, and once the reflection of sunlight from the villa's roof. There was nothing to be learned from aloft. So Sam took a deep breath and equipped himself with arms so that he would be inconspicuously a walking arsenal. It was wryly humorous to think that if the police found him his weapons would be proof of criminality, and if a betweeen-worlds door closed on him the weapons would be useless. But he carried them just the same. He went down to the street to begin his search.

Then an idea struck him. He could give himself more time before the police hunted actively for him. He stepped into a phone booth and dialed his original hotel.

"Desk?" he said briskly. "Todd speaking. I have suite 406, you know. I've been suddenly called out of town. Cleveland and possibly Chicago afterward. Hold my mail for a forwarding address, won't you? I'll wire it."

The desk clerk said hurriedly: "Yes, sir. But Mr. Todd! Your secretary has called three times in the past hour. She says it is desperately important for you to call her at once, sir. Extremely urgent."

Sam's hair stood upon his head. Nancy Holt was his secretary. Four days ago she'd vanished in a pool of quicksilver. And nobody who vanished like that ever came back. Nobody! It would be a trap—

"Very well," said Sam Todd, his throat tightening. "I'll call her. Did she leave a number?"

"No sir."

"Thanks," said Sam.

He hung up, his lips twisted. Then the oddity of it hit him. Nancy hadn't left a phone number. She didn't need to, of course. He knew the number of her phone. But anybody impersonating Nancy, or Nancy under duress, would have left a number. Anybody who forced Nancy to call would think it suspicious if she didn't leave a number Sam could call. So—incredibly enough—it was possible that it was straight. Or it was possible that some compulsion more terrible than he could guess at would have enslaved Nancy's mind as well as her body.

It was a decision of importance vastly greater than merely his own safety. Sam felt that the wrong decision might mean slavery and degradation and shame and horror for generations yet unborn. He had to play it out.

He called her number from the other side of town, with a taxi waiting to carry him away the instant he dashed out of the booth. He heard the crisp buzzings that meant her phone was ringing. Then her voice. It was unquestionably Nancy's voice, strained and tense.

"Hello?"

"Nancy!" he said hoarsely. "This is Sam Todd."

He heard her give a cry of pure relief.

"Sam! I've been going crazy, trying to reach Dick, and I couldn't—the Museum doesn't know where he is—and—"

"He went after you," said Sam flatly.

She laughed without amusement, almost hysterically.

"He couldn't. He couldn't, Sam! He's going to think I'm crazy— "

"Another world," said Sam. "Manhattan Island with no buildings on it. Slaves. Animals like dogs or wolves that have as much sense as men. Jungle all around. Right?"

"Sam!" she gasped. "How did you know?"

"Dick's gone there," he repeated. "The people who live there just kidnapped Maltby. How'd you get back?"

He kept listening for a false note in her voice. There weren't any false notes. Either this was the first escape in five thousand years, or it was Nancy made into a traitor to Earth and all her kind.

"Sam!" she panted. "They have ways like doors from that world to this. They set traps for people to drop into! I—I got back through one of those traps. It was—like the one I fell into when I was on the street with you. If—you hurry we can get the trap and—"

Sam said flatly, "Where is the trap? In terms of this world, Nancy. Where were you when you got back?"

"A little alley between two old houses—" She told him, almost incoherently, the exact location. "Why?"

"I'll be seeing you," he said. "Right away. That's what you want, isn't it?"

"Y-yes. I brought back a slave with me. A man who was a slave there. Where are you, Sam?"

"I'm on the way," said Sam grimly. "I'll be right over."

He hung up. He went out and got into the cab. He stopped it two blocks from where she said she'd come back to earth. There was again an office building handy. Sam bribed an elevator operator and was admitted to a men's room normally accessible only to tenants of the building. In privacy there, he peered through his peephole. He looked directly into the Other World from a height above the jungle trees. At first he saw nothing, but there was a small gap among the branches through which he glimpsed squared, fresh lumber. It was a crude and clumsy cage, of hand-hewn timbers mortised together so that anything inside could not possibly get out. He stared at it, and saw a movement nearby. There were beasts around it. The wolflike beasts he'd seen at the villa and engaged in the galley fight of that morning. There were several beasts. At one time he saw three, one lying peacefully on the ground, and one sitting up thoughtfully licking at its paw, and another pacing restlessly up and down.

He went very pale indeed. He went down to the street again and rode the six blocks to Nancy's home. He approached it cautiously, several times using the peephole in his handkerchief as if he had a speck of dust in his eye.

The part of the Other World corresponding to Nancy's apartment house was empty of beasts or cages or beings of the Other World. The space corresponding to her apartment itself was empty of anything but tree branches. But there were Other World beasts waiting where she said she'd returned to Earth. And she'd brought back a man.

It was Sam's duty to be suspicious, but he felt rather sick. He liked Nancy. He'd been naïve before, when he went to Brooklyn, and he'd almost been picked up. There were just two possibilities here. It might be quite straight, and a break of incredible importance, or—Nancy had been in the Other World for four days, and she might have been the victim of contrivances or concoctions developed during five thousand years of pure villainy, and she might have become enslaved in the most literal possible sense.

Sam took a deep breath. He hoped desperately that everything was all right. But he held his pistols fast as he went into the apartment house. He was unhappily ready to kill Nancy as an act of kindness, if it should be necessary.

There was sunshine streaming in a window. There was dust on a polished table on which the sunbeams smote. There was a man with shaggy, uncombed hair and beard seated at the table, clad in a quilted dressing gown which obviously belonged to Nancy. He was eating ferociously with his fingers. Nancy was nowhere in sight. The man looked up. Sam backed against a wall and said: "Well?"

His fingers were ready to pull the triggers. The man stared at Sam. He swallowed convulsively and spoke. "You Sam Todd?"

"Yes," said Sam. "I am. Who're you?"

"Name's Kelly," said the long-haired man huskily. "I been a slave—yonder. She got me back here. She's—washin', I guess. She said she felt filthy."

Nancy's voice called, "Sam?"

"Here!" said Sam. It didn't seem like a trap.

"Just a minute!" she called. "Get Kelly to tell you!"

"Right. Go ahead," said Sam to the man. But he kept his back against the wall.

"I was a slave," said the man in the dressing gown. "I—here!" He stood up and slipped off the garment. He wore a loincloth underneath, and nothing else. There were horrible, crisscross, purplish marks upon his back, laid over and over each other. "They're floggin's," he said briefly. "The overseer said I was hard to break an' the *ruhks*'d get me sure. But they didn't. I was choppin' wood when this *ruhk* come up an' told my guard a master wanted me. So I went with the *ruhk*."

"What's a *ruhk*?" asked Sam warily. The man drew the dressing gown about his shoulders and sat down again.

"A creature of the devil!" said Kelly in a hard voice. "Critters that look like police dogs, only twice their size. They got sense like men. They can talk to each other an' we slaves hadda learn to understan' their orders."

Sam waited. He felt very lonely. It had seemed to him that he was the only man left with the purpose of fighting the Other World. He wanted to believe this man, but he did not quite dare. Not yet.

"The *ruhk* took me to—her." He nodded in the general direction from which Nancy's voice had come. "There she was. White as a sheet but game, talkin' to the *ruhks* who were lookin' at her an' waggin' their tails an' crawlin' on the ground when she looked at them. I never seen a *ruhk* wag his tail before. An' she was dressed." He was eating again, but at Sam's expression he explained: "Slaves get stripped soon as they're caught. Men an' women both. That's a sign they're slaves. Overseers wear things like shirts. Long ones. But she was dressed like N'York, so she wasn't no slave, an' she wasn't no master, either."

The word "master" evidently referred to males and females alike, of a class of humans concerning which Kelly had evidently only indefinite ideas.

"When I got there, she says to me, 'I—I'm here and I don't know where here is, and—I'm afraid I've gone insane. These—animals seem to understand when I talk. Can you—tell me what's happened?' "

That was convincing. It sounded like Nancy.

"What had happened?" asked Sam. His hands weren't clenched so tightly on his pistol butts now.

"She'd found herself in a cage trap," said Kelly. "Same as me. When they want slaves they set a trap somewheres where only one fella at a time is likely to be. Or they fix it for times when there won't be many folks around. You get in the trap space an' somethin' drops over you, an' you are—yonder. There's a *ruhk* watchin' the trap. Always. He makes sure you don't do nothin' funny. Me—when I was caught the *ruhk* just snarled every time I moved, then some more *ruhks* come with a overseer. They turned me outa the trap an' the *ruhks* threw me, neat, an' tore my clothes off. I thought they was gonna kill me, but when I was stripped they marched me to the slave pen. A man that's been stripped an' herded by *ruhks* has all the starch took out of him somehow. For a woman it's worse. It took a long time to figger out why when she"—again the nod toward the other room—"found herself in a cage trap the *ruhk* on watch pulled the latch an' let her out right away an' whined anxious tryin' to say he was sorry. Acted like a puppy, she said. There was moonlight enough for her to see his tail waggin' like crazy. Come mornin', she started to walk away, scared, an' he follered her, an' presently a couple more *ruhks* come up, trailin' by scent, an' they acted like bashful puppies, too."

Kelly took a mouthful of food. What he said was not reasonable, but Sam found that he believed it. He tried to guess at an explanation.

"It was the next day before she asked 'em pretty if they would bring her somebody human to talk to. She'd found out they could understand better'n dogs. As good as men. They just can't say words, not havin' the throat for it. Anyhow, one of 'em run off an' brought her me. An' I told her where she was an' what'd happened as best I knew, but it took two days to figure out what made them *ruhks* act like they did. They caught some animals an' brought 'em when she said she was hungry. I managed to make a fire an' cook. The *ruhks* hung around like they were crazy about her. When we got things figured out, we made 'em crazy about me!"

He laughed suddenly.

"What was it?" asked Sam.

"Her grandma's perfume," said Kelly sardonically. "The perfume she used that she had made up after her grandma's recipe. They're crazy about it. When I'd told her everything I knew, she said she must smell like the masters they had—the masters that boss *ruhks* an' overseers together. I never seen a master, but she said the *ruhks* acted like cats with the smell of catnip, or dogs with the smell of—what is it? Anise? Maybe *ruhks* are bred to be crazy about that scent, like dogs are bred to be crazy about the scent of different animals they're s'pposed to hunt. She said if that kinda breedin' was kept up long enough—"

"Five thousand years, more or less," said Sam quietly. "That's long enough to breed in a special instinct, all right! And it's clever. Damnably clever! That's why they can trust the beasts. That's why there can't even be a revolt of overseers; much less slaves! Go on!"

"That's all," said Kelly. "When she had it all figured out—she had a little perfume thing in her purse. She sprayed some smell-stuff on me. Her kind. Them *ruhks* got bewildered, then. I'd been a slave, an' all of a sudden I was a master. All of a sudden they loved me. They hadda do like I said. It was bred in 'em. An' still underneath the master-smell I stunk like a slave! Funny, huh? So that part was okay an' we told 'em to take us to a cage trap that was set, an' we went in, an' they let down the thing on us, an' we were back in New York. We stepped off an' I was in a fix without enough clo'es on to walk a block. She grabbed a taxi an' we come here."

He poured a huge glass of milk—it was strange to see this brawny, hair man drinking milk—and turned from the table.

"I'm goin' back," he added coldly. "We kinda agreed on that. She's goin' to get some more of that perfume—gallons an' gallons of it—an' I got use for it! We got those particular *ruhks* waitin' by that trap for us. I don't know how long they will. We got to hurry. We need guns. . . ."

Sam felt sick again, but now it was relief. This narrative had just that quality of convincing unreason that nobody in the world would devise to deceive him. So much more plausible stories could have been contrived! And he had been so horribly afraid that Nancy would have been enslaved in a fashion akin to drug addiction!

She came into the room, smiling.

She had been his secretary for almost a year, and he had admired her efficiency and respected her intelligence, but he hadn't thought about her as a girl. She was helping him get set to be a consulting criminologist. But for four days he'd felt horrible self-reproach because she'd been the victim of a crime literally within arms' reach of him, and he'd been unable to help her. Now—she was beautiful.

She was freshly bathed and brushed. She was dressed in a sort of whipcord costume. She looked tense, but without fear. She looked at him, smiled, and then said urgently:

"Sam! You said Dick's in the Other World after me! Where and how, Sam? We've got to catch up with him and give him some of that master-scent so he'll be safe from the *ruhks!* And we've simply got to do something about the slaves, Sam! People from right here are made into work animals and—and worse, Sam! Kelly told me!"

Sam Todd released his two pistols. He took a deep breath.

"List what you need, Nancy," he said grimly. "I'll get a suit for Kelly first. I've got plenty of money for that and anything else we need. Then—Kelly, can we move that doorway if we've both got the master-smell on us?"

"If you mean the thing we come through, sure!" said Kelly. "There's always a *ruhk* on guard over them things in case somebody managed to get outa a cage after bein' caught. An' in case a slave got loose an' found one. No slave is ever loose outside a slave pen without a *ruhk* guardin' him. But *ruhks* won't bother us now!"

"I've already ordered the perfume made up," said Nancy crisply. "I phoned a drugstore that makes it up for me. This time I ordered all they could make. It should be ready any minute."

"Then—clothes for Kelly," snapped Sam, "so we can get to the trap and into it, and we'll go. Call and nag them about the scent while I see what I can do."

He went downstairs and found the superintendent of Nancy's apartment house. He bargained with him extravagantly. He came back with a coat and sweater and trousers—none of them clean.

"No shoes," he reported. "You're a nature boy, Kelly, but in this part of town it's allowable to be a little crazy. The scent?"

"It's ready," said Nancy.

They went out together, Kelly wriggling a little from the unaccustomed feel of clothing on his legs and body.

They got the scent-stuff from the drugstore, where it had been compounded, and a number of smaller empty bottles to transfer it to for dispensing.

"Now," said Sam, as the cab started off again, "here's some money. It's advance salary. Nancy, I want you to go to some small town and stay there until Dick and I get back. New York City isn't safe for you. But it's not likely that there'll be *ruhk-*

Egyptian setups anywhere but near big towns. You'll be safest in a small one."

Nancy said firmly, "I'm safe in the Other World, Sam. *Ruhks* would fight for me. And Dick's there!"

"I could give you the peephole so you could watch out," said Sam miserably, "but I can't hope to get what we'll need without it. If from this world I can look into the Other World with it, from the Other World I should be able to look back into this. And I'm going to need to do just that!"

"Of course you will!" agreed Nancy comfortably. "But since Dick went after me, not even knowing what he'd find, it's only fair for me to go after him, since I do know! I'm going!"

Kelly said woodenly:

"Even with the stuff on me, fella, they minded her better than me. She's right that they'll fight for her. If you got a gun for her—we need her. And fella—for what I'm goin' back there for, I'll take anybody along that'll help!"

Sam fumbled out pistols and shells for Kelly. He'd made himself into a walking arsenal, and he proved it. The cab swerved suddenly and stopped. The driver looked around. He saw the weapons being passed over. Sam's eyes fell upon him and he swallowed and said:

"I—didn't see nothin'. I didn't see a thing!"

But Sam knew that he had seen. And the passing-out of pistols in a taxicab in New York has only one meaning. People who are not planning holdups do not exchange or examine pistols in taxicabs. But Sam could do nothing. He shrugged his shoulders and passed over a twenty-dollar bill. No matter what the driver did or did not do, if the cage-trap doorway was where it had been, and if the beasts were subject to Kelly and himself, it wouldn't matter about the police. It wouldn't matter anyhow, after he'd vanished in a pool of quicksilver.

They got out of the cab, and it jerked away with the flag still down. The brakes squealed at the corner, where a traffic cop was on duty. Sam saw the cab stop within inches of the cop, and saw the chauffeur jabber excitedly. The cop jerked his head around. He fumbled at his hip and started toward them.

Sam put the peephole to his eye. Yes. The cage trap, with its doorway open. Six beasts—*ruhks*—waited on the ground about it. Sam saw exactly where the doorway was, and how it was contrived to work.

The cop blew his whistle shrilly. A radio car, going cross-town, swerved sharply. It turned against all traffic rules and

darted toward Sam. The taxi stayed in the middle of the inter-
section, the driver staring avidly back.

"Okay, Kelly," said Sam wearily. "We go through the door,
and fast. Nancy, you haven't a gun and they can't do a thing.
Just act dumb. Come on, Kelly! Here goes!"

He stepped into place, Kelly beside him. Something seemed
to flash into being over their heads and to drop soundlessly
upon them. As the other cosmos came swiftly into view—actually,
it seemed to be unveiled about them—Sam knew that to Nancy
they had seemed to vanish in a double pool of quicksilver.

Bloodcurdling snarls filled the air. Six *ruhks* gazed at him
with feral, deadly eyes. They were monstrous creatures, far
larger than any wolves could be. Sam felt an angry horror of
them. Then Kelly said harshly:

"I washed! Damn! Where's that smell-stuff?"

Sam fumbled, and went cold. He'd been watching the driver.
Then he'd been watching the traffic cop. He'd been scared for
Nancy. His blood felt icy in his veins as he realized that he
hadn't even brought the scent-stuff out of the cab. He said
bitterly:

"We muffed it! But they've got to come in the door, these
beasts. Maybe we can kill them all before they call somebody—"

But he didn't even hope it. And then something fell against
him, hard, and Nancy was with them in the cage, and the
snarling of the *ruhks* did not change at all but rather grew
louder. Because she didn't have the master-scent on her, either.
She too, had bathed and changed.

The galley lay at anchor in the Hudson, having stroked its
way past the top of Manhattan Island. The two cutters trailed
astern. Men fished, moved restlessly about, and uneasily scanned
the river and the shores for signs of pursuit. But most of them
talked. They babbled. They shouted, perhaps because as slaves
they had been forbidden to speak.

Some had been so long enslaved and so broken in spirit that
they babbled hysterically and then were struck dumb and cringed
and looked fearfully over their shoulders. But there was one
group in earnest, low-voiced discussion, and there were a few in
grim consultation with Dick.

There had been only the three boats in all the harbor which
should have been New York. The cutters had been used as
ferries from Manhattan to the villa on the Brooklyn shore. The
larger galley carried heavy stores, and on rare occasions one of

that family of aloof and remote persons who were the masters of the palace and the overseers and the slaves and *ruhks*. But there were no motorboats. There were no airplanes. There were no cars or other means of fast transportation—or pursuit.

"*Ruhks*, prob'ly, can keep pace with us on shore," said a man with a crooked nose, "but there's nothin' else that can. We can go anyplace we want an' they can't stop us."

Another man said sourly:

"Go what place? An' do what when we get there?"

There was silence. A shout astern. A fisherman hauled to the deck a fishlike creature almost his own length. It writhed and snapped on the planking.

"The masters can get all the boats they want," pointed out Dick. "They can drag PT boats into this world if they feel like it."

"Who'll run 'em?" demanded a man with a scarred face. "Not slaves! They don't even know which of us knows how to do what, and *they* can't run machinery! It didn't matter when all they wanted was slaves to row and dig and cut wood. They didn't use PT boats then, and they can't use 'em now. They can't even use galleys until they train new crews—if they know how to do that!"

"I hadn't thought of that," admitted Dick. "It makes sense, though. But we can count on their having plenty of guns. Maybe grenades. Certainly machine guns."

"Yes?" demanded the man with the scarred face. "They'd have to get slaves to teach 'em how to use grenades. They'd have to find slaves who knew how. And then—would they trust grenades in slaves' hands, or use them themselves on slaves' instructions? And how about machine guns? They can't use them and don't dare trust slaves to teach them. They'll stick to regular guns. What we can't lick are the *ruhks*."

Dick said shortly, "We did today."

"Sure! Twice. But once we had 'em swimmin'," said another man gloomily. "The other time you had tear gas. Got any more tear gas?"

"N-no," admitted Dick. "But I could get in touch with my friends—"

There was sardonic, mirthless laughter. If any man in the Other World had been able to get in touch with his friends on Earth, the fact of the Other World's existence wouldn't have remained a secret, and it would have been the object of the research of all the scientists on Earth for centuries or millennia.

All Earthly science would have been focused upon it, and it would have been reached and conquered long ago.

"What keeps the *ruhks* loyal?" demanded Dick. "Why do they work for the masters? If they're so intelligent, why don't they go off and be happy savage beasts?"

Nobody knew the secret.

"I never saw a master," growled a short, brawny man, "but the *ruhks* do. Every *ruhk* gets to stay at the palace awhile every so often. The overseers see to that! And let me tell you, the overseers are scared of the *ruhks*, too! Plenty scared! It ain't but three or four years ago that a overseer was given to the *ruhks* to play with. They had a swell game with him. I watched. First time I ever enjoyed watchin' a *ruhk* game! There's some trick the masters got to keep the *ruhks* crazy about 'em—"

"Wait a minute!" said Dick sharply. "Overseers are scared of them? And still give them orders? Why do *ruhks* take orders from them and not from slaves?"

A tall man said with precise, academic detachment:

"It's the robes. Police dogs learn to obey any man in uniform. Only overseers wear robes. That's a uniform. Maybe the cloth has a special smell the *ruhks* recognize, but a robe would be enough. Slaves are nearly naked. A new-caught slave is stripped at once. That's what makes him a slave in the *ruhks'* minds."

"But they're supposed to be intelligent," objected Dick. "Would that be enough—"

"Why not?" asked the tall man. "They're intelligent, but they're not educated. Illiterate peasants would accept a badge like that. In fact, they do. They obey any man in a policeman's uniform. It doesn't mean lack of brains. It just means lack of information. There are no schools for *ruhks*. They're intelligent like men with limited educations." Then he said deliberately: "Yes. I think that any of us with an overseer's robe—we might need a bath, too—would be obeyed within limits by the *ruhks*. I would be quite willing to try to deceive them. I think it could be done at least for a time."

"Good!" said Dick. "We'll pick a few among ourselves to impersonate overseers, then. Right?"

The tall man said, "Overseers shave. That's another badge. No slave ever has a blade he could use to shave—or cut his throat with."

Dick fumbled mentally. He had an idea. It might or might not work. He put it forward diffidently. But to his surprise, there was no enthusiasm.

"That's not what we want," growled the man with the broken nose. "Get back to Earth? Sure! But only after we wipe out this gang! If I was by myself, I'd jump at the chance to escape. But there's a lot of us here, and I aim to see some *ruhks* an' overseers get theirs before I duck!"

Growled agreement echoed his words. A man who has been enslaved and degraded wants two things above all others. One is freedom, to be sure, but the others is to get back his self-respect, which means the destruction of the cause of his degradation.

"We'll try the trick I mentioned," said Dick, grimly. "I've got a pocket knife of sorts. We'll hone it up for shaving and use the robes of the overseers we've killed, and make more if we find suitable stuff on board here. Let's get to work."

His counselors rose. But the tall man lingered. He touched Dick on the shoulder.

"Just a moment. I used to be professor of physics. If you can tell me how your friend set about making that doorway between worlds. . . . it can't call for elaborate apparatus if it could be worked out five thousand years ago, as you explained."

Dick began helplessly to tell him what he knew. It was not much. Maltby had explained that the trick was a freak orientation of the molecules of an alloy. The tall man listened. Dick added that Maltby, working drearily and close to exhaustion, had said that what we call dimensions happen actually to be merely a set of directions in which the forces we know of work. Forms of energy interchange at right angles to each other. Electricity and magnetism, for example. One wraps wire around an iron core so that a current in the wire will always be at right angles to the length of the core. The magnetic field which results is parallel to the core and at right angles to the current flow.

The tall man said, "Of course. It goes farther than that. There's what they call the three-finger rule in elementary physics. Go on! What's next?"*

Dick frowned, trying to recall what Maltby had said. When Maltby had made his explanation, however, he had been already tired and Dick had been close to madness because of Nancy's disappearance. He hadn't really tried to understand that abstract principles Maltby was wearily putting into words.

"All I can remember," said Dick, "is that he said that the

---

*This of course, is the well-known principle by which dynamos, motors, amme-ters, etc., work. The three-finger rule will be found in same form in any physics textbook which treats of electricity and magnetism. —**Murray Leinster**.

three forms of energy you mentioned as following the three-finger rule—electricity, magnetism, and kinetic energy—simply have to operate at right angles to each other. And he said that if two of them or all three were interdependent and yet somehow the apparatus was contrived so that they were not at right angles in our cosmos, then the whole system would tend to rotate into a cosmos in which they could be at right angles. And that such a system could be made to bend anything introduced into it into other cosmos. Does that make sense to you?"

The tall man clasped his hands feverishly.

"Of course! Of course! Go on!" Then as Dick looked at him in doubt, he said irritably, "The most obvious thing in the world!"

"I—suppose so," said Dick doubtfully. "Anyhow, Maltby said he thought he could produce the setup he wanted with electricity and magnetism and so on because there wasn't any—" He paused and said uncertainly, "Hall effect? Because there's no Hall effect in liquids?"

The tall man tensed.

"There isn't! Go on!"

"I don't remember anything else," admitted Dick ruefully. "The only thing that had seemed strange to him was that the *crux ansata* we started with had bismuth in it. Actually, it was a freak bronze. Very early, perhaps earlier than the Fifth Dynasty. The Egyptians didn't have tin at the beginning, you know. Egyptology is my speciality, though, and I could tell him that they had bismuth and antimony almost as early as they had copper. They used antimony for *kohl*—for eye shadow, for the women to make their eyes look larger," he finished unnecessarily.

The tall man stared at him, his eyes intent. He reached up and thoughtfully tugged at one ear.

"I shall have to think," he said slowly. "I think I see the principle. Copper is just a trifle diamagnetic, and bismuth is much more so. Yes . . . but—"

"Maltby," added Dick, "was pretty much astonished to know that the ancients knew one metal would displace another from solution. They actually electroplated gold and silver—using meteoric iron to displace the noble metals because it was considered magic."*

The tall man's eyes were still intent.

"That would be it," he said slowly. "Yes. No Hall effect in

*This is fact. Electroplated objects have been found in ancient Egyptian tombs.
—Murray Leinster.

liquids. Displacement deposition from liquids. The same as electroplating of a mixed metal. Absolutely. Given copper and bismuth, I think I could do it myself." Then his features turned wry. "Where'll I find some bismuth? The masters won't let it loose, one may be sure! I've no idea even where its ore is found or what it looks like! But any drugstore on Earth could supply me with at least some bismuth compounds!" He asked hopelessly, "Would you know bismuth ore?"

Dick shook his head.

"Given time, we might find a slave who could. Probably not here, though. In some other slave pen of some other villa. Which gives an aspect of reason to my acquired instinct to kill overseers and *ruhks*. I shall concentrate on that. We will try to destroy our master here, and then wage a holy war on others—for bismuth!"

"We're going to try to capture a doorway back to Earth from a cage trap," protested Dick.

The tall man shook his head, in turn.

"Our masters are fools—our masters and all the others," he observed dispassionately. "They waste all the intelligence of their slaves by brutality which has no purpose but the protection of their stupidity. But they are not such fools as to keep any slave traps out, with doorways to Earth in them, while there's a galley full of slaves at large and in revolt! They'll have called in all slave traps and the doorways in them. Every one will be at the villa. And they'll destroy every one of them if they have to run away from us to get help to destroy us. In absolute emergency they might even retreat to Earth. But I don't think they'd like Earth!"

He grinned at that idea and went to the others. Dick turned his attention to the immediate problem of preparing to shave and otherwise disguise as many slaves as they had costumes for, to play the part of overseers.

Men continued to fish and to babble at the top of their voices. The galley was perhaps two hundred yards from shore, but this was the shore that was the Bronx on Earth. It was separate alike from Manhattan Island and from the Long Island equivalent where Queens should have existed, and on which the villa of the master stood. With all the known boats of the villa in their hands, Dick's followers had no reason to fear bullets from the shore.

But now, suddenly, a naked figure appeared on a bluff where deep water apparently came close to the land. The figure was bent low and running. Behind it, gaining at every bound, there was the snarling shape of a *ruhk*. The naked man ran like a deer, reached the edge of the bluff no more than three yards ahead of the beast, and leaped magnificently. The *ruhk* seemed to falter in its stride, and then plunged savagely after the man. Its faltering had come with a glimpse of the galley at anchor offshore. But it plunged. Man and beast were in the air at the same time, though the man splashed and went deep before the *ruhk* touched water. The beast had estimated with cold ferocity that he should be able to overtake and kill the man before help could come from the galley.

The man stayed under for seconds. The *ruhk* rose almost instantly and paddled dog-fashion, snarling as it looked about for the man to reappear. On the galley and in the cutters howlings arose. Dick's voice straightened out the confusion. Men piled into a single cutter and hastily shipped oars, while one with a spear crouched at the bow, grinning savagely. The cutter got under way.

The fugitive broke water, flinging back his head. The *rukh* started for him, blood-curdling sounds coming from its throat. The man in the water faced it. He dived suddenly. The men in the cutter strained at their oars as they had never strained even under their overseer's lashes. The *ruhk* growled and made for where the man had been. It swam, of course, but diving was not a part of its instinct or of its intelligence.

It screamed suddenly, and thrashed violently in the water. The man's head momentarily appeared, five feet away. He gasped for breath and dived again. The *ruhk* suddenly swam powerfully for the shore. But the man rose behind it. He grabbed fiercely at its tail. His other arm rose and fell, and rose and fell, and the *ruhk* whirled, snarling, and a confusion of spray and foam erupted.

From the galley, Dick could see nothing but spray and battling portions of man and beast. The cutter sped for the spot, its crew straining every nerve. Then, abruptly, a sobbing cry sounded, and there was only stillness with ripples around something quite unrecognizable.

Then the man's head popped up. The men in the cutter extended hands to him as the boat's bow reached the floating thing. The spearman in the bow stabbed it and stabbed it and stabbed it. It did not stir.

Minutes later the cutter came back with the man who had been swimming. He was pale, but grinning. He held fast to one arm with the hand of the other, to stop the blood that came welling out from a deep bite in the flesh. A galley slave shouted, "Bring him here! I'm a doctor!"

They handed him up. Cloth that would have made part of an overseer's robe went to make a bandage—a tight compress dipped in the salt tidal water overside for lack of a better antiseptic. Dick went to the improvised surgery and asked questions.

The newly escaped slave, still grinning, told his tale. He had been sent—with a *ruhk* as guard—to carry a message to the nearest other villa up the Hudson. It should have been a two days' journey. There was a small, one-man boat still at the villa, and it had put him and his guard ashore. He'd started upriver. He'd made the journey before. As the trail ran close by the water, over a rise in the ground he caught a glimpse of the galley and the cutters at anchor. He knew of the bluff beyond him and the deep water below it. The *ruhk,* its eye level lower than his, had not seen the galley. When it heard the chattering, babbling noise the exuberant slaves were making, it stopped short to listen. The slave had gone on. When it growled to him to stop, he'd started to run. It had been close, but he'd made it to the water.

"And I was in the Pacific, once," he said, grinning more widely still. "Stationed on an atoll with a lotta natives that could swim from way back. I learned some tricks from them. I'd been figurin' on tryin' a getaway anyhow. I hadda dagger-thorn hid in my hair. I figured if I could kill a shark, I oughta handle a *ruhk*. An' I did. . . ."

The dagger-thorn was a monstrosity, all of ten inches long with a point like a needle. Since slaves were never barbered, he had been able to conceal it in his long hair. No tree of Earth ever bore such thorns, but here—

"What was the message you carried?" asked Dick. His face was tense. Their situation was bad enough without help coming to this villa from others.

The messenger brought out a packet neatly wrapped in modern oiled silk. Inside was a brightly polished section of chromium-plated brass tubing, with a cork in each end. The corks yielded readily. A rolled-up sheet tumbled into Dick's hand.

"It's no good," said the messenger. "It's crazy picturewriting. I know that much!"

But Dick regarded it professionally. It was a parchmentlike paper, the most beautiful and thick and glossy of handmade writing material. It was written on in colored inks, very beautifully, and the beginning and end glittered with gold dust or gold filings dropped upon adhesive ink while it was still wet. It was written in hieroglyphic Egyptian characters.

They were not all familiar to Dick, to be sure. There were forms which doubtless dated back to the Fifth Dynasty, but the pictographs had been debased, and the language had undoubtedly changed, and there were probably abbreviations and quite certainly some entirely new words. But it was definitely derived from ancient Egyptian—and Dick was one of no more than a hundred men on all of Earth who would be able to puzzle out its meaning.

"I think," said Dick, "that I'll be able to decipher this. It's possibly a break. It's especially a break because they'd never dream either that it wouldn't be delivered, or that anybody but one of themselves would be able to read it. I only hope it's explicit about their plans!"

It was explicit, but it took him two hours to work out the meaning. He had to guess at words that had no parallel in ancient times from the stylized ideographic elements of the writing. But he read it.

He was pale when he had finished. It was not a message to encourage him. It called for action in a hurry. And it meant that no help could possibly be had from Earth, unless he was prepared to call down on the civilized planet such turmoil and devastation as would make even the lootings and enslavings of the past five thousand years seem trivial.

The *ruhks* which snarled at Sam Todd and Nancy and Kelly were intelligent animals, whose minds worked exactly in the pattern of illiterate intelligent peasants. When the three humans appeared in the cage trap, they did not recognize Nancy as a member of the master race because she no longer had the master-race scent upon her. Common-sense logic, that.

Sam snapped to Kelly:

"Look! I'll hold the doorway if they try to get in. You heave Nancy up back through the doorway! The cops'll grab her and take her somewhere else—"

Then he heard a very tiny hissing sound. It was the sound of a woman's purse perfume dispenser. A curiously clean, pungently pleasant smell smote his nostrils.

And the snarlings died. Snuffings took their place. The *ruhks* were puzzled. Then they were abashed. And Nancy said to them severely:

"You should be ashamed! You know better than to snarl at anyone with this scent on them!"

And the *ruhks,* their ears flattened abjectly, groveled and whimpered before her. They made whining conversational noises. Kelly said curtly:

"They say they're sorry. Spray some of that stuff on me."

Sam Todd gasped a little. Then he turned to Nancy. She was very pale, but she smiled with a tiny silver object in her hand.

"Your forgot, Sam. But I wanted to come here particularly to give the master-scent to Dick. So I brought it!"

And she showed him the jug in which all of one drugstore's supply of the needed odorous substances had been combined to make a gallon of master-scent solution.

Their actions now were based upon a complete change in the situation. Kelly stepped out of the cage trap. He was clad in garments which to the *ruhks* meant that he should be flung to the ground and stripped, but he smelled of godhead. They fawned upon him. Sam Todd stepped out next, his hands gripping pistols. But though his suspicions did not lessen, his apprehension inevitably died away as the beasts groveled at his feet.

But as a matter of sheer common sense he refused to take any further action at all—even the dismantling of the doorway between worlds which had dropped them into the cage—until he had filled all the empty small bottles in his pocket from the larger container. He had Nancy slip off her jacket, too, and hold it underneath as he poured, so that if any stray drops should spill, they would add to her divinity in the opinion of the *ruhks.* And his hands trembled a little, and drops did spill, so that when he had finished pouring all the air around Nancy was redolent of the fragrance that five thousand years of breeding had turned into a talisman of godhead that no *ruhk* could possibly deny. She was in no danger from anything or anybody as long as a *ruhk* was near her.

"See if these beasts know anything about the galley," Sam told Kelly. He couldn't speak to them directly because he wouldn't understand their yelping.

While Kelly spoke authoritatively to the fawning beasts, Sam went to the cage trap. There was a round disk which was the doorway, at the roof of the cage. There was a pole by which it could be lifted out of reach from below. His hands in his pockets still holding his pistols, Sam inspected it. If it wasn't lifted in time, an agile man might climb back out. But most men would be far too terrified to think of such a thing immediately.

Kelly came over.

"The galley's somewhere in the Hudson," he reported. "They heard howlings that carried the news. That's all they knew."

There, again, would be an oddity. Wolf-howlings would carry news even faster than messengers, if *ruhks* were searching for a thing over a large area.

"That's good enough," said Sam morosely, "but we've got a job ahead of us. We've got to get this damned doorway off the end of this pole and find out how to carry it through what'll be streets of New York without bringing fat women and stray cats and odd brickwork through it. Then we'll go to the nearest precinct police station—I'll find it with the peephole—and rob it of tear-gas bombs and maybe some riot guns. We'll use this same doorway for that. And then—"

He fumbled in his pocket. He put the peephole to his eye. He saw out into the street in New York from which the three of them had come. There were many police around now. It seemed that he could reach out and touch any one. He flinched involuntarily. But they did not see him, of course. They were hunting feverishly for the three people who had disappeared so mysteriously.

Sam regarded them wryly. Then he shrugged and put away the peephole. With Kelly, he experimented cautiously. It was simple enough, however. The disk was a doorway on one face only. Objects could enter it only from one side, on Earth, and that side was unsubstantial—like, when he thought of it, the phantom disk six inches from the disk of the *crux ansata*. With the other side forward they could walk through the jungle unconcernedly, even though they marched through the space occupied on Earth by solid buildings. Of course, anything that ran into the reverse face of the disk, in the Other World, would emerge on Earth.

As a matter of fact, it is rather likely that some small fauna such as flying midges and the like did suddenly find themselves in a totally strange world of streets and stone buildings. And they would never be able to adjust themselves to it all.

The three humans headed roughly west, and presently there were some little, glittering pools of quicksilver in a precinct police station, and some tear-gas bombs were missing on Earth. Then some other glitterings, and Sam and Kelly had two riot guns apiece, and ammunition for them. The men off duty in the squad room would later catch the devil for letting such things be stolen under their very noses, but Sam and the other two went on. Six great, deadly beasts trotted all about them, sometimes breasting the brushwood ahead and sometimes trailing a little behind, but always coming back to sniff at the master-scent it was bred into them to adore, and to wag their huge, shaggy tails worshipfully.

Presently even Sam almost took them for granted. He began to worry. He was going to need a boat. He could steal anything he needed from Earth. In the present emergency he had no qualms. But how could he get a boat big enough for his purposes through an interdimensional doorway designed to be a trap only for men?

From time to time he looked through the peephole for guidance through the other-dimensional New York. And then, on the bank of the Hudson as it existed on Earth, he found the answer. There was a small boathouse in a most unlikely place, storing canoes for apartment-house dwellers nearby. The boathouse was locked.

It was two hours after their arrival through the doorway before they reached the Hudson, and it took an hour and a half to make a platform and fix the outboard motor to it and lash it across the two canoes. But then they pushed off. They had a catamaran with a motor driving it from between the two canoes. It was moderately seaworthy, and not even very slow. When it moved out from the shore the *ruhks* howled at being left behind.

Sam pulled on the cranking cord of the motor. Rather surprisingly, it caught instantly and ran smoothly. The improvised craft swung out into the river and headed upstream. The *ruhks*, howling their desolation, crashed through the brushwood, following. But presently they were lost to sight.

The motor made a steady roar. Sam headed out for a longer look up and down the river, and they had not gone far when they saw the galley. It was at anchor off Manhattan Island somewhere near what would be Seventieth Street on Earth. There was no movement visible. The two cutters were tethered to its stern.

The double canoe headed on a straight course for it. The tide was at full flood and the motor roared valiantly. It made excellent speed, but as they drew near men howled defiance at them. Oar blades waved menacingly.

"Dick ought to recognize me, anyhow," said Nancy uneasily. "What do you suppose—"

Then Kelly stood up in the bow of the right-hand canoe. He bellowed. His voice rose above the din of shouting and the motor together. The shouting died. There were not too many men on the galley—not many more than a dozen. They stared blankly as the motor cut off and the double canoe floated up to the galley under its own momentum. Kelly matter-of-factly climbed over the side. The other two heard his voice, harsh and argumentative. They saw him strip off his coat and sweater, showing the lash marks on his skin. But his most convincing argument was the riot guns he handed over in the most casual way in the world.

He came back to the rail.

"The gang's gone ashore. Some are dressed up like overseers. They took all the guns an' spears they had. They're hopin' to rush the slave pen and then fight off the *ruhks* until they find out where a cage trap is, an' then they'll try to get hold of the doorway an' get guns through that."

"We've got to go after them!" cried Nancy. "With the scent—"

"All right," snapped Sam. "Come along if you're coming! Any of you other men who want to come along too, do so. Make it quick!"

Kelly spoke urgently, and climbed down. Half the men on the galley followed. He snapped again, and the rest followed sheepishly.

"They got nothin' to fight with," he said tonelessly. "All that have are plenty anxious to come."

The catamaran's motor sputtered. It headed for the beach. It touched, and men splashed to the shore. Nancy looked at them and shivered a little. She had seen Kelly naked save for a loincloth and with stripes on his flesh, but he had come as a human being when she was in terror of the *ruhks*—even though they fawned on her. These men, scarred and gaunt and terrible, were another matter. Kelly said briefly. "Put some scent on 'em. Better pass out a bottle or two. When they see how it works—"

It was late afternoon, near to sunset. The extraordinarily assorted group started on through the jungle. Kelly and Sam had riot guns and pistols. Two others had riot guns. Then Sam brought out the rest of the arsenal he had been carrying. He saw one man caress a stubby pistol as if it were an infinitely precious thing.

They went on. Giant trees. Strange, improbable underbrush. Unfamiliar cries in the treetops. Discordant bellowings at unpredictable intervals in the distance.

They had gone perhaps half a mile when they heard shots ahead. Many shots. Then they began to run. The shooting rose in volume. Sam panted to a galley slave:

"How many guns did our gang have?"

"F-Fourteen," gasped the slave. "The rest were spears."

"Plenty more'n that up there!" said Sam. "Faster!"

They pelted toward the tumult. The sounds grew louder. They heard shrieks. There must have been fifty weapons in action up ahead.

There were. It was only logical that there should be. Because an expedition specially ordered by the master of the villa had been brought to Manhattan Island early that morning to kidnap Maltby. It had been composed exclusively of overseers and *ruhks*. It had captured Maltby, but it couldn't get back to the villa because the big galley was in revolt. So the party, in very bad temper, had taken refuge in the slave compound ahead.

Dick Blair and his party of pseudo-overseers and the slaves they would pretend they had recaptured—all of them together ran into forty armed men in the slave camp, every man armed with spear and pistol against the fourteen firearms of the attackers. And there were the *ruhks*.

It was sheer slaughter. It was a retreat from the beginning. It would have been a rout save that no man would turn his back while there remained a chance to kill a *ruhk* or an overseer with a bullet. So no armed man would run away. And no unarmed slave would actually flee while he hoped for one of the armed men to be killed so that he would have a firearm to use.

Leaping forms in the brush alongside the trail. Snarls and rushings. Then the *ruhks* stopped short. They tried to fawn on Sam Todd and Nancy and on Kelly. They whimpered and groveled before the slaves who had come from the galley with these three of Earth. The slaves fired vengefully. *Ruhks* whimpered, and were killed. Some ran away, howling. Five millenniums of breeding to be worshipers of creatures bearing that particular scent made too strong a compulsion. They could not attack or resist a creature that more than two thousand of their generations had learned must be obeyed. Frenzied panic seized the beasts—because godlings slew them.

The tumult came nearer as the smaller party ran. A slave, staggering with two *ruhks* at his flanks, fell as they came upon him. Sawed-off shotguns freed him. Nancy flicked droplets of the magic odorous stuff upon him. Then he was safe. They ran on. And they came upon pandemonium.

There was shooting ahead where the pitifully few men with firearms fought in the jungle to make a retreat possible. But jungle fighting was the *ruhks'* specialty. The spear-armed slaves had had to close up together, back to back, making a hedge of spearpoints against the *ruhks,* who could creep close and spring almost unseen in the shadowy undergrowth. *Ruhks* died, to be sure, but men died too. Yet there were many more men than weapons, and no weapon went unused because its owner fell.

It was all stark confusion and lunatic noise. When the newscomers plunged toward the embattled, despairing slaves, *ruhks* leaped—and then groveled before them. They made yelping sounds which warned off other *ruhks.*

They plunged into the mass of fighting men. And those who had just come from the galley had come to believe in their immunity from the *ruhks.* Roaring laughter, they plunged among the animals, killing zestfully. Sam and Nancy forced their way through the close-packed crowd of slaves who waited for spears that they might fight with them. Nancy battled through them to Dick, and drenched him with the master-scent. She panted in his ear. Sam thrust ahead of him and his riot gun crashed.

"Sprinkle that damned stuff!" he roared over his shoulder at Nancy. "Get busy!"

Kelly was already at it. Sam brought down a robed overseer, and a slave darted forward to get his weapons. A *rukh* pounced from behind a treetrunk—and then could not attack as the odor reached its nostrils. The slave squirmed over and fired upward. The beast screamed.

And then, strangely, even the slaves not yet redolent of divinity ceased to be attacked. There was the master-scent about this spot. The *ruhks* drew off, whimpering, and the overseers commanded them to attack, and they yelped and whined. Then Kelly ran out from the knot of slaves. Godhead was upon him. He reeked of deity to the beasts. He commanded attack upon the overseers, waving on the animals with gestures.

That did it. Where a knot of naked slaves had fought despairingly, resolved only to fight until they were killed, and where robed men had angrily but still cautiously pressed upon the rebels, now the tide turned abruptly. Nancy ran about among the slaves, incongruously slapping at them with a scent-drenched lacy handkerchief. Dick groped to understand her panted, inadequate explanation, and suddenly caught her meaning. He bellowed to his followers and led a furious charge.

The retreat that had been almost a rout became an attack again. This time the *ruhks* were with the slaves. They flung themselves upon the robed men—all the robed men not infallibly declared by *ruhk* nostrils to be divine. The overseers knew terror and horror akin to madness. They broke and ran, and those whom the slaves did not overtake the *ruhks* did. With each dead overseer there was another slave armed with spear or pistol or both, and the flight of the overseers ended before the swiftest of them could reach the slave pen again.

There were more overseers there, but not many, and there were robed men among those who approached. The disguise of the slaves had seemed vain, before, but it was not vain now. Approaching, with *ruhks* fawning upon them, they entered the barred gate. They left the *ruhks* outside. They killed the overseers who had remained at the slave camp. The *ruhk* guards inside the pen groveled before them. They killed those, too. And they let in other humans who went about among the stupefied slaves, sprinkling them with sweet-smelling stuff until every slave reeked of the odor which to *ruhks* was sanctity.

Then they let in the *ruhks*—and killed them. For five thousand years the *ruhks* had been the victims of a discovery made when magicians first moved between worlds. The scent had ensured their absolute loyalty to a race which ruled over *ruhks* and overseers and human slaves alike. And now they could not believe that men with the smell of the gods upon them could destroy them. Some whimpered as the slaves stabbed and shot. A few fought halfheartedly, almost paralyzed by the instinct five thousand years had made immutable. Some seemed to go insane at the impossibility they saw and smelled, their own massacre by men who smelled like those they must worship. But they died. All of them.

Night had fallen now, and great fires blazed in the slave pen. In their crimson light, hordes of more than half naked men and women howled and leaped and gloried in the havoc that had been wrought. Some of them prowled among the dead bodies of the *ruhks*, clubbing and stabbing the dead things when they could persuade themselves that a spark of life remained in a furry carcass.

But Dick rounded up the men who on the galley had seemed

instinctively leaders. There was a man with a scarred face, and a short and brawny man, and one who had been a professor of physics.

Dick found Maltby and freed him, and Nancy doused him with scent. They found the spidery device that no slave should ever see—and Sam knew something of it. So Dick told his followers what he wanted to do next, and they scattered and rounded up suitable men from the rejoicing mob. It was a still-shouting gang which went back through the jungle toward their ship. They carried torches, and they pushed and pulled and wrestled through the jungle the device by which anything at all that was desired by the masters of this world could be brought here from Earth. Sam Todd had even found on a dead overseer a curious pair of goggles which he recognized.

He marched through the jungle with those goggles in place over his eyes, and he was able to see at the same time the flame-lit trunks of mighty trees as bare-bodied men swaggered through the jungle, and the electric-lit streets and motor traffic of crosstown streets in that Manhattan Island which was on Earth.

The triumphant men reached the river, and torches flared upon its flood. They got the cutters ashore, made a platform of oars between them, wrestled the spidery device upon it, and the double canoe towed it out to the galley. By main strength they loaded it on the galley, and then it was up anchor and down the long, moonlit jungle shore of Manhattan Island. Sam Todd returned the alloy peephole to Dick. With the goggles from a dead overseer which looked more efficiently between two worlds, he conned the galley through the night, guided by the lights on Earth.

The galley beached alongside a barren rock at midnight, and men sweated and strained to get the spidery thing ashore on what should have been Governor's Island. Sam led men off into the darkness, again guided by lights on another planet which happened to be the twin of this. Because, of course, Governor's Island on Earth is an army post and an air field, and in these days it is kept equipped for any emergency. There would be guns and ammunition and hand grenades and other things more precious than fine gold to the men of the galley and cutters. The Army lost valuable equipment that night, before Sam Todd came back and gleeful men made trip after trip to load their booty on the galley and in the smaller craft.

Dick did not share in that. He had to talk to Nancy, to

suggest anxiously that, as soon as the loading of the galley was finished, she let him put her back on Earth down by the Battery, which was just across the stream from here. Of course the place that *should* have been the Battery on the Other World was dark forest from which eerie cries and a curious semblance of the sound of bells came faintly. But she resolutely refused to go back to Earth. When he told her why neither he nor any other man from the galley would go back to Earth to stay, just yet, she shuddered and seized upon the explanation as an additional reason why she should remain.

They were a little awkward with each other because Dick had merely resolved that nobody else could possibly be allowed to marry Nancy, and had not explained the matter to her. But suddenly he said anxiously, "Of course we'll have to slip back long enough to get married—"

And then that was all right too.

When the galley's oars spread out and she and the cutters went on through the dark once more, Dick had things to do. He called each cutter's crew alongside and gave specific instructions. Then the expedition really began.

The moon sank low, though the waters were still streaked with flashes of its light. All three craft hugged the Manhattan shore, at first. When the dim lights of the villa first became visible, though, one of the cutters turned and streaked straight across to the Brooklyn shore. Lest any *ruhks* sight them and give the alarm, men landed and marched along the shore so that *ruhks* would sight them and creep up to spring—and remain to grovel and to die.

The galley made fast at the wharf on the Manhattan shore where Dick had killed his first overseer and taken the first cutter. A scented, murderous band of armed men marched along the trail to the slave pen inland from it. Nancy, for once, willingly stayed behind. She talked to Maltby, bringing him up to date on her adventures.

A wounded *ruhk* came staggering down the trail and out upon the wharf. A member of the galley guard walked casually toward it. It smelled divinity. It staggered feebly toward him, making noises which told of disaster at the slave pen.

The sentry killed it.

Meanwhile the second cutter went on upriver well past the villa, and cut straight across like the first, and landed most of its crew. And Dick's plan went forward.

It was simple. Men moved through the jungle to make a great half-circle behind the villa, far past the range of human guards. There would be *ruhk* patrols there. The *ruhks* would detect the men and instantly become subject to them. In ones or twos, they would be killed as they groveled. In greater numbers, they might be led back to the cutters and their boat guards on the shore. Or they could simply be commanded to go to the boat guards and obey them. They would do so.

As the night wore on, there were no more *ruhks* patrolling the forest behind the villa, and it did not matter if there were. There was a single shot from a slave pen where gardener-slaves were imprisoned. And after that a line of freed slaves with a strange smell on them went through the jungle to where a cutter waited with firearms for every man who wanted them. Every man did, and many women, too. But the villa did not take alarm.

In the villa, the master was not disturbed. He was, at worst, annoyed. A man had been found spying upon the villa through an interdimensional window. Later he was found free on Manhattan Island, with arms in his hands. He had escaped capture. He had left a note for someone, pinned to a tree trunk with a dagger-thorn. Apparently some independent experimenter had discovered that there was an Other World and had managed to reach it and arranged to communicate with fellows still on Earth. When this fact was discovered, a note from an Earthling companion could not reach the thorn-pinned message without attracting attention—hence the discovery must still be a secret on Earth. The master of the villa had astutely commanded that this companion be seized. The number of persons in the secret would be learned from him, and where they were to be found. If practicable, they would be brought to this Other World and given to the *ruhks* as a suitable reward for their meddling. If there were many, the measures long ago decided upon for use in case of a discovery by Earthlings would be used.

No word had reached the villa of the capture of either cutter or even of the capture of the galley—which had taken place with Welfare Island screening the battle from the villa. The master of the villa was merely annoyed. He had not been kept informed by the regular procedure of events as they happened. Some overseers would be given to the *ruhks* for this inefficiency!

When the galley crossed the river during the last hours of darkness it was loaded to the limit with beings who had been civilized men one, two, five or seven years before. Now they were half-naked, hairy, murderous incarnations of vengeance. And every man had a modern repeating rifle with ammunition for it, and those with experience in such matters had hand grenades besides.

Runners to the two cutters learned of the number of men they had freed and armed. Strong parties went inland just in case anybody tried to leave the villa on the land side.

Then the sun rose. It lighted a world of green forest and blue waters and seeming infinite peace.

There was the tiny, popping sound of a single shot. Then the army of former slaves moved on the villa.

From nearby, the villa was very splendid and very spacious. It was built of brick in the style of gimcrack magnificence most approved of some sixty or seventy-five years ago in these same United States of America. In a parasitic race such as the slavers from antiquity there would be no racial culture nor racial art in any form. The gardens were vast, intricately laid out and tended with infinite expenditure of labor. There were trees bent and trained into preposterous resemblances to animals and to men. There was statuary looted from Earth, and there were sunken gardens, and reflection pools which reflected nothing in particular.

Over this lawn and into these gardens the freed slaves surged. There were shoutings here and there where a man with past experience in combat led some others toward the villa and guided them so they were not exposed to fire from the windows.

A sudden crackling of rifle fire from the huge mansion. No parley, of course. The slaves could not be treated with. There could be no terms of surrender. In all probability the master of the villa did not even think of it. After all, in five thousand years some slave revolts must have been attempted and one or two may have attained to some success. Certainly overseers knew there could be no surrender for them. They were frightened, to be sure, and they were doomed and knew it. But they made no vain attempts to delay the attack which nothing could delay.

They shot from the upper windows. Slaves fell. But there was instinctive discipline among the attackers. Not everywhere, but in spots. Groups of men flung themselves down behind flower beds and hedges, and a single flash of a gun from a window brought storms of lead. Those volleys smashed the glass and the sash and filled the opening with death. This was a tactic the defenders, who did not know combat but only murder, could not cope with. Many robed men died from these volleys fired by the quite impromptu combat units of the attackers.

The horde of hairy avengers infiltrated the gardens. There was an elaborate maze of clipped hedge in which fifty men crawled to within a hundred yards of the house. There were tall beds of ornamental plants which sheltered dozens more. There were screens of shrubs. There were fountains whose stone basins were bulletproof breastworks. There were graceful terraces which were cover.

The sound of shooting became a steady, popping noise. There was little other sound. The slaves filtered forward here, and trickled closer there, and when a shot came from the house there was a hail of lead in reply.

Presently the forward movement ceased. Every bit of cover near the house was filled with men all ready for the kill. Then, suddenly, it seemed that the ground erupted *ruhks*—the palace beasts. The animals brought to the villa to see their master and smell the scent of godhead had been filled with ecstasy at his sight and smell. Now he sent them out to disperse the rebel slaves.

They ran into a withering fire. A dozen went down or rolled over, snapping at their wounds. The balance reached the attackers. And then they cowered and quivered in bewilderment, because they could not attack these men. . . .

A desperate rush of robed men on their heels. If they could cut through the ring of slaves, presumably thrown into confusion by the charge of *ruhks*, they could swing sidewise about the mansion, taking the attackers in flank and rolling them up before them, while fire from the windows could begin again.

Perhaps against some antagonists it would have served well enough. But there was a leavening of former professional fighting men among the slaves. The charge of the *ruhks* had been a fiasco. The survivors quivered with uneasiness but made no attack whatever once they were among the slaves. Those hardbitten men ignored them unless to kill them with scornful satisfaction. So the charge of the overseers was no better. Indeed, it was worse, because as the last of them raced out into the open a lobbed grenade fell among them.

A man with matted hair stood up, yelling defiantly. He heaved another grenade. It went in a window and exploded inside. Howls of joy arose. Another grenade in another window. A third and fourth—

And then there was one tremendous roar of fury, and the slaves swarmed into the building from every side and through every opening, grenades blasting a way for them.

There were noises inside, for a while, but not for very long. In one place there was a nursery suite, and shivering young slave girls shrilly told the invaders that they were slaves, too, and they were unharmed. Another place a giant overseer stood at bay with a spear, his pistol empty, and a grinning young man with icy gray eyes snapped for others to stand back and fought it out, using bayonet tactics with a rifle that had no bayonet on it against an eight-foot spear. The rifleman won, after fighting his way inside the spear's length. He killed his antagonist with a gun butt. Some overseers hid, and were dragged out and killed, and others barricaded themselves in a cellar, not realizing what would happen when grenades with pulled-out pins were dropped down among them.

There was one room where women of the master race were found, very frail and delicate to look at, splendidly dressed in soft stuffs. They were dead, preferring that to the fate their servants had administered to so many slaves, and which they feared for themselves.

The last of the fighting took place in what must have been the armory of the villa. The last surviving overseers fought desperately here. When at last a surging tide of ex-slaves poured in upon them, the reason was clear. Here were the doorways between worlds. Here were the passageways to Earth. And while the slaves battered their way in, the master of the villa had been destroying them. Seared by a flame, apparently the freakish molecular orientation ceased to be. A great bonfire of garments and furniture burned in the middle of the stone floor. And there was a child here, an imperious, wide-eyed six-year-old girl, clinging to a man with the delicate features of that inbred race of masters. There was already but one of the doorways to Earth remaining. But the child's father, while his servants fought until they were killed, emptied some small bag of treasure. He strung glittering necklaces about the child's neck. He filled the small pockets of her healthily brief jumper full of gems, and then he thrust her forcibly through a great disk of copper alloy some three feet in diameter. She vanished. And then he heaved the disk into the mounting flames, seized a weapon from the floor, and plunged into the fighting. He, with the others, was dead within minutes.

What followed freedom was inevitably an anticlimax. There were some of the freedmen who—their vengeance sated— demanded immediate return to Earth. There were others—

especially women—who bitterly protested against return. Many men, also, were ashamed. And the number who felt that their vengeance was complete grew smaller as hours passed. Most found themselves still lusting to kill more *ruhks* and overseers, and there were not a few who hungrily discussed the fact that there were other villas in the Other World. There was one up the Hudson near Albany. There was one near Philadelphia, and one near Boston. There were other men in slave pens—

Then Dick Blair showed the translation of the message in hieroglyphic script he had gotten from a messenger sent to take it up-river. The translation was explicit.

From Zozer, son of Haton, of the race of lords of men and ruhks, to Khafre, son of Siut, the son of Zozer's uncle, greeting:

There is a slave from the land of slaves (Earth, or New York) at large in my land. He came from the land of the slaves of his own contrivance, not by being enslaved. There is one other who remains in the land of the slaves who knows of his coming.

I have sent ruhks and servants to seize him and to bring his companion from the land of the slaves for questioning. Do you have the news writings of the slave-people near you brought to your interpreters each day to be searched for word of this event or of the discovery by the slave-people of our world.

If such news should appear, tell all of our race, that they may spread fire and death and pestilence in the land of the slaves, in every house and every city, so that they will forget to think of our land in their study of their own griefs. Do this in the manner arranged in the time of our fathers.

Do not do this unless the news writings speak of our world. Farewell.

> *Zozer, the son of Haton, of the race of lords of ruhks and men, to Khafre, son of Suit the son of Zozer's uncle.*

Dick said bluntly:

"There are other villas and certainly other slaves. This business started in Egypt, and it spread. And the one thing these masters are afraid of is that on our Earth the people will find out about them and come and wipe them out. So if they're spoken of on Earth, they'll start to work to destroy it. They won't wipe out humanity, of course. But they can put a fire in every cellar of every house, in every warehouse, every building, every fuel store, every petroleum tank. They can put germs into all drinking water, foul all food, and spread disease beyond any possibility of our stopping them. They could steal bombs from any store of bombs on earth, and introduce and explode them anywhere they pleased.

"Nobody could stop them. The price of our going back to Earth is just that sort of catastrophe everywhere there are villas on this world. They wouldn't destroy humanity, but they'd come damn near destroying civilization before they were through. So—let's start smashing them up from here. We'll go upriver and smash the villa up there. We'll have more men, then. We'll smash the villas at Boston and Philadelphia. We'll spread out, smashing the slave pens and killing the *ruhks* until at least our own country's safe from their revenge! And maybe we'll carry on past that. If we destroy every slave pen and free every slave on this world, we can go back to Earth as conquerors instead of victims—"

He glared about him. The argument was hot. But before sunset of the day of victory, he saw men carrying bodies out of the villa and arranging to bury them, as if there were no question but that life was to go on here. He became busy planning the expedition upriver. It would be a good deal simpler than the affair here had been. For one thing, it would be an absolute surprise. A hundred armed men with the master-scent upon them would be ample. No *ruhk* would give warning of their coming. No force of overseers would be gathered to oppose them. . . .

The tall man who had been a professor of physics stopped him as he left a conference where Sam had made it clear that he was going to be in the expedition upriver.

"Nobody really plans to go back to Earth," he told Dick dryly. "I don't. No man or woman who's ever been a slave will want to go back. They'd be ashamed. The thing to do is to arrange, very discreetly, for someone to buy bulldozers and tractors and clothes and books and safety razors and canned goods and get them through some doorway to here. There's gold and jewelry enough in the palace yonder to pay for everything we need. And send us some bismuth. I've been talking to your friend Maltby. We can make doorways we can even get small oceangoing craft through. We've a job here that's worth doing. In five thousand years those devils have set up villas in maybe hundreds and possibly thousands of places. They've got to be cleared out!"

Dick said, "Still, if people want to go back . . ."

"They can't go back right away!" said the tall man. "We put it to a vote. No question. Everybody stays, at least for a while. Actually, I doubt that any of us will ever go. We'll get to realizing what will happen if Earth ever learns about this planet. Can you picture the stampede of the nations for pieces of this world? Can you picture them dumping bombs through doorways on us, or piling into this world to dump bombs back on Earth?"

Dick winced. Then the tall man said:

"We can stop any war on Earth. I think we will. We've had enough of killing and cruelty. I think—'"

"I've been talking to several people," admitted Dick. "They are inclined to think as you do."

"Surely," said the tall man. "But for the time being we'll just tell ourselves we're staying here until we free all the other slaves, and make sure there's no interdimensional attack on Earth in case we want to go back. We'll need somebody to buy things for us, and maybe to advise us from time to time. We'll need somebody around who never was a slave. We're apt to be pretty extreme."

"To tell the truth," said Dick, "I thought I'd go back with Maltby and arrange for buying the sort of stuff we need here, and—well—get married, and come back. . . ."

The tall man nodded.

That was the way it was. They returned the spidery device to its former storage place in the villa. It would never again be used to rob Earth. They began to clean up the bloodstains. There were hundreds of things to be done. Dick himself had a list of literally thousands of items that would somehow, without creating curiosity, have to be bought for this Other World.

A cutter rowed them across to the Manhattan shore just at sundown. There was a doorway there which they would ultimately set up in a closet in the house Dick and Nancy would presently acquire for the benefit of the people in the Other World.

None of the brawny figures with them showed any sign of wanting to go back to New York with them. They were going upriver in the morning, to attack another villa. They grinned when Maltby went back to Earth. He had borrowed Sam Todd's clothes; Sam was wearing a loincloth and a riot gun and enjoying it. Nancy went through, Kelly went through, with a parcel. Dick went through, and they were in New York, in a narrow, smelly small alley only feet from a well-frequented street.

"Wedding present," said Kelly. "I picked it up at the first slave pen we took. Thought you might like it."

"What is it?" asked Nancy.

"A *crux ansata*," said Dick. "On Earth it belongs to Maltby, but Kelly rates it as spoils of war. He's right. It is. Maltby shan't have it. I'll turn it into a hand mirror for you to look at yourself in."

"Kelly," said Nancy, "don't you want to stay for the wedding?"

"No," said Kelly laconically. "I got a date upriver."

Maltby went out of the alley into the street.

"See you next week," said Dick.

"Okay," said Kelly. "Good luck."

He vanished in a pool of quicksilver. There didn't seem to be anything else to say. Dick took Nancy's hand and went out of the alley. He held up three fingers and whistled at a passing vehicle.

"Taxi!" said Dick.

TARGET: BERLIN!
The Role of the Air Force Four-Door Hardtop
by George Alec Effinger

Born in Cleveland in 1947, George Alec Effinger is one of science fiction's premier satirists and humorists. He began publishing in the early 1970s and quickly established a reputation as an absurdist and a twister of sf conventions. His more than twenty novels and story collections attest to his considerable talent and ability to turn life upside down. Perhaps his best-known novel remains his first, What Entropy Means to me *(1972);* The Wolves of Memory *(1981) is also excellent. But it is as a short story writer (at least until now) that he truly excels, and collections like* Irrational Numbers *(1976) and* Dirty Tricks *(1978) are a joy to read. He is also one of the very few science fiction writers to specialize in sports stories, and his latest collection,* Idle Pleasures *(1983), is a feast for lovers of this seemingly odd combination of genres.*

Preface

Feeling neglected, my wife left me during those terrible months. I also lost the friendship of several colleagues, but we succeeded in modifying a Lincoln Continental four-door sedan into our first great bomber of the war, the B-17 Flying Fortress. It was a trying time, but I'll tell you about it if you care to listen.

Effinger WWII Book Gossipy, Rambling

Reviewed for the Rusty Brook, N.J., *Sun* by Louis J. Arphouse

The opening words of Effinger's memoir, the very first paragraph of his preface, give the flavor of the remainder of the book. After a chapter or two, it is not a pleasant flavor. This is the first eyewitness document we have gotten from the war, at least from so notorious a participant. One could have hoped for a more disciplined, less discursive book. Effinger was personally involved in many of the tactical decisions and technical inventions that shaped the Second World War. He has seen fit in his history of those years to give us instead his meager snapshots of great figures, mere glimpses of elbows and coats rushing out of the frame while momentous consequences remain hinted at in the background.

One might even think that Effinger's book was written well before the end of the war, as a kind of hedging of his bets. In places it seems like the author is placating his former enemies, smoothing over their errors in the hopes that, had they emerged victorious, they might have gone easier on Effinger in whatever hypothetical war crimes trials that might have ensued. It's unlikely that the book would have had even that effect. Instead, it is too stilted to be read with any pleasure as a personal memoir, and not strict enough to be of value as a history text. It is fortunate for Effinger, and for the free world, that his talents during the war were used in other directions.

Preface (Continued)

The decision not to hold the Second World War in the nineteen-forties was made by mutual consent of all combatant parties, and a general agreement was signed in Geneva. Simply speaking, most nations felt it would just be better to wait. But there were often more probing reasons, situations which reflected sophisticated and convoluted paths of national policy. The Japanese, for example, at the Maryknoll conference, were rankled at the oil embargo a suspicious United States had placed on that island empire. A Japanese delegate rose from his seat at one point and abandoned his polite but false diplomatic manner. "What's the matter?" he said in a loud voice. "I can't understand it. Your own Admiral Perry opened us up to trade. Now you won't sell us what we want. That's stupid." And the irate delegate walked out of the conference room, blushing at his own brazenness.

There was a stunned silence, and then a great deal of muttering from the American side of the table. One of the American delegates cleared his throat. "You know," he said, "we never looked at it that way. He has a point."

The conference went on more smoothly from there and eventually achieved a compromise that both sides could accept enthusiastically. Japan no longer felt threatened economically, and war with the United States was averted. However, there were other causes for the sudden mending of political fences, many of which might have seemed laughable at the time but which cannot be underestimated in the light of successive events. One of the emperor's younger nephews, a member of the Imperial War Office, was a great baseball fan, as were many of his countrymen; this influential person believed that it would be a shame to interrupt the career of such a star as Joe DiMaggio. The emperor's nephew, too, was a voice that counseled patience.

In Nazi Germany, the citizens were made aware of the activities of Heinrich Himmler and Reinhard Heydrich. These men, chiefs of the SS and the Security Police, were assembling vast dossiers on millions upon millions of people: Nazis, anti-Nazis, politicians, common people, rich, poor, old, young. No one in the Reich could escape their scrutiny. Of course, this news made the people of Germany nervous; at the first opportunity, the Nazis were removed from office. "Thank God for the American news services," said many German citizens afterward, for it was through the American newspapers and radio broadcasts that the Germans were alerted to the shenanigans of the Nazis. "The Americans are the sentinels of liberty. Once again they have had to save our necks." The political structure of Germany reformed, moving from the extreme right, stopping comfortably just left of middle; the new rulers in Berlin made it embarrassingly clear to Washington that there was no further reason to seek war. Italy, her trains humming along on schedule, followed suit a few months later. The trains got all fouled up, but tourists in Italy reported that otherwise things had changed for the better, except around Venice during July and August, and even Mussolini hadn't been able to do anything about that.

AT LAST, THE WAR AS IT WAS!

TARGET: BERLIN!
BY GEORGE ALEC EFFINGER
OFERMOD PRESS, $12.95
ILLUSTRATED

At long last, Ofermod Press is proud to announce the publication of the first genuine firsthand documentary to come out of the war. A searing indictment of the conservative voices in President Roosevelt's cabinet and of the timid liberal partisans, both groups which almost led the United States to ruin. MORE! A caustic attack on the fearful counselors who would allow other nations in this postwar world to maintain a superiority in number and type of bombing weapon. MORE! A vital book for all thoughtful citizens, a shocking, sometimes amusing glimpse into the world of high-pressure politics and top-level decision-making. MORE! This book is much more because it was written by one of the most influential men of the Second World War, and it contains an urgent message for all Americans.

NATIONAL ADVERTISING,
PROMOTION, AND TWENTY-FOUR-CITY
AUTHOR TOUR

$12.95, Pub Date Sept. 9, 1981

Preface (Continued)

I could see how the war was going to go, even at the very beginning. I know that isn't the kind of thing one should say about oneself, especially in a book like this. But in this case there isn't anyone else around to say it and, after all, my opinion was later seconded by President Roosevelt himself, in addition to a handful of lesser dignitaries. "Well, George," said the President, "you guessed which turn this war would take quite a while ago, didn't you?" I had to agree. And, in the same way, I can see which way this book is going, too, not that it does me any more good. Because during the war I had what I came to call a Cassandra complex. I'll discuss that in more detail later; let me just say now that I had a sense of the magnitude of the war's climax, but I never felt certain of the moral implications.

It must be made clear, prefatorily, that international disagreements had not been completely resolved without open conflict. No, rather, the war had merely been shelved. The more bloodthirsty members of Japan's Imperial War Office went underground for some years, as did their counterparts in France and Great Britain, in the Soviet Union, the war-seekers in the United States, Hitler's colleagues and Mussolini's. The world at large slumbered in three decades of what the Twenties and Thirties had been—a mixed bag of peace, prosperity, anxiety, and depression. Franklin Delano Roosevelt, relieved of many of his heaviest political worries, continued in office, as hearty as ever, a visual reminder, along with Winston Churchill, of a nostalgic time. The forties passed, and the Fifties, and the frenetic Sixties. Then the Seventies began, and it looked once more as if the world were edging closer to that irrevocable stumble into total war. In Germany the populace, tired of thirty years of liberal politics and the rowdiness it induced in the younger generation, began a slow retreat toward fascism. Adolf Hitler, now eight-five years old, came out of retirement to lead his country. Himmler dusted off his old dossiers. The people of Germany who recalled the old days smiled and nudged their neighbors. Hitler was something they could understand, not like the glittery transvestite singing stars of their children's generation. Hitler would show those guys something. The older people settled back to watch.

In Japan, the emperor's nephew no longer followed American baseball. He had taken up golf. With a worldwide fuel shortage in 1974, Japan found herself back in the same situation that she had been in the early Forties. "What the hell," muttered the Imperial War Office. "What the hell," muttered the emperor. Secret plans were made.

France watched nervously, Great Britain watched confidently, the Soviet Union watchly slyly. The United States didn't seem to be watching at all, but it was difficult to be sure.

Events moved quickly thereafter, resuming their inexorable march to war along the very same lines that had been abandoned three decades before. But there were a few alterations, thanks to the progress of both technology and human relations.

Hermann Goering, leader of Hitler's Luftwaffe, studied detailed maps of Poland and France. Goering, now eighty-one years old, looked somewhat ridiculous in his refurbished uniforms. His fat face was masked by broad striations of wrinkles. His hands wavered noticeably as he lifted small replicas of aircraft, moving them from bases within the Reich to proposed targets all over the mapboard. He beamed happily as he set an airplane down in Paris, another in London, a third in Prague. An aide moved still another airplane to Moscow, too far for Goering to reach by himself. The air marshal's aides whispered behind his back. Someone would have to tell the Führer's trusted lieutenant about the Luftwaffe's weak point. The young men, fearful of the senile yet powerful man, contested among themselves. Eventually the least assertive and most vulnerable of them presented Goering with a special file, one which had been placed on his desk several times before and which Goering had chosen to ignore. He could ignore it no longer.

FROM THE DESK OF . . .

. . . HERMANN GOERING
Reich Master of the Hunt

June 10, 1974

Dear George:

It's been a long time since I've seen you. How are things in the Free World? Things are moving along at a rapid pace here, under the banner of National Socialism. I'm sure you're keeping up with events, but I'll bet we still surprise you. The next few years will be momentous ones in the history of the world. Isn't it kind of exciting, being on the inside?

Talk of war is heard on all sides. I'm sure you're keeping up to date on our air force, its size and capabilities, just as I receive reports on you and the others. I wonder if your reports are any better than mine. You must know that the Luftwaffe is in no shape to face a long-drawn-out war now. But there's no talking to Adolf these days. He has this timetable, he keeps telling us. Ah, well, we do our best. You know just how difficult this job is.

You probably also know that we've scrapped the idea of long-range heavy bombers. I don't suppose I'm giving away any secrets in saying that. We'd have to restructure our entire automotive industry. You've already beaten us there. But don't count us out altogether! You might wake up some morning to the sound of Volkswagen six-passenger luxury bombers driving by under your window. You know us. We have more Situation Contingency Plans than anyone even knows about—including me, Adolf, the OKW, or anybody. If we could just get everything indexed and sorted, we'd be in great shape. Too many personalities clashing for that, though, I'm afraid. . . .

Tell Diana that my Emmy tried her recipe for Mad Dog Chili last week. Emmy saw it in the New York *Post*. It was so good that I was in bed recovering for three days. That was a very nice profile on Diana, too. She must be happy. Emmy can't get anything like it here, in the *Beobachter*. I think Emmy's jealous.

If there isn't war by then, I'll see you in the fall in Milan for the air show. I wish I had your youth; nowadays, a few days away from Emmy means only that I'll end up with diarrhea. Regards to your . . . President (I almost wrote you-know-what).

Best,
H.

Preface (Continued)

In Tokyo, the War Office studied a photographed copy of Goering's file. The Japanese conclusions were the same as the German: the Imperial Air Force would also have to be drastically restructured. As things turned out, that did not prove to be so large an obstacle.

Finally, here in the United States, the clamor to arms did not sound so loudly. Nevertheless, President Roosevelt was aware of what the potential belligerent nations were doing and spurred production. The Air Force followed in the footsteps of Germany and Japan and turned from the development of aircraft to the exploration of the motorcar as a tactical weapon, both as long-range bomber and as fighter escort. The reasons were the same; the Air Force generals were astonished by the statistics concerning the vast amounts of petroleum products that an all-out war would demand. Oil was scarce, and supplies were dangerously low. There was no guarantee that overseas oil-producing nations would remain friendly. Automobiles could bring about the same results as aircraft and with much greater economy. All that was necessary was a certain basic alteration in military thinking. Naturally enough, because of the conservative outlook of the military mind, this change met some resistance. But when the facts were made clear and the economic and political ramifications were explained, the real business of realigning the Air Force began, in Washington as well as Berlin, Tokyo, Moscow, Paris, and London.

It was against the background, then, that I began my work. I was given a suite of offices in the Pentagon; that was on February 18, 1974. Across the United States, huge lines of cars waited at service stations, unable to purchase gasoline with the freedom the American motorist had come to enjoy. On the way home each day I saw hundreds of automobiles still queued up hopefully; I remember thinking that it was ironic that the same gasoline shortage that paralyzed these motorists had made an all-out war equally impractical and that the common solution of all the leading nations had been to replace their aircraft with automobiles. Billions of gallons of gasoline would be saved in this way—involuntarily, of course, as the gasoline was not actually available to be saved in the first place; still, I wondered if the man in the street would react as we hoped, would rise up in patriotic sacrifice and curtail his pleasure driving for the war effort, should hostilities become official.

Chapter Two

George Alec Effinger, *Special Assistant to President Roosevelt:* Then you were involved with the early Luftwaffe attacks on Poland?

Oberleutnant Rolf Mulp, *pilot of the German Nazi Luftwaffe:* Yes, indeed, certainly so. I commanded a *kette* in an attack—

Effinger: *"Kette"?*

Mulp: Yes. I'm sorry. It's a German word. Don't worry about it. Anyway, we were taking these three Stukas against a bridge just across the Polish border. This was September 1,1974. The first day of the war.

Effinger: And the Stuka, the old terror bomber—

Mulp: Was now the 1973 Opel 53 four-door sedan. We had made the change in strategy and procedures very quickly, thanks to our basic German love of discipline. We practiced a lot, driving around shopping centers, aiming our fingers at people—

Effinger: And with Hitler and Goering and everybody back in power, it was like old times.

Mulp: I wouldn't know firsthand, of course, I was too young in the Thirties to remember them. But my parents told me stories of what it had been like. And we all joined in, and we all settled down quickly. It was so comfortable to have those familiar faces back, now grown so old, but still so familiar. Comfortable, like an old boot.

Effinger: A high black one, no doubt.

Mulp: It comes just below the knee. Ah, I see that you understand, do you not? Ha, ha, ha.

Effinger: Ha, ha, ha. We can laugh, now that the war's over.

Mulp: Ha, ha, ha. Indeed, yes. But those were terrible years. Me, driving the Opel at top speed. My tail gunner sitting in the back seat worried, nervous, chattering nonsense while I was trying to keep my mind on the road. We had a constant fear of enemy fighters screaming toward us around the next bend in the road. And then the business of having to pitch bombs at bridges or whatever, or stopping the car and getting out to toss the things. It took a lot of skill and a lot of luck.

Effinger: And a lot of daring.

Mulp: I'm glad that you can appreciate that now. I'd like to ask you a question, if I may.

Effinger: Certainly. I'll bet I know which one, too.

Mulp: You were almost single-handedly responsible—

Effinger: No, for crying out loud, I don't want to hear it. I'm tired of hearing it already.

From the Cormorant, Indiana, *Flash-Comet*

ONE THE TOWNE

by Craig Towne

The column's reporter went to an unusual promo party last week. In town for a few days pushing a new book was a former aide of the late President Roosevelt. The author, George Effinger, visited our little city once several years ago, before the war. I recall meeting him then, shaking his hand, and hearing him say that he was "glad I could make it." This reporter was very gratified that Mr. Effinger, too, remembered that brief acquaintanceship. Also, his book seems very handsome. But remember when books cost five bucks?

Chapter Four

Effinger: What was it like?

Maginna: It was awful, what do you think? Really awful. Anybody who lived through it would tell you the same thing. About how awful it was. We were all thinking such idiotic things while it was happening. And now, looking back, it's kind of hard to straighten it all out in my mind. I remember thinking, "God, they're all going to think we were idiots here." I was afraid that people would laugh or something, because we let it happen. That Pearl Harbor would go down in history as our fault.

Effinger: Of course, there was a certain lack of communication.

Maginna: Things seemed worse at the time. I've read about the attack since, many times. I'm glad, of course, that the whole thing wasn't as bad as it looked to me then. But the accounts never convey the real feeling we had, the loud awfulness. I thought, "There goes the shortest war in the world." I thought the Navy was sunk.

Effinger: Can you describe what it looked like?

Maginna: Sure. Nothing easier. It was mostly these Honda Civics—we called them Kates during the war—that did most of the bombing. And these Toyota Corolla 1200 coupes, what we called Zeroes, were the fighter escorts. It was such a quiet morning. I don't know, I can't remember what I had planned for the afternoon. Anyway, these Jap cars started driving up in long lines from Honolulu, a couple of hundred of them at least. They roared through the sentry posts, the Zeroes shooting down soldiers, sailors, a lot of civilians, even. The Kates screeched their brakes at the end of the piers, threw their bombs, and drove away. All the time their Zeroes, those Toyota coupes, were demolishing our planes before our pilots could get them started. Most of the damage was done real quick. We never knew what hit us.

Effinger: And you have no trouble recalling your feelings.

Maginna: No trouble at all. That's something I'll remember

until the day I die. That's the reason I don't like to read about Pearl Harbor, because the accounts just don't capture it.

Effinger: I'm giving you the chance to correct that.

Maginna: Sure. A lot of us that saw the *Arizona* get hit— some of us had friends on her—were glad of what you did at the end of the war. We would have voted for you for President. And you're right these days, about not letting other countries do that to us all over again. Sure. We ought to screw them down while we have the chance.

Effinger: That's not exaclty what I—

Maginna: I wouldn't want that to happen all over again.

Effinger: Me, neither.

Maginna: Right. Right. *(Pause)* Are you okay?

Dear Mr. Effinger:

I recently borrowed your book *Target: Berlin!* from the library. It isn't such a big library, here in Springfield, not so big as you'd think with a college right in town, but then the college has its own, of course, but we had your book, and since my husband was a pilot in the war I thought I'd read your book. My husband was killed in one of the raids over Germany that you talk about in Chapter Eight late in the war. We were married only a little while before Pearl Harbor, and when my husband was killed, it was a tremendous loss, but I have learned to live with it and accept it as God's will, something that a lot of us wives have trouble doing but I don't. That's just the way I was raised, I guess.

I liked your book a lot. A lot of us wives had trouble understanding just why our husbands were dying, dropping bombs on tiny towns that didn't look like they'd be worth anything to anybody. I liked your book because it made me understand for the first time that my husband was actually contributing and doing something important instead of just throwing his life away which is what we all thought for so long.

I'm glad at last that somebody told us something. We all are, though a lot of us wives have trouble believing it, even still.

But I know that if Lawrence was alive today, he'd like your book too, on account of he was a part of what you describe so well. And the fact that it was you, personally, that did so much to help our country win the war, not only coming up with the idea of the big bombing missions but also making the decision to go ahead with the A-bomb, I know that would have impressed him no end. Of course, I didn't know who you were then, during the war I mean, and I doubt that Lawrence did, either, but I know that if he wasn't dead, he'd know who you are now and be grateful. I know that I am.

God bless you. I hope things work out all right for you.

Very truly yours,
Mrs. Catherine M. Tuposky

Chapter Seven

Dr. Nelson: I walked into the project director's office that first Monday, I recall it very clearly, and I was mad as a drowning hornet. I said, "Who is this jerk?" I figured I'd worked for twenty years, and now was no time for some idiot with no experience and a lot of nerve to come and tell me what to do, war or no war. It was the wrong way for the President to go about things, I thought. Roosevelt was always like that, even in his first five or six terms, if you'll remember. But, like I say, the matter was settled, and I didn't have anything to say about it. We were at war. We needed another heavy bomber to fill in on certain kinds of missions on which the B-17 had demonstrated a kind of vulnerability. The project director said to me, "This guy Effinger wants you to make something out of this." He tossed me a picture of a 1974 Chrysler Imperial Le Baron four-door hardtop. A beauty of a car. Well, I didn't know as much about the situation as the President or you did. I thought about all the work we did to rig up a heavy bomber out of the Lincoln Continental. I didn't want to have to go through all of that again. But what could I say?

Dr. Johnson: This was my first big project. I was very excited about it. I can still picture Dr. Nelson fuming and raging at his desk, but I never shared that feeling. I was still very much impressed by your development of the long-range bombing attacks against the enemies' industrial complexes. That showed a certain sophistication that I admired. Up until that point, the bomber was used only to support troops and armored attacks—in short, limited raids. But both Germany and Japan were learning the hard way that we meant business.

Dr. Nelson: It was a kind of perverse rebellion that forced me to include many of the Le Baron's luxury extras as standard equipment on what eventually came to be the B-24 Liberator. It was only later that I learned from B-24 crew members that these things which I intended as a harmless slap at the government, hitting it in the budget so to speak, actually saved many lives and greatly added to the crews' driving pleasure.

Dr. Green: The B-24 had certain advantages over the B-17, although some B-17 pilots say the same about their own bombers. Still, the Liberator was fitted out better in some respects, particularly the leather trim inside, rear radio speaker, glove compartment vanity mirror, carpeted luggage space in the trunk, and an interior gas cap lock release. These things had been left off the B-17 for monetary reasons, but they showed up on the B-24 as Dr. Nelson's little joke.

Dr. Nelson: Still, they saved many lives and undoubtedly shortened the war.

Dr. Johnson: And you, Mr. Effinger, you were with us through all of it, with the B-17, the B-24, and, later, with the B-29. I'll never forget how much I hated your guts.

Dr. Green: Still, our country will always be grateful.

Dr. Nelson: Still.

FROM THE OFFICE OF THE PRESIDENT   Feb. 7, 1981

Dear. George:

It's been a long time, I know, since we've last had the time to talk. Well, after all, I'm President now, you know. I sometimes miss the old days, before FDR died and I accepted the burden that so wears me down these days. I miss the pinball contests in the Executive Mansion. I miss the table-tennis matches with the Senate Majority Leader whose name I've forgotten, he's dead now. I miss being able to sneak out for some miniature golf and not being recognized.

It's silly to live in the past. They all tell me that, every day. Even Miss Brant says the same thing. Am I living in the past? That's a kind of mental illness, isn't it? I suspect that they're trying to convince me that I'm unstable. Sometimes I'm thankful that we don't have the vote of confidence in this country.

What brought all this on was I found the enclosed while moving a file cabinet this morning. Thought you'd like to have it. We *all* live in the past, just a little.

Regards,
Bob

Robert L. Jennings
President of the United States

RLJ/eb
Enc.

FROM THE OFFICE OF THE PRESIDENT

August 21, 1979

Dear George:

How are things going with the you-know-what? Have you heard from the Manhattan District boys lately? Are you working on the delivery vehicle for the you-know-what? I suppose you are, but I can't help worrying that Uncle Adolf will beat us to it. Hitler is an even ninety years old this year. He dodders when he speaks these days, you can see it in the newscasts. I'm ninety-seven, but at least I have an excuse not to have to stand up. I do all my doddering with a shawl on my lap.

War is hell, did you know that? It's also futile. And inhuman, if you listen to the right people. But it can be glorious, and no one can deny that marvelous things come out of war. For instance, if you recall your history, the elimination of a lot of odd little Balkan states (a wonderful thing, I wish they'd thought of

*that in my childhood) and, of course, the you-know-what. Hurry
it up, will you?*

*I hope you're not feeling the weight of responsibility for the
you-know-what. I mean, it'll shorten the war, won't it? Try to
think of it like that.*

*I remember when it looked like this war was going to be
fought forty years ago. I thought about all the wonderful patriotic movies that could have been made: Fred MacMurray as a
pilot, Pat O'Brien as a tough old naval officer, John Wayne in
the Marines, James Stewart as a bashful hero. Who do we have
today? Robert Redford? O'Toole? Newman? Gatelin? I miss
radio.*

*Eleanor tried Diana's recipe for chicken in honey sauce. In
fact, she tried it on some Englishman over here for something or
other. He said he knew for a fact that it was a dish that Rudolf
Hess asks for a lot in prison. Hess calls it Poulet au Roehm; he
always gets a laugh from ordering it, poor man.*
*So. Keep up the good work. Push on with the you-know-what,
keep me posted, and let's have you over for supper some evening
when I'm back on solid food.*

Hello to Diana.

Best,
F.

Franklin Delano Roosevelt
President of the United States

FDR/sf

Chapter Nine

Major Erich von Locher, *German fighter pilot:* I am frequently . . . Can you hear me? I am frequently . . . How is that?

Effinger: Fine. Fine.

Von Locher: All right, I suppose. I am frequently asked

these days to comment on what I feel to be the reasons for the sudden deterioration of the Luftwaffe after the Battle of Britain. I generally avoid that question. It is too complex. I would be doing my former comrades an injustice by trying to answer.

Instead, let me speculate on the relative strengths of our "aircraft," such as they were. I feel I have more experience and more confidence to discuss such a concrete problem.

The chief workhorses of our fighter-interceptor arm were the Me 109, which the Messerschmitt people had built from the beautiful little Porsche 911-T, and the FW 190, which came later, a development of the ungainly Volkswagen Beetle. With the introduction of disposable fuel tanks, these two fighters had great range, great mobility. They were unmatched in the air during the early part of the war. However, it was not long before the Allies came up with planes that equaled and, finally, surpassed them. Much has been made of the supposed even match between our Porsche and the English Triumph Spitfire "Spitfire." As far as I'm concerned, it was an even match only when neither was destroyed. That did not happen often.

I piloted a Volkswagen during most of the war, first in the west, then on the Russian front. Is that all right?

Effinger: You're doing fine.

Von Locher: You don't think I'm being too pedantic? I don't want to sound like a professor or something.

Effinger: No, no. Just keep going like you were. It's fine.

Von Locher: Where was I?

Effinger: Here, I'll play it back.

Von Locher: *Was destroyed. That did not happen often. I piloted a Volkswagen during most of the war, first in the west, then on the Russian front. Is that all—*
Oh, yes. Well. I remember one particular battle. A whole gang of American bombers was coming east, along the northern route. Our spotters along the way had counted over five hundred bombers, all Lincoln Continentals and Chrysler Imperials, the big ones. They had landed in France and driven across Belgium, then southeast toward Augsburg. This was '79, when the Allied bombing missions were going on night and day,

without much resistance from the weakened Luftwaffe. Anyway, our Operations people had the facts on this wave, but all we could do was wait. That was the hard part, sitting in our Volkswagens with the engines revving, waiting.

Suddenly we got the call: The bombers had taken the freeway to Berlin. I felt a cold chill; this was the first actual attack on our capital. It had a tremendous symbolic meaning for us. We all gritted our teeth and swore to defend Berlin. Still, even then, all we could do was wait. The drive from France to Berlin was very long, even on the good roads. The Allied crews would have to stop in motels along the way. Our nerves were worn thin, if that is possible with nerves. At last our group leaders ordered us to pull out. We drove in squadrons, spaced out over all four lanes of the divided highway. We did not anticipate running into any civilian traffic, so we drove on both sides of the median strip. The civilians were mostly taking the trains at the end of the war, leaving the highways to the Luftwaffe.

We met the Allied bombers about one hundred and seventy miles from Berlin. There we got the greatest and most horrifying surprise of the war. The bombers were escorted by fighter planes, the Ford Mustang "Mustang." Until this time the bombers were escorted by Plymouth Duster "Thunderbolts" and Chevy Vega "Tomahawks," which could not carry enough fuel to make a long journey into Germany and then return. The bombers were usually on their own during the last stages of their missions. That's when we had our greatest success. But the "Mustangs" changed that. Even Goering realized this fact. That's when he finally admitted that the end had come. And besides their range, the "Mustangs" were our superior in most offensive categories as well.

We did our best, weary and low in morale as we were. We were defending Berlin. I ignored the "Mustangs" and went straight for the bombers. I drove at about eighty-five miles per hour, approaching at a right angle to the path of a Lincoln ahead of me. The bomber's gunner began firing, but my Volkswagen made a small target. I also could turn quicker than he could; it was shortly after dawn, and the sun was rising in the Lincoln pilot's eyes. I drove out of the sun, swung in to him, and raked the side of the car with my 20-mm cannons. The bomber exploded, then swerved off the road and through the guardrail. The battle was less than five minutes old, and already I had a confirmed kill. My squadron leader congratulated me over the radio. I did not take time to relax. A "Mustang" was trying to position itself on my tail. All around me the battle raged; tires screamed as evasive maneuvers were made; burned cars, American and German, littered the highway, making tactics and strategy more difficult. By the end of the morning I had six kills. The Americans lost hundreds of planes, but enough got through to Berlin to shock our leaders into an awareness of just how defenseless the Reich had become.

We drove back to our base in a subdued—

Effinger: I'm sorry, I think the tape's running out. Let me change . . . no, doggone it, that's the last one.

Von Locher: I wanted to talk about the time I held off three Ford Pintos while my machine guns were jammed.

Effinger: Tomorrow. As soon as I g—

June 18, 1980

Dear George:

I hope you understand. I just can't take it any more, that's all. I suppose people will think I'm unpatriotic, but they don't know how much I've given to the war effort. I sit home every night alone, watching television, wondering what you're doing. And you're always saying that you're with those scientists of yours, trying to come up with a better airplane. Well, we're supposed to be married. Germany surrendered already, remember? Japan isn't going to last much longer, either, as far as I can see. Still, you have to go have "meetings." I'm beginning to wonder.

Last Monday you said you were going to have a meeting with the President. But did you know that at just the time you were supposed to be huddling with him in the Oval Office he was on TV addressing the nation? Did you know that? I won't even bother to ask you where you were. It doesn't matter anymore. I've left you before, and the Secret Service boys always convinced me to come back, for reasons of national security. But what about *my* security? Nobody seems to worry about that.

You spend all day tinkering with Imperials and things, and what does the government give us to drive? A Mercury Comet. I think it's ridiculous.

Don't think that I don't love you, because I still do. But it's just gotten to be too much. I really mean it.

What's-her-name, that old bag secretary of yours, can take care of you. She can learn to make macaroni and cheese, and after that you won't miss me at all. That's about all you needed me for, anyway. And don't worry about money or things like that. I'm not going to bleed you. I think I'll go back to Matamoras for a while, and then I think I'll go into the theater. I've already got an offer of a job from Mickey.

> All good wishes,
> Your wife,
> Diana

Chapter Twelve

Tanora Keigi, *Japanese fighter pilot:* Now here's an interesting point. Today in America many people believe that the kamikaze pilots were religious fanatics or superpatriotic men hypnotized by their devotion to the emperor. As I recall it, this was not the case. We were merely defending our homeland and our families. The B-29 bases in the South Pacific were too numerous and too well defended to be destroyed. With the fall of Iwo Jima to the Americans, the long-range "Mustang" fighters could be based close enough to the Japanese home islands to accompany the bombers on their missions. All that the dwindling Japanese air force could accomplish were attacks against the aircraft carriers that ferried bombers and fighters from the more distant American bases. And ammunition production was down, and fuel was scarce. We suicide pilots took our inspiration from several high-ranking officers who crashed their planes against American craft in demonstration of their love for their countrymen. It was not long before suicide squadrons were organized on a regular basis.

It was very difficult to crash an automobile against a ship, especially if the ship were still at sea. Therefore, our tactics called for waiting until the American ships dropped anchor near our shores, and the bomber cars and the fighter cars were landed on the beach. We could attack these enemy cars, or the landing craft, or, with the aid of the navy and our own motorized rafts, we might be able to crash into the American ships themselves. Few of us were that lucky.

We had very strange procedures, once these decisions to give our lives in suicidal attacks were made. A friend of mine who drove a Toyota Corolla "Zero" was given a large bomb to throw. The idea was that he would toss the bomb, the bomb would damage his target, and a few seconds later he would crash his Toyota into the same target. Of course, he had to throw the bomb from very short range. The odds were that the target would be shooting back at my friend. As it turned out, he threw the bomb too soon, the bomb hit the ground and bounced up, my friend's "Zero" hit the bomb, which exploded. My friend was already dead when the flaming mass of his car struck his target. He was a hero, and we praised his name from a position of safety about a half mile away.

I had my opportunity to emulate my friend the next day, but bad luck caused me to overshoot my target and waste my precious bomb. Three days later I was ordered to drive my Datsun into a flight of Cadillac Fleetwood "Superfortresses." Again, the gods willed otherwise. Although I weaved through the American bombers for nearly an hour, I did not hit a single target. The bombers passed me by, and I was left out of gas on a highway seven miles from the small town of Gogura.

I kept trying. My commanding officers were very sympathetic. One by one my comrades met glorious death, while I found only frustration. At last the war ended before I found my own moment of honorable sacrifice.

Today I am a moderately successful and prosperous automobile dealer, with a Toyota showroom in San Diego, California. I bear no ill will toward the people who slew so many of my friends and relatives. They seem to harbor no resentment toward me, at the same time. Years have passed, and old disagreements are forgotten. A group of fellow businessmen from Japan have joined me in forming a syndicate, and we are currently buying golf courses in America, athletic teams, and opening franchised fast-food stands. Everything is fine. Everyone is happy. The emperor must have been right, after all. My service mates did not die in vain.

December 10, 1983

Mr. George Alec Effinger
c/o Ofermod Press
409 E. 147th Street
Cleveland, Ohio
        44010

Dear Mr. Effinger:

I recently had the pleasure of reading your book, *Target: Berlin!*, which was published a few years ago. I don't exactly know why I picked it up, except for the fact that I enjoy reading memoirs of famous people. Sort of like high-class gossip. Also, I've had acquaintances with several people mentioned in your book. I liked your book very much, though much of it was way over my head. I learned a lot from it.

This letter is being written for more than one reason. I don't know if you'll recall, but a couple of years ago I prosecuted a paternity suit against then White House aide Arthur Whitewater, who figures often in your work. Because of governmental pressure, the case was eventually dismissed. Another typical example of administrative self-preservation at the expense of the common man. In the following year I brought L. Daniel Dresser, former presidential press secretary to President Jennings during the close of the war, to court on similar grounds. Again, the case was thrown out before I ever had a fair chance to prove my charges. But I've learned to accept the facts that high-up officials can do just about anything these days. That's why I really liked your book, because it shows these people in everyday life, fallible and slightly stupid.

I saw you on a late-night talk show with Don McCarey, and I thought you were terrific, even if you only had four minutes. Just think, a few years ago you were one of the most influential men in the country. Now you're lucky to get four minutes of time at one o'clock in the morning. Still, that's more than I'll ever get.

Did you have any trouble publishing your book? I mean, did the government censors hassle you or threaten you at all? I bet they did. You have a lot of integrity, and I admire that. That's why I'm sure you'll behave with more honor than either Whitewater or Dresser. I can't say anything for certain as yet, but I go to the doctor the day after tomorrow, and I may have some important news for you then.

Keep up the good work. I know that in the years since the

war you've had a constant guilt thing about being responsible for the dropping of the A-bombs on Japan. It shows up all the time in your book. I just want to say that we all have things to be guilty about, and we just have to learn to stifle those feelings before they interfere with regular life. So your situation is a little more extreme than most everyone else's. In a way, we're all responsible for those tragedies. Did you ever think of it like that? It probably doesn't make any difference to you, but I wish I could make you happier. I'd like to meet you in person someday.

Like I said, you'll get the results of the doctor's examination, and we can proceed from there. Surely the royalties on your book would be more than enough to cover the minor expenses that I might cost you. It's no big thing. It happens to people all the time. I don't hold any personal grudge. After all, you never really did anything; we've never been in the same state together. Still, you must admit that, as a famous celebrity, you're a target. This is just part of the circumstances you agreed to accept along with your notoriety. So there isn't any personal animosity between us. I want you to understand that.

Anyway, I'm looking forward to your new book. I saw an ad for it in the *Plain Dealer. The Lighter Side of Hiroshima.* Lots of humorous anecdotes collected in the years since 1980. That takes a little nerve, too, you know. I'm impressed. The wild, wacky world of nuclear holocaust. Perhaps it's good therapy for you, though. Who am I to say?

Hoping to hear from you soon (I enclosed a self-addressed, stamped envelope for your convenience),

Heather Oroszco

Chapter Fourteen

Colonel Holbrook Leaf, *pilot of the B-29 Enola Gay:* I think that I was the only man in the entire 509th Composite Group that knew of the existence of the atomic bomb. I was the commanding officer of the Group, of course, and we had been assembled specially for the purpose of delivering the bomb on certain selected targets in Japan. We went through what seemed to the regular crews unusual training procedures and special treatment. I imagine that it must have been a hard time for the three other members of my crew.

Major Charles W. Bartz, *co-pilot of the Enola Gay:* It sure
was. The other men on the base on Tinian laughed at us and
called us names. They couldn't understand what we were contributing to the war effort. We weren't going on regular bombing runs. We were contributing, but even we, except for Colonel
Leaf, were unaware of just how. But everybody suspected that
something special was in preparation. We never guessed that it
was the order of the A-bomb, though.

Major Andrew Douglas Swayne, *bombardier:* The B-29 was
a beautiful car. The Cadillac Fleetwood. After flying B-17s
during the early part of the war, it was like a vacation to be
transferred to the 509. But we had to take a lot of ribbing from
the guys. It's funny. When you meet those fellows today, they
never remember all of that that happened before the dropping
of the bomb. They just remembered the awe and the pride.

Bartz: I've had to describe that moment to my kid at least a
hundred times.

Leaf: Me, too. Your kid never gets tired of hearing about it.

Swayne: As bombardier, and with just the single bomb, I
took over the job of navigator. They put us ashore in some
godforsaken rural area of Japan. I didn't even know where we
were. It was Colonel Leaf and Major Bartz in the front seat,
and me and Captain Ealywine in the large, comfortable back
seat. We drove for nearly an hour before we saw a sign. It put
us on the road to the main road to Hiroshima. We were really
afraid that we'd run out of gas before we got there. The *Enola
Gay* wasn't going to make the return trip with us, but it still had
to get us to the target.

Captain Solomon Ealywine, *gunner:* The back seat wasn't as
comfortable as most B-29s, because the A-bomb itself was
nearly ten feet long, and a hole had been cut to allow the nose
of the thing to extend out from the trunk and across the seat. It
separated Swayne and me. It was an eerie feeling, driving along
with that thing under my right arm.

Swayne: And it made navigation more difficult. I had to sit in
the back seat with the road maps spread out on my lap, and I
didn't really have room to operate. In those days in Japan, the

road-map markings and the routes they represented bore little relation to each other. Just finding our way to Hiroshima was a tough job. No divided highways with large green overhead signs.

Bartz: Still, we got there. I didn't have much to do, as it turned out. We weren't bothered the whole time. No enemy fighters to meet us or anything. It was like a weekend drive in the country. It seemed like a shame to abandon such a nice car, but we left the Cadillac in the parking lot of a largish shopping center in Hiroshima, where it would blend in with a lot of other cars, many of them prewar American.

Swayne: I had been trained to operate the bomb, although during the instruction drills I never had any idea of the magnitude of the bomb I'd be working with. I set it to explode in ninety minutes. ConComOp had worked out the schedule with almost split-second precision. That was their thing, even though it rarely worked in practice. Still, we kept amazingly to the schedule. We got out of the car, keeping our eyes on the ground, trying to be inconspicuous in enemy territory. We said goodbye to the faithful *Enola Gay,* slammed and locked the doors, and walked across the parking lot to where we could catch the bus back to the village of Horoshiga. There would be a submarine waiting for us offshore. That's the last we saw of the plane, but ninety minutes later, many miles away, riding on the bus, we saw the sky turn pinkish-white. It happened with a suddenness like a bolt of lightning. We turned and shook hands all around. We knew that stroke would crumble the Japanese will to continue the war.

Effinger: Do you ever feel the least bit guilty about killing and maiming so many thousands of innocent Japanese civilians?

(Pause)

Swayne: Guilty? Innocent?

Ealywine: We had the weapon. We had the Cadillac to deliver it. Our soldiers and marines, not to mention our fellow aircraft crews, were still dying in large numbers. For four years the Japanese had mercilessly waged war against us. Here we had the chance to end it all, with one shot, tie it up neatly with one hit.

Bartz: There were civilians killed at Pearl Harbor. There were civilians killed everywhere.

Effinger: But the numbers—

Ealywine: All right. According to your thinking there are numbers of civilian dead that ought to make us feel bad, like at Hiroshima. That implies that there are numbers of civilian dead that ought not to make us feel bad, that we ought to accept. Somewhere in the middle those feelings change. Say, if we kill five thousand civilians, it's all right, but if we kill five thousand and five hundred, we'll be haunted for the rest of our lives. You just can't analyze it like that.

Leaf: You may regret heading up the Manhattan Project, and you may regret encouraging President Jennings to drop the bomb, but I can tell you for a fact that none of the United States Air Force fliers, and none of the rest of the wartime servicemen, and, most likely, truthfully, none of the Japanese people regret the dropping of the bomb. They all appreciate how many lives it saved by avoiding a longer, more protracted war.

Effinger: You know, I've never been able to visualize it like that. But now I think I can begin to learn to live with it.

Swayne: That's the first step.

Effinger: Thank you all very much.

Leaf: Not at all. That's what we're here for. Don't give the dead Japanese another thought. After all, they started it, didn't they? It's not often that we get involved in a situation with so clearly marked good and bad sides.

Ealywine: I'm glad we were on the right side.

Effinger: I'm sure that makes it unanimous. Good night, my friends, good night.

NOW, FOR THE FIRST TIME IN PAPERBACK!

SKIES FULL OF DEATH (Original title: TARGET: BER-LIN!)

The fascinating story of World War II as told by one of the most influential leaders of America's struggle for freedom.

SKIES FULL OF DEATH, by George Alec Effinger, a Gemsbok Book.

"The taste of truth pervades each page in a way that simply can't be found in works by mere observers. Effinger was there, and he tells it all the way it happened."

—The Destrehan *Sun-Star*

SKIES FULL OF DEATH is an amazing account of Effinger's efforts to hold Germany and Japan at bay, and the relationships he endured with less far-sighted members of our nation's leadership.

SKIES FULL OF DEATH will be published March 2, 1983. $1.95, wherever good books are sold. A Gemsbok Book.

TARGET: BERLIN! An eyewitness account of the some-times madcap goings-on at the top of the executive heap during the Second World War, written by a member of President Roosevelt's inner circle. A must for hobbyists and collectors.
PUB. ED. $12.95   Our remainder price: **ONLY $2.95**

ADEPT'S GAMBIT

by Fritz Leiber

Fritz Leiber (1910–   ) is perhaps the most honored writer in the science fiction/fantasy field, the winner of the following major awards: six Hugos; four Nebulas of the Science Fiction Writers of America, including that organization's Grand Master Award; two World Fantasy Awards; the Ann Radcliffe Award; the Gandalf Award; and the August Derleth Award. No other writer has worked as successfully across the spectrum of speculative fiction—hard science fiction, social science fiction, sword and sorcery (a field he helped found), and both high and dark fantasy. His "Change War" stories were very influential and created an entire subgenre of science fiction. And best of all, he is still going strong at seventy-six.

The Wrong Branch

It is rumored by the wise-brained rats which burrow the citied earth and by the knowledgeable cats that stalk its shadows and by the sagacious bats that wing its night and by the sapient zats which soar through airless space, slanting their metal wings to winds of light, that those two swordsmen and blood-brothers, Fafhrd and the Gray Mouser, have adventured not only in the World of Nehwon with its great empire of Lankhmar, but also in many other worlds and times and dimensions, arriving at these through certain secret doors far inside the mazy caverns of Ningauble of the Seven Eyes—whose great cave, in this sense, exists simultaneously in many worlds and times. It is a Door, while Ningauble glibly speaks the languages of many worlds and universes, loving the gossip of all times and places.

In each new world, the rumor goes, the Mouser and Fafhrd awaken with knowledge and speaking skills and personal memories suitable to it, and Lankhmar then seems to them only a dream and they know not its languages, though it is ever their primal homeland.

It is even whispered that on one occasion they lived a life in that strangest of worlds variously called Gaia, Midgard, Terra, and Earth, swashbuckling there along the eastern shore of an inner sea in kingdoms that were great fragments of a vasty empire carved out a century before by one called Alexander the Great.

So much Srith of the Scrolls has to tell us. What we know from informants closer to the source is as follows:

After Fafhrd and the Gray Mouser escaped from the sea-king's wrath, they set a course for chilly No-Ombrulsk, but by midnight the favoring west wind had shifted around into a blustering northeaster. It was Fafhrd's judgment, at which the Mouser sneered, that this thwarting was the beginning of the sea-king's revenge on them. They perforce turned tail (or stern, as finicky sailormen would have us say) and ran south under jib alone, always keeping the grim mountainous coast in view to larboard, so they would not be driven into the trackless Outer Sea, which they had crossed only once in their lives before, and then in dire circumstance, much farther south.

Next day they reentered the Inner Sea by way of the new strait that had been created by the fall of the curtain rocks. That they were able to make this perilous and unchartered passage without holing the *Black Treasurer,* or even scraping her keel, was cited by the Mouser as proof that they had been forgiven or forgotten by the sea-king, if such a formidable being indeed existed. Fafhrd, contrariwise, murkily asserted that the sea-queen's weedy and polygynous husband was only playing cat and mouse with them, letting them escape one danger so as to raise their hopes and then dash them even more devilishly at some unknown future time.

Their adventurings in the Inner Sea, which they knew almost as well as a queen of the east her turquoise and golden bathing pool, tended more and more to substantiate Fafhrd's pessimistic hypothesis. They were becalmed a score of times and hit by threescore sudden squalls. They had thrice to outsail pirates and once best them in bloody hand-to-hand encounter. Seeking to reprovision in Ool Hrusp, they were themselves accused of piracy by the Mad Duke's harbor patrol, and only the moonless night and some very clever tacking—and a generous measure of luck—allowed the *Black Treasurer* to escape, its side bepricked

and its sails transfixed with arrows enough to make it resemble
a slim aquatic ebon hedgehog, or a black needlefish.

Near Kvarch Nar they did manage to reprovision, though
only with coarse food and muddy river water. Shortly thereafter
the seams of the *Black Treasurer* were badly strained and two
opened by glancing collision with an underwater reef which
never should have been where it was. The only possible point
where they could careen and mend their ship was the tiny beach
on the southeast side of the Dragon Rocks, and it took them
two days of nip-and-tuck sailing and bailing to get them there
with deck above water. Whereupon while one patched or napped,
the other must stand guard against inquisitive two- and three-
headed dragons and even an occasional monocephalic. When
they got a cauldron of pitch seething for final repairs, the
dragons all deserted them, put off by the black stuff's stink—a
circumstance which irked rather than pleased the two adventurers, since they hadn't had the wit to keep a pot of pitch a-boil
from the start. (They were most touchy and thin-skinned now
from their long run of ill fortune.)

A-sail once more, the Mouser at long last agreed with Fafhrd
that they truly had the sea-king's curse on them and must seek
sorcerous aid in getting it removed—because if they merely
forsook sea for land, the sea-king might well pursue them
through his allies the Rivers and the Rainstorms, and they
would still be under the full curse whenever they again took to
ocean.

It was a close question as to whether they should consult
Sheelba of the Eyeless Face, or Ningauble of the Seven Eyes.
But since Sheelba laired in the Salt Marsh next to the city of
Lankhmar, where their recent close connection with Pulg and
Issekianity might get them into more trouble, they decided to
consult Ningauble in his caverns in the low mountains behind
Ilthmar.

Even the sail to Ilthmar was not without dangers. They were
attacked by giant squids and by flying fish of the poison-spined
variety. They also had to use all their sailor skill and expend all
the arrows which the Ool Hruspians had given them, in order
to stand off yet one more pirate attack. The brandy was all
drunk.

As they were anchoring in Ilthmar harbor, the *Black Treasurer*
literally fell apart like a joke-box, starboard side parting from
larboard like two quarters of a split melon, while the mast and
cabin, weighted by the keel, sank speedily as a rock.

Fafhrd and Mouser saved only the clothes they were in, their swords, dirk, and ax. And it was well they hung on to the latter, for while swimming ashore they were attacked by a school of sharks, and each man had to defend self and comrade while swimming encumbered. Ilthmarts lining the quays and moles cheered the heroes and the sharks impartially, or rather as to how they had laid their money, the odds being mostly three-to-one against both heroes surviving, with various shorter odds on the big man, the little man, or one or the other turning the trick.

Ilthmarts are a somewhat heartless people and much given to gambling. Besides, they welcome sharks into their harbor, since it makes for an easy way of disposing of common criminals, robbed and drunken strangers, slaves grown senile or otherwise useless, and also assures that the shark-god's chosen victims will always be spectacularly received.

When Fafhrd and the Mouser finally staggered ashore panting, they were cheered by such Ilthmarts as had won money on them. A larger number were busy booing the sharks.

The cash they got by selling the wreckage of the *Black Treasurer* was not enough to buy or hire them horses, though sufficient to provide food, wine, and water for one drunk and a few subsequent days of living.

During the drunk they more than once toasted the *Black Treasurer*, a faithful ship which had literally given its all for them, worked to death by storms, pirate attacks, the gnawing of sea-things, and other sacraments of the sea-king's rage. The Mouser drank curses on the sea-king, while Fafhrd crossed his fingers. They also had more or less courteously to fight off the attentions of numerous dancing girls, most of them fat and retired.

It was a poor drunk, on the whole. Ilthmar is a city in which even a minimally prudent man dare not sleep soused, while the endless repetitions of its rat-god, more powerful even than its shark-god, in sculptures, murals, and smaller decor (and in large live rats silent in the shadows or a-dance in the alleys) make for a certain nervousness in newcomers after a few hours.

Thereafter it was a dusty two-day trudge to the caverns of Ningauble, especially for men untrained to trampling by many months a-sea and with the land becoming sandy desert toward the end.

The coolth of the hidden-mouthed rocky tunnel leading to Ningauble's deep abode was most welcome to men weary, dry, and powdered with fine sand. Fafhrd, being the more knowledgeable of Ningauble and his mazy lair, led the way, hands groping above and before him for stalactites and sharp rock edges which might inflict grievous head-bashings and other wounds. Ningauble did not approve the use by others of torch or candle in his realm.

After avoiding numerous side-passages they came to a Y-shaped branching. Here the Mouser, pressing ahead, made out a pale glow far along the left-hand branch and insisted they explore that tunnel.

"After all," he said, "if we find we've chosen wrong, we can always come back."

"But the right-hand branch is the one leading to Ningauble's auditorium," Fafhrd protested. "That is, I'm almost certain it is. That desert sun curdled my brain."

"A plague on you for a pudding-head and a know-not-know," the Mouser snapped, himself irritable still from the heat and dryness of their trampling, and strode confidently a-crouch down the left-hand branch. After two heartbeats, Fafhrd shrugged and followed.

The light grew ever more coolly bright ahead. Each experienced a brief spell of dizziness and a momentary unsettling of the rock underfoot, as if there were a very slight earthquake.

"Let's go back," Fafhrd said.

"Let's at least *see*," the Mouser retorted. "We're already there."

A few steps more and they were looking down another slope of desert. Just outside the entrance arch there stood with preternatural calm a richly caparisoned white horse, a smaller black one with silver harness buckles and rings, and a sturdy mule laden with water-bags, pots, and parcels looking as though they contained provender for man and four-foot beast. By each of the saddles hung a bow and quiver of arrows, while to the white horse's saddle was affixed a most succinct note on a scrap of parchment:

> *The sea-king's curse is lifted. Ning.*

There was something very strange about the writing, though neither could wholly define wherein the strangeness lay. Perhaps it was that Ningauble had written down the sea-king as Poseidon, but that seemed a most acceptable alternate. And yet . . .

"It is most peculiar of Ningauble," Fafhrd said, his voice sounding subtly odd to the Mouser and to himself too, "—most peculiar to do favors without demanding much information and even service in return."

"Let us not look gift-steeds in the mouth," the Mouser advised. "Nor even a gift mule, for that matter."

The wind had changed while they had been in the tunnels, so that it was not now blowing sultry from the east, but cool from the west. Both men felt greatly refreshed, and when they discovered that one of the mule's bags contained not branch water, but delicious strong water, their minds were made up. They mounted, Fafhrd the white, the Mouser the black, and single-footed confidently west, the mule tramping after.

A day told them that something unusual had happened, for they did not fetch Ilthmar or even the Inner Sea.

Also, they continued to be bothered by something strange about the words they were using, though each understood the other clearly enough.

In addition, both realized that something was happening to his memories and even common knowledge, though they did not at first reveal to each other this fear. Desert game was plentiful, and delicious when broiled, enough to quiet wonderings about an indefinable difference in the shape and coloration of the animals. And they found a rarely sweet desert spring.

It took a week, and also encounter with a peaceful caravan of silk-and-spice merchants, before they realized that they were speaking to each other not in Lankhmarese, pidgin Mingol, and Forest Tongue, but in Phoenician, Aramaic, and Greek; and that Fafhrd's childhood memories were not of the Cold Waste, but of lands around a sea called Baltic; the Mouser's not of Tovilyis, but Tyre; and that here the greatest city was not called Lankhmar, but Alexandria.

And even with those thoughts, the memory of Lankhmar and the whole world of Nehwon began to fade in their minds, become a remembered dream or series of dreams.

Only the memory of Ningauble and his caverns stayed sharp and clear. But the exact nature of the trick he had played on them became cloudy.

No matter, the air here was sharp and clean, the food good, the wine sweet and adding, the men built nicely enough to promise interesting women. What if the names and the new words seemed initially weird? Such feelings diminished even as one thought about them.

Here was a new world, promising unheard-of adventures. Though even as one thought "new," it became a world more familiar.

They cantered down the white sandy track of their new, yet foreordained, destiny.

1: Tyre

It happened that while Fafhrd and the Gray Mouser were dallying in a wine shop near the Sidonian Harbor of Tyre, where all wine shops are of doubtful repute, a long-limbed yellow-haired Galatian girl lolling in Fafhrd's lap turned suddenly into a wallopingly large sow. It was a singular occurrence, even in Tyre. The Mouser's eyebrows arched as the Galatian's breasts, exposed by the Cretan dress that was the style revival of the hour, became the uppermost pair of slack white dugs, and he watched the whole proceeding with unfeigned interest.

The next day four camel traders, who drank only water disinfected with sour wine, and two purple-armed dyers, who were cousins of the host, swore that no transformation took place and that they saw nothing, or very little out of the ordinary. But three drunken soldiers of King Antiochus and four women with them, as well as a completely sober Armenian juggler, attested the event in all its details. An Egyptian mummy-smuggler won brief attention with the claim that the oddly garbed sow was only a semblance, or phantom, and made dark references to visions vouchsafed men by the animal gods of his native land, but since it was hardly a year since the Selucids had beaten the Ptolomies out of Tyre, he was quickly shouted down. An impecunious traveling lecturer from Jerusalem took up an even more attenuated position, maintaining that the sow was not a sow, or even a semblance, but only the semblance of a semblance of a sow.

Fafhrd, however, had no time for such metaphysical niceties. When, with a roar of disgust not unmingled with terror, he had shoved the squealing monstrosity halfway across the room so that it fell with a great splash into the water tank, it turned back again into a long-limbed Galatian girl and a very angry one, for the stale water in which the sow had floundered drenched her garments and plastered down her yellow hair (the Mouser murmured, "Aphrodite!") and the sow's uncorsetable bulk had split the tight Cretan waist. The stars of midnight were peeping through the skylight above the tank, and the wine cups had been many times refilled, before her anger was dissipated. Then, just as Fafhrd was impressing a reintroductory kiss upon her melting lips, he felt them once again become slobbering and tusky. This time she picked herself up from between two wine casks and, ignoring the shrieks, excited comments, and befuddled stares as merely part of a rude mystification that had been carried much too far, she walked with Amazonian dignity from the room. She paused only once, on the dark and deep-worn threshold, and then but to hurl at Fafhrd a small dagger, which he absentmindedly deflected upward with his copper goblet, so that it struck full in the mouth a wooden satyr on the wall, giving that deity the appearance of introspectively picking his teeth.

Fafhrd's sea-green eyes became likewise thoughtful as he wondered what magician had tampered with his love life. He slowly scanned the wine shop patrons, face by sly-eyed face, pausing doubtfully when he came to a tall, dark-haired girl beyond the water tank, finally returning to the Mouser. There he stopped, and a certain suspiciousness became apparent in his gaze.

The Mouser folded his arms, flared his snub nose, and returned the stare with all the sneering suavity of a Parthian ambassador. Abruptly he turned, embraced and kissed the cross-eyed Greek girl sitting beside him, grinned wordlessly at Fafhrd, dusted from his coarse-woven gray silk robe the antimony that had fallen from her eyelids, and folded his arms again.

Fafhrd began softly to beat the base of his goblet against the butt of his palm. His wide, tight-laced leather belt, wet with the sweat that stained his white linen tunic, creaked faintly.

Meanwhile murmured speculation as to the person responsible for casting a spell on Fafhrd's Galatian eddied around the tables and settled uncertainly on the tall, dark-haired girl, probably because she was sitting alone and therefore could not join in the suspicious whispering.

"She's an odd one," Chloe, the cross-eyed Greek, confided to the Mouser. "Silent Salmacis they call her, but I happen to know that her real name is Ahura."

"A Persian?" asked the Mouser.

Chloe shrugged. "She's been around for years, though no one knows exactly where she lives or what she does. She used to be a gay, gossipy little thing, though she never would go with men. Once she gave me an amulet, to protect me from someone, she said—I still wear it. But then she was away for a while," Chloe continued garrulously, "and when she came back she was just like you see her now—shy, and tight-mouthed as a clam, with a look in her eyes of someone peering through a crack in a brothel wall."

"Ah," said the Mouser. He looked at the dark-haired girl, and continued to look, appreciatively, even when Chloe tugged at his sleeve. Chloe gave herself a mental bastinado for having been so foolish as to call a man's attention to another girl.

Fafhrd was not distracted by this byplay. He continued to stare at the Mouser with the stony intentness of a whole avenue of Egyptian colossi. The cauldron of his anger came to a boil.

"Scum of wit-weighted culture," he said, "I consider it the nadir of base perfidy that you should try out on me your puking sorcery."

"Softly, man of strange loves," purred the Mouser. "This unfortunate mishap has befallen several others besides yourself, among them an ardent Assyrian warlord whose paramour was changed into a spider between the sheets, and an impetuous Ethiop who found himself hoisted several yards into the air and kissing a giraffe. Truly, to one who knows the literature, there is nothing new in the annals of magic and thaumaturgy."

"Moreover," continued Fafhrd, his low-pitched voice loud in the silence, "I regard it an additional treachery that you should practice your pig-trickery on me in an unsuspecting moment of pleasure."

"And even if I should choose sorcerously to discommode your lechery," hypothesized the Mouser, "I do not think it would be the woman that I would metamorphose."

"Furthermore," pursued Fafhrd, leaning forward and laying his hand on the sheathed dirk beside him on the bench, "I judge it an intolerable and direct affront to myself that you should pick a Galatian girl, member of a race that is cousin to my own."

"It would not be the first time," observed the Mouser portentously, slipping his fingers inside his robe, "that I have had to fight you over a woman."

"But it would be the first time," asserted Fafhrd, with an even greater portentousness, "that you had to fight me over a pig!"

For a moment he maintained his belligerent posture, head lowered, jaw outthrust, eyes slitted. Then he began to laugh.

It was something, Fafhrd's laughter. It began with windy

snickers through the nostrils, next spewed out between clenched teeth, then became a series of jolting chortles, swiftly grew into a roar against which the barbarian had to brace himself, legs spread wide, head thrown back, as if against a gale. It was a laughter of the storm-lashed forest or the sea, a laughter that conjured up wide visions, that seemed to blow from a more primeval, heartier, lusher time. It was the laughter of the Elder Gods observing their creature man and noting their omissions, miscalculations and mistakes.

The Mouser's lips began to twitch. He grimaced wryly, seeking to avoid the infection. Then he joined in.

Fafhrd paused, panted, snatched up the wine pitcher, drained it.

"Pig-trickery!" he bellowed, and began to laugh all over again.

The Tyrian riffraff gawked at them in wonder—astounded, awestruck, their imaginations cloudily stirred.

Among them, however, was one whose response was noteworthy. The dark-haired girl was staring at Fafhrd avidly, drinking in the sound, the oddest sort of hunger and baffled curiosity—and calculation—in her eyes.

The Mouser noticed her and stopped his laughter to watch. Mentally Chloe gave herself an especially heavy swipe on the soles of her bound, naked feet.

Fafhrd's laughter trailed off. He blew out the last of it soundlessly, sucked in a normal breath, hooked his thumbs in his belt.

"The dawn stars are peeping," he commented to the Mouser, ducking his head for a look through the skylight. "It's time we were about the business."

And without more ado he and Mouser left the shop, pushing out of their way a newly arrived and very drunken merchant of Pergamum, who looked after them bewilderedly, as if he were trying to decide whether they were a tall god and his dwarfish servitor, or a small sorceror and the great-thewed automaton who did his bidding.

Had it ended there, two weeks would have seen Fafhrd claiming that the incident of the wine shop was merely a drunken dream that had been dreamed by more than one—a kind of coincidence with which he was by no means unfamiliar. But it did not. After "the business" (which turned out to be much more complicated than had been anticipated, evolving from a fairly simple affair of Sidonian smugglers into a glittering intrigue studded with Cilician pirates, a kidnapped Cappadocian princess, a forged letter of credit on a Syracusian financier, a bargain with a female Cyprian slave-dealer, a rendezvous that turned into an ambush, some priceless tomb-filched Egyptian jewels that no one ever saw, and a band of Idumean brigands who came galloping out of the desert to upset everyone's calculations) and after Fafhrd and the Gray Mouser had returned to the soft embraces and sweet polyglot of the seaport ladies, pig-trickery befell Fafhrd once more, this time ending in a dagger brawl with some men who thought they were rescuing a pretty Bithynian girl from death by salty and odorous drowning at the hands of a murderous red-haired giant—Fafhrd had insisted on dipping the girl, while still metamorphosed, into a hogshead of brine remaining from pickled pork. This incident suggested to the Mouser a scheme he never told Fafhrd: namely, to engage an amiable girl, have Fafhrd turn her into a pig, immediately sell her to a butcher, next sell her to an amorous merchant when she had escaped the bewildered butcher as a furious girl, have Fafhrd sneak after the merchant and turn her back into a pig (by this time he ought to be able to do it merely by making eyes at her), then sell her to another butcher and begin all over again. Low prices, quick profits.

For a while Fafhrd stubbornly continued to suspect the Mouser, who was forever dabbling in black magic and carried a gray leather case of bizarre instruments picked from the pockets of wizards and recondite books looted from Chaldean libraries— even though long experience had taught Fafhrd that the Mouser seldom read systematically beyond the prefaces in the majority of his books (though he often unrolled the later portions to the accompaniment of penetrating glances and trenchant criticisms) and that he was never able to evoke the same results two times running with his enchantments. That he could manage to transform two of Fafhrd's lights of love was barely possible; that he should get a sow each time was unthinkable. Besides, the thing happened more than twice; in fact, there never was a time when it did not happen. Moreover, Fafhrd did not really believe in magic, least of all the Mouser's. And if there was any doubt left in his mind, it was dispelled when a dark and satiny-skinned Egyptian beauty in the Mouser's close embrace was transformed into a giant snail. The Gray One's disgust at the slimy tracks on his silken garments was not to be mistaken, and was not lessened when two witnesses, traveling horse doctors, claimed that they had seen no snail, giant or ordinary, and

agreed that the Mouser was suffering from an obscure kind of
wet rot that induced hallucinations in its victim, and for which
they were prepared to offer a rare Median remedy at the
bargain price of nineteen drachmas a jar.

Fafhrd's glee at his friend's discomfiture was short-lived, for
after a night of desperate and far-flung experimentation, which,
some said, blazed from the Sidonian harbor to the Temple of
Melkarth a trail of snail tracks that next morning baffled all the
madams and half the husbands in Tyre, the Mouser discovered
something he had suspected all the time, but had hoped was not
the whole truth: namely, that Chloe alone was immune to the
strange plague his kisses carried.

Needless to say, this pleased Chloe immensely. An arrogant
self-esteem gleamed like two clashing swords from her crossed
eyes and she applied nothing but costly scented oil to her poor,
mentally bruised feet—and not only mental oil, for she quickly
made capital of her position by extorting enough gold from the
Mouser to buy a slave whose duty it was to do very little else.
She no longer sought to avoid calling the Mouser's attention to
other women, in fact she rather enjoyed doing so, and the next
time they encountered the dark-haired girl variously called Ahura
and Silent Salmacis, as they were entering a tavern known as
the Murex Shell, she volunteered more information.

"Ahura's not so innocent, you know, in spite of the way she
sticks to herself. Once she went off with some old man—that
was before she gave me the charm—and once I heard a
primped-up Persian lady scream at her, 'What have you done
with your brother?' Ahura didn't answer, just looked at the
woman coldly as a snake, and after a while the woman ran out.
Brr! You should have seen her eyes!"

But the Mouser pretended not to be interested.

Fafhrd could have undoubtedly have had Chloe for the polite
asking, and Chloe was more than eager to extend and cement
in this fashion her control over the twain. But Fafhrd's pride
would not allow him to accept such a favor from his friend, and
he had frequently in past days, moreover, railed against Chloe
as a decadent and unappetizing contemplater of her own nose.

So he perforce led a monastic life and endured contemptuous
feminine glares across the drinking table and fended off painted
boys who misinterpreted his misogyny and was much irritated
by a growing rumor to the effect that he had become a secret
eunuch priest of Cybele. Gossip and speculation had already
fantastically distorted the truer accounts of what had happened,

and it did not help when the girls who had been transformed denied it for fear of hurting their business. Some people got the idea that Fafhrd had committed the nasty sin of bestiality and they urged his prosecution in the public courts. Others accounted him a fortunate man who had been visited by an amorous goddess in the guise of a swine, and who thereafter scorned all earthly girls. While still others whispered that he was a brother of Circe and that he customarily dwelt on a floating island in the Tyrrhenian Sea, where he kept cruelly transformed into pigs a whole herd of beautiful shipwrecked maidens. His laughter was heard no more and dark circles appeared in the white skin around his eyes and he began to make guarded inquiries among magicians in hopes of finding some remedial charm.

"I think I've hit on a cure for your embarrassing ailment," said the Mouser carelessly one night, laying aside a raggedy brown papyrus. "Came across it in this obscure treatise, 'The Demonology of Isaiah ben Elshaz.' It seems that whatever change takes place in the form of the woman you love, you should continue to make love to her, trusting to the power of your passion to transform her back to her original shape."

Fafhrd left off honing his great sword and asked, "Then why don't you try kissing snails?"

"It would be disagreeable and, for one free of barbarian prejudices, there is always Chloe."

"Pah! You're just going with her to keep your self-respect. I know you. For seven days now you'd had thoughts for no one but that Ahura wench."

"A pretty chit, but not to my liking," said the Mouser icily. "It must be your eye she's the apple of. However, you really should try my remedy; I'm sure you'd prove so good at it that the shes of all the swine in the world would come squealing after you."

Whereupon Fafhrd did go so far as to hold firmly at arm's length the next sow his pent passion created, and feed it slops in the hope of accomplishing something by kindness. But in the end he had once again to admit defeat and assuage with owl-stamped Athenian silver didrachmas an hysterically angry Scythian girl who was sick at the stomach. It was then that an ill-advised curious young Greek philosopher suggested to the Northman that the soul or inward form of the thing loved is alone of importance, the outward form having no ultimate significance.

"You belong to the Socratic school?" Fafhrd questioned gently. The Greek nodded.

"Socrates was the philosopher who was able to drink unlimited quantities of wine without blinking?"

Again the quick nod.

"That was because his rational soul dominated his animal soul?"

"You are learned," replied the Greek, with a more respectful but equally quick nod.

"I am not through. Do you consider yourself in all ways a true follower of your master?"

This time the Greek's quickness undid him. He nodded, and two days later he was carried out of the wine shop by friends, who found him cradled in a broken wine barrel, as if new-born in no common manner. For days he remained drunk, time enough for a small sect to spring up who believed him a reincarnation of Dionysus and as such worshiped him. The sect was dissolved when he became half sober and delivered his first oracular address, which had as its subject the evils of drunkenness.

The morning after the deification of the rash philosopher, Fafhrd awoke when the first hot sunbeams struck the flat roof on which he and the Mouser had chosen to pass the night. Without sound or movement, suppressing the urge to groan out for someone to buy him a bag of snow from the white-capped Lebanons (over which the sun was even now peeping) to cool his aching head, he opened an eye on the sight that he in his wisdom had expected: the Mouser sitting on his heels and looking at the sea.

"Son of a wizard and a witch," he said, "it seems that once again we must fall back upon our last resource."

The Mouser did not turn his head, but he nodded it once, deliberately.

"The first time we did not come away with our lives," Fafhrd went on.

"The second time we lost our souls to the Other Creatures," the Mouser chimed in, as if they were singing a dawn chant to Isis.

"And the last time we were snatched away from the bright dream of Lankhmar."

"He may trick us into drinking the drink, and we not awake for another five hundred years."

"He may send us to our deaths and we not to be reincarnated for another two thousand," Fafhrd continued.

"He may show us Pan, or offer us to the Elder Gods, or whisk us beyond the stars, or send us into the underworld of Quarmall," the Mouser concluded.

There was a pause of several moments.

Then the Gray Mouser whispered, "Nevertheless, we must visit Ningauble of the Seven Eyes."

And he spoke truly, for as Fafhrd had guessed, his soul was hovering over the sea dreaming of dark-haired Ahura.

2: Ningauble

So they crossed the snowy Lebanons and stole three camels, virtuously choosing to rob a rich landlord who made his tenants milk rocks and sow the shores of the Dead Sea, for it was unwise to approach the Gossiper of the Gods with an overly dirty conscience. After seven days of pitching and tossing across the desert, furnace days that made Fafhrd curse Muspelheim's fire gods, in whom he did not believe, they reached the Sand Combers and the Great Sand Whirlpools, and warily slipping past them while they were only lazily twirling, climbed the Rocky Islet. The city-loving Mouser ranted at Ningauble's preference for "a godforsaken hole in the desert," although he suspected that the Newsmonger and his agents came and went by a more hospitable road than the one provided for visitors, and although he knew as well as Fafhrd that the Snarer of Rumors (especially the false, which are the more valuable) must live as close to India and the infinite garden lands of the Yellow Men as to barbaric Britain and marching Rome, as close to the heaven-steaming trans-Ethiopian jungle as to the mystery of lonely tablelands and star-scraping mountains beyond the Caspian Sea.

With high expectations they tethered their camels, took torches, and fearlessly entered the Bottomless Caves, for it was not so much in the visiting of Ningauble that danger lay as in the tantalizing charm of his advice, which was so great that one had to follow wherever it led.

Nevertheless Fafhrd said, "An earthquake swallowed Ningauble's house and it stuck in his throat. May he not hiccup."

As they were passing over the Trembling Bridge spanning the Pit of Ultimate Truth, which could have devoured the light of ten thousand torches without becoming any less black, they met and edged wordlessly past a helmeted, impassive fellow whom they recognized as a far-journeying Mongol. They speculated as to whether he too were a visitor of the Gossiper, or a spy—Fafhrd had no faith in the clairvoyant powers of the seven eyes, averring that they were merely a sham to awe fools and that Ningauble's information was gathered by a corps of peddlers, panders, slaves, urchins, eunuchs, and midwives, which outnumbered the grand armies of a dozen kings.

They reached the other side with relief and passed a score of tunnel mouths, which the Mouser eyed most wistfully.

"Mayhap we should choose one at random," he muttered, "and seek yet another world. Ahura's not Aphrodite, nor yet Astarte—quite."

"Without Ning's guidance?" Fafhrd retorted. "And carrying our curses with us? Press on!"

Presently they saw a faint light flickering on the stalactited roof, reflected from a level above them. Soon they were struggling toward it up the Staircase of Error, an agglomeration of great rough rocks. Fafhrd stretched his long legs; the Mouser leaped catlike. The little creatures that scurried about their feet, brushed their shoulders in slow flight, or merely showed their yellow, insatiably curious eyes from crevice and rocky perch multiplied in number; for they were nearing the Arch-eavesdropper.

A little later, having wasted no time in reconnoitering, they stood before the Great Gate, whose iron-studded upper reaches disdained the illumination of the tiny fire. It was not the gate, however, that interested them, but its keeper, a monstrously paunched creature sitting on the floor beside a vast heap of potsherds, and whose only movement was a rubbing of what seemed to be his hands. He kept them under the shabby but voluminous cloak which also completely hooded his head. A third of the way down the cloak, two large bats clung.

Fafhrd cleared his throat.

The movement ceased under the cloak.

Then out of the top of it sinuously writhed something that seemed to be a serpent, only in place of a head it bore an opalescent jewel with a dark central speck. Nevertheless, one might finally have judged it a serpent, were it not that it also resembled a thick-stalked exotic bloom. It restlessly turned this way and that until it pointed at the two strangers. Then it went rigid and the bulbous extremity seemed to glow more brightly. There came a low purring and five similar stalks twisted rapidly from under the hood and aligned themselves with their companion. Then the six black pupils dilated.

"Fat-bellied rumor monger!" hailed the Mouser nervously. "Must you forever play at peep show?"

For one could never quite get over the faint initial uneasiness that came with meeting Ningauble of the Seven Eyes.

"That is an incivility, Mouser," a voice from under the hood quavered thinly. "It is not well for men who come seeking sage counsel to cast fleers before them. Nevertheless, I am today in a merry humor and will give ear to your problem. Let me see, now, what world do you and Fafhrd come from?"

"Earth, as you very well know, you king of shreds of lies and patches of hypocrisy," the Mouser retorted thinly, stepping nearer. Three of the eyes closely followed his advance, while a fourth kept watch on Fafhrd.

At the same time, "Further incivilities," Ningauble murmured sadly, shaking his head so that his eyestalks jogged. "You think it easy to keep track of the times and spaces and of the worlds manifold? And speaking of time, is it not time indeed that you ceased to impose on me, because you once got me an unborn ghoul that I might question it of its parentage? The service to me was slight, accepted only to humor you; and I, by the name of the Spoorless God, have repaid it twenty times over."

"Nonsense, Midwife of Secrets," retorted the Mouser, stepping forward familiarly, his gay impudence almost restored. "You know as well as I that deep in your great paunch you are trembling with delight at having a chance to mouth your knowledge to two such appreciative listeners as we."

"That is as far from the truth as I am from the Secret of the Sphinx," commented Ningauble, four of his eyes following the Mouser's advance, one keeping watch on Fafhrd, while the sixth looped back around the hood to reappear on the other side and gaze suspiciously behind them.

"But, Ancient Tale-bearer, I am sure you have been closer to the Sphinx than any of her stony lovers. Very likely she first received her paltry riddle from your great store."

Ningauble quivered like jelly at this tickling flattery.

"Nevertheless," he piped, "today I am in a merry humor and will give ear to your question. But remember that it will almost certainly be too difficult for me."

"We know your great ingenuity in the face of insurmountable obstacles," rejoined the Mouser in the properly soothing tones.

"Why doesn't your friend come forward?" asked Ningauble, suddenly querulous again.

Fafhrd had been waiting for that question. It always went against his grain to have to behave congenially toward one who called himself the Mightiest Magician as well as the Gossiper of the Gods. But that Ningauble should let hang from his shoulders two bats whom he called Hugin and Munin in open burlesque of Odin's ravens was too much for him. It was more a patriotic than religious matter with Fafhrd. He believed in Odin only during moments of sentimental weakness.

"Slay the bats or send them slithering and I'll come, but not before," he dogmatized.

"Now I'll tell you nothing," said Ningauble pettishly, "for, as all know, my health will not permit bickering."

"But, Schoolmaster of Falsehood," purred the Mouser, darting a murderous glance at Fafhrd, "that is indeed to be regretted, especially since I was looking forward to regaling you with the intricate scandal that the Friday concubine of the satrap Philip withheld even from her body slave."

"Ah well," conceded the Many-Eyed One, "it is time for Hugin and Munin to feed."

The bats reluctantly unfurled their wings and flew lazily into the darkness.

Fafhrd stirred himself and moved forward, sustaining the scrutiny of the majority of the eyes, all six of which the Northman considered artfully manipulated puppet-orbs. The seventh no man had seen, or boasted of having seen, save the Mouser, who claimed it was Odin's other eye, stolen from sagacious Mimer—this not because he believed it, but to irk his Northern comrade.

"Greetings, Snake Eyes," Fafhrd boomed.

"Oh, is it you, Hulk?" said Ningauble carelessly. "Sit down, both, and share my humble fire."

"Are we not to be invited beyond the Great Gate and share your fabulous comforts too?"

"Do not mock me, Gray One. As all know, I am poor, penurious Ningauble."

So with a sigh the Mouser settled himself on his heels, for he well knew that the Gossiper prized above all else a reputation for poverty, chastity, humility, and thrift, therefore playing his own doorkeeper, except on certain days when the Great Gate muted the tinkle of impious sistrum and the lascivious wail of flute and the giggles of those who postured in the shadow shows.

But now Ningauble coughed piteously and seemed to shiver and warmed his cloaked members at the fire. And the shadows flickered weakly against iron and stone, and the little creatures crept rustling in, making their eyes wide to see and their ears cupped to hear; and upon their rhythmically swinging, weaving stalks pulsated the six eyes. At intervals, too, Ningauble would pick up, seemingly at random, a potsherd from the great pile and rapidly scan the memorandum scribbled on it, without breaking the rhythm of the eyestalks or, apparently, the thread of his attention.

The Mouser and Fafhrd crouched on their hams.

As Fafhrd started to speak, Ningauble questioned rapidly, "And now, my children, you had something to tell me concerning the Friday concubine—"

"Ah, yes, Artist of Untruth," the Mouser cut in hastily. "Concerning not so much the concubine as three eunuch priests of Cybele and a slave girl from Samos—a tasty affair of wondrous complexity, which you must give me leave to let simmer in my mind so that I may serve it up to you skimmed of the slightest fat of exaggeration and with all the spice of true detail."

"And while we wait for the Mouser's mind-pot to boil," said Fafhrd casually, at last catching the spirit of the thing, "you may the more merrily pass the time by advising us as to a trifling difficulty." And he gave a succinct account of their tantalizing bedevilment by sow- and snail-changed maidens.

"And you say that Chloe alone proved immune to the spell?" queried Ningauble thoughtfully, tossing a potsherd to the far side of the pile. "Now that brings to my mind—"

"The exceedingly peculiar remark at the end of Diotima's fourth epistle to Socrates?" interrupted the Mouser brightly. "Am I not right, Father?"

"You are not," replied Ningauble coldly. "As I was about to observe, when this tick of the intellect sought to burrow the skin of my mind, there must be something that throws a protective influence around Chloe. Do you know of any god or demon in whose special favor she stands, or any incantation or rune she habitually mumbles, or any notable talisman, charm, or amulet she customarily wears or inscribes on her body?"

"She did mention one thing," the Mouser admitted diffidently after a moment. "An amulet given her years ago by some Persian, or Greco-Persian, girl. Doubtless a trifle of no consequence."

"Doubtless. Now, when the first sow-change occurred, did Fafhrd laugh the laugh? He did? That was unwise, as I have many times warned you. Advertise often enough your connection with the Elder Gods and you may be sure that some greedy searcher from the pit . . ."

"But what *is* our connection with the Elder Gods?" asked the Mouser, eagerly, though not hopefully. Fafhrd grunted derisively.

"Those are matters best not spoken of," Ningauble ordained. "Was there anyone who showed a particular interest in Fafhrd's laughter?"

The Mouser hesitated. Fafhrd coughed. Thus prodded, the Mouser confessed, "Oh, there was a girl who was perhaps a trifle more attentive than the others to his bellowing. A Persian girl. In fact, as I recall, the same one who gave Chloe the amulet."

"Her name is Ahura," said Fafhrd. "The Mouser's in love with her."

"A fable!" the Mouser denied laughingly, double-daggering Fafhrd with a superstitious glare. "I can assure you, Father, that she is a very shy, stupid girl, who cannot possibly be concerned in any way with our troubles."

"Of course, since you say so," Ningauble observed, his voice icily rebuking. "However, I can tell you this much: the one who has placed the ignominious spell upon you is, insofar as he partakes of humanity, a man . . ."

(The Mouser was relieved. It was unpleasant to think of dark-haired, lithe Ahura being subjected to certain methods of questioning which Ningauble was reputed to employ. He was irked at his own clumsiness in trying to lead Ningauble's attention away from Ahura. Where she was concerned, his wit failed him.)

". . . and an adept," Ningauble concluded. "Yes, my sons, an adept—a master practitioner of blackest magic without faintest blink of light."

The Mouser started. Fafhrd groaned. "Again?"

"Again," Ningauble affirmed. "Though why, save for your connection with the Elder Gods, you should interest those most recondite of creatures, I cannot guess. They are not men who wittingly will stand in the glaringly illuminated foreground of history. They seek—"

"But who is it?" Fafhrd interjected.

"Be quiet, Mutilator of Rhetoric. They seek the shadows, and surely for good reason. They are the glorious amateurs of high magic, disdaining practical ends, caring only for the satisfaction of their insatiable curiosities, and therefore doubly dangerous. They are . . ."

"But what's his name?"

"Silence, Trampler of Beautiful Phrases. They are in their fashion fearless, irreligiously considering themselves the co-equals of destiny and having only contempt for the Demigoddess of Chance, the Imp of Luck, and the Demon of Improbability. In short, they are adversaries before whom you should certainly tremble and to whose will you should unquestionably bow."

"But his name, Father, his name!" Fafhrd burst out, and the Mouser, his impudence again in the ascendant, remarked, "Is it he of the Sabihoon, is it not, Father?"

"It is not. The Sabihoon are an ignorant fisher folk who inhabit the hither shore of the far lake and worship the beast god Wheen, denying all others," a reply that tickled the Mouser, for to the best of his knowledge he had just invented the Sabihoon.

"No, his name is . . ." Ningauble paused and began to chuckle. "I was forgetting that I must under no circumstances tell you his name."

Fafhrd jumped up angrily. "What?"

"Yes, children," said Ningauble, suddenly making his eye-stalks staringly rigid, stern, and uncompromising. "And I must furthermore tell you that I can in no way help you in this matter . . ." (Fafhrd clenched his fists) ". . . and I am very glad of it too . . ." (Fafhrd swore) ". . . for it seems to me that no more fitting punishment could have been devised for your abominable lecheries, which I have so often bemoaned . . ." (Fafhrd's hand went to his sword hilt) ". . . in fact, if it had been up to me to chastise you for your manifold vices, I would have chosen the very same enchantment . . ." (But now he had gone too far; Fafhrd growled, "Oh, so it is you who are behind it!" ripped out his sword and began to advance slowly on the hooded figure) ". . . Yes, my children, you must accept your lot without rebellion or bitterness . . ." (Fafhrd continued to advance) ". . . Far better that you should retire from the world as I have and give yourselves to meditation and repentance . . ." (The sword, flickering with firelight, was only a yard away) ". . . Far better that you should live out the rest of this incarnation in solitude, each surrounded by his faithful band of sows or snails . . ." (The sword touched the ragged robe) ". . .

devoting your remaining years to the promotion of a better understanding between mankind and the lower animals. However—" (Ningauble sighed and the sword hesitated) ". . . if it is still your firm and foolhardy intention to challenge this adept, I suppose I must aid you with what little advice I can give, though warning you that it will plunge you into maelstroms of trouble and lay upon you geases you will grow gray in fulfilling, and incidentally be the means of your deaths."

Fafhrd lowered his sword. The silence in the black cave grew heavy and ominous. Then, in a voice that was distant yet resonant, like the sound that came from the statue of Memnon at Thebes when the first rays of the morning sun fell upon it, Ningauble began to speak.

"It comes to me, confusedly, like a scene in a rusted mirror; nevertheless, it comes, and thus: You must first possess yourselves of certain trifles. The shroud of Ahriman, from the secret shrine near Persepolis—"

"But what about the accursed swordsmen of Ahriman, Father?" put in the Mouser. "There are twelve of them. Twelve, Father, and all very accursed and hard to persuade."

"Do you think I am setting toss-and-fetch problems for puppy dogs?" wheezed Ningauble angrily. "To proceed: You must secondly obtain powdered mummy from the Demon Pharaoh, who reigned for three horrid and unhistoried midnights after the death of Ikhnaton—"

"But, Father," Fafhrd protested, blushing a little, "you know who owns that powdered mummy, and what she demands of any two men who visit her."

"Shh! I'm your elder, Fafhrd, by eons. Thirdly, you must get the cup from which Socrates drank the hemlock; fourthly, a sprig from the original Tree of Life, and lastly . . ." He hesitated as if his memory had failed him, dipped up a potsherd from the pile, and read from it: "And lastly, you must procure the woman who will come when she is ready."

"What woman?"

"The woman who will come when she is ready." Ningauble tossed back the fragment, starting a small landslide of shards.

"Corrode Loki's bones!" cursed Fafhrd, and the Mouser said, "But, Father, no woman comes when she's ready. She always waits."

Ningauble sighed merrily and said, "Do not be downcast, children. Is it ever the custom of your good friend the Gossiper to give simple advice?"

"It is not," said Fafhrd.

"Well, having all these things, you must go to the Lost City of Ahriman that lies east of Armenia—whisper not its name—"

"Is it Khatti?" whispered the Mouser.

"No, Blowfly. And furthermore, why are you interrupting me when you are supposed to be hard at work recalling all the details of the scandal of the Friday concubine, the three eunuch priests, and the slave girl from Samos?"

"Oh truly, Spy of the Unmentionable, I labor at that until my mind becomes a weariness and a wandering, and all for love of you." The Mouser was glad of Ningauble's question, for he had forgotten the three eunuch priests, which would have been most unwise, as no one in his senses sought to cheat the Gossiper of even a pinch of misinformation promised.

Ningauble continued, "Arriving at the Lost City, you must seek out the ruined black shrine, and place the woman before the great tomb, and wrap the shroud of Ahriman around her, and let her drink the powdered mummy from the hemlock cup, diluting it with a wine you will find where you find the mummy, and place in her hand the sprig from the Tree of Life, and wait for the dawn."

"And then?" rumbled Fafhrd.

"And then the mirror becomes all red with rust. I can see no further, except that someone will return from a place which it is unlawful to leave, and that you must be wary of the woman."

"But, Father, all this scavenging of magical trumpery is a great bother," Fafhrd objected. "Why shouldn't we go at once to the Lost City?"

"Without the map on the shroud of Ahriman?" murmured Ningauble.

"And you still can't tell us the name of the adept we seek?" the Mouser ventured. "Or even the name of the woman? Puppy dog problems indeed! We give you a bitch, Father, and by the time you return her, she's dropped a litter."

Ningauble shook his head ever so slightly, the six eyes retreated under the hood to become an ominous multiple gleam, and the Mouser felt a shiver crawl on his spine.

"Why is it, Riddle-Vendor, that you always give us half knowledge?" Fafhrd pressed angrily. "Is it that at the last moment our blades may strike with half force?"

Ningauble chuckled.

"It is because I know you too well, children. If I said one word more, Hulk, you could be cleaving with your great sword—at the wrong person. And your cat-comrade would be brewing his child's magic—the wrong child's magic. It is no simple creature you foolhardily seek, but a mystery, no single identity but a mirage, a stony thing that has stolen the blood and substance of life, a nightmare crept out of dream."

For a moment it was as if, in the far reaches of that nighted cavern, something that waited stirred. Then it was gone.

Ningauble purred complacently, "And now I have an idle moment, which, to please you, I will pass in giving ear to the story that the Mouser has been impatiently waiting to tell me."

So, there being no escape, the Mouser began, first explaining that only the surface of the story had to do with the concubine, the three priests, and the slave girl; the deeper portion touching mostly, though not entirely, on four infamous handmaidens of Ishtar and a dwarf who was richly compensated for his deformity. The fire grew low and a little, lemurlike creature came edging in to replenish it, and the hours stretched on, for the Mouser always warmed to his own tales. There came a place where Fafhrd's eyes bugged with astonishment, and another where Ningauble's paunch shook like a small mountain in earthquake, but eventually the tale came to an end, suddenly and seemingly in the middle, like a piece of foreign music.

Then farewells were said and final questions refused answer, and the two seekers started back the way they had come. And Ningauble began to sort in his mind the details of the Mouser's story, treasuring it the more because he knew it was an improvisation, his favorite proverb being "He who lies artistically treads closer to the truth than ever he knows."

Fafhrd and the Mouser had almost reached the bottom of the boulder stair when they heard a faint tapping and turned to see Ningauble peering down from the verge, supporting himself with what looked like a cane and rapping with another.

"Children," he called, and his voice was tiny as the note of the lone flute in the Temple of Baal, "it comes to me that something in the distant spaces lusts for something in you. You must guard closely what commonly needs no guarding."

"Yes, Godfather of Mystification."

"You will take care?" came the elfin note. "Your beings depend on it."

"Yes, Father."

And Ningauble waved once and hobbled out of sight. The little creatures of his great darkness followed him, but whether to report and receive orders or only to pleasure him with their gentle antics, no man could be sure. Some said that Ningauble had been created by the Elder Gods for men to guess about and so sharpen their imaginations for even tougher riddles. None knew whether he had the gift of foresight, or whether he merely set the stage for future events with such a bewildering cunning that only an efreet or an adept could evade acting the part given him.

3: The Woman Who Came

After Fafhrd and the Gray Mouser emerged from the Bottomless Caves into the blinding upper sunlight, their trail for a space becomes dim. Material relating to them has, on the whole, been scanted by annalists, since they were heroes too disreputable for classic myth, too cryptically independent ever to let themselves be tied to a folk, too shifty and improbable in their adventurings to please the historian, too often involved with a riffraff of dubious demons, unfrocked sorcerers, and discredited deities—a veritable underworld of the supernatural. And it becomes doubly difficult to piece together their actions during a period when they were engaged in thefts requiring stealth, secrecy, and bold misdirection. Occasionally, however, one comes across the marks they left upon the year.

For instance, a century later the priests of Ahriman were chanting, although they were too intelligent to believe it themselves, the miracle of Ahriman's snatching of his own hallowed shroud. One night the twelve accursed swordsmen saw the blackly scribbled shroud rise like a pillar of cobwebs from the altar, rise higher than mortal man, although the form within seemed anthropoid. Then Ahriman spoke from the shroud, and they worshiped him, and he replied with obscure parables and finally strode giantlike from the secret shrine.

The shrewdest of the century-later priests remarked, "I'd say a man on stilts, or else—" (happy surmise!) "—one man on the shoulders of another."

Then there were things that Nikri, body slave to the infamous False Laodice, told the cook while she anointed the bruises of her latest beating. Things concerning two strangers who visited her mistress, and the carousal her mistress proposed to them, and how they escaped the black eunuch scimitarmen she had set to slay them when the carousal was done.

"They were magicians, both of them," Nikri averred, "for at

the peak of the doings they transformed my lady into a hideous, wiggly-horned sow, a horrid chimera of snail and swine. But that wasn't the worst, for they stole her chest of aphrodisiac wines. When she discovered that the demon mummia was gone with which she'd hoped to stir the lusts of Ptolemy, she screamed in rage and took her back-scratcher to me. Ow, but that hurts!"

The cook chuckled.

But as to who visited Hieronymus, the greedy tax farmer and connoisseur of Antioch, or in what guise, we cannot be sure. One morning he was found in his treasure room with his limbs stiff and chill, as if from hemlock, and there was a look of terror on his fat face, and the famous cup from which he had often caroused was missing, although there were circular stains on the table before him. He recovered, but would never tell what had happened.

The priests who tended the Tree of Life in Babylon were a little more communicative. One evening just after sunset they saw the topmost branches shake in the gloaming and heard the snick of a pruning knife. All around them, without other sound or movement, stretched the desolate city, from which the inhabitants had been herded to nearby Seleucia three-quarters of a century before and to which the priests crept back only in great fear to fulfill their sacred duties. They instantly prepared, some of them to climb the Tree armed with tempered golden sickles, others to shoot down with gold-tipped arrows whatever blasphemer was driven forth, when suddenly a large gray batlike shape swooped from the Tree and vanished behind a jagged wall. Of course, it might conceivably have been a gray-cloaked man swinging on a thin, tough rope, but there were too many things whispered about the creatures that flapped by night through the ruins of Babylon for the priests to dare pursuit.

Finally Fafhrd and the Gray Mouser reappeared in Tyre, and a week later they were ready to depart on the ultimate stage of their quest. Indeed, they were already outside the gates, lingering at the landward end of Alexander's mole, spine of an ever-growing isthmus. Gazing at it, Fafhrd remembered how once an unintroduced stranger had told him a tale about two fabulous adventurers who had aided mightily in the foredoomed defense of Tyre against Alexander the Great more than a hundred years ago. The larger had heaved heavy stone blocks on the attacking ships, the smaller had dove to file through the chains with which they were anchored. Their names, the stranger

had said, were Fafhrd and the Gray Mouser. Fafhrd had made
no comment.

It was near evening, a good time to pause in adventurings, to
recall past escapades, to hazard misty, wild, rosy speculations
concerning what lay ahead.

"I think any woman would do," insisted the Mouser, bickering. "Ningauble was just trying to be obscure. Let's take Chloe."

"If only she'll come when she's ready," said Fafhrd, half
smiling.

The sun was dipping ruddy-golden into the rippling sea. The
merchants who had pitched shop on the landward side in order
to get first crack at the farmers and inland traders on market
day were packing up wares and taking down canopies.

"Any woman will eventually come when she's ready, even
Chloe," retorted the Mouser. "We'd only have to take along a
silk tent for her and a few pretty conveniences. No trouble at
all."

"Yes," said Fafhrd, 'We could probably manage it without
more than one elephant."

Most of Tyre was darkly silhouetted against the sunset, although there were gleams from the roofs here and there, and
the gilded peak of the Temple of Melkarth sent a little water-
borne glitter track angling in toward the greater one of the sun.
The fading Phoenician port seemed entranced, dreaming of
past glories, only half listening to today's news of Rome's
implacable eastward advance, and Philip of Macedon's loss of
the first round at the Battle of the Dog's Heads, and now
Antiochus preparing for the second, with Hannibal come to
help him from Tyre's great fallen sister Carthage across the sea.

"I'm sure Chloe will come if we wait until tomorrow," the
Mouser continued. "We'll have to wait in any case, because
Ningauble said the woman wouldn't come until she was ready."

A cool little wind came out of the wasteland that was Old
Tyre. The merchants hurried; a few of them were already going
home along the mole, their slaves looking like hunchbacks and
otherwise misshapen monsters because of the packs on their
shoulders and heads.

"No," said Fafhrd, "we'll start. And if the woman doesn't
come when she's ready, then she isn't the woman who will
come when she's ready, of if she is, she'll have to hump herself
to catch up."

The three horses of the adventurers moved restlessly and the
Mouser's whinnied. Only the great camel, on which were slung

the wine-sacks, various small chests, and snugly wrapped weapons, stood sullenly still, Fafhrd and the Mouser casually watched the one figure on the mole that moved against the homing stream; they were not exactly suspicious, but after the year's doings they could not overlook the possibility of death-dealing pursuers, taking the form either of accursed swordsmen, black eunuch scimitarmen, gold-weaponed Babylonian priests, or such agents as Hieronymus of Antioch might favor.

"Chloe would have come on time, if only you'd helped me persuade her," argued the Mouser. "She likes you, and I'm sure she must have been the one Ningauble meant, because she has that amulet which works against the adept."

The sun was a blinding sliver on the sea's rim, then went under. All the little glares and glitters on the roofs of Tyre winked out. The Temple of Melkarth loomed black against the fading sky. The last canopy was being taken down and most of the merchants were more than halfway across the mole. There was still only one figure moving shoreward.

"Weren't seven nights with Chloe enough for you?" asked Fafhrd. "Besides, it isn't she you'll be wanting when we kill the adept and get this spell off us."

"That's as it may be," retorted the Mouser. "But remember we have to catch our adept first. And it's not only I whom Chloe's company could benefit."

A faint shout drew their attention across the darkling water to where a lateen-rigged trader was edging into the Egyptian Harbor. For a moment they thought the landward end of the mole had been emptied. Then the figure moving away from the city came out sharp and black against the sea, a slight figure, not burdened like the slaves.

"Another fool leaves sweet Tyre at the wrong time," observed the Mouser. "Just think what a woman will mean in those cold mountains we're going to, Fafhrd, a woman to prepare dainties and stroke your forehead."

Fafhrd said, "It isn't your forehead, little man, you're thinking of."

The cool wind came again and the packed sand moaned at its passing. Tyre seemed to crouch like a beast against the threats of darkness. A last merchant searched the ground hurriedly for some lost article.

Fafhrd put his hand on his horse's shoulder and said, "Come on."

The Mouser made a last point. "I don't think Chloe would

insist on taking the slave girl to oil her feet, that is, if we handled it properly."

Then they saw the other fool leaving sweet Tyre was coming toward them, and that it was a woman, tall and slender, dressed in stuffs that seemed to melt into the waning light, so that Fafhrd found himself wondering whether she truly came from Tyre or from some aerial realm whose inhabitants may venture to earth only at sunset. Then, as she continued to approach at an easy, swinging stride, they saw that her face was fair and that her hair was raven; and the Mouser's heart gave a great leap and he felt that this was the perfect consummation of their waiting, that he was witnessing the birth of an Aphrodite, not from the foam but the dusk; for it was indeed his dark-haired Ahura of the wine shops, no longer staring with cold, shy curiosity, but eagerly smiling.

Fafhrd, not altogether untouched by similar feelings, said slowly, "So you are the woman who came when she was ready?"

"Yes," added the Mouser gaily, "and did you know that in a minute more you'd have been too late?"

4: The Lost City

During the next week, one of steady northward journeying along the fringe of the desert, they learned little more of the motives or history of their mysterious companion than the dubious scraps of information Chloe had provided. When asked why she had come, Ahura replied that Ningauble had sent her, that Ningauble had nothing to do with it and that it was all an accident, that certain dead Elder Gods had dreamed her a vision, that she sought a brother lost in a search for the Lost City of Ahriman; and often her only answer was silence, a silence that seemed sometimes sly and sometimes mystical. However, she stood up well to hardship, proved a tireless rider, and did not complain at sleeping on the ground with only a large cloak snuggled around her. Like some especially sensitive migratory bird, she seemed possessed of an even greater urge than their own to get on with the journey.

Whenever opportunity offered, the Mouser paid assiduous court to her, limited only by the fear of working a snail-change. But after a few days of this tantalizing pleasure, he noticed that Fafhrd was vying for it. Very swiftly the two comrades became rivals, contesting as to who should be the first to offer Ahura assistance on those rare occasions when she needed it, striving to top each other's brazenly boastful accounts of incredible adventures, constantly on the alert lest the other steal a moment alone. Such a spate of gallantry had never before been known on their adventurings. They remained good friends—and they were aware of that—but very surly friends—and they were aware of that too. And Ahura's shy, or sly, silence encouraged them both.

They forded the Euphrates south of the ruins of Carchemish, and struck out for the headwaters of the Tigris, intersecting but swinging east away from the route of Xenophon and the Ten Thousand. It was then that their surliness came to a head. Ahura had roamed off a little, letting her horse crop the dry herbage, while the two sat on a boulder, and expostulated in whispers, Fafhrd proposing that they both agree to cease paying court to the girl until their quest was over, the Mouser doggedly advancing his prior claim. Their whispers became so heated that they did not notice a white pigeon swooping toward them until it landed with a downward beat of wings on an arm Fafhrd had flung wide to emphasize his willingness to renounce the girl temporarily—if only the Mouser would.

Fafhrd blinked, then detached a scrap of parchment from the pigeon's leg, and read, "There is danger in the girl. You must both forgo her."

The tiny seal was an impression of seven tangled eyes.

"Just *seven* eyes!" remarked the Mouser. "Pah, he is modest!" And for a moment he was silent, trying to picture the gigantic web of unknown strands by which the Gossiper gathered his information and conducted his business.

But this unsuspected seconding of Fafhrd's argument finally won from him a sulky consent, and they solemnly pledged not to lay hand on the girl, or each in any way to further his cause, until they had found and dealt with the adept.

They were now in townless land that caravans avoided, a land like Xenophon's, full of chill misty mornings, dazzling noons, and treacherous twilights, with hints of shy, murderous, mountain-dwelling tribes recalling the omnipresent legends of "little people" as unlike men as cats are unlike dogs. Ahura seemed unaware of the sudden cessation of the attentions paid her, remaining as provocatively shy and indefinite as ever.

The Mouser's attitude toward Ahura, however, began to undergo a gradual but profound change. Whether it was the souring of his inhibited passion, or the shrewder insight of a mind no longer a-bubble with the fashioning of compliments and witticisms, he began to feel more and more that the Ahura he loved was only a faint spark almost lost in the darkness of a stranger who daily became more riddlesome, dubious, and even, in the end, repellent. He remembered the other name Chloe had given Ahura, and found himself brooding oddly over the legend of Hermaphroditus bathing in the Carian fountain and becoming joined in one body with the nymph Salmacis. Now when he looked at Ahura he could see only the avid eyes that peered secretly at the world through a crevice. He began to think of her chuckling soundlessly at night at the mortifying spell that had been laid upon himself and Fafhrd. He became obsessed with Ahura in a very different way, and took to spying on her and studying her expression when she was not looking, as if hoping in that way to penetrate her mystery.

Fafhrd noticed it and instantly suspected that the Mouser was contemplating going back on his pledge. He restrained his indignation with difficulty and took to watching the Mouser as closely as the Mouser watched Ahura. No longer when it became necessary to procure provisions was either willing to hunt alone. The easy amicability of their friendship deteriorated. Then, late one afternoon while they were traversing a shadowy ravine east of Armenia, a hawk dove suddenly and sank its talons in Fafhrd's shoulder. The Northerner killed the creature in a flurry of reddish feathers before he noticed that it too carried a message.

"Watch out for the Mouser," was all it said, but coupled with the smart of the talon-pricks, that was quite enough for Fafhrd. Drawing up beside the Mouser while Ahura's horse pranced skittishly away from the disturbance, he told the Mouser his full suspicions and warned him that any violation of their agreement would at once end their friendship and bring them into deadly collision.

The Mouser listened like a man in a dream, still moodily watching Ahura. He would have liked to have told Fafhrd his real motives, but was doubtful whether he could make them intelligible. Moreover, he was piqued at being misjudged. So when Fafhrd's direful outburst was finished, he made no comment. Fafhrd interpreted this as an admission of guilt and cantered on in a rage.

They were now nearing that rugged vantage-land from which the Medes and the Persians had swooped down on Assyria and Chaldea, and where, if they could believe Ningauble's geography, they would find the forgotten lair of the Lord of Eternal Evil. At first the archaic map on the shroud of Ahriman proved more maddening than helpful, but after a while, clarified in part by a curiously erudite suggestion of Ahura, it began to make disturbing sense, showing them a deep gorge where the foregoing terrain led one to expect a saddle-backed crest, and a valley where ought to have been a mountain. If the map held true, they would reach the Lost City in a very few days.

All the while, the Mouser's obsession deepened, and at last took definite and startling form. He believed that Ahura was a man.

It was very strange that the intimacy of camp life and the Mouser's own zealous spying should not long ago have turned up concrete proof or disproof of this clear-cut supposition. Nevertheless, as the Mouser wonderingly realized on reviewing events, they had not. Granted, Ahura's form and movements, all her least little actions were those of a woman, but he recalled painted and padded minions, sweet not simpering, who had aped femininity almost as well. Preposterous—but there it was. From that moment his obsessive curiosity became a compulsive sweat and he redoubled his moody peering, much to the anger of Fafhrd, who took to slapping his sword hilt at unexpected intervals, though without ever startling the Mouser into looking away. Each in his way stayed as surly sullen as the camel that displayed a more and more dour balkiness at this preposterous excursion from the healthy desert.

Those were nightmare days for the Gray One, as they advanced ever closer through gloomy gorges and over craggy crests toward Ahriman's primeval shrine. Fafhrd seemed an ominous, white-faced giant reminding him of someone he had known in waking life, and their whole quest a blind treading of the more subterranean routes of dream. He still wanted to tell the giant his suspicions, but could not bring himself to it, because of their monstrousness and because the giant loved Ahura. And all the while Ahura eluded him, a phantom fluttering just beyond reach; though, when he forced his mind to make the comparison, he realized that her behavior had in no way altered, except for an intensification of the urge to press onward, like a vessel nearing its home port.

Finally there came a night when he could bear his torturing curiosity no longer. He writhed from under a mountain of oppressive unremembered dreams and, propped on an elbow, looked around him, quiet as the creature for which he was named.

It would have been cold if it had not been so still. The fire had burned to embers. It was rather the moonlight that showed him Fafhrd's tousled head and elbow outthrust from shaggy bearskin cloak. And it was the moonlight that struck full on Ahura stretched beyond the embers, her lidded, tranquil face fixed on the zenith, seeming hardly to breathe.

He waited a long time. Then, without making a sound, he laid back his gray cloak, picked up his sword, went around the fire, and kneeled beside her. Then, for another space, he dispassionately scrutinized her face. But it remained the hermaphroditic mask that had tormented his waking hours—if he were still sure of the distinction between waking and dream. Suddenly his hands grasped at her—and as abruptly checked. Again he stayed motionless for a long time. Then, with movements as deliberate and rehearsed-seeming as a sleep-walker's, but more silent, he drew back her woolen cloak, took a small knife from his pouch, lifted her gown at the neck, careful not to touch her skin, slit it to her knee, treating her chiton the same.

The breasts, white as ivory, that he had known would not be there, were there. And yet, instead of his nightmare lifting, it deepened.

It was something too profound for surprise, this wholly unexpected further insight. For as he knelt there, somberly studying, he knew for a certainty that this ivory flesh too was a mask, as cunningly fashioned as the face and for as frighteningly incomprehensible a purpose.

The ivory eyelids did not flicker, but the edges of the teeth showed in what he fancied was a deliberate, flickery smile.

He was never more certain than at this moment that Ahura was a man.

The embers crunched behind him.

Turning, the Mouser saw only the streak of gleaming steel poised above Fafhrd's head, motionless for a moment, as if with superhuman forbearance a god should give his creature a chance before loosing the thunderbolt.

The Mouser ripped out his own slim sword in time to ward the titan blow. From hilt to point, the two blades screamed.

And in answer to that scream, melting into, continuing, and augmenting it, there came from the absolute calm of the west a gargantuan gust of wind that sent the Mouser staggering forward and Fafhrd reeling back, and rolled Ahura across the place where the embers had been.

Almost as suddenly the gale died. As it died, something whipped batlike toward the Mouser's face and he grabbed at it. But it was not a bat, or even a large leaf. It felt like papyrus.

The embers, blown into a clump of dry grass, had perversely started a blaze. To its flaring light he held the thin scrap that had fluttered out of the infinite west.

He motioned frantically to Fafhrd, who was clawing his way out of a scrub pine.

There was squid-black writing on the scrap, in large characters, above the tangled seal.

"By whatever gods you revere, give up this quarrel. Press onward at once. Follow the woman."

They became aware that Ahura was peering over their abutting shoulders. The moon came gleamingly from behind the small black tatter of cloud that had briefly obscured it. She looked at them, pulled together chiton and gown, belted them with her cloak. They collected their horses, extricated the fallen camel from the cluster of thorn bushes in which it was satisfiedly tormenting itself, and set out.

After that the Lost City was found almost too quickly; it seemed like a trap or the work of an illusionist. One moment Ahura was pointing out to them a boulder-studded crag; the next, they were looking down a narrow valley choked with crazily leaning, moonsilvered monoliths and their accomplice shadows.

From the first it was obvious that "city" was a misnomer. Surely men had never dwelt in those massive stone tents and huts, though they may have worshiped there. It was a habitation for Egyptian colossi, for stone automata. But Fafhrd and the Mouser had little time to survey its entirety, for without warning Ahura sent her horse clattering and sliding down the slope.

Thereafter it was a harebrained, drunken gallop, their horses plunging shadows, the camel a lurching ghost, through forests of crude-hewn pillars, past teetering single slabs big enough for palace walls, under lintels made for elephants, always following the elusive hoofbeat, never catching it, until they suddenly emerged into clear moonlight and drew up in an open space between a great sarcophagus-like block or box with steps leading up to it, and a huge, crudely man-shaped monolith.

But they had hardly begun to puzzle out the things around

them before they became aware that Ahura was gesturing impatiently. They recalled Ningauble's instructions, and realized that it was almost dawn. So they unloaded various bundles and boxes from the shivering, snapping camel, and Fafhrd unfolded the dark, cobwebby shroud of Ahriman and wrapped it around Ahura as she stood wordlessly facing the tomb, her face a marble portrait of eagerness, as if she sprang from the stone around her.

While Fafhrd busied himself with other things, the Mouser opened the ebony chest they had stolen from the False Laodice. A fey mood came upon him and, dancing cumbrously in imitation of a eunuch serving man, he tastefully arrayed a flat stone with all the little jugs and jars and tiny amphorae that the chest contained. And in an appropriate falsetto he sang:

> "I laid a board for the Great Seleuce,
> I decked it pretty and abstruse;
> And he must have been pleased,
> For when stuffed, he wheezed,
> 'As punishment castrate the man.'

"You thee, Fafhwd," he lisped, "the man had been cathtwated ath a boy, and tho it wath no punithment at all. Becauthe of pweviouth cathtwathion—"

"I'll castrate your wit-engorged top end," Fafhrd cried, raising the next implement of magic, but thought better of it.

Then Fafhrd handed him Socrates' cup and, still prancing and piping, the Mouser measured into it the mummy powder and added the wine and stirred them together, and, dancing fantastically toward Ahura, offered it to her. When she made no movement, he held it to her lips and she greedily gulped it without taking her eyes from the tomb.

Then Fafhrd came with the sprig from the Babylonian Tree of Life, which still felt marvelously fresh and firm-leafed to his touch, as if the Mouser had only snipped it a moment ago. And he gently pried open her clenched fingers and placed the sprig inside them and folded them again.

Thus ready, they waited. The sky reddened at the edge and seemed for a moment to grow darker, the stars fading and the moon turning dull. The outspread aphrodisiacs chilled, refusing the night breeze their savor. And the woman continued to watch the tomb, and behind her, seeming to watch the tomb too, as if it were her fantastic shadow, loomed the man-shaped monolith, which the Mouser now and then scrutinized uneasily over his shoulder, being unable to tell whether it were of primevally crude workmanship or something that men had laboriously defaced because of its evil.

The sky paled until the Mouser could begin to make out some monstrous carvings on the side of the sarcophagus—of men like stone pillars and animals like mountains—and until Fafhrd could see the green of the leaves in Ahura's hand.

Then he saw something astounding. In an instant the leaves withered and the sprig became a curled and blackened stick. In the same instant Ahura trembled and grew paler still, snow pale, and to the Mouser it seemed that there was a tenuous black cloud forming around her head, that the riddlesome stranger he hated was pouring upward like a smoky jinni from her body, the bottle.

The thick stone cover of the sarcophagus groaned and began to rise.

Ahura began to move toward the sarcophagus. To the Mouser it seemed that the cloud was drawing her along like a black sail.

The cover was moving more swiftly, as if it were the upper jaw of a stone crocodile. The black cloud seemed to the Mouser to strain triumphantly toward the widening slit, dragging the white wisp behind it. The cover opened wide. Ahura reached the top and then either peered down inside or, as the Mouser saw it, was almost sucked in along with the black cloud. She shook violently. Then her body collapsed like an empty dress.

Fafhrd gritted his teeth, a joint cracked in the Mouser's wrist. The hilts of their swords, unconsciously drawn, bruised their palms.

Then, like an idler from a day of bowered rest, an Indian prince from the tedium of the court, a philosopher from quizzical discourse, a slim figure rose from the tomb. His limbs were clad in black, his body in silvery metal, his hair and beard raven and silky. But what first claimed the sight, like an ensign on a masked man's shield, was a chatoyant quality of his youthful olive skin, a silvery gleaming that turned one's thoughts to fishes' bellies and leprosy—that, and a certain familiarity.

For the face of this black and silver stranger bore an unmistakable resemblance to Ahura.

5: Anra Devadoris

Resting his long hands on the edge of the tomb, the new-comer surveyed them pleasantly and nodded as if they were intimates. Then he vaulted lightly over and came striding down the steps, treading on the shroud of Ahriman without so much as a glance at Ahura.

He eyed their swords. "You anticipate danger?" he asked, politely stroking the beard which, it seemed to the Mouser, could never have grown so bushily silky except in a tomb.

"You are an adept?" Fafhrd retorted, stumbling over the words a little.

The stranger disregarded the question and stopped to study amusedly the zany array of aphrodisiacs.

"Dear Ningauble," he murmured, "is surely the father of all seven-eyed Lechers. I suppose you know him well enough to guess that he had you fetch these toys because he wants them for himself. Even in his duel with me, he cannot resist the temptation of a profit on the side. But perhaps this time the old pander had curtsied to destiny unwittingly. At least, let us hope so."

And with that he unbuckled his sword belt and carelessly laid it by, along with the wondrously slim, silver-hilted sword. The Mouser shrugged and sheathed his own weapon, but Fafhrd only grunted.

"I do not like you," he said. "Are you the one who put the swine-curse on us?"

The stranger regarded him quizzically.

"You are looking for a cause," he said. "You wish to know the name of an agent you feel has injured you. You plan to unleash your rage as soon as you know. But behind every cause is another cause, and behind the last agent is yet another agent. An immortal could not slay a fraction of them. Believe me, who have followed that trail further than most and who have had some experience of the special obstacles that are placed in the way of one who seeks to live beyond the confines of his skull and the meager present—the traps that are set for him, the titanic enmities he awakens. I beseech you to wait awhile before warring, as I shall wait before answering your second question. That I am an adept I freely admit."

At this last statement the Mouser felt another light-headed impulse to behave fantastically, this time in mimicry of a magi-cian. Here was the rare creature on whom he could test the rune against adepts in his pouch! He wanted to hum a death spell between his teeth, to flap his arms in an incantational gesture, to spit at the adept and spin widdershins on his left heel thrice. But he too chose to wait.

"There is always a simple way of saying things," said Fafhrd ominously.

"But there is where I differ with you," returned the adept, almost animatedly. "There are no ways of saying certain things, and others are so difficult that a man pines and dies before the right words are found. One must borrow phrases from the sky, words from beyond the stars. Else were all an ignorant, imprisoning mockery."

The Mouser stared at the adept, suddenly conscious of a monstrous incongruity about him—as if one should glimpse a hint of double-dealing in the curl of Solon's lips, or cowardice in the eyes of Alexander, or imbecility in the face of Aristotle. For although the adept was obviously erudite, confident, and powerful, the Mouser could not help thinking of a child morbidly avid for experience, a timid, painfully curious small boy. And the Mouser had the further bewildering feeling that this was the secret for which he had spied so long on Ahura.

Fafhrd's sword-arm bulged and he seemed about to make an even pithier rejoinder. But instead he sheathed his sword, walked over to the woman, held his fingers to her wrists for a moment, then tucked his bearskin cloak around her.

"Her ghost has gone only a little way," he said. "It will soon return. What did you do to her, you black and silver popinjay?"

"What matters what I've done to her or you, or me?" retorted the adept, almost peevishly. "You are here, and I have business with you." He paused. "This, in brief, is my proposal: that I make you adepts like myself, sharing with you all knowledge of which your minds are capable, on condition only that you continue to submit to such spells as I have put upon you and may put upon you in future, to further our knowledge. What do you say to that?"

"Wait, Fafhrd!" implored the Mouser, grabbing his comrade's arm. "Don't strike yet. Let's look at the statue from all sides. Why, magnanimous magician, have you chosen to make this offer to us, and why have you brought us out here to make it, instead of getting your yes or no in Tyre?"

"An adept," roared Fafhrd, dragging the Mouser along. "Offers to make me an adept! And for that I should go on kissing swine! Go spit down Fenris' throat!"

"As to why I have brought you here," said the adept coolly, "there are certain limitations on my powers of movement, or at least on my powers of satisfactory communication. There is, moreover, a special reason, which I will reveal to you as soon as we have concluded our agreement—though I may tell you that, unknown to yourselves, you have already aided me."

"But why pick on *us*? Why?" persisted the Mouser, bracing himself against Fafhrd's tugging.

"Some whys, if you follow them far enough, lead over the rim of reality," replied the black and silver one. "I have sought knowledge beyond the dreams of ordinary men; I have ventured far into the darkness that encircles minds and stars. But now, midmost of the pitchy windings of that fearsome labyrinth, I find myself suddenly at my skein's end. The tyrant powers who ignorantly guard the secret of the universe without knowing what it is, have scented me. Those vile wardens of whom Ningauble is the merest agent and even Ormadz a cloudy symbol have laid their traps and built their barricades. And my best torches have snuffed out, or proved too flickery-feeble. I need new avenues of knowledge."

He turned upon them eyes that seemed to be changing to twin holes in a curtain. "There is something in the inmost core of you, something that you, or others before you, have close-guarded down the ages. Something that lets you laugh in a way that only the Elder Gods ever laughed. Something that makes you see a kind of jest in horror and disillusionment and death. There is much wisdom to be gained by the unraveling of that something."

"Do you think us pretty woven scarves for your slick fingers to fray," snarled Fafhrd, "so you can piece out that rope you're at the end of, and climb all the way down to Niflheim?"

"Each adept must fray himself, before he may fray others," the stranger intoned unsmilingly. "You do not know the treasure you keep virgin and useless within you, or spill in senseless laughter. There is much richness in it, many complexities, destiny-threads that lead beyond the sky to realms undreamt." His voice became swift and invoking.

"Have you no itch to understand, no urge for greater adventuring than schoolboy rambles? I'll give you gods for foes, stars for your treasure-trove, if only you will do as I command. All men will be your animals; the best, your hunting pack. Kiss snails and swine? That's but an overture. Greater than Pan, you'll frighten nations, rape the world. The universe will tremble at your lust, but you will master it and force it down. That ancient laughter will give you the might—"

"Filth-spewing pimp! Scabby-lipped pander! Cease!" bellowed Fafhrd.

"Only submit to me and to my will," the adept continued rapturously, his lips working so that his black beard twitched rhythmically. "All things we'll twist and torture, know their cause. The lechery of gods will pave the way we'll tramp through windy darkness till we find the one who lurks in senseless Odin's skull twitching the strings that move your lives and mine. All knowledge will be ours, all for us three. Only give up your wills, submit to me!"

For a moment the Mouser was hypnotized by the glint of ghastly wonders. Then he felt Fafhrd's biceps, which had slackened under his grasp—as if the Northerner were yielding too—suddenly tighten, and from his own lips he heard words projected coldly into the echoing silence.

"Do you think a rhyme is enough to win us over to your nauseous titillations? Do you think we care a jot for your high-flown muck-peering? Fafhrd, this slobberer offends me, past ills that he had done us aside. It only remains to determine which one of us disposes of him. I long to unravel him, beginning with the ribs."

"Do you not understand what I have offered you, the magnitude of the boon? Have we no common ground?"

"Only to fight on. Call up your demons, sorcerer, or else look to your weapon."

An unearthly lust receded, rippling from the adept's eyes, leaving behind only a deadliness. Fafhrd snatched up the cup of Socrates and dropped it for a lot, swore as it rolled toward the Mouser, whose cat-quick hand went softly to the hilt of the slim sword called Scalpel. Stooping, the adept groped blindly behind him and regained his belt and scabbard, drawing from it a blade that looked as delicate and responsive as a needle. He stood, a lank and icy indolence, in the red of the risen sun, the black anthropomorphic monolith looming behind him for his second.

The Mouser drew Scalpel silently from its sheath, ran a finger caressingly down the side of the blade, and in so doing noticed an inscription in black crayon which read, "I do not approve of this step you are taking. Ningauble." With a hiss of annoyance the Mouser wiped it off on his thigh and concentrated his gaze

on the adept—so preoccupiedly that he did not observe the
eyes of the fallen Ahura quiver open.

"And now, Dead Sorcerer," said the Gray One lightly, "my
name is the Gray Mouser."

"And mine is Anra Devadoris."

Instantly the Mouser put into action his carefully weighed
plan: to take two rapid skips forward and launch his blade-
tipped body at the adept's sword, which was to be deflected,
and at the adept's throat, which was to be sliced. He was
already seeing the blood spurt when, in the middle of the
second skip, he saw, whirring like an arrow toward his eyes, the
adept's blade. With a belly-contorted effort he twisted to one
side and parried blindly. The adept's blade whipped in greedily
around Scalpel, but only far enough to snag and tear the skin at
the side of the Mouser's neck. The Mouser recovered balance
crouching, his guard wide open, and only a backward leap
saved him from Anra Devadoris' second serpentlike strike. As
he gathered himself to meet the next attack, he gaped amazedly,
for never before in his life had he been faced by superior speed.
Fafhrd's face was white. Ahura, however, her head raised a
little from the furry cloak, smiled with a weak and incredulous,
but evil joy—a frankly vicious joy wholly unlike her former sly,
intangible intimations of cruelty.

But Anra Devadoris smiled wider and nodded with a patron-
izing gratefulness at the Mouser, before gliding in. And now it
was the blade Needle that darted in unhurried lightning attack,
and Scalpel that whirred in frenzied defense. The Mouser retreated in jerky, circling stages, his face sweaty, his throat hot,
but his heart exulting, for never before had he fought this
well—not even on that stifling morning when, his head in a
sack, he had disposed of a whimsically cruel Egyptian kidnapper.

Inexplicably, he had the feeling that his days spent in spying
on Ahura were now paying off.

Needle came slipping in and for the moment the Mouser
could not tell upon which side of Scalpel it skirred and so
sprang backward, but not swiftly enough to escape a prick in
the side. He cut viciously at the adept's withdrawing arm—and
barely managed to jerk his own arm out of the way of a stop
thrust.

In a nasty voice so low that Fafhrd hardly heard her, and the
Mouser heard her not at all, Ahura called, "The spiders tickled
your flesh ever so lightly as they ran, Anra."

Perhaps the adept hesitated almost imperceptibly, or perhaps

it was only that his eyes grew a shade emptier. At all events,
the Mouser was not given that opportunity, for which he was
desperately searching, to initiate a counterattack and escape the
deadly whirling of his circling retreat. No matter how intently
he peered, he could spy no gap in the sword-woven steel net his
adversary was tirelessly casting toward him, nor could he dis-
cern in the face behind the net any betraying grimace, any
flicker of eye hinting at the next point of attack, any flaring of
nostrils or distension of lips telling of gasping fatigue similar to
his own. It was inhuman, unalive, the mask of a machine built
by some Daedalus, or of a leprously silver automaton stepped
out of myth. And like a machine, Devadoris seemed to be
gaining strength and speed from the very rhythm that was
sapping his own.

The Mouser realized that he must interrupt that rhythm by a
counterattack, any counterattack, or fall victim to a swiftness
become blinding.

And then he further realized that the proper opportunity for
that counterattack would never come, that he would wait in
vain for any faltering in his adversary's attack, that he must risk
everything on a guess.

His throat burned, his heart pounded on his ribs for air, a
stinging, numbing poison seeped through his limbs.

Devadoris started a feint, or a deadly thrust, at his face.

Simultaneously, the Mouser heard Ahura jeer, "They hung
their webs on your beard and the worms knew your secret
parts, Anra."

He guessed—and cut at the adept's knee.

Either he guessed right, or else something halted the adept's
deadly thrust.

The adept easily parried the Mouser's cut, but the rhythm
was broken and his speed slackened.

Again he developed speed, again at the last possible moment
the Mouser guessed. Again Ahura eerily jeered, "The maggots
made you a necklace, and each marching beetle paused to peer
into your eye, Anra."

Over and over it happened, speed, guess, macabre jeer, but
each time the Mouser gained only momentary respite, never
the opportunity to start an extended counterattack. His circling
retreat continued so uninterruptedly that he felt as if he had
been caught in a whirlpool. With each revolution, certain fixed
landmarks swept into view: Fafhrd's blanched agonized face;
the hulking tomb; Ahura's hate-contorted, mocking visage; the

red stab of the risen sun; the gouged, black, somber monolith, with its attendant stony soldiers and their gigantic stone tents; Fafhrd again. . . .

And now the Mouser knew his strength was failing for good and all. Each guessed counterattack brought him less respite, was less of a check to the adept's speed. The landmarks whirled dizzily, darkened. It was as if he had been sucked to the maelstrom's center, as if the black cloud which he had fancied pouring from Ahura were enveloping him vampirously; choking off his breath.

He knew that he would be able to make only one more countercut, and must therefore stake all on a thrust at the heart.

He readied himself.

But he had waited too long. He could not gather the necessary strength, summon the speed.

He saw the adept preparing the lightning deathstroke.

His own thrust was like the gesture of a paralyzed man seeking to rise from his bed.

Then Ahura began to laugh.

It was a horrible, hysterical laugh; a giggling, snickering laugh; a laugh that made him dully wonder why she should find such joy in his death; and yet, for all the difference, a laugh that sounded like a shrill, distorted echo of Fafhrd's or his own.

Puzzledly, he noted that Needle had not yet transfixed him, that Devadoris' lightning thrust was slowing, slowing, as if the hateful laughter were falling in cumbering swathes around the adept, as if each horrid peal dropped a chain around his limbs.

The Mouser leaned on his own sword and collapsed, rather than lunged, forward.

He heard Fafhrd's shuddering sigh.

Then he realized that he was trying to pull Scalpel from the adept's chest and that it was an almost insuperably difficult task, although the blade had gone in as easily as if Anra Devadoris had been a hollow man. Again he tugged, and Scalpel came clear, fell from his nerveless fingers. His knees shook, his head sagged, and darkness flooded everything.

Fafhrd, sweat-drenched, watched the adept. Anra Devadoris' rigid body teetered like a stone pillar, slim cousin to the monolith behind him. His lips were fixed in a frozen, foreknowing smile. The teetering increased, yet for a while, as if he were an incarnation of death's ghastly pendulum, he did not fall. Then he swayed too far forward and fell like a pillar, without collapse. There was a horrid, hollow crash as his head struck the black pavement.

Ahura's hysterical laughter burst out afresh.

Fafhrd ran foward calling to the Mouser, anxiously shook the slumped form. Snores answered him. Like some spent Theban phalanx-man drowsing over his pike in the twilight of the battle, the Mouser was sleeping the sleep of complete exhaustion. Fafhrd found the Mouser's gray cloak, wrapped it around him, and gently laid him down.

Ahura was shaking convulsively.

Fafhrd looked at the fallen adept, lying there so formally outstretched, like a tomb-statue rolled over. Devadoris' lankness was skeletal. He had bled hardly at all from the wound given him by Scalpel, but his forehead was crushed like an eggshell. Fafhrd touched him. The skin was cold, the muscles hard as stone.

Fafhrd had seen men go rigid immediately upon death— Macedonians who had fought too desperately and too long. But they had become weak and staggering toward the end. Anra Devadoris had maintained the appearance of ease and perfect control up to the last moment, despite the poisons that must have been coursing through his veins almost to the exclusion of blood. All through the duel, his chest had hardly heaved.

"By Odin crucified!" Fafhrd muutered. "He was something of a man, even though he was an adept."

A hand was laid on his arm. He jerked around. It was Ahura come behind him. The whites showed around her eyes. She smiled at him crookedly, then lifted a knowing eyebrow, put her finger to her lips, and dropped suddenly to her knees beside the adept's corpse. Gingerly she touched the satin smooth surface of the tiny blood-clot on the adept's breast. Fafhrd, noting afresh the resemblance between the dead and the crazy face, sucked in his breath. Ahura scurried off like a startled cat.

Suddenly she froze like a dancer and looked back at him, and a gloating, transcendent vindictiveness came into her face. She beckoned to Fafhrd. Then she ran lightly up the steps to the tomb and pointed into it and beckoned again. Doubtfully the Northerner approached, his eyes on her strained and unearthly face, beautiful as an efreet's. Slowly he mounted the steps.

Then he looked down.

Looked down to feel that the wholesome world was only a film on primary abominations. He realized that what Ahura was showing him had somehow been her ultimate degradation

and the ultimate degradation of the thing that had named itself
Anra Devadoris. He remembered the bizarre taunts that Ahura
had thrown at the adept during the duel. He remembered her
laughter, and his mind eddied along the edge of suspicions of
pit-spawned improprieties and obscene intimacies. He hardly
noticed that Ahura had slumped over the wall of the tomb, her
white arms hanging down as if pointing all ten slender fingers in
limp horror. He did not know that the blackly puzzled eyes of
the suddenly awakened Mouser were peering up at him.

Thinking back, he realized that Devadoris' fastidiousness and
exquisitely groomed appearance had made him think of the
tomb as an eccentric entrance to some luxurious underground
palace.

But now he saw that there were no doors in that cramping
cell into which he peered, nor cracks indicating where hidden
doors might be. Whatever had come from there, had lived
there, where the dry corners were thick with webs and the floor
swarmed with maggots, dung beetles, and furry black spiders.

6: The Mountain

Perhaps some chuckling demon, or Ningauble himself, planned
it that way. At all events, as Fafhrd stepped down from the
tomb, he got his feet tangled in the shroud of Ahriman and
bellowed wildly (the Mouser called it "bleating") before he
noticed the cause, which was by that time ripped to tatters.

Next, Ahura, aroused by the tumult, set them into a brief
panic by screaming that the black monolith and its soldiery
were marching toward them to grind them under stony feet.

Almost immediately afterwards the cup of Socrates momentarily froze their blood by rolling around in a semicircle, as if its
learned owner were visibly pawing for it, perhaps to wet his
throat after a spell of dusty disputation in the underworld. Of
the withered sprig from the Tree of Life there was no sign,
although the Mouser jumped as far and as skittishly as one of
his namesakes when he saw a large black walking-stick insect
crawling away from where the sprig might have fallen.

But it was the camel that caused the biggest commotion, by
suddenly beginning to prance about clumsily in a most unchar-
acteristically ecstatic fashion, finally cavorting up eagerly on
two legs to the mare, which fled in squealing dismay. Afterwards it became apparent that the camel must have gotten into

the aphrodisiacs, for one of the bottles was bashed as if by a hoof, with only a scummy licked patch showing where its leaked contents had been, and two of the small clay jars were vanished entirely. Fafhrd set out after the two beasts on one of the remaining horses, hallooing crazily.

The Mouser, left alone with Ahura, found his glibness put to the test in saving her sanity by a barrage of small talk, mostly well-spiced Tyrian gossip, but including a wholly apocryphal tale of how he and Fafhrd and five small Ethiopian boys once played Maypole with the eyestalks of a drunken Ningauble, leaving him peering about in the oddest directions. (The Mouser was wondering why they had not heard from their seven-eyed mentor. After victories Ningauble was always particularly prompt in getting in his demands for payment; and very exacting too—he would insist on a strict accounting for the three missing aphrodisiac containers.)

The Mouser might have been expected to take advantage of this opportunity to press his suit with Ahura, and if possible assure himself that he was now wholly free of the snail-curse. But, her hysterical condition aside, he felt strangely shy with her, as if, although this was the Ahura he loved, he were now meeting her for the first time. Certainly this was a wholly different Ahura from the one with whom they had journeyed to the Lost City, and the memory of how he had treated that other Ahura put a restraint on him. So he cajoled and comforted her as he might have some lonely Tyrian waif, finally bringing two funny little hand-puppets from his pouch and letting them amuse her for him.

And Ahura sobbed and stared and shivered, and hardly seemed to hear what nonsense the Mouser was saying, yet grew quiet and sane-eyed and appeared to be comforted.

When Fafhrd eventually returned with the still giddy camel and the outraged mare, he did not interrupt, but listened gravely, his gaze occasionally straying to the dead adept, the black monolith, the stone city, or the valley's downward slope to the north. High over their heads a flock of birds was flying in the same direction. Suddenly they scattered wildly, as if an eagle had dropped among them. Fafhrd frowned. A moment later he heard a whirring in the air. The Mouser and Ahura looked up too, momentarily glimpsed something slim hurtling downward. They cringed. There was a thud as a long whitish arrow buried itself in a crack in the pavement hardly a foot from Fafhrd and stuck there vibrating.

After a moment Fafhrd touched it with shaking hand. The shaft was crusted with ice, the feathers stiff, as if, incredibly, it had sped for a long time through frigid supramundane air. There was something tied snugly around the shaft. He detached and unrolled an ice-brittle sheet of papyrus, which softened under his touch, and read, "You must go farther. Your quest is not ended. Trust in omens. Ningauble."

Still trembling, Fafhrd began to curse thunderously. He crumpled the papyrus, jerked up the arrow, broke it in two, threw the parts blindly away. "Misbegotten spawn of a eunuch, an owl, and an octopus!" he finished. "First he tries to skewer us from the skies, then he tells us our quest is not ended—when we've just ended it!"

The Mouser, well knowing these rages into which Fafhrd was apt to fall after battle, especially a battle in which he had not been able to participate, started to comment coolly. Then he saw the anger abruptly drain from Fafhrd's eyes, leaving a wild twinkle which he did not like.

"Mouser!" said Fafhrd eagerly. "Which way did I throw the arrow?"

"Why, north," said the Mouser without thinking.

"Yes, and the birds were flying north, and the arrow was coated with ice!" The wild twinkle in Fafhrd's eyes became a berserk brilliance. "Omens, he said? We'll trust in omens all right! We'll go north, north, and still north!"

The Mouser's heart sank. Now would be a particularly difficult time to combat Fafhrd's long-standing desire to take him to "that wonderously cold land where only brawny, hot-blooded men may live and they but by the killing of fierce, furry animals"—a prospect poignantly disheartening to a lover of hot baths, the sun, and southern nights.

"This is the chance of all chances," Fafhrd continued, intoning like a skald. "Ah, to rub one's naked hide with snow, to plunge like walrus into ice-garnished water. Around the Caspian and over greater mountains than these goes a way that men of my race have taken. Thor's gut, but you will love it! No wine, only hot mead and savory smoking carcasses, skin-toughening furs to wear, cold air at night to keep dreams clear and sharp, and great strong-hipped women. Then to raise sail on a winter ship and laugh at the frozen spray. Why have we so long delayed? Come! By the icy member that begot Odin, we must start at once!"

The Mouser stifled a groan. "Ah, blood-brother," he intoned, not a whit less brazen-voiced, "my heart leaps even more than yours at the thought of nerve-quickening snow and all the other niceties of the manly life I have long yearned to taste. But"—here his voice broke sadly—"we forget this good woman, whom in any case, even if we disregard Ningauble's injunction, we must take safely back to Tyre."

He smiled inwardly.

"But I don't want to go back to Tyre," interrupted Ahura, looking up from the puppets with an impishness so like a child's that the Mouser cursed himself for ever having treated her as one. "This lonely spot seems equally far from all builded places. North is as good a way as any."

"Flesh of Freya!" bellowed Fafhrd, throwing his arms wide. "Do you hear what she says, Mouser? By Idun, that was spoken like a true snow-land woman! Not one moment must be wasted now. We shall smell mead before a year is out. By Frigg, a woman! Mouser, you good for one so small, did you not notice the pretty way she put it?"

So it was bustle about and pack and (for the present, at least, the Mouser conceded) no way out of it. The chest of aphrodisiacs, the cup, and the tattered shroud were bundled back onto the camel, which was still busy ogling the mare and smacking its great leathery lips. And Fafhrd leaped and shouted and clapped the Mouser's back as if there were not an eon-old dead stone city around them and a lifeless adept warming in the sun.

In a matter of moments they were jogging off down the valley, with Fafhrd singing tales of snowstorms and hunting and monsters big as icebergs and giants as tall as frost mountains, and the Mouser dourly amusing himself by picturing his own death at the hands of some overly affectionate "great strong-hipped" woman.

Soon the way became less barren. Scrub trees and the valley's downward trend hid the city behind them. A surge of relief which the Mouser hardly noticed went through him as the last stony sentinel dipped out of sight, particularly the black monolith left to brood over the adept. He turned his attention to what lay ahead—a conical mountain barring the valley's mouth and wearing a high cap of mist, a lonely thunderhead which his imagination shaped into incredible towers and spires.

Suddenly his sleepy thoughts snapped awake. Fafhrd and Ahura had stopped and were staring at something wholly unexpected—a low wooden windowless house pressed back among the scrubby trees, with a couple of tilled fields behind it.

The rudely carved guardian spirits at the four corners of the roof and topping the kingposts seemed Persian, but Persian purged of all southern influence—ancient Persian.

And ancient Persian too appeared the thin features, straight nose, and black-streaked beard of the aged man watching them circumspectly from the low doorway. It seemed to be Ahura's face he scanned most intently—or tried to scan, since Fafhrd mostly hid her.

"Greetings, Father," called the Mouser. "Is this not a merry day for riding, and yours good lands to pass?"

"Yes," replied the aged man dubiously, using a rusty dialect. "Though there are none, or few, who pass."

"Just as well to be far from the evil stinking cities," Fafhrd interjected heartily. "Do you know the mountain ahead, Father? Is there an easy way past it that leads north?"

At the word "mountain" the aged man cringed. He did not answer.

"Is there something wrong about the path we are taking?" the Mouser asked quickly. "Or something evil about that misty mountain?"

The aged man started to shrug his shoulders, held them contracted, looked again at the travelers. Friendliness seemed to fight with fear in his face, and to win, for he leaned forward and said hurriedly, "I warn you, sons, not to venture farther. What is the steel of your swords, the speed of your steeds, against—but remember"—he raised his voice—"I accuse no one." He looked quickly from side to side. "I have nothing at all to complain of. To me the mountain is a great benefit. My fathers returned here because the land is shunned by thief and honest man alike. There are no taxes on this land—no money taxes. I question nothing."

"Oh, well, Father, I don't think we'll go farther," sighed the Mouser wilily. "We're but idle fellows who follow our noses across the world. And sometimes we smell a strange tale. And that reminds me of a matter in which you may be able to give us generous lads some help." He chinked the coins in his pouch. "We have heard a tale of a demon that inhabits here—a young demon dressed in black and silver, pale, with a black beard."

As the Mouser was saying these things the aged man was edging backward and at the finish he dodged inside and slammed the door, though not before they saw someone pluck at his sleeve. Instantly there came muffled angry expostulation in a girl's voice.

The door burst open. They heard the aged man say ". . . bring it down upon us all." Then a girl of about fifteen came running toward them. Her face was flushed, her eyes anxious and scared

"You must turn back!" she called to them as she ran. "None but wicked things go to the mountain—or the doomed. And the mist hides a great horrible castle. And powerful, lonely demons live there. And one of them—"

She clutched at Fafhrd's stirrup. But just as her fingers were about to close on it, she looked beyond him straight at Ahura. An expression of abysmal terror came into her face. She screamed, "He! The black beard!" and crumpled to the ground.

The door slammed and they heard a bar drop into place.

They dismounted. Ahura quickly knelt by the girl, signed to them after a moment that she had only fainted. Fafhrd approached the barred door, but it would not open to any knocking, pleas, or threats. He finally solved the riddle by kicking it down. Inside he saw: the aged man cowering in a dark corner; a woman attempting to conceal a young child in a pile of straw; a very old woman sitting on a stool, obviously blind, but frightenedly peering about just the same; and a young man holding an ax in trembling hands. The family resemblance was very marked.

Fafhrd stepped out of the way of the young man's feeble ax-blow and gently took the weapon from him.

The Mouser and Ahura brought the girl inside. At sight of Ahura there were further horrified shrinkings.

They laid the girl on the straw, and Ahura fetched water and began to bathe her head.

Meanwhile, the Mouser, by playing on her family's terror and practically identifying himself as a mountain demon, got them to answer his questions. First he asked about the stone city. It was a place of ancient devil-worship, they said, a place to be shunned. Yes, they had seen the black monolith of Ahriman, but only from a distance. No, they did not worship Ahriman—see the fire-shrine they kept for his adversary Ormadz? But they dreaded Ahriman, and the stones of the devil-city had a life of their own.

Then he asked about the misty mountain, and found it harder to get satisfactory answers. The cloud always shrouded its peak, they insisted. Though once toward sunset, the young man admitted, he thought he had glimpsed crazily leaning green towers and twisted minarets. But there was danger up there, horrible danger. What danger? He could not say.

The Mouser turned to the aged man. "You told me," he said harshly, "that my brother demons exact no money tax from you for this land. What kind of tax, then, do they exact?"

"Lives," whispered the aged man, his eyes showing more white.

"Lives, eh? How many? And when do they come for them?"

"They never come. We go. Maybe every ten years, maybe every five, there comes a yellow-green light on the mountaintop at night, and a powerful calling in the air. Sometimes after such a night one of us is gone—who was too far from the house when the green light came. To be in the house with others helps resist the calling. I never saw the light except from our door, with a fire burning bright at my back and someone holding me. My brother went when I was a boy. Then for many years afterwards the light never came, so that even I began to wonder whether it was not a boyhood legend of illusion.

"But seven years ago," he continued quaveringly, staring at the Mouser, "there came riding late one afternoon, on two gaunt and death-wearied horses, a young man and an old—or rather the semblances of a young man and an old, for I knew without being told, knew as I crouched trembling inside the door, peering through the crack, that the masters were returning to the Castle Called Mist. The old man was bald as a vulture and had no beard. The young man had the beginnings of a silky black one. He was dressed in black and silver, and his face was very pale. His features were like—" Here his gaze flickered fearfully toward Ahura. "He rode stiffly, his lanky body rocking from side to side. He looked as if he were dead.

"They rose on toward the mountain without a sideward glance. But ever since that time the greenish-yellow light has glowed almost nightly from the mountaintop, and many of our animals have answered the call—and the wild ones too, to judge from their diminishing numbers. We have been careful, always staying near the house. It was not until three years ago that my eldest son went. He strayed too far in hunting and let darkness overtake him.

"And we have seen the black-bearded young man many times, usually at a distance, treading along the skyline or standing with head bowed upon some crag. Though once when my daughter was washing at the stream she looked up from her clothes-pounding and saw his dead eyes peering through the reeds. And once my eldest son, chasing a wounded snow-leopard into a thicket, found him talking with the beast. And once, rising early on a harvest morning, I saw him sitting by the well, staring at our doorway, although he did not seem to see me emerge. The old man we have seen too, though not so often. And for the last two years we have seen little or nothing of either, until—" And once again his gaze flickered helplessly toward Ahura.

Meanwhile the girl had come to her senses. This time her terror of Ahura was not so extreme. She could add nothing to the aged man's tale.

They prepared to depart. The Mouser noted a certain veiled vindictiveness toward the girl, especially in the eyes of the woman with the child, for having tried to warn them. So turning in the doorway he said, "If you harm one hair of the girl's head, we will return, and the black-bearded one with us, and the green light to guide us by and wreak terrible vengeance."

He tossed a few gold coins on the floor and departed.

(And so, although, or rather because her family looked upon her as an ally of demons, the girl from then on led a pampered life, and came to consider her blood as superior to theirs, and played shamelessly on their fear of the Mouser and Fafhrd and Black-beard, and finally made them give her all the golden coins, and with them purchased seductive garments after fortunate passage to a faraway city, where by clever stratagem she became the wife of a satrap and lived sumptuously ever afterwards—something that is often the fate of romantic people, if only they are romantic enough.)

Emerging from the house, the Mouser found Fafhrd making a brave attempt to recapture his former berserk mood. "Hurry up, you little apprentice-demon!" he welcomed. "We've a tryst with the good land of snow and cannot lag on the way!"

As they rode off, the Mouser rejoined good-naturedly, "But what about the camel, Fafhrd? You can't very well take it to the ice country. It'll die of the phlegm."

"There's no reason why snow shouldn't be as good for camels as it is for men," Fafhrd retorted. Then, rising in his saddle and turning back, he waved toward the house and shouted, "Lad! You that held the ax! When in years to come your bones feel a strange yearning, turn your face to the north. There you will find a land where you can become a man indeed."

But in their hearts both knew that this talk was a pretense, that other planets now loomed in their horoscopes—in particular one that shone with a greenish-yellow light. As they pressed on up the valley, its silence and the absence of animal and insect life now made sinister, they felt mysteries hovering all around. Some, they knew, were locked in Ahura, but both refrained from questioning her, moved by vague apprehensions of terrifying upheavals her mind had undergone.

Finally the Mouser voiced what was in the thoughts of both of them. "Yes, I am much afraid that Anra Devadoris, who sought to make us his apprentices, was only an apprentice himself and apt, apprentice-wise, to take credit for his master's work. Black-beard is gone, but the beardless one remains. What was it Ningauble said? . . . no simple creature, but a mystery? . . . no single identity, but a mirage?"

"Well, by all the fleas that bite the Great Antiochus, and all the lice that tickle his wife!" remarked a shrill, insolent voice behind them. "You doomed gentlemen already know what's in this letter I have for you."

They whirled around. Standing beside the camel—he might conceivably have been hidden, it is true, behind a nearby boulder—was a pertly grinning brown urchin, so typically Alexandrian that he might have stepped this minute out of Rakotis with a skinny mongrel sniffing at his heels. (The Mouser half expected such a dog to appear at the next moment.)

"Who sent you, boy?" Fafhrd demanded. "How did you get here?"

"Now who and how would you expect?" replied the urchin. "Catch." He tossed the Mouser a wax tablet. "Say, you two, take my advice and get out while the getting's good. I think so far as your expedition's concerned, Ningauble's pulling up his tent pegs and scuttling home. Always a friend in need, my dear employer."

The Mouser ripped the cords, unfolded the tablet, and read:

"Greetings, my brave adventurers. You have done well, but the best remains to be done. Hark to the calling. Follow the green light. But be very cautious afterwards. I wish I could be of more assistance. Send the shroud, the cup, and the chest back with the boy as first payment."

"Loki-brat! Regin-spawn!" burst out Fafhrd. The Mouser looked up to see the urchin lurching and bobbing back toward the Lost City on the back of the eagerly fugitive camel. His impudent laughter returned shrill and faint.

"There," said the Mouser, "rides off the generosity of poor, penurious Ningauble. Now we know what to do with the camel."

"Zutt!" said Fafhrd. "Let him have the brute and the toys. Good riddance to his gossiping!"

"Not a very high mountain," said the Mouser an hour later, "but high enough. I wonder who carved this neat little path and who keeps it clear?"

As he spoke, he was winding loosely over his shoulder a long thin rope of the sort used by mountain climbers, ending in a hook.

It was sunset, with twilight creeping at their heels. The little path, which had grown out of nothing, only gradually revealing itself, now led them sinuously around great boulders and along the crests of ever steeper rock-strewn slopes. Conversation, which was only a film on wariness, had played with the methods of Ningauble and his agents—whether they communicated with one another directly, from mind to mind, or by tiny whistles that emitted a note too high for human ears to hear, but capable of producing a tremor in any brother whistle or in the ear of the bat.

It was a moment when the whole universe seemed to pause. A spectral greenish light gleamed from the cloudy top ahead— but that was surely only the sun's sky-reflected afterglow. There was a hint of all-pervading sound in the air, a might susurrus just below the threshold of hearing, as if an army of unseen insects were tuning up their instruments. These sensations were as intangible as the force that drew them onward, a force so feeble that they knew they could break it like a single spider-strand, yet did not choose to try.

As if in response to some unspoken word, both Fafhrd and the Mouser turned toward Ahura. Under their gaze she seemed to be changing momently, opening like a night flower, becoming ever more childlike, as if some master hypnotist were stripping away the outer, later petals of her mind, leaving only a small limpid pool, from whose unknown depths, however, dark bubbles were dimly rising.

They felt their infatuation pulse anew, but with a shy restraint on it. And their hearts fell silent as the hooded heights above, as she said, "Anra Devadoris was my twin brother."

7: Ahura Devadoris

"I never knew my father. He died before we were born. In one of her rare fits of communicativeness my mother told me, 'Your father was a Greek, Ahura. A very kind and learned man. He laughed a great deal.' I remember how stern she looked as she said that, rather than how beautiful, the sunlight glinting from her ringleted, black-dyed hair.

"But it seemed to me that she had slightly emphasized the word 'Your.' You see, even then I wondered about Anra. So I asked Old Berenice the housekeeper about it. She told me she had seen Mother bear us, both on the same night.

"Old Berenice went on to tell me how my father had died. Almost nine months before we were born, he was found one morning beaten to death in the street just outside the door. A gang of Egyptian longshoremen who were raping and robbing by night were supposed to have done it, although they were never brought to justice—that was back when the Ptolemies had Tyre. It was a horrible death. He was almost bashed to a pulp against the cobbles.

"At another time Old Berenice told me something about my mother, after making me swear by Athena and by Set and by Moloch, who would eat me if I did, never to tell. She said that Mother came from a Persian family whose five daughters in the old times were all priestesses, dedicated from birth to be the wives of an evil Persian god, forbidden the embraces of mortals, doomed to spend their nights alone with the stone image of the god in a lonely temple 'halfway across the world,' she said. Mother was away that day and Old Berenice dragged me down into a little basement under Mother's bedroom and pointed out three ragged gray stones set among the bricks and told me they came from the temple. Old Berenice liked to frighten me, although she was deathly afraid of Mother.

"Of course I instantly went and told Anra, as I always did."

The little path was leading sharply upward now, along the spine of a crest. Their horses went at a walk, first Fafhrd's then Ahura's, last the Mouser's. The lines were smoothed in Fafhrd's face, although he was still very watchful, and the Mouser looked almost like a quaint child.

Ahura continued, "It is hard to make you understand my relationship with Anra, because it was so close that even the word 'relationship' spoils it. There was a game we would play in the garden. He would close his eyes and guess what I was looking at. In other games we would change sides, but never in this one.

"He invented all sorts of versions of the game and didn't want to play any others. Sometimes I would climb up by the olive tree onto the tiled roof—Anra couldn't make it—and watch for an hour. Then I'd come down and tell him what I'd seen—some dyers spreading out wet green cloth for the sun to turn it purple, a procession of priests around the Temple of Melkarth, a galley from Pergamum setting sail, a Greek official impatiently explaining something to his Egyptian scribe, two henna-handed ladies giggling at some kilted sailors, a mysterious and lonely Jew—and he would tell me what kind of people they were and what they had been thinking and what they were planning to do. It was a very special kind of imagination, for afterwards when I began to go outside I found out that he was usually right. At the time I remember thinking that it was as if he were looking at the pictures in my mind and seeing more than I could. I liked it. It was such a gentle feeling.

"Of course our closeness was partly because Mother, especially after she changed her way of life, wouldn't let us go out at all or mix with other children. There was more reason for that than just her strictness. Anra was very delicate. He once broke his wrist and it was a long time healing. Mother had a slave come in who was skilled in such things, and he told Mother he was afraid that Anra's bones were becoming too brittle. He told about children whose muscles and sinews gradually turned to stone, so that they became living statues. Mother struck him in the face and drove him from the house—an action that cost her a dear friend, because he was an important slave.

"And even if Anra had been allowed to go out, he couldn't have. Once after I had begun to go outside I persuaded him to come with me. He didn't want to, but I laughed at him, and he could never stand laughter. As soon as we climbed over the garden wall he fell down in a faint and I couldn't rouse him from it, though I tried and tried. Finally I climbed back so I could open the door and drag him in, and Old Berenice spotted me and I had to tell her what had happened. She helped me carry him in, but afterwards she whipped me because she knew I'd never dare tell Mother I'd taken him outside. Anra came to his senses while she was whipping me, but he was sick for a week afterwards. I don't think I ever laughed at him after that, until today.

"Cooped up in the house, Anra spent most of his time

studying. While I watched from the roof or wheedled stories from Old Berenice and the other slaves, or later on went out to gather information for him, he would stay in Father's library, reading, or learning some new language from Fathers grammars and translations. Mother taught both of us to read Greek, and I picked up a speaking knowledge of Aramaic and scraps of other tongues from the slaves and passed them on to him. But Anra was far cleverer than I at reading. He loved letters as passionately as I did the outside. For him, they were alive. I remember him showing me some Egyptian hieroglyphs and telling me that they were all animals and insects. And then he showed me some Egyptian hieratics and demotics and told me those were the same animals in disguise. But Hebrew, he said, was best of all, for each letter was a magic charm. That was before he learned Old Persian. Sometimes it was years before we found out how to pronounce the languages he learned. That was one of my most important jobs when I started to go outside for him.

"Father's library had been kept just as it was when he died. Neatly stacked in canisters were all the renowned philosophers, historians, poets, rhetoricians, and grammarians. But tossed in a corner along with potsherds and papyrus scraps like so much trash were rolls of a very different sort. Across the back of one of them my father had scribbled, derisively I'm sure, in his big impulsive hand, 'Secret Wisdom!' It was those that from the first captured Anra's curiosity. He would read the respectable books in the canisters, but chiefly so he could go back and take a brittle roll from the corner, blow off the dust, and puzzle out a little more.

"They were very strange books that frightened and disgusted me and made me want to giggle all at once. Many of them were written in a cheap and ignorant style. Some of them told what dreams meant and gave directions for working magic—all sorts of nasty things to be cooked together. Others—Jewish rolls in Aramaic—were about the end of the world and wild adventures of evil spirits and mixed-up, messy monsters—things with ten heads and jeweled cartwheels for feet, things like that. Then there were Chaldean star-books that told how all the lights in the sky were alive and their names and what they did to you. And one jerky, half illiterate roll in Greek told about something horrible, which for a long while I couldn't understand, connected with an ear of corn and six pomegranate seeds. It was in another of those sensational Greek rolls that Anra first found out about Ahriman and his eternal empire of evil, and after that he couldn't wait until he'd mastered Old Persian. But none of the few Old Persian rolls in Father's library were about Ahriman, so he had to wait until I could steal such things for him outside.

"My going outside was after Mother changed her way of life. That happened when I was seven. She was always a very moody and frightening woman, though sometimes she'd be very affectionate toward me for a little while, and she always spoiled and pampered Anra, though from a distance, through the slaves, almost as if she were afraid of him.

"Now her moods became blacker and blacker. Sometimes I'd surprise her looking in horror at nothing, or beating her forehead while her eyes were closed and her beautiful face was all taut, as if she were going mad. I had the feeling she'd been backed up to the end of some underground tunnel and must find a door leading out, or lose her mind.

"Then one afternoon I peeked into her bedroom and saw her looking into her silver mirror. For a long, long while she studied her face in it and I watched her without making a sound. I knew that something important was happening. Finally she seemed to make some sort of difficult inward effort and the lines of anxiety and sternness and fear disappeared from her face, leaving it smooth and beautiful as a mask. Then she unlocked a drawer I'd never seen into before and took out all sorts of little pots and vials and brushes. With these she colored and whitened her face and carefully smeared a dark, shining powder around her eyes and painted her lips reddish-orange. All this time my heart was pounding and my throat was choking up, I didn't know why. Then she laid down her brushes and dropped her chiton and felt of her throat and breasts in a thoughtful way and took up the mirror and looked at herself with a cold satisfaction. She was very beautiful, but it was a beauty that terrified me. Until now I'd always thought of her as hard and stern outside, but soft and loving within, if only you could manage to creep into that core. But now she was all turned inside out. Strangling my sobs, I ran to tell Anra and find out what it meant. But this time his cleverness failed him. He was as puzzled and disturbed as I.

"It was right afterwards that she became even stricter with me, and although she continued to spoil Anra from a distance, kept us shut up from the world more than ever. I wasn't even allowed to speak to the new slave she'd bought, an ugly, smirking, skinny-legged girl named Phryne who used to massage her and sometimes play the flute. There were all sorts of visitors coming to the house now at night, but Anra and I were always locked in our little bedroom high up by the garden. We'd hear them yelling through the wall and sometimes screaming and bumping around the inner court to the sound of Phryne's flute. Sometimes I'd lie staring at the darkness in an inexplicable sick terror all night long. I tried every way to get Old Berenice to tell me what was happening, but for once her fear of mother's anger was too great. She'd only leer at me.

"Finally Anra worked out a plan for finding out. When he first told me about it, I refused. It terrified me. That was when I discovered the power he had over me. Up until that time the things I had done for him had been part of a game I enjoyed as much as he. I had never thought of myself as a slave obeying commands. But now when I rebelled, I found out not only that my twin had an obscure power over my limbs, so that I could hardly move them at all, or imagined I couldn't, if he were unwilling, but also that I couldn't bear the thought of him being unhappy or frustrated.

"I realize now that he had reached the first of those crises in his life when his way was blocked and he pitilessly sacrificed his dearest helper to the urgings of his insatiable curiosity.

"Night came. As soon as we were locked in I let a knotted cord out the little high window and wriggled out and climbed down. Then I climbed the olive tree to the roof. I crept over the tiles down to the square skylight of the inner court and managed to squirm over the edge—I almost fell—into a narrow, cobwebby space between the ceiling and the tiles. There was a faint murmur of talk from the dining room, but the court was empty. I lay still as a mouse and waited."

Fafhrd uttered a smothered exclamation and stopped his horse. The others did likewise. A pebble rattled down the slope, but they hardly heard it. Seeming to come from the heights above them and yet to fill the whole darkening sky was something that was not entirely a sound, something that tugged at them like the Sirens' voices at fettered Odysseus. For a while they listened incredulously, then Fafhrd shrugged and started forward again, the others following.

Ahura continued, "For a long time nothing happened, except occasionally slaves hurried in and out with full and empty dishes, and there was some laughter, and I heard Phryne's flute. Then suddenly the laughter grew louder and changed to singing, and there was the sound of couches pushed back and the patter of footsteps, and there swept into the court a Dionysiac rout.

"Phryne, naked, piped the way. My mother followed, laughing, her arms linked with those of two dancing young men, but clutching to her a bosom a large silver wine-bowl. The wine sloshed over and stained purple her white silk chiton around her breasts, but she only laughed and reeled more wildly. After those came many others, men and women, young and old, all singing and dancing. One limber young man skipped high, clapping his heels, and one fat old grinning fellow panted and had to be pulled by girls, but they kept it up three times around the court before they threw themselves down on the couches and cushions. Then while they chattered and laughed and kissed and embraced and played pranks and watched a naked girl prettier than Phryne dance, my mother offered the bowl around for them to dip their wine cups.

"I was astounded—and entranced. I had been almost dead with fear, expecting I don't know what cruelties and horrors. Instead, what I saw was wholly lovely and natural. The revelation burst on me, 'So this is the wonderful and important thing that people do.' My mother no longer frightened me. Though she still wore her new face, there was no longer any hardness about her, inside or out, only joy and beauty. The young men were so witty and gay I had to put my fist in my mouth to keep from screaming with laughter. Even Phryne, squatting on her heels like a skinny boy as she piped, seemed for once unmalicious and likable. I couldn't wait to tell Anra.

"There was only one disturbing note, and that was so slight I hardly noticed it. Two of the men who took the lead in the joking, a young red-haired fellow and an older chap with a face like a lean satyr, seemed to have something up their sleeves. I saw them whisper to some of the others. And once the younger grinned at Mother and shouted, 'I know something about you from way back!' And once the older called at her mockingly, 'I know something about your great-grandmother, you old Persian you!' Each time Mother laughed and waved her hand derisively, but I could see that she was bothered underneath. And each time some of the others paused momentarily, as if they had an inkling of something, but didn't want to let on. Eventually the two men drifted out, and from then on there was nothing to mar the fun.

"The dancing became wilder and staggering, the laughter louder, more wine was spilled than drank. Then Phryne threw away her flute and ran and landed in the fat man's lap with a jounce that almost knocked the wind out of him. Four or five of the others tumbled down.

"Just at that moment there came a crashing and a loud rending of wood, as if a door were being broken in. Instantly everyone was as still as death. Someone jerked around and a lamp snuffed out, throwing half the court into shadow.

"Then loud, shaking footsteps, like two paving blocks walking, sounded through the house, coming nearer and nearer.

"Everyone was frozen, staring at the doorway. Phryne still had her arm around the fat man's neck. But it was in Mother's face that the truly unbearable terror showed. She had retreated to the remaining lamp and dropped to her knees there. The whites showed around her eyes. She began to utter short, rapid screams, like a trapped dog.

"Then through the doorway clomped a great ragged-edged, square-limbed, naked stone man fully seven feet high. His face was just expressionless black gashes in a flat surface, and before him was thrust a mortary stone member. I couldn't bear to look at him, but I had to. He tramped echoingly across the room to Mother, jerked her up, still screaming, by the hair, and with the other hand ripped down her wine-stained chiton. I fainted.

"But it must have ended about there, for when I came to, sick with terror, it was to hear everyone laughing uproariously. Several of them were bending over Mother, at once reassuring and mocking her, the two men who had gone out among them, and to one side was a jumbled heap of cloth and thin boards, both crusted with mortar. From what they said I understood that the red-haired one had worn the horrible disguise, while satyr-face had made the footsteps by rhythmically clomping on the floor with a brick, and had simulated the breaking door by jumping on a propped-up board.

" 'Now tell us your great-grandmother wasn't married to a stupid old stone demon back in Persia!' he jeered pleasantly, wagging his finger.

"Then came something that tortured me like a rusty dagger and terrified me, in a very quiet way, as much as the image. Although she was white as milk and barely able to totter, Mother did her best to pretend that the loathsome trick they'd played on her was just a clever joke. I knew why. She was horribly afraid of losing their friendship and would have done anything rather than be left alone.

"Her pretense worked. Although some of them left, the rest

yielded to her laughing entreaties. They drank until they sprawled out snoring. I waited until almost dawn, then summoned all my courage, made my stiff muscles pull me onto the tiles, cold and slippery with dew, and with what seemed the last of my strength, dragged myself back to our room.

"But not to sleep. Anra was awake and avid to hear what had happened. I begged him not to make me, but he insisted. I had to tell him everything. The pictures of what I'd seen kept bobbing up in my wretchedly tired mind so vividly that it seemed to be happening all over again. He asked all sorts of questions, wouldn't let me miss a single detail. I had to relive that first thrilling revelation of joy, tainted now by the knowledge that the people were mostly sly and cruel.

"When I got to the part about the stone image, Anra became terribly excited. But when I told him about it all being a nasty joke, he seemed disappointed. He became angry, as if he suspected me of lying.

"Finally he let me sleep.

"The next night I went back to my cubbyhole under the tiles."

Again Fafhrd stopped his horse. The mist masking the mountaintop had suddenly begun to glow, as if a green moon were rising, or as if it were a volcano spouting green flames. The hue tinged their upturned faces. It lured like some vast cloudy jewel. Fafhrd and the Mouser exchanged a glance of fatalistic wonder. Then all three proceeded up the narrowing ridge.

Ahura continued, "I'd sworn by all the gods I'd never do it. I'd told myself I'd rather die. But . . . Anra made me.

"Daytimes I wandered around like a stupefied little ghost-slave. Old Berenice was puzzled and suspicious and once or twice I thought Phryne grimaced knowingly. Finally even Mother noticed and questioned me and had a physician in.

"I think I would have gotten really sick and died, or gone mad, except that then, in desperation at first, I started to go outside, and a whole new world opened to me."

As she spoke on, her voice rising in hushed excitement at the memory of it, there was painted in the minds of Fafhrd and the Mouser a picture of the magic city that Tyre must have seemed to the child—the waterfront, the riches, the bustle of trade, the hum of gossip and laughter, the ships and strangers from foreign lands.

"Those people I had watched from the roof—I could touch almost anywhere. Every person I met seemed a wonderful mystery, something to be smiled and chattered at. I dressed as a slave-child, and all sorts of folk got to know me and expect my coming—other slaves, tavern wenches and sellers of sweet-meats, street merchants and scribes, errand boys and boatmen, seamstresses and cooks. I made myself useful, ran errands myself, listened delightedly to their endless talk, passed on gossip I'd heard, gave away bits of food I'd stolen at home, became a favorite. It seemed to me I could never get enough of Tyre. I scampered from morning to night. It was generally twilight before I climbed back over the garden wall.

"I couldn't fool Old Berenice, but after a while I found a way to escape her whippings. I threatened to tell Mother it was she who had told red-hair and satyr-face about the stone image. I don't know if I guessed right or not, but the threat worked. After that, she would only mumble venomously whenever I sneaked in after sunset. As for Mother, she was getting farther away from us all the time, alive only by night, lost by day in frightened brooding.

"Then, each evening, came another delight. I would tell Anra everything I had heard and seen, each new adventure, each little triumph. Like a magpie I repeated for him all the bright colors, sounds, and odors. Like a magpie I repeated for him the babble of strange languages I'd heard, the scraps of learned talk I'd caught from priests and scholars. I forgot what he'd done to me. We were playing the game again, the most wonderful version of all. Often he helped me, suggesting new places to go, new things to watch for, and once he even saved me from being kidnapped by a couple of ingratiating Alexandrian slave-dealers whom anyone but me would have suspected.

"It was odd how that happened. The two had made much of me, were promising me sweetmeats if I would go somewhere nearby with them, when I thought I heard Anra's voice whisper 'Don't.' I became cold with terror and darted down an alley.

"It seemed as though Anra were now able sometimes to see the pictures in my mind even when I was away from him. I felt ever so close to him.

"I was wild for him to come out with me, but I've told you what happened the one time he tried. And as the years passed, he seemed to become tied even tighter to the house. Once when Mother vaguely talked of moving to Antioch, he fell ill and did not recover until she had promised we would never, never go.

"Meanwhile he was growing up into a slim and darkly handsome youth. Phryne began to make eyes at him and sought excuses to go to his room. But he was frightened and rebuffed her. However, he coaxed me to make friends with her, to be near her, even share her bed those nights when Mother did not want her. He seemed to like that.

"You know the restlessness that comes to a maturing child, when he seeks love, or adventure, or the gods, or all three. That restlessness had come to Anra, but his only gods were in those dusty, dubious rolls my father had labeled 'Secret Wisdom!' I hardly knew what he did by day any more except that there were odd ceremonies and experiments mixed with his studies. Some of them he conducted in the little basement where the three gray stones were. At such times he had me keep watch. He no longer told me what he was reading or thinking, and I was so busy in my new world that I hardly noticed the difference.

"And yet I could see the restlessness growing. He sent me on longer and more difficult missions, had me inquire after books the scribes had never heard of, seek out all manner of astrologers and wise-women, required me to steal or buy stranger and stranger ingredients from the herb doctors. And when I did win such treasures for him, he would only snatch them from me unjoyfully and be twice as gloomy the evening after. Gone were such days of rejoicing as when I had brought him the first Persian rolls about Ahriman, the first lodestone, or repeated every syllable I had overheard of the words of a famous philosopher from Athens. He was beyond all that now. He sometimes hardly listened to my detailed reports, as if he had already glanced through them and knew they contained nothing to interest him.

"He grew haggard and sick. His restlessness took the form of a frantic pacing. I was reminded of my mother trapped in that blocked-off, underground corridor. It made my heart hurt to watch him. I longed to help him, to share with him my new exciting life, to give him the thing he so desperately wanted.

"But it was not my help he needed. He had embarked on a dark, mysterious quest I did not understand, and he had reached a bitter, corroding impasse where of his own experience he could go no farther.

"He needed a teacher."

8: The Old Man Without a Beard

"I was fifteen when I met the Old Man Without a Beard. I called him that then and I still call him that, for there is no other distinguishing characteristic my mind can seize and hold. Whenever I think of him, even whenever I look at him, his face melts into the mob. It is as if a master actor, after portraying every sort of character in the world, should have hit on the simplest and most perfect of disguises.

"As to what lies behind that too-ordinary face—the something you can sometimes sense but hardly grasp—all I can say is a satiety and an emptiness that are not of this world."

Fafhrd caught his breath. They had reached the end of the ridge. The leftward slope had suddenly tilted upward, become the core of the mountain. While the rightward slope had swung downward and out of sight, leaving an unfathomable black abyss. Between, the path continued upward, a stony strip only a few feet wide. The Mouser touched reassuringly the coil of rope over his shoulder. For a moment their horses hung back. Then, as if the faint green glow and the ceaseless murmuring that bathed them were an intangible net, they were drawn on.

"I was in a wine shop. I had just carried a message to one of the men-friends of the Greek girl Chloe, hardly older than myself, when I noticed him sitting in a corner. I asked Chloe about him. She said he was a Greek chorister and commercial poet down on his luck, or, no, that he was an Egyptian fortune-teller, changed her mind again, tried to remember what a Samian pander had told her about him, gave him a quick puzzled look, decided that she didn't really know him at all and that it didn't matter.

"But his very emptiness intrigued me. Here was a new kind of mystery. After I had been watching him for some time, he turned around and looked at me. I had the impression that he had been aware of my inquiring gaze from the beginning, but had ignored it as a sleepy man a buzzing fly.

"After that one glance he slumped back into his former position, but when I left the shop he walked at my side.

" 'You're not the only one who looks through your eyes, are you?' he said quietly.

"I was so startled by his question that I didn't know how to reply, but he didn't require me to. His face brightened without becoming any more individualized and he immediately began to talk to me in the most charming and humorous way, though his words gave no clue as to who he was or what he did.

"However, I gathered from hints he let fall that he possessed some knowledge of those odd sorts of things that always interested Anra and so I followed him willingly, my hand in his.

"But not for long. Our way led up a narrow twisting alley, and I saw a sideways glint in his eye, and felt his hand tighten on mine in a way I did not like. I became somewhat frightened and expected at any minute the danger warning from Anra.

"We passed a lowering tenement and stopped at a rickety three-story shack leaning against it. He said his dwelling was at the top. He was drawing me toward the ladder that served for stairs, and still the danger warning did not come.

"Then his hand crept toward my wrist and I did not wait any longer, but jerked away and ran, my fear growing greater with every step.

"When I reached home, Anra was pacing like a leopard. I was eager to tell him all about my narrow escape, but he kept interrupting me to demand details of the Old Man and angrily flirting his head because I could tell him so little. Then, when I came to the part about my running away, an astounding look of tortured betrayal contorted his features, he raised his hands as if to strike me, then threw himself down on the couch, sobbing.

"But as I leaned over him anxiously, his sobs stopped. He looked around at me, over his shoulder, his face white but composed, and said, 'Ahura, I must know everything about him.'

"In that one moment I realized all that I had overlooked for years—that my delightful airy freedom was a sham—that it was not Anra, but I, that was tethered—that the game was not a game, but a bondage—that while I had gone about so open and eager, intent only on sound and color, form and movement, he had been developing the side I had no time for, the intellect, the purpose, the will—that I was only a tool to him, a slave to be sent on errands, an unfeeling extension of his own body, a tentacle he could lose and grow again, like an octopus—that even my misery at his frantic disappointment, my willingness to do anything to please him, was only another lever to be coldly used against me—that our very closeness, so that we were only two halves of one mind, was to him only another tactical advantage.

"He had reached the second great crisis in his life, and again he unhesitatingly sacrificed his nearest.

"There was something uglier to it even than that, as I could see in his eyes as soon as he was sure he had me. We were like brother and sister kings in Alexandria or Antioch, playmates from infancy, destined for each other, but unknowingly, and the boy crippled and impotent—and now, too soon and horridly had come the bridal night.

"The end was that I went back to the narrow alley, the lowering tenement, the rickety shack, the ladder, the third story, and the Old Man Without a Beard.

"I didn't give in without a struggle. Once I was out of the house I fought every inch of the way. Up until now, even in the cubbyhole under the tiles, I had only to spy and observe for Anra. I had not to do things.

"But in the end it was the same. I dragged myself up the last rung and knocked on the warped door. It swung open at my touch. Inside, across a fumy room, behind a large empty table, by the light of a single ill-burning lamp, his eyes as unwinking as a fish's, and upon me, sat the Old Man Without a Beard."

Ahura paused, and Fafhrd and the Mouser felt a clamminess descend upon their skins. Looking up, they saw uncoiling downward from dizzy heights, like the ghosts of constrictive snakes or jungle vines, thin tendrils of green mist.

"Yes," said Ahura, "there is always mist or smokiness of some sort where he is.

"Three days later I returned to Anra and told him everything—a corpse giving testimony as to its murderer. But in this instance the judge relished the testimony, and when I told him of a certain plan the Old Man had in mind, an unearthly joy shimmered on his face.

"The Old Man was to be hired as a tutor and physician for Anra. This was easily arranged, as Mother always acceded to Anra's wishes and perhaps still had some hope of seeing him stirred from his seclusion. Moreover, the Old Man had a mixture of unobtrusiveness and power that I am sure would have won him entry everywhere. Within a matter of weeks he had quietly established a mastery over everyone in the house—some, like Mother, merely to be ignored; others, like Phryne, ultimately to be used.

"I will always remember Anra on the day the Old Man came. This was to be his first contact with the reality beyond the garden wall, and I could see that he was terribly frightened. As the hours of waiting passed, he retreated to his room, and I think it was mainly pride that kept him from calling the whole thing off. We did not hear the Old Man coming—only Old Berenice, who was counting the silver outside, stopped her muttering. Anra threw himself back on the couch in the farthest corner of the room, his hands gripping its edge, his eyes fixed on the doorway. A shadow lurched into sight there, grew darker and more definite. Then the Old Man put down on the threshold the two bags he was carrying and looked beyond me at Anra. A moment later my twin's painful gasps died in a faint hiss of expired breath. He had fainted.

"That evening his new education began. Everything that had happened was, as it were, repeated on a deeper, stranger level. There were languages to be learned, but not any languages to be found in human books; rituals to be intoned, but not to any gods that ordinary men have worshiped; magic to be brewed, but not with herbs that I could buy or steal. Daily Anra was instructed in the ways of inner darkness, the sicknesses and unknown powers of the mind, the eon-buried emotions that must be due to insidious impurities the gods overlooked in the earth from which they made man. By silent stages our home became a temple of the abominable, a monastery of the unclean.

"Yet there was nothing of tainted orgy, of vicious excess about their actions. Whatever they did, was done with strict self-discipline and mystic concentration. There was no looseness anywhere about them. They aimed at a knowledge and a power, born of darkness, true, but one which they were willing to make any self-sacrifice to obtain. They were religious, with this difference: their ritual was degradation, their aim a world chaos played upon like a broken lyre by their master minds, their god the quintessence of evil, Ahriman, the ultimate pit.

"As if performed by sleepwalkers, the ordinary routine of our home went on. Indeed, I sometimes felt that we were all of us, except Anra, merely dreams behind the Old Man's empty eyes—actors in a deliberate nightmare where men portrayed beasts; beasts, worms; worms, slime.

"Each morning I went out and made my customary way through Tyre, chattering and laughing as before, but emptily, knowing that I was no more free than if visible chains leashed me to the house, a puppet dangled over the garden wall. Only at the periphery of my masters' intentions did I dare oppose them even passively—once I smuggled the girl Chloe a protective amulet because I fancied they were considering her as a subject for such experiments as they had tried on Phryne. And daily the periphery of their intentions widened—indeed, they would long since have left the house themselves, except for Anra's bondage to it.

"It was to the problem of breaking that bondage that they now devoted themselves. I was not told how they hoped to manage it, but I soon realized that I was to play a part.

"They would shine glittering lights into my eyes and Anra would chant until I slept. Hours or even days later I would awake to find that I had gone unconsciously about my daily business, my body a slave to Anra's commands. At other times Anra would wear a thin leathermask which covered all his features, so that he could only see, if at all, through my eyes. My sense of oneness with my twin grew steadily with my fear of him.

"Then came a period in which I was kept closely pent up, as if in some savage prelude to maturity or death or birth, or all three. The Old Man said something about 'not to see the sun or touch the earth.' Again I crouched for hours in the cubbyhole under the tiles or on reed mats in the little basement. And now it was my eyes and ears that were covered rather than Anra's. For hours I, whom sights and sounds had nourished more than food, could see nothing but fragmentary memories of the child—Anra sick, or the Old Man across the fumy room, or Phryne writhing on her belly and hissing like a snake. But worst of all was my separation from Anra. For the first time since our birth I could not see his face, hear his voice, feel his mind. I withered like a tree from which the sap is withdrawn, an animal in which the nerves have been killed.

"Finally came a day or night, I know not which, when the Old Man loosened the mask from my face. There could hardly have been more than a glimmer of light, but my long-blindfolded eyes made out every detail of the little basement with a painful clarity. The three gray stones had been dug out of the pavement. Supine beside them lay Anra, emaciated, pale, hardly breathing, looking as though he were about to die."

The three climbers stopped, confronted by a ghostly green wall. The narrow path had emerged onto what must be the mountain's tablelike top. Ahead stretched a level expanse of dark rock, mist-masked after the first few yards. Without a word they dismounted and led their trembling horses forward into a moist realm which, save that the water was weightless, most resembled a faintly phosphorescent sea bottom.

"My heart leaped out toward my twin in pity and horror. I realized that despite all tyranny and torment I still loved him more than anything in the world, loved him as a slave loves the weak, cruel master who depends for everything on that slave, loved him as the ill-used body loves the despot mind. And I felt more closely linked to him, our lives and deaths interdependent, than if we had been linked by bonds of flesh and blood, as some rare twins are.

"The Old Man told me I could save him from death if I chose. For the present I must merely talk to him in my usual fashion. This I did, with an eagerness born of days without him. Save for an occasional faint fluttering of his sallow eyelids, Anra did not move, yet I felt that never before had he listened as intently, never before had he understood me as well. It seemed to me that all my previous speech with him had been crude by contrast. Now I remembered and told him all sorts of things that had escaped my memory or seemed too subtle for language. I talked on and on, haphazardly, chaotically, ranging swiftly from local gossip to world history, delving into myriad experiences and feelings, not all of them my own.

"Hours, perhaps days passed—the Old Man may have put some spell of slumber or deafness on the other inmates of the house to guard against interruption. At times my throat grew dry and he gave me drink, but I hardly dared pause for that, since I was appalled at the slight but unremitting change for the worse that was taking place in my twin and I had become possessed with the idea that my talking was the cord between life and Anra, that it created a channel between our bodies, across which my strength could flow to revive him.

"My eyes swam and blurred, my body shook, my voice ran the gamut of hoarseness down to an almost inaudible whisper. Despite my resolve I would have fainted, save that the Old Man held to my face burning aromatic herbs which caused me to come shudderingly awake.

"Finally I could no longer speak, but that was no release, as I continued to twitch my cracked lips and think on and on in a rushing feverish stream. It was as if I jerked and flung from the depths of my mind scraps of ideas from which Anra sucked the tiny life that remained to him.

"There was one persistent image—of a dying Hermaphroditus approaching Salmacis' pool, in which he would become one with the nymph.

"Farther and farther I ventured out along the talk-created channel between us, nearer and nearer I came to Anra's pale, delicate, cadaverous face, until, as with a despairing burst of effort I hurled my last strength to him, it loomed large as a green-shadowed ivory cliff falling to engulf me—"

Ahura's words broke off in a gasp of horror. All three stood still and stared ahead. For rearing up before them in the thickening mist, so near that they felt they had been ambushed, was a great chaotic structure of whitish, faintly yellowed stone, through whose narrow windows and wide-open door streamed a baleful greenish light, source of the mist's phosphorescent glow. Fafhrd and the Mouser thought of Karnak and its obelisks, of the Pharos lighthouse, of the Acropolis, of the Ishtar Gate in Babylon, of the ruins of Khatti, of the Lost City of Ahriman, of those doomful mirage-towers that seamen see where are Scylla and Charybdis. Of a truth, the architecture of the strange structure varied so swiftly and to such unearthly extremes that it was lifted into an insane stylistic realm all its own. Mist-magnified, its twisted ramps and pinnacles, like a fluid face in a nightmare, pushed upward toward where the stars should have been.

9: The Castle Called Mist

"What happened next was so strange that I felt sure I had plunged from feverish consciousness into the cool retreat of a fanciful dream," Ahura continued as, having tethered their horses, they mounted a wide stairway toward that open door which mocked alike sudden rush and cautious reconnoitering. Her story went on with as calm and drugged a fatalism as their step-by-step advance. "I was lying on my back beside the three stones and watching my body move around the little basement. I was terribly weak, I could not stir a muscle, and yet I felt delightfully refreshed—all the dry burning and aching in my throat was gone. Idly, as one will in a dream, I studied my face. It seemed to be smiling in triumph, very foolishly I thought. But as I continued to study it, fear began to intrude into my pleasant dream. The face was mine, but there were unfamiliar quirks of expression. Then, becoming aware of my gaze, it grimaced contemptuously and turned and said something to the Old Man, who nodded matter-of-factly. The intruding fear engulfed me. With a tremendous effort I managed to roll my eyes downward and look at my real body, the one lying on the floor.

"It was Anra's."

They entered the doorway and found themselves in a huge,

many-nooked and niched stone room—though seemingly no
nearer the ultimate source of the green glow, except that here
the misty air was bright with it. There were stone tables and
benches and chairs scattered about, but the chief feature of the
place was the mighty archway ahead, from which stone groin-
ings curved upward in baffling profusion. Fafhrd's and the
Mouser's eyes momentarily sought the keystone of the arch,
both because of its great size and because there was an odd
dark recess toward its top.

The silence was portentous, making them feel uneasily for
their swords. It was not merely that the luring music had
ceased—here in the Castle Called Mist there was literally no
sound, save what rippled out futilely from their own beating
hearts. There was instead a fogbound concentration that froze
into the senses, as though they were inside the mind of a titanic
thinker, or as if the stones themselves were entranced.

Then, since it seemed as unthinkable to wait in that silence as
for lost hunters to stand motionless in deep winter cold, they
passed under the archway and took at random an upward-
leading ramp.

Ahura continued, "Helplessly I watched them make certain
preparations. While Anra gathered some small bundles of manu-
scripts and clothing, the Old Man lashed together the three
mortar-crusted stones.

"It may have been that in the moment of victory he relaxed
habitual precautions. At all events, while he was still bending
over the stones, my mother entered the room. Crying out,
'What have you done to him?' she threw herself down beside
me and felt at me anxiously. But that was not to the Old Man's
liking. He grabbed her shoulders and roughly jerked her back.
She lay huddled against the wall, her eyes wide, her teeth
chattering—especially when she saw Anra, in my body, grotes-
quely lift the lashed stones. Meanwhile the Old Man hoisted
me, in my new, wasted form, to his shoulder, picked up the
bundles, and ascended the short stair.

"We walked through the inner court, rose-strewn and filled
with Mother's perfumed, wine-splashed friends, who stared at
us in befuddled astonishment, and so out of the house. It was
night. Five slaves waited with a curtained litter in which the Old
Man placed me. My last glimpse was of Mother's face, its paint
tracked by tears, peering horrifiedly through the half-open door."

The ramp issued onto an upper level and they found themselves wandering aimlessly through a mazy series of rooms. Of

little use to record here the things they thought they saw through
shadowy doorways, or thought they heard through metal doors
with massy complex bolts whose drawing they dared not fathom.
There was a disordered, high-shelved library, certain of the
rolls seeming to smoke and fume as though they held in their
papyrus and ink the seeds of a holocaust; the corners were piled
with sealed canisters of greenish stone and age-verdigrised brass
tablets. There were instruments that Fafhrd did not even bother
to warn the Mouser against touching. Another room exuded a
fearful animal stench; upon its slippery floor they noted a
sprinkling of short, incredibly thick black bristles. But the only
living creature they saw at any time was a little hairless thing
that looked as if it had once sought to become a bear cub; when
Fafhrd stooped to pet it, it flopped away whimpering. There
was a door that was thrice as broad as it was high, and its height
hardly that of a man's knee. There was a window that let upon
a blackness that was neither of mist nor of night, and yet
seemed infinite; peering in, Fafhrd could faintly see rusted iron
handholds leading upward. The Mouser uncoiled his climbing
rope to its full length and swung it around inside the window,
without the hook striking anything.

Yet the strangest impression this ominously empty stronghold
begot in them was also the subtlest, and one which each new
room or twisting corridor heightened—a feeling of architectural
inadequacy. It seemed impossible that the supports were equal
to the vast weights of the great stone floors and ceilings, so
impossible that they almost became convinced that there were
buttresses and retaining walls they could not see, either invisible or existing in some other world altogether, as if the Castle
Called Mist had only partially emerged from some unthinkable
outside. That certain bolted doors seemed to lead where no
space could be added to this hinting.

They wandered through passages so distorted that, though
they retained a precise memory of landmarks, they lost all
sense of direction.

Finally Fafhrd said, "This gets us nowhere. Whatever we
seek, whomever we wait for—Old Man or demon—it might as
well be in that first room of the great archway."

The Mouser nodded as they turned back, and Ahura said,
"At least we'll be at no greater disadvantage there. Ishtar, but
the Old Man's rhyme is true! 'Each chamber is a slavering
maw, each arch a toothy jaw.' I always greatly feared this

place, but never thought to find a mazy den that sure as death has stony mind and stony claws.

"They never chose to bring me here, you see, and from the night I left our home in Anra's body, I was a living corpse, to be left or taken where they wished. They would have killed me, I think, at least there came a time when Anra would, except it was necessary that Anra's body have an occupant—or my rightful body when he was out of it, for Anra was able to reenter his own body and walk about in it in this region of Ahriman. At such times I was kept drugged and helpless at the Lost City. I believe that something was done to his body at that time—the Old Man talked of making it invulnerable—for after I returned to it, I found it seeming both emptier and stonier than before."

Starting back down the ramp, the Mouser thought he heard from somwhere ahead, against the terrible silence, the faintest of windy groans.

"I grew to know my twin's body very well, for I was in it most of seven years in the tomb. Somewhere during that black period all fear and horror vanished—I had become habituated to death. For the first time in my life my will, my cold intelligence, had time to grow. Physically fettered, existing almost without sensation, I gained inward power. I began to see what I could never see before—Anra's weaknesses.

"For he could never cut me wholly off from him. The chain he had forged between our minds was too strong for that. No matter how far away he went, no matter what screens he raised up, I could always see into some sector of his mind, dimly, like a scene at the end of a long, narrow, shadowy corridor.

"I saw his pride—a silver-armored wound. I watched his ambition stalk among the stars as if they were jewels set on black velvet in his treasure house to be. I felt, almost as if it were my own, his choking hatred of the bland, miserly gods—almighty fathers who lock up the secrets of the universe, smile at our pleas, frown, shake their heads, forbid, chastise; and his groaning rage at the bonds of space and time, as if each cubit he could not see and tread upon were a silver manacle on his wrist, as if each moment before or after his own life were a silver crucifying nail. I walked through the gale-blown halls of his loneliness and glimpsed the beauty that he cherished—shadowy, glittering forms that cut the soul like knives—and once I came upon the dungeon of his love, where no light came to show it was corpses that were fondled and bones kissed. I grew familiar with his desires, which demanded a universe of

miracles peopled by unveiled gods. And his lust, which quivered at the world as at a woman, frantic to know each hidden
part.

"Happily, for I was learning at long last to hate him, I noted
how, though he possessed my body, he could not use it easily
and bravely as I had. He could not laugh, or love, or dare. He
must instead hang back, peer, purse his lips, withdraw."

More than halfway down the ramp, it seemed to the Mouser
that the groan was repeated, louder, more whistlingly.

"He and the Old Man started on a new cycle of study and
experience that took them, I think, to all corners of the world
and that they were confident, I'm sure, would open to them
those black realms wherein their powers would become infinite.
Anxiously from my cramped vantage-point I watched their quest
ripen and then, to my delight, rot. Their outstretched fingers
just missed the next handhold in the dark. There was something
that both of them lacked. Anra became bitter, blamed the Old
Man for their lack of success. They quarreled.

"When I saw Anra's failure become final, I mocked him with
my laughter, not of lips but of mind. From here to the stars he
could not have escaped it—it was then he would have killed
me. But he dared not while I was in his own body, and I now
had the power to bar him from that.

"Perhaps it was my faint thought-laughter that turned his
desperate mind to you and to the secret of the laughter of the
Elder Gods—that, and his need of magical aid in regaining his
body. For a while then I almost feared he had found a new
avenue of escape—or advance—until this morning before the
tomb, with sheer cruel joy, I saw you spit on his offers, challenge, and, helped by my laughter, kill him. Now there is only
the Old Man to fear."

Passing again under the massive multiple archway with its
oddly recessed keystone, they heard the whistling groan once
more repeated, and this time there was no mistaking its reality,
its nearness, its direction. Hastening to a shadowy and particularly misty corner of the chamber, they made out an inner
window set level with the floor, and in that window they saw a
face that seemed to float bodiless on the thick fog. Its features
defied recognition—it might have been a distillation of all the
ancient, disillusioned faces in the world. There was no beard
below the sunken cheeks.

Coming close as they dared, they saw that it was perhaps not
entirely bodiless or without support. There was the ghostly

suggestion of tatters of clothing or flesh trailing off, a pulsating sack that might have been a lung, and silver chains with hooks or claws.

Then the one eye remaining to that shameful fragment opened and fixed upon Ahura, and the shrunken lips twisted themselves into the caricature of a smile.

"Like you, Ahura," the fragment murmured in the highest of falsettos, "he sent me on an errand I did not want to run."

As one, moved by a fear they dared not formulate, Fafhrd and the Mouser and Ahura half turned round and peered over their shoulders at the mist-clogged doorway leading outside. For three, four heartbeats they peered. Then, faintly, they heard one of the horses whinny. Whereupon they turned fully round, but not before a dagger, sped by the yet unshaking hand of Fafhrd, had buried itself in the open eye of the tortured thing in the inner window.

Side by side they stood, Fafhrd wild-eyed, the Mouser taut, Ahura with the look of someone who, having successfully climbed a precipice, slips at the very summit.

A slim shadowy bulk mounted into the glow outside the doorway.

"Laugh!" Fafhrd hoarsely commanded Ahura. "Laugh!" He shook her, repeating the command.

Her head flopped from side to side, the cords in her neck jerked, her lips twitched, but from them came only a dry croaking. She grimaced despairingly.

"Yes," remarked a voice they all recognized, "there are times and places where laughter is an easily blunted weapon—as harmless as the sword which this morning pierced me through."

Death-pale as always, the tiny blood-clot over his heart, his forehead crumbled in, his black garb travel-dusted, Anra Devadoris faced them.

"And so we come back to the beginning," he said slowly, "but now a wider circle looms ahead."

Fafhrd tried to speak, to laugh, but the words and laughter choked in his throat.

"Now you have learned something of my history and my power, as I intended you should," the adept continued. "You have had time to weigh and reconsider. I still await your answer."

This time it was the Mouser who sought to speak or laugh and failed.

For a moment the adept continued to regard them, smiling confidently. Then his gaze wandered beyond them. He frowned suddenly and strode forward, pushed past them, knelt by the inner window.

As soon as his back was turned Ahura tugged at the Mouser's sleeve, tried to whisper something—with no more success than one deaf and dumb.

They heard the adept sob, "He was my nicest."

The Mouser drew a dagger, prepared to steal on him from behind, but Ahura dragged him back, pointing in a very different direction.

The adept whirled on them. "Fools!" he cried. "Have you no inner eye for the wonders of darkness, no sense of the grandeur of horror, no feeling for a quest beside which all other adventurings fade in nothingness, that you should destroy my greatest miracle—slay my dearest oracle? I let you come here to Mist, confident its mighty music and glorious vistas would win you to my view—and thus I am repaid. The jealous, ignorant powers ring me round—you are my great hope fallen. There were unfavorable portents as I walked from the Lost City. The white, idiot glow of Ormadz faintly dirtied the black sky. I heard in the wind the senile clucking of the Elder Gods. There was a fumbling abroad, as if even incompetent Ningauble, last and stupidest of the hunting pack, were catching up. I had a charm in reserve to thwart them, but it needed the Old Man to carry it. Now they close in for the kill. But there are still some moments of power left me and I am not wholly yet without allies. Though I am doomed, there are still those bound to me by such ties that they must answer me if I call upon them. You shall not see the end, if end there be." With that he lifted his voice in a great eerie shout: "Father! Father!"

The echoes had not died before Fafhrd rushed at him, his great sword swinging.

The Mouser would have followed suit except that, just as he shook Ahura off, he realized at what she was so insistently pointing.

The recess in the keystone above the mighty archway.

Without hesitation he unslipped his climbing rope, and running lightly across the chamber, made a whistling cast.

The hook caught in the recess.

Hand over hand he climbed up.

Behind him he heard the desperate skirl of swords, heard also another sound, far more distant and profound.

His hand gripped the lip of the recess; he pulled himself up and thrust in head and shoulders, steadying himself on hip and elbow. After a moment, with his free hand, he whipped out his dagger.

Inside, the recess was hollowed like a bowl. It was filled with a foul greenish liquid and encrusted with glowing minerals. At the bottom, covered by the liquid, were several objects—three of them rectangular, the other irregularly round and rhythmically pulsating.

He raised his dagger, but for the moment did not, could not, strike. There was too crushing a weight of things to be realized and remembered—what Ahura had told about the ritual marriage in her mother's family—her suspicion that, although she and Anra were born together, they were not children of the same father—how her Greek father had died (and now the Mouser guessed at the hands of what) —the strange affinity for stone the slave-physician had noted in Anra's body—what she had said about an operation performed on him—why a heart-thrust had not killed him—why his skull had cracked so hollowly and egg-shell easy—how he had never seemed to breathe —old legends of other sorcerers who had made themselves invulnerable by hiding their hearts—above all, the deep kinship all of them had sensed between Anra and this half-living castle— the black, man-shaped monolith in the Lost City—

He saw Anra Devadoris, spitted on Fafhrd's blade, hurling himself closer along it, and Fafhrd desperately warding off Needle with a dagger.

As if pinioned by a nightmare, he helplessly heard the clash of swords rise toward a climax, heard it blotted out by the other sound—a gargantuan stony clomping that seemed to be following their course up the mountain, like a pursuing earthquake—

The Castle Called Mist began to tremble, and still he could not strike—

Then, as if a surging across infinity from that utmost rim beyond which the Elder Gods had retreated, relinquishing the world to younger deities, he heard a mighty, star-shaking laughter that laughed at all things, even at this; and there was power in the laughter, and he knew the power was his to use.

With a downward sweep of his arm he sent his dagger plunging into the green liquid and tearing through the stone-crusted heart and brain and lungs and guts of Anra Devadoris.

The liquid foamed and boiled, the castle rocked until he was almost shaken from the niche, the laughter and stony clomping rose to a pandemonium.

Then, in an instant it seemed, all sound and movement

ceased. The Mouser's muscles went weak. He half fell, half slid, to the floor. Looking about dazedly, making no attempt to rise, he saw Fafhrd wrench his sword from the fallen adept and totter back until his groping hand found the support of a table-edge, saw Ahura, still gasping from the laughter that had possessed her, go up and kneel beside her brother and cradle his crushed head on her knees.

No word was spoken. Time passed. The green mist seemed to be slowly thinning.

Then a small black shape swooped into the room through a high window and the Mouser grinned.

"Hugin," he called luringly.

The shape swooped obediently to his sleeve and clung there, head down. He detached from the bat's leg a tiny parchment.

"Fancy, Fafhrd, it's from the commander of our rear guard," he announced gaily. "Listen:

" 'To my agents Fafhrd and the Gray Mouser, funeral greetings! I have regretfully given up all hope for you, and yet—token of my great affection—I risk my own dear Hugin in order to get this last message through. Incidentally, Hugin, if given opportunity, will return to me from Mist—something I am afraid you will not be able to do. So if, before you die, you see anything interesting—and I am sure you will—kindly scribble me a memorandum. Remember the proverb: Knowledge takes precedence over death. Farewell for two thousand years, dearest friends. Ningauble' "

"That demands drink," said Fafhrd, and walked out into the darkness. The Mouser yawned and stretched himself, Ahura stirred, printed a kiss on the waxen face of her brother, lifted the trifling weight of his head from her lap, and laid it gently on the stone floor. From somewhere in the upper reaches of the castle they heard a faint crackling.

Presently Fafhrd returned, striding more briskly, with two jars of wine under his arm.

"Friends," he announced, "the moon's come out, and by its light this castle begins to look remarkably small. I think the mist must have been dusted with some green drug that made us see sizes wrong. We must have been drugged, I'll swear, for we never saw something that's standing plain as day at the bottom of the stairs with its foot on the first step—a black statue that's twin brother to the one in the Lost City."

The Mouser lifted his eyebrows. "And if we went back to the Lost City . . . ?" he asked.

"Why," said Fafhrd, "we might find that those fool Persian farmers, who admitted hating the thing, had knocked down the statue there, and broken it up, and hidden the pieces." He was silent for a moment. Then, "Here's wine," he rumbled, "to sluice the green drug from our throats."

The Mouser smiled. He knew that hereafter Fafhrd would refer to their present adventure as "the time we were drugged on a mountaintop."

They all three sat on a table-edge and passed the two jars endlessly round. The green mist faded to such a degree that Fafhrd, ignoring his claims about the drug, began to argue that even it was an illusion. The crackling from above increased in volume; the Mouser guessed that the impious rolls in the library, no longer shielded by the damp, were bursting into flame. Some proof of this was given when the abortive bear cub, which they had completely forgotten, came waddling frightenedly down the ramp. A trace of decorus down was already sprouting from its naked hide. Fafhrd dribbled some wine on its snout and held it up to the Mouser.

"It wants to be kissed," he rumbled.

"Kiss it yourself, in memory of pig-trickery," replied the Mouser.

This talk of kissing turned their thoughts to Ahura. Their rivalry forgotten, at least for the present, they persuaded her to help them determine whether her brother's spells were altogether broken. A moderate number of hugs demonstrated this clearly.

"Which reminds me," said the Mouser brightly, "now that our business here is over, isn't it time we started, Fafhrd, for your lusty Northland and all that bracing snow?"

Fafhrd drained one jar dry and picked up the other.

"The Northland?" he ruminated. "What is it but a stamping ground of petty, frost-whiskered kinglets who know not the amenities of life? That's why I left the place. Go back? By Thor's smelly jerkin, not now!"

The Mouser smiled knowingly and sipped from the remaining jar. Then, noticing the bat still clinging to his sleeve, he took stylus, ink, and a scrap of parchment from his pouch, and, with Ahura giggling over his shoulder, wrote:

"To my aged brother in petty abominations, greetings! It is with the deepest regret that I must report the outrageously lucky and completely unforeseen escape of two rude and unsympathetic fellows from the Castle Called Mist. Before leaving, they expressed to me the intention of returning to someone

called Ningauble—you are Ningauble, master, are you not?
—and lopping off six of his seven eyes for souvenirs. So I think
it only fair to warn you. Believe me, I am your friend. One of
the fellows was very tall and at times, his bellowings seemed to
resemble speech. Do you know him? The other fancied a gray
garb and was of extreme wit and personal beauty, given to . . ."

Had any of them been watching the corpse of Anra Devadoris
at this moment, they would have seen a slight twitching of the
lower jaw. At last the mouth came open, and out leaped a tiny
black mouse. The cublike creature, to whom Fafhrd's fondling
and the wine had imparted the seeds of self-confidence, lurched
drunkenly at it, and the mouse began a squeaking scurry toward the wall. A wine jar, hurled by Fafhrd, shattered on the
crack into which it shot; Fafhrd had seen, or thought he had
seen, the untoward place from which the mouse had come.

"Mice in his mouth," he hiccuped. "What dirty habits for a
pleasant young man! A nasty, degrading business, this thinking
oneself an adept."

"I am reminded," said the Mouser, "of what a witch told me
about adepts. She said that, if an adept chances to die, his soul
is reincarnated in a mouse. If, as a mouse, he managed to kill a
rat, his soul passes over into a rat. As a rat, he must kill a cat;
as a cat, a wolf; as a wolf, a panther; and, as a panther, a man.
Then he can recommence his adeptry. Of course, it seldom
happens that anyone gets all the way through the sequence, and
in any case it takes a very long time. Trying to kill a rat is
enough to satisfy a mouse with mousedom."

Fafhrd solemnly denied the possibility of such foolery, and
Ahura cried until she decided that being a mouse would interest
rather than dishearten her peculiar brother. More wine was
drunk from the remaining jar. The crackling from the rooms
above had become a roar, and a bright red glow consumed the
dark shadows. The three adventurers prepared to leave the
place.

Meantime the mouse, or another very much like it, thrust its
head from the crack and began to lick the wine-damp shards,
keeping a fearful eye upon those in the great room, but especially upon the strutting little would-be bear.

The Mouser said, "Our quest's done. I'm for Tyre."

Fafhrd said, "I'm for Ning's Gate and Lankhmar. Or is that a
dream?"

The Mouser shrugged. "Mayhap Tyre's the dream. Lankhmar sounds as good."

Ahura said, "Could a girl go?"

A great blast of wind, cold and pure, blew away the last lingering of Mist. As they went through the doorway they saw, outspread above them, the self-consistent stars.

LAST ENEMY

H. Beam Piper

H. Beam Piper (1904–1964) is one of the tragic figures in the history of science fiction. He took his own life at the age of sixty because he was too proud to ask for financial help at a time when his work was largely unknown. Years later, primarily in the 1970s, he was rediscovered, and his Terran Federation novels and stories—which include Little Fuzzy *(1962),* Space Viking *(1963), and* The Other Human Race *(1964)—became hugely popular. New collections like* Empire *and* Paratime *were published as late as the 1980s, and he has developed something of a cult following. He also wrote an excellent mystery novel,* Murder in the Gun Room *(1953).*

Along the U-shaped table, the subdued clatter of dinnerware and the buzz of conversation was dying out; the soft music that drifted down from the overhead sound outlets seemed louder as the competing noises diminished. The feast was drawing to a close, and Dallona of Hadron fidgeted nervously with the stem of her wineglass as last-moment doubts assailed her.

The old man at whose right she sat noticed, and reached out to lay his hand on hers.

"My dear, you're worried," he said softly. "You of all people, shouldn't be, you know."

"The theory isn't complete," she replied. "And I could wish for more positive verification. I'd hate to think I'd got you into this—"

Garnon of Roxor laughed. "No, no!" he assured her. "I'd decided upon this long before you announced the results of your experiments. Ask Girzon; he'll bear me out."

"That's true," the young man who sat at Garnon's left said,

leaning forward. "Father has meant to take this step for a long time. He was waiting until after the election, and then he decided to do it now, to give you an opportunity to make experimental use of it."

The man on Dallona's right added his voice. Like the others at the table, he was of medium stature, brown-skinned and dark-eyed, with a wide mouth, prominent cheekbones and a short, square jaw. Unlike the others, he was armed, with a knife and pistol on his belt, and on the breast of his black tunic he wore a scarlet oval patch on which a pair of black wings, with a tapering silver object between them had been super-imposed.

"Yes, Lady Dallona; the Lord Garnon and I discussed this, oh, two years ago at the least. Really, I'm surprised that you seem to shrink from it, now. Of course, you're Venus-born, and customs there may be different, but with your scientific knowledge—"

"That may be the trouble, Dirzed," Dallona told him. "A scientist gets in the way of doubting, and one doubts one's own theories most of all."

"That's the scientific attitude, I'm told," Dirzed replied, smiling. "But somehow, I cannot think of you as a scientist." His eyes traveled over her in a way that would have made most women, scientists or otherwise, blush. It gave Dallona of Hadron a feeling of pleasure. Men often looked at her that way, especially here at Darsh. Novelty had something to do with it—her skin was considerably lighter than usual, and there was a pleasing oddness about the structure of her face. Her alleged Venusian origin was probably accepted as the explanation of that, as of so many other things.

As she was about to reply, a man in dark gray, one of the upper-servants who were accepted as social equals by the Akor-Neb nobles, approached the table. He nodded respectfully to Garnon of Roxor.

"I hate to seem to hurry things, sir, but the boy's ready. He's in a trance-state now," he reported, pointing to the pair of visiplates at the end of the room.

Both of the ten-foot-square plates were activated. One was a solid luminous white; on the other was the image of a boy of twelve or fourteen, seated at a big writing machine. Even allowing for the fact that the boy was in a hypnotic trance, there was an expression of idiocy on his loose-lipped, slack-jawed face, a pervading dullness.

"One of our best sensitives," a man with a beard, several places down the table on Dallona's right, said. "You remember him, Dallona; he produced that communication from the discarnate Assassin, Sirzim. Normally, he's a low-grade imbecile, but in trance-state he's wonderful. And there can be no argument that the communications he produces originate in his own mind; he doesn't have mind enough, of his own, to operate that machine."

Garnon of Roxor rose to his feet, the others rising with him. He unfastened a jewel from the front of his tunic and handed it to Dallona.

"Here, my dear Lady Dallona; I want you to have this," he said. "It's been in the family of Roxor for six generations, but I know that you will appreciate and cherish it." He twisted a heavy ring from his left hand and gave it to his son. He unstrapped his wrist watch and passed it across the table to the gray-clad upper-servant. He gave a pocket case, containing writing tools, slide rule and magnifier, to the bearded man on the other side of Dallona. "Something you can use, Dr. Harnosh," he said. Then he took a belt, with a knife and holstered pistol, from a servant who had brought it to him, and gave it to the man with the red badge. "And something for you, Dirzed. The pistol's by Farnor of Yand, and the knife was forged and tempered on Luna."

The man with the winged-bullet badge took the weapons, exclaiming in appreciation. Then he removed his own belt and buckled on the gift.

"The pistol's fully loaded," Garnon told him.

Dirzed drew it and checked—a man of his craft took no statement about weapons without verification—then slipped it back into the holster.

"Shall I use it?" he asked.

"By all means; I'd had that in mind when I selected it for you."

Another man, to the left of Girzon, received a cigarette case and lighter. He and Garnon hooked fingers and clapped shoulders.

"Our views haven't been the same, Garnon," he said, "but I've always valued your friendship. I'm sorry you're doing this, now; I believe you'll be disappointed."

Garnon chuckled. "Would you care to make a small wager on that, Nirzav?" he asked. "You know what I'm putting up. If

I'm proven right, will you accept the Volitionalist theory as verified?"

Nirzav chewed his mustache for a moment. "Yes, Garnon, I will." He pointed toward the blankly white screen. "If we get anything conclusive on that, I'll have no other choice."

"All right, friends," Garnon said to those around him. "Will you walk with me to the end of the room?"

Servants removed a section from the table in front of him, to allow him and a few others to pass through; the rest of the guests remained standing at the table, facing toward the inside of the room. Garnon's son, Girzon, and the gray-mustached Nirzav of Shonna walked on his left; Dallona of Hadron and Dr. Harnosh of Hosh on his right. The gray-clad upper-servant, and two or three ladies, and a nobleman with a small chin-beard, and several others, joined them; of those who had sat close to Garnon, only the man in the black tunic with the scarlet badge hung back. He stood still, by the break in the table, watching Garnon of Roxor walk away from him. Then Dirzed the Assassin drew the pistol he had lately received as a gift, hefted it in his hand, thumbed off the safety, and aimed at the back of Garnon's head.

They had nearly reached the end of the room when the pistol cracked. Dallona of Hadron started, almost as though the bullet had crashed into her own body, then caught herself and kept on walking. She closed her eyes and laid a hand on Dr. Harnosh's arm for guidance, concentrating her mind upon a single question. The others went on as though Garnon of Roxor were still walking among them.

"Look!" Harnosh of Hosh cried, pointing to the image in the visiplate ahead. "He's under control!"

They all stopped short, and Dirzed, holstering his pistol, hurried forward to join them. Behind, a couple of servants had approached with a stretcher and were gathering up the crumpled figure that had, a moment ago, been Garnon.

A change had come over the boy at the writing machine. His eyes were still glazed with the stupor of the hypnotic trance, but the slack jaw had stiffened, and the loose mouth was compressed in a purposeful line. As they watched, his hands went out to the keyboard in front of him and began to move over it, and as they did, letters appeared on the white screen on the left.

Garnon of Roxor, discarnate, communicating, they read. The machine stopped for a moment, then began again. *To Dallona*

*of Hadron: The question you asked, after I discarnated, was:
What was the last book I read, before the feast? While waiting
for my valet to prepare my bath, I read the first ten verses of the
fourth Canto of* Splendor of Space, *by Larnov of Horka, in my
bedroom. When the bath was ready, I marked the page with a
strip of message tape, containing a message from the bailiff of
my estate on the Shevva River, concerning a breakdown at the
power plant, and laid the book on the ivory-inlaid table beside
the big red chair.*

Harnosh of Hosh looked at Dallona inquiringly; she nodded.

"I rejected the question I had in my mind, and substituted
that one, after the shot," she said.

He turned quickly to the upper-servant. "Check on that,
right away, Kirzon," he directed.

As the upper-servant hurried out, the writing machine started
again.

*And to my son, Girzon: I will not use your son, Garnon, as a
reincarnation-vehicle; I will remain discarnate until he is grown
and has a son of his own; if he has no male child, I will
reincarnate in the first available male child of the family of
Roxor, or of some family allied to us by marriage. In any case, I
will communicate before reincarnating.*

*To Nirzav of Shonna: Ten days ago, when I dined at your
home, I took a small knife and cut three notches, two close
together and one a little apart from the others, on the underside
of the table. As I remember, I sat two places down on the left. If
you find them, you will know that I have won that wager that I
spoke of a few minutes ago.*

"I'll have my butler check on that, right away," Nirzav said.
His eyes were wide with amazement, and he had begun to
sweat; a man does not casually watch the beliefs of a lifetime
invalidated in a few moments.

To Dirzed the Assassin: the machine continued. *You have
served me faithfully, in the last ten years, never more so than
with the last shot you fired in my service. After you fired, the
thought was in your mind that you would like to take service
with the Lady Dallona of Hadron, who you believe will need the
protection of a member of the Society of Assassins. I advise you
to do so, and I advise her to accept your offer. Her work, since
she has come to Darsh, has not made her popular in some
quarters. No doubt Nirzav of Shonna can bear me out on that.*

"I won't betray things told me in confidence, or said at the

Councils of the Statisticalists, but he's right," Nirzav said. "You need a good Assassin, and there are few better than Dirzed."

I see that this sensitive is growing weary, the letters on the screen spelled out. *His body is not strong enough for prolonged communication. I bid you all farewell, for the time; I will communicate again. Good evening, my friends, and I thank you for your presence at the feast.*

The boy, on the other screen, slumped back in his chair, his face relaxing into its customary expression of vacancy.

"Will you accept my offer of service, Lady Dallona?" Dirzed asked. "It's as Garnon said; you've made enemies."

Dallona smiled at him. "I've not been too deep in my work to know that. I'm glad to accept your offer, Dirzed."

Nirzav of Shonna already turned away from the group and was hurrying from the room, to call his home for confirmation on the notches made on the underside of his dining table. As he went out the door, he almost collided with the upper-servant, who was rushing in with a book in his hand.

"Here it is," the latter exclaimed, holding up the book. "Larnov's *Splendor of Space,* just where he said it would be. I had a couple of servants with me as witnesses; I can call them in now, if you wish." He handed the book to Harnosh of Hosh. "See, a strip of message tape in it, at the tenth verse of the Fourth Canto."

Nirzav of Shonna reentered the room; he was chewing his mustache and muttering to himself. As he rejoined the group in front of the now dark visiplates, he raised his voice, addressing them all generally.

"My butler found the notches, just as the communication described," he said. "This settles it! Garnon, if you're where you can hear me, you've won. I can't believe in the Statisticalist doctrines after this, or in the political program based upon them. I'll announce my change of attitude at the next meeting of the Executive Council, and resign my seat. I was elected by Statisticalist votes, and I cannot hold office as a Volitionalist."

"You'll need a couple of Assassins, too," the nobleman with the chin-beard told him. "Your former colleagues and fellow party members are regrettably given to the forcible discarnation of those who differ with them."

"I've never employed personal Assassins before," Nirzav replied, "but I think you're right. As soon as I get home, I'll call Assassins' Hall and make the necessary arrangements."

"Better do it now," Girzon of Roxor told him, lowering his voice. "There are over a hundred guests here, and I can't vouch for all of them. The Statisticalists would be sure to have a spy planted among them. My father was one of their most dangerous opponents, when he was on the Council; they've always been afraid he'd come out of retirement and stand for reelection. They'd want to make sure he was really discarnate. And if that's the case, you can be sure your change of attitude is known to old Mirzark of Bashad by this time. He won't dare allow you to make a public renunciation of Statisticalism." He turned to the other nobleman. "Prince Jirzyn, why don't you call the Volitionist headquarters and have a couple of our Assassins sent here to escort Lord Nirzav home?"

"I'll do that immediately," Jirzyn of Starpha said. "It's as Lord Girzon says; we can be pretty sure there was a spy among the guests, and now that you've come over to our way of thinking, we're responsible for your safety."

He left the room to make the necessary visiphone call. Dallona, accompanied by Dirzed, returned to her place at the table, where she was joined by Harnosh of Hosh and some of the others.

"There's no question about the results," Harnosh was exulting. "I'll grant that the boy might have picked up some of that stuff telepathically from the carnate minds present here; even from the mind of Garnon, before he was discarnated. But he could not have picked up enough data, in that way, to make a connected and coherent communication. It takes a sensitive with a powerful mind of his own to practice telesthesia, and that boy's almost an idiot." He turned to Dallona. "You asked a question, mentally, after Garnon was discarnate, and got an answer that could have been contained only in Garnon's mind. I think it's conclusive proof that the discarnate Garnon was fully conscious and communicating."

"Dirzed also asked a question, mentally, after the discarnation, and got an answer. Dr. Harnosh, we can state positively that the surviving individuality is fully conscious in the discarnate state, is telephathically sensitive, and is capable of telepathic communication with other minds," Dallona agreed. "And in view of our earlier work with memory-recalls, we're justified in stating positively that the individual is capable of exercising choice in reincarnation vehicles."

"My father had been considering voluntary discarnation for a long time," Girzon of Roxor said. "Ever since the discarnation of my mother. He deferred that step because he was unwilling to deprive the Volitionalist Party of his support. Now it would seem that he had done more to combat Statisticalism by discarnating than he ever did in his carnate existence."

"I don't know, Girzon," Jirzyn of Starpha said, as he joined the group. "The Statisticalists will denounce the whole thing as a prearranged fraud. And if they can discarnate the Lady Dallona before she can record her testimony under truth hypnosis or on a lie detector, we're no better off then we were before. Dirzed, you have a great responsibility in guarding the Lady Dallona; some extraordinary security precautions will be needed."

In his office, in the First Level city of Dhergabar, Tortha Karf, Chief of Paratime Police, leaned forward in his chair to hold his lighter for his special assistant, Verkan Vall, then lit his own cigarette. He was a man of middle age—his three hundredth birthday was only a decade or so off—and he had begun to acquire a double chin and a bulge at his waistline. His hair, once black, had turned a uniform iron-gray and was beginning to thin in front.

"What do you know about the Second Level Akor-Neb Sector, Vall?" he inquired. "Ever work in that paratime-area?"

Verkan Vall's handsome features became even more immobile than usual as he mentally pronounced the verbal trigger symbols which should bring hypnotically acquired knowledge into his conscious mind. Then he shook his head.

"Must be a singularly well-behaved sector, sir," he said. "Or else we've been lucky, so far. I never was on an Akor-Neb operation; don't even have a hypno-mech for that sector. All I know is from general reading.

"Like all the Second Level, its time-lines descend from the probability of one or more shiploads of colonists having come to Terra from Mars about seventy-five to a hundred thousand years ago, and then having been cut off from the home planet and forced to develop a civilization of their own here. The Akor-Neb civilization is of a fairly high culture-order, even for Second Level. An atomic-power, interplanetary culture; gravity-counteraction, direct conversion of nuclear energy to electrical power, that sort of thing. We buy fine synthetic plastics and fabrics from them." He fingered the material of his smartly cut green police uniform. "I think this cloth is Akor-Neb. We sell a lot of Venusian zerfa-leaf; they smoke it, straight and mixed with tobacco. They have a single System-wide government, a single race, and a universal language. They're a dark-brown race, which evolved in its present form about fifty thousand years ago; the present civilization is about ten thousand years old, developed out of the wreckage of several earlier civilizations which decayed or fell through wars, exhaustion of resources, et cetera. They have legends, maybe historical records, of their extraterrestrial origin."

Tortha Karf nodded. "Pretty good, for consciously acquired knowledge," he commented. "Well, our luck's run out, on that sector; we have troubles there, now. I want you to go iron them out. I know, you've been going pretty hard, lately—that nighthound business, on the Fourth Level Europo-American Sector, wasn't any picnic. But the fact is that a lot of my ordinary and deputy assistants have a little too much regard for the alleged sanctity of human life, and this is something that may need some pretty drastic action."

"Some of our people getting out of line?" Varkan Vall asked.

"Well, the data isn't too complete, but one of our people has run into trouble on that sector, and needs rescuing—a psychic-science researcher, a young lady name Hadron Dalla. I believe you know her, don't you?" Tortha Karf asked innocently.

"Slightly," Vergan Vall dead-panned. "I enjoyed a brief but rather hectic companionate-marriage with her, about twenty years ago. What sort of a jam's little Dalla got herself into, now?"

"Well, frankly, we don't know. I hope she's still alive, but I'm not unduly optimistic. It seems that about a year ago, Dr. Hadron transposed to the Second Level, to study alleged proof of reincarnation which the Akor-Neb people were reported to possess. She went to Gindrabar, on Venus, and transposed to the Second Paratime Level, to a station maintained by Outtime Import & Export Trading Corporation—a zerfa plantation just east of the High Ridge country. There she assumed an identity as the daughter of a planter, and took the name of Dallona of Hadron. Parenthetically, all Akor-Neb family-names are prepositional; family names were originally place-names. I believe that ancient Akor-Neb marital relations were too complicated to permit exact establishment of paternity. And all Akor-Neb men's personal names have -irz- or -arn- inserted in the middle, and women's names end in -itra or -ona. You could call yourself Virzal of Verkan, for instance.

"Anyhow, she made the Second Level Venus-Terra trip on a regular passenger liner, and landed at the Akor-Neb city of

Ghamma, on the upper Nile. There she established contact with the Outtime Trading Corporation representative, Zortan Brend, locally known as Brarnend of Zorda. He couldn't call himself Brarnend of Zortan—in the Akor-Neb language, *zortan* is a particularly nasty dirty word. Hadron Dalla spent a few weeks at his residence, briefing herself on local conditions. Then she went to the capital city, Darsh, in eastern Europe, and enrolled as a student at something called the Independent Institute for Reincarnation Research, having secured a letter of introduction to its director, a Dr. Harnosh of Hosh.

"Almost at once, she began sending in reports to her home organization, the Rhogom Memorial Foundation of Psychic Science, here at Dhergabar, through Zortan Brend. The people there were wildly enthusiastic. I don't have more than the average intelligent—I hope—layman's knowledge of psychics, but Dr. Volzar Darv, the director of Rhogom Foundation, tells me that even in the present incomplete form, her reports have opened whole new horizons in the science. It seems that these Akor-Neb people have actually demonstrated, as a scientific fact, that the human individuality reincarnates after physical death—that your personality, and mine, have existed, as such, for ages, and will exist for ages to come. More, they have means of recovering, from almost anybody, memories of past reincarnations.

"Well, after about a month, the people at this Reincarnation Institute realized that this Dallona of Hadron wasn't any ordinary student. She probably had trouble keeping down to the local level of psychic knowledge. So, as soon as she'd learned their techniques, she was allowed to undertake experimental work of her own. I imagine she let herself out on that; as soon as she'd mastered the standard Akor-Neb methods of recovering memories of past reincarnations, she began refining and developing them more than the local yokels had been able to do in the past thousand years. I can't tell you just what she did, because I don't know the subject, but she must have lit things up properly. She got quite a lot of local publicity; not only scientific journals, but general newscasts.

"Then, four days ago, she disappeared, and her disappearance seems to have been coincident with an unsuccessful attempt on her life. We don't know as much about this as we should; all we have is Zortan Brend's account.

"It seems that on the evening of her disappearance, she had been attending the voluntary discarnation feast—suicide party—of a prominent nobleman named Garnon of Roxor. Evidently when the Akor-Neb people get tired of their current reincarnation they invite in their friends, throw a big party, and then do themselves in in an atmosphere of general conviviality. Frequently they take poison or inhale lethal gas; this fellow had his personal trigger man shoot him through the head. Dalla was one of the guests of honor, along with this Harnosh of Hosh. They'd made rather elaborate preparations, and after the shooting they got a detailed and apparently authentic spirit-communication from the late Garnon. The voluntary discarnation was just a routine social event, it seems, but the communication caused quite an uproar, and rated top place on the System-wide newscasts, and started a storm of controversy.

"After the shooting and the communication, Dalla took the officiating gun artist, one Dirzed, into her own service. This Dirzed was spoken of as a generally respected member of something called the Society of Assassins, and that'll give you an idea of what things are like on that sector, and why I don't want to send anybody who might develop trigger-finger cramp at the wrong moment. She and Dirzed left the home of the gentleman who had just had himself discarnated, presumably for Dalla's apartment, about a hundred miles away. That's the last that's been heard of either of them.

"This attempt on Dalla's life occurred while the premortem revels were still going on. She lived in a six-room apartment, with three servants, on one of the upper floors of a three-thousand-foot tower—Akor-Neb cities are built vertically, with considerable interval between units—and while she was at this feast, a package was delivered at the apartment, ostensibly from the Reincarnation Institute and made up to look as though it contained record tapes. One of the servants accepted it from a service employee of the apartments. The next morning, a little before noon, Dr. Harnosh of Hosh called her on the visiphone and got no answer, he then called the apartment manager, who entered the apartment. He found all three of the servants dead, from a lethal-gas bomb which had exploded when one of them had opened this package. However, Hadron Dalla had never returned to the apartment, the night before."

Verkan Vall was sitting motionless, his face expressionless as he ran Tortha Karf's narrative through the intricate semantic and psychological processes of the First Level mentality. The fact that Hadron Dalla had been a former wife of his had been relegated to one corner of his consciousness and contained there; it was not a fact that would, at the moment, contribute to the problem or to his treatment of it.

"The package was delivered while she was at this suicide party," he considered. "It must, therefore, have been sent by somebody who either did not know she would be out of the apartment, or who did not expect it to function until after her return. On the other hand, if her disappearance was due to hostile action, it was the work of somebody who knew she was at the feast and did not want her to reach her apartment again. This would seem to exclude the sender of the package bomb."

Tortha Karf nodded. He had reached that conclusion himself.

"Thus," Verkan Vall continued, "if her disappearance was the work of an enemy, she must have two enemies, each working in ignorance of the other's plans."

"What do you think she did to provoke such enmity?"

"Well, of course, it just might be that Dalla's normally complicated love-life had got a little more complicated than usual and short-circuited on her," Verkan Vall said, out of the fullness of personal knowledge, "but I doubt that, at the moment. I would think that this affair has political implications."

"So?" Tortha Karf had not thought of politics as an explanation. He waited for Verkan Vall to elaborate.

"Don't you see, chief?" the special assistant asked. "We find a belief in reincarnation on many time-lines, as a religious doctrine, but these people accept it as a scientific fact. Such acceptance would carry much more conviction; it would influence a people's entire thinking. We see it reflected in their disregard for death—suicide as a social function, this Society of Assassins, and the like. It would naturally color their political thinking, because politics is nothing but common action to secure more favorable living conditions, and to these people, the term 'living conditions' includes not only the present life, but also an indefinite number of future lives as well. I find this title, 'Independent' Institute, suggestive. Independent of what? Possibly of partisan affiliation."

"But wouldn't these people be grateful to her for her new discoveries, which would enable them to plan their future reincarnations more intelligently?" Tortha Karf asked.

"Oh, chief!" Verkan Vall reproached. "You know better than that! How many times have our people got in trouble on other time-lines because they divulged some useful scientific fact that conflicted with the locally revered nonsense? You show me ten men who cherish some religious doctrine or political ideology, and I'll show you nine men whose minds are utterly impervious to any factual evidence which contradicts their beliefs, and who regard the producer of such evidence as a criminal who ought to be suppressed. For instance, on the Fourth Level Europo-American Sector, where I was just working, there is a political sect, the Communists, who, in the territory under their control, forbid the teaching of certain well-established facts of genetics and heredity, because those facts do not fit the world-picture demanded by their political doctrines. And on the same sector, a religious sect recently tried, in some sections successfully, to outlaw the teaching of evolution by natural selection."

Tortha Karf nodded. "I remember some stories my grandfather told me, about his narrow escapes from an organization called the Holy Inquisition, when he was a paratime trader on the Fourth Level, about four hundred years ago. I believe that thing's still operating, on the Europo-American Sector, under the name of NKVD. So you think Dalla may have proven something that conflicted with local reincarnation theories, and somebody who had a vested interest in maintaining those theories is trying to stop her?"

"You spoke of a controversy over the communication alleged to have originated with this voluntarily discarnated nobleman. That would suggest a difference of opinion on the manner of nature of reincarnation or the discarnate state. This difference may mark the dividing line between the different political parties. Now, to get to this Darsh place, do I have to go to Venus, as Dalla did?"

"No. The Outtime Trading Corporation has transposition facilities at Ravvanan, on the Nile, which is spatially coexistent with the city of Ghamma on the Akor-Neb Sector, where Zortan Brend is. You transpose through there, and Zortan Brend will furnish you transportation to Darsh. It'll take you about two days, here, getting your hypnomech indoctrinations and having your skin pigmented, and your hair turned black. I'll notify Zortan Brend at once that you're coming through. Is there anything special you'll want?"

"Why, I'll want an abstract of the reports Dalla sent back to Rhogom Foundation. It's likely that there is some clue among them as to whom her discoveries may have antagonized. I'm going to be a Venusian *zerfa*-planter, a friend of her father's; I'll want full hypno-mech indoctrination to enable me to play that part. And I'll want to familiarize myself with Akor-Neb weapons and combat techniques. I think that will be all, chief."

The last of the tall city-units of Ghamma were sliding out of sight as the ship passed over them—shaftlike buildings that rose two or three thousand feet above the ground in clumps of three or four or six, one at each corner of the landing stages set in series between them. Each of these units stood in the middle of a wooded park some five miles square; no unit was much more or less than twenty miles from its nearest neighbor, and the land between was the uniform golden-brown of ripening grain, crisscrossed with the threads of irrigation canals and dotted here and there with sturdy farm-village buildings and tall, stacklike granaries. There were a few other ships in the air at the fifty-thousand-foot level, and below, swarms of small airboats darted back and forth on different levels, depending upon speed and direction. Far ahead, to the northeast, was the shimmer of the Red Sea and the hazy bulk of Asia Minor beyond.

Verkan Vall—the Lord Virzal of Verkan, temporarily—stood at the glass front of the observation deck, looking down. He was a different Verkan Vall from the man who had talked with Tortha Karf in the latter's office, two days before. The First Level cosmeticists had worked miracles upon him with their art. His skin was a soft chocolate-brown, now; his hair was jet-black, and so were his eyes. And in his subconscious mind, instantly available to consciousness, was a vast body of knowledge about conditions on the Akor-Neb sector, as well as a complete command of the local language, all hypnotically acquired.

He knew that he was looking down upon one of the minor provincial cities of a very respectably advanced civilization. A civilization which built its cities vertically, since it had learned to counteract gravitation. A civilization which still depended upon natural cereals for food, but one which had learned to make the most efficient use of its soil. The network of dams and irrigation canals which he saw was as good as anything on his own paratime level. The wide dispersal of buildings, he knew, was a heritage of a series of disastrous atomic wars of several thousand years before; the Akor-Neb people had come to love the wide inter-vistas of open country and forest, and had continued to scatter their buildings, even after the necessity had passed. But the slim, towering buildings could only have been reared by a people who had banished nationalism and, with it, the threat of total war. He contrasted them with the ground-hugging dome cities of the Khiftan civilization, only a few thousand parayears distant.

Three men came out of the lounge behind him and joined him. One was, like himself, a disguised paratimer from the First level—the Outtime Export and Import man, Zortan Brend, here known as Brarnend of Zorda. The other two were Akor-Neb people, and both wore the black tunics and the winged-bullet badges of the Society of Assassins. Unlike Verkan Vall and Zortan Brend, who wore shoulder holsters under their short tunics, the Assassins openly displayed pistols and knives on their belts.

"We heard that you were coming two days ago, Lord Virzal," Zortan Brend said. "We delayed the takeoff of this ship, so that you could travel to Darsh as inconspicuously as possible. I also booked a suite for you at the Solar Hotel, at Darsh. And these are your Assassins—Olirzon, and Marnik."

Verkan Vall hooked fingers and clapped shoulders with them.

"Virzal of Verkan," he identified himself. "I am satisfied to entrust myself to you."

"We'll do our best for you, Lord Virzal," the older of the pair, Olirzon, said. He hesitated for a moment, then continued: "Understand, Lord Virzal, I only ask for information useful in serving and protecting you. But is this of the Lady Dallona a political matter?"

"Not from our side," Verkan Vall told him. "The Lady Dallona is a scientist, entirely nonpolitical. The Honorable Brarnend is a businessman; he doesn't meddle with politics as long as the politicians leave him alone. And I'm a planter on Venus; I have enough troubles, with the natives, and the weather, and blue-rot in the *zerfa* plants, and poison roaches, and javelin bugs, without getting into politics. But psychic science is inextricably mixed with politics, and the Lady Dallona's work had evidently tended to discredit the theory of Statistical Reincarnation."

"Do you often make understatements like that, Lord Virzal?" Olirzon grinned. "In the last six months, she's knocked Statistical Reincarnation to splinters."

"Well, I'm not a psychic scientist, and as I said, I don't know much about Terran politics," Verkan Vall replied. "I know that the Statisticalists favor complete socialization and political control of the whole economy, because they want everybody to have the same opportunities in every reincarnation. And the

Volitionalists believe that everybody reincarnates as he pleases, and so they favor continuance of the present system of private ownership of wealth and private profit under a system of free competition. And that's about all I do know. Naturally, as a landowner and the holder of a title of nobility, I'm a Volitionalist in politics, but the socialization issue isn't important on Venus. There is still too much unseated land there, and too many personal opportunities, to make socialism attractive to anybody."

"Well, that's about it," Zortan Brend told him. "I'm not enough of a psychicist to know what the Lady Dallona's been doing, but she's knocked the theoretical basis from under Statistical Reincarnation, and that's the basis, in turn, of Statistical Socialism. I think we'll find that the Statisticalist Party is responible for whatever happened to her."

Marnik, the younger of the two Assassins, hesitated for a moment, then addressed Verkan Vall:

"Lord Virzal, I know none of the personalities involved in this matter, and I speak without wishing to give offense, but is it not possible that the Lady Dallona and the Assassin Dirzed may have gone somewhere together voluntarily? I have met Dirzed, and he has many qualities which women find attractive, and he is by no means indifferent to the opposite sex. You understand, Lord Virzal—"

"I understand all too perfectly, Marnik," Verkan Vall replied, out of the fullness of experience. "The Lady Dallona has had affairs with a number of men, myself among them. But under the circumstances, I find that explanation unthinkable."

Marnik looked at him in open skepticism. Evidently, in his book, where an attractive man and a beautiful woman were concerned, that explanation was never unthinkable.

"The Lady Dallona is a scientist," Verkan Vall elaborated. "She is not above diverting herself with love affairs, but that's all they are—a not too important form of diversion. And, if you recall, she had just participated in a most significant experiment; you can be sure that she had other things on her mind at the time than pleasure jaunts with good-looking Assassins."

The ship was passing around the Caucasus Mountains, with the Caspian Sea in sight ahead, when several of the crew appeared on the observation deck and began preparing the shielding to protect the deck from gunfire. Zortan Brend inquired of the petty officer in charge of the work as to the necessity.

"We've been getting reports of trouble at Darsh, sir," the man said. "Newscast bulletins every couple of minutes; rioting in different parts of the city. Started yesterday afternoon, when a couple of Statisticalist members of the Executive Council resigned and went over to the Volitionalists. Lord Nirzav of Shonna, the only nobleman of any importance in the Statisticalist Party, was one of them; he was shot immediately afterward, while leaving the Council Chambers, along with a couple of Assassins who were with him. Some people in an airboat sprayed them with a machine rifle as they came out onto the landing stage."

The two Assassins exclaimed in horrified anger over this.

"That wasn't the work of members of the Society of Assassins!" Olirzon declared. "Even after he'd resigned, the Lord Nirzav was still immune till he left the Government Building. There's too blasted much illegal assassination going on!"

"What happened next?" Verkan Vall wanted to know.

"About what you'd expect, sir. The Volitionalists weren't going to take that quietly. In the past eighteen hours, four prominent Statisticalists were forcibly discarnated, and there was even a fight in Mirzark of Bashad's house, when Volitionalist Assassins broke in; three of them and four of Mirzark's Assassins were discarnated."

"You know, something is going to have to be done about that, too," Olirzon said to Marnik. "It's getting to a point where these political faction fights are being carried on entirely between members of the Society. In Ghamma alone, last year, thirty or forty of our members were discarnated that way."

"Plug in a newscast visiplate, Karnil," Zortan Brend told the petty officer. "Let's see what's going on in Darsh now."

In Darsh, it seemed, an uneasy peace had been established. Verkan Vall watched heavily armed airboats and light combat ships patrolling among the high towers of the city. He saw a couple of minor riots being broken up by the blue-uniformed Constabulary, with considerable shooting and a ruthless disregard for who might get shot. It wasn't exactly the sort of policing that would have been tolerated in the First Level Civil Order Section, but it seemed to suit Akor-Neb conditions. And he listened to a series of angry recriminations and contradictory statements by different policitians, all of whom blamed the disorders on their opponents. The Volitionalists spoke of the Statisticalists as "insane criminals" and "underminers of social stability," and the Statisticalists called the Volitionalists "reactionary criminals," and "enemies of social progress." Politicians, he had observed, differed little in their vocabularies from one time-line to another.

This kept up all the while the ship was passing over the Caspian Sea; as they were turning up the Volga valley, one of the ship's officers came down from the control deck, above.

"We're coming into Darsh now," he said, and as Verkan Vall turned from the visiplate to the forward windows, he could see the white and pastel-tinted towers of the city rising above the hardwood forests that covered the whole Volga basin on this sector. "Your luggage has been put into the airboat, Lord Virzal and Honorable Assassins, and it's ready for launching whenever you are." The officer glanced at his watch. "We dock at Commercial Center in twenty minutes; we'll be passing the Solar Hotel in ten."

They all rose, and Verkan Vall hooked fingers and clapped shoulders with Zortan Brend.

"Good luck, Lord Virzal," the latter said. "I hope you find the Lady Dallona safe and carnate. If you need help, I'll be at Mercantile House for the next day or so; if you get back to Ghamma before I do, you know who to ask for there."

A number of Assassins loitered in the hallways and offices of the Independent Institute of Reincarnation Research when Verkan Vall, accompanied by Marnik, called there that afternoon. Some of them carried submachine guns or sleep-gas projectors, and they were stopping people and questioning them. Marnik needed only to give them a quick gesture and the words "Assassins' Truce," and he and his client were allowed to pass. They entered a lifter tube and floated up to the office of Dr. Harnosh of Hosh, with whom Verkan Vall had made an appointment.

"I'm sorry, Lord Virzal," the director of the Institute told him, "but I have no idea what has befallen the Lady Dallona, or even if she is still carnate. I am quite worried; I admired her extremely, both as an individual and as a scientist. I do hope she hasn't been discarnated; that would be a serious blow to science. It is fortunate that she accomplished as much as she did, while she was with us."

"You think she is no longer carnate, then?"

"I'm afraid so. The political effects of her discoveries—" Harnosh of Hosh shrugged sadly. "She was devoted, to a rare degree, to her work. I am sure that nothing but her discarnation could have taken her away from us, at this time, with so many important experiments still uncompleted."

Marnik nodded to Verkan Vall, as much as to say: "You were right."

"Well, I intend acting upon the assumption that she is still carnate and in need of help, until I am positive to the contrary," Verkan Vall said. "And in the latter case, I intend finding out who discarnated her, and send him to apologize for it in person. People don't forcibly discarnate my friends with impunity."

"Sound attitude," Dr. Harnosh commented. "There's certainly no positive evidence that she isn't still carnate. I'll gladly give you all the assistance I can, if you'll only tell me what you want."

"Well, in the first place," Verkan Vall began, "just what sort of work was she doing?" He already knew the answer to that, from the reports she had sent back to the First Level, but he wanted to hear Dr. Harnosh's version. "And what, exactly, are the political effects you mentioned? Understand, Dr. Harnosh, I am really quite ignorant of any scientific subject unrelated to *zerfa* culture, and equally so of Terran politics. Politics, on Venus, is mainly a question of who gets how much graft out of what."

Dr. Harnosh smiled; evidently he had heard about Venusian politics. "Ah, yes, of course. But you are familiar with the main differences between Statistical and Volitional reincarnation theories?"

"In a general way. The Volitionalists hold that the discarnate individuality is fully conscious, and is capable of something analogous to sense-perception, and is also capable of exercising choice in the matter of reincarnation vehicles, and can reincarnate or remain in the discarnate state as it chooses. They also believe that discarnate individualities can communicate with one another, and with at least some carnate individualities, by telepathy," he said. "The Statisticalists deny all this; their opinion is that the discarnate individuality is in a more or less somnambulistic state, that it is drawn by a process akin to tropism to the nearest available reincarnation vehicle, and that it must reincarnate in and only in that vehicle. They are labeled Statisticalists because they believe that the process of reincarnation is purely at random, or governed by unknown and uncontrollable causes, and is unpredictable except as to aggregates."

"That's a fairly good generalized summary," Dr. Harnosh of

Hosh grudged, unwilling to give a mere layman too much credit. He dipped a spoon into a tobacco humidor, dusted the tobacco lightly with dried *zerfa,* and rammed it into his pipe. "You must understand that our modern Statisticalists are the intellectual heirs of those ancient materialistic thinkers who denied the possibility of any discarnate existence, or of any extraphysical mind, or even of extrasensory perception. Since all these things have been demonstrated to be facts, the materialistic dogma has been broadened to include them, but always strictly within the frame of materialism.

"We have proven, for instance, that the human individuality can exist in a discarnate state, and that it reincarnates into the body of an infant, shortly after birth. But the Statisicalists cannot accept the idea of discarnate consciousness, since they conceive of consciousness purely as a function of the physical brain. So they postulate an unconscious discarnate personality, or, as you put it, one in a somnambulistic state. They have to concede memory to this discarnate personality, since it was by recovery of memories of previous reincarnations that discarnate existence and reincarnation were proven to be facts. So they picture the discarnate individuality as a material object, or physical event, of negligible but actual mass, in which an indefinite number of memories can be stored as electrical charges. And they picture it as being drawn irresistibly to the body of the nearest non-incarnated infant. Curiously enough, the reincarnation vehicle chosen is almost always of the same sex as the vehicle of the previous reincarnation, the exceptions being cases of persons who had a previous history of psychological sex-inversion."

Dr. Harnosh remembered the unlighted pipe in his hand, thrust it into his mouth, and lit it. For a moment, he sat with it jutting out of his black beard, until it was drawing to his satisfaction. "This belief in immediate reincarnation leads the Statisticalists, when they fight duels or perform voluntary discarnation, to do so in the neighborhood of maternity hospitals," he added. "I know, personally, of one reincarnation memory-recall, in which the subject, a Statisticalist, voluntarily discarnated by lethal-gas inhaler in a private room at one of our local maternity hospitals, and reincarnated twenty years later in the city of Jeddul, three thousand miles away." The square black beard jiggled as the scientist laughed.

"Now, as to the political implications of these contradictory theories: Since the Statisicalists believe that they will reincarnate entirely at random, their aim is to create an utterly classless social and economic order, in which, theoretically, each individuality will reincarnate into a condition of equality with everybody else. Their political program, therefore, is one of complete socialization of all means of production and distribution, abolition of hereditary titles and inherited wealth—eventually, all private wealth—and total government control of all economic, social and cultural activities. Of course," Dr Harnosh apologized, "politics isn't my subject; I wouldn't presume to judge how that would function in practice."

"I would," Verkan Vall said shortly, thinking of all the different time-lines on which he had seen systems like that in operation. "You wouldn't like it, doctor. And the Volitionalists?"

"Well, since they believe that they are able to choose the circumstances of their next reincarnations for themselves, they are the party of the *status quo*. Naturally, almost all the nobles, almost all the wealthy trading and manufacturing families, and almost all professional people are Volitionalists; most of the workers and peasants are Statisticalists. Or, at least, they were, for the most part, before we began announcing the results of the Lady Dallona's experimental work."

"Ah, now we come to it," Verkan Vall said as the story clarified.

"Yes. In somewhat oversimplified form, the situation is rather like this," Dr. Harnosh of Hosh said. "The Lady Dallona introduced a number of refinements and some outright innovations into our technique of recovering memories of past reincarnations. Previously, it was necessary to keep the subject in an hypnotic trance, during which he or she would narrate what was remembered of past reincarnations, and this would be recorded. On emerging from the trance, the subject would remember nothing; the tape recording would be all that would be left. But the Lady Dallona devised a technique by which these memories would remain in what might be called the forepart of the subject's subconscious mind, so that they could be brought to the level of consciousness at will. More, she was able to recover memories of past discarnate existences, something we had never been able to do heretofore." Dr. Harnosh shook his head. "And to think, when I first met her, I thought that she was just another sensation-seeking young lady of wealth, and was almost about to refuse her enrollment!"

He wasn't the only one whom little Dalla had surprised, Verkan Vall thought. At least, he had been pleasantly surprised.

"You see, this entirely disproves the Statistical Theory of Reincarnation. For example, we got a fine set of memory-recalls from one subject, for four previous reincarnations and four intercarnations. In the first of these, the subject had been a peasant on the estate of a wealthy noble. Unlike most of his fellows, who reincarnated into other peasant families almost immediately after discarnation, this man waited for fifty years in the discarnate state for an opportunity to reincarnate as the son of an over-servant. In his next reincarnation, he was the son of a technician, and received a technical education; he became a physics researcher. For his next reincarnation, he chose the son of a nobleman by a concubine as his vehicle; in his present reincarnation, he is a member of a wealthy manufacturing family, and married into a family of the nobility. In five reincarnations, he has climbed from the lowest to the next-to-highest rung of the social ladder. Few individuals of the class from whence he began this ascent possess so much persistence or determination. Then, of course, there was the case of Lord Garnon of Roxor."

He went on to describe the last experiment in which Hadron Dalla had participated.

"Well, that all sounds pretty conclusive," Verkan Vall commented. "I take it the leaders of the Volitionalist Party here are pleased with the result of the Lady Dallona's work?"

"Pleased? My dear Lord Virzal, they're fairly bursting with glee over it!" Harnosh of Hosh declared. "As I pointed out, the Statisticalist program of socialization is based entirely on the proposition that no one can choose the circumstances of his next reincarnation, and that's been demonstrated to be utter nonsense. Until the Lady Dallona's discoveries were announced, they were the dominant party, controlling a majority of the seats in Parliament and on the Executive Council. Only the Constitution kept them from enacting their entire socialization program long ago, and they were about to legislate constitutional changes which would remove that barrier. They had expected to be able to do so after the forthcoming general elections. But now, social inequality has become desirable; it gives people something to look forward to in the next reincarnation. Instead of wanting to abolish wealth and privilege and nobility, the proletariat want to reincarnate into them." Harnosh of Hosh laughed happily. "So you can see how furious the Statisticalist Party organization is!"

"There's a catch to this, somewhere," Marnik the Assassin,

speaking for the first time, declared. "They can't all reincarnate as princes, there aren't enough vacancies to go round. And no noble is going to reincarnate as a tractor driver to make room for a tractor driver who wants to reincarnate as a noble."

"That's correct," Dr. Harnosh replied. "There is a catch to it; a catch most people would never admit, even to themselves. Very few individuals possess the willpower, the intelligence or the capacity for mental effort displayed by the subject of the case I just quoted. The average man's interests are almost entirely on the physical side; he actually finds mental effort painful, and makes as little of it as possible. And that is the only sort of effort a discarnate individuality can exert. So, unable to endure the fifty or so years needed to make a really good reincarnation, he reincarnates in a year or so, out of pure boredom, into the first vehicle he can find, usually one nobody else wants." Dr. Harnosh dug out the heel of his pipe and blew through the stem. "But nobody will admit his own mental inferiority, even to himself. Now, every machine operator and field hand on the planet thinks he can reincarnate as a prince or a millionaire. Politics isn't my subject, but I'm willing to bet that since Statistical Reincarnation is an exploded psychic theory, Statisticalist Socialism has been caught in the blast area and destroyed along with it."

Olirzon was in the drawing room of the hotel suite when they returned, sitting on the middle of his spinal column in a reclining chair, smoking a pipe, dressing the edge of his knife with a pocket-hone, and gazing lecherously at a young woman in the visiplate. She was an extremely well-designed young woman, in a rather fragmentary costume, and she was heaving her bosom at the invisible audience in anger, sorrow, scorn, entreaty, and numerous other emotions.

". . . this revolting crime," she was declaiming, in a husky contralto, as Verkan Vall and Marnik entered, "foul even for the criminal beasts who conceived and perpetrated it!" She pointed an accusing finger. "This murder of the beautiful Lady Dallona of Hadron!"

Verkan Vall stopped short, considering the possibility of something having been discovered lately of which he was ignorant. Olirzon must have guessed his thought; he grinned reassuringly.

"Think nothing of it, Lord Virzal," he said, waving his knife at the visiplate. "Just political propaganda; strictly for the sparrows. Nice propagandist, though."

"And now," the woman with the magnificent natural resources lowered her voice reverently, "we bring you the last image of the Lady Dallona, and of Dirzed, her faithful Assassin, taken just before they vanished, never to be seen again."

The plate darkened, and there were strains of slow, dirgelike music; then it lighted again, presenting a view of a broad hallway, thronged with men and women in bright vari-colored costumes. In the foreground, wearing a tight skirt of deep blue and a short red jacket, was Hadron Dalla, just as she had looked in the solidographs taken in Dhergabar after her alteration by the First Level cosmeticians to conform to the appearance of the Malayoid Akor-Neb people. She was holding the arm of a man who wore the black tunic and red badge of an Assassin, a handsome specimen of the Akor-Neb race. Trust little Dalla for that, Verkan Vall thought. The figures were moving with exaggerated slowness, as though a very fleeting picture were being stretched out as far as possible. Having already memorized his former wife's changed appearance, Verkan Vall concentrated on the man beside her until the picture faded.

"All right, Olirzon; what did you get?" he asked.

"Well, first of all, at Assassins' Hall," Olirzon said, rolling up his left sleeve, holding his bare forearm to the light, and shaving a few fine hairs from it to test the edge of his knife. "Of course, they never tell one Assassin anything about the client of another Assassin; that's standard practice. But I was in the Lodge Secretary's office, where nobody but Assassins is ever admitted. They have a big panel in there, with the names of all the Lodge members on it in light-letters; that's standard in all Lodges. If an Assassin is unattached and free to accept a client, his name's in white light. If he has a client, the light's changed to blue, and the name of the client goes up under his. If his whereabouts are unknown, the light's changed to amber. If he is discarnated, his name's removed entirely, unless the circumstances of his discarnation are such as to constitute an injury to the Society. In that case, the name's in red light until he's been properly avenged, or, as we say, till his blood's been mopped up. Well, the name of Dirzed is up in blue light, with the name of Dallona of Hadron under it. I found out that the light had been amber for two days after the disappearance, and then had been changed back to blue. Get it, Lord Virzal?"

Verkan Vall nodded. "I think so. I'd been considering that as a possibility from the first. Then what?"

"Then I was about and around for a couple of hours, buying drinks for people—unattached Assassins, Constabulary detectives, political workers, newscast people. You owe me fifteen System Monetary Units for that, Lord Virzal. What I got, when it's all sorted out—I taped it in detail, as soon as I got back—reduces to this: The Volitionalists are moving mountains to find out who was the spy at Garnon of Roxor's discarnation feast, but are doing nothing but nothing at all to find the Lady Dallona or Dirzed. The Statisticalists are making all sorts of secret efforts to find out what happened to her. The Constabulary blame the Statistos for the package-bomb; they're interested in that because of the discarnation of the three servants by an illegal weapon of indiscriminate effect. They claim that the disappearance of Dirzed and the Lady Dallona was a publicity hoax. The Volitionalists are preparing a line of publicity to deny this."

Verkan Vall nodded. "That ties in with what you learned at Assassins' Hall," he said. "They're hiding out somewhere. Is there any chance of reaching Dirzed through the Society of Assassins?"

Olirzon shook his head. "If you're right—and that's the way it looks to me, too—he's probably just called in and notified the Society that he's still carnate and so is the Lady Dallona, and called off any search the Society might be making for him."

"And I've got to find the Lady Dallona as soon as I can. Well, if I can't reach her, maybe I can get her to send word to me," Verkan Vall said. "That's going to take some doing, too."

"What did you find out, Lord Virzal?" Olirzon asked. He had a piece of soft leather now, and was polishing his blade lovingly.

"The Reincarnation Research people don't know anything," Verkan Vall replied. "Dr. Harnosh of Hosh thinks she's discarnate. I did find out that the experimental work she's done, so far, has absolutely disproved the theory of Statistical Reincarnation. The Volitionalists' theory is solidly established."

"Yes, what do you think, Olirzon?" Marnik added. "They have a case on record of a man who worked up from field hand to millionaire in five reincarnations. Deliberately, that is." He went on to repeat what Harnosh of Hosh had said; he must have possessed an almost eidetic memory, for he gave the bearded psychicist's words verbatim, and threw in the gestures and voice inflections.

Olirzon grinned. "You know, there's a chance for the easy-money boys," he considered. " 'You, too, can reincarnate as a millionaire! Let Dr. Nirzutz of Futzbutz help you! Only 49.98 System Monetary Units for the Secret, Infallible, Autosuggestive Formula' And would it sell!" He put away the hone and the bit of leather and slipped his knife back into its sheath. "If I weren't a respectable Assassin, I'd give it a try myself."

Verkan Vall looked at his watch. "We'd better get something to eat," he said. "We'll go down to the main dining room; the Martian Room, I think they call it. I've got to think of some way to let the Lady Dallona know I'm looking for her."

The Martian Room, fifteen stories down, was a big place, occupying almost half of the floor space of one corner tower. It had been fitted to resemble one of the ruined buildings of the ancient and vanished race of Mars who were the ancestors of Terran humanity. One whole side of the room was a gigantic cine-solidograph screen, on which the gullied desolation of a Martian landscape was projected; in the course of about two hours, the scene changed from sunrise through daylight and night to sunrise again.

It was high noon when they entered and found a table; by the time they had finished their dinner, the night was ending and the first glow of dawn was tinting the distant hills. They sat for a while, watching the light grow stronger, then got up and left the table.

There were five men at the table near them; they had come in before the stars had grown dim, and the waiters were just bringing their first dishes. Two were Assassins, and the other three were of a breed Verkan Vall had learned to recognize on any time-line—the arrogant, cocksure, ambitious, leftist politician, who knows what is best for everybody better than anybody else does, and who is convinced that he is inescapably right and that whoever differs with him is not only an ignoramus but a venal scoundrel as well. One was a beefy man in a gold-laced cream-colored dress tunic; he had thick lips and a too-ready laugh. Another was a rather monkish-looking young man who spoke earnestly and rolled his eyes upward, as though at some celestial vision. The third had the faint powdering of gray in his black hair which was, among the Akor-Neb people, almost the only indication of advanced age.

"Of course it is; the whole thing is a fraud," the monkish young man was saying angrily. "But we can't prove it."

"Oh, Sirzob here, can probe anything, if you give him time," the beefy one laughed. "The trouble is, there isn't too much time. We know that that communication was a fake, prearranged by the Volitionalists, with Dr. Harnosh and this Dallona of Hadron as their tools. They fed the whole thing to that idiot boy hypnotically, in advance, and then, on a signal, he began typing out this spurious communication. And then, of course, Dallona and this Assassin of hers ran off somewhere together, so that we'd be blamed with discarnating or abducting them, and so that they wouldn't be made to testify about the communication on a lie detector."

A sudden happy smile touched Verkan Vall's eyes. He caught each of his Assassins by an arm.

"Marnik, cover my back," he ordered. "Olirzon, cover everybody at the table. Come on!"

Then he stepped forward, halting between the chairs of the young man and the man with the gray hair and facing the beefy man in the light tunic.

"You!" he barked. "I mean *you*."

The beefy man stopped laughing and stared at him; then sprang to his feet. His hand, streaking toward his left armpit, stopped and dropped to his side as Olirzon aimed a pistol at him. The others sat motionless.

"You," Verkan Vall continued, "are a complete, deliberate, malicious, and unmitigated liar. The Lady Dallona of Hadron is a scientist of integrity, incapable of falsifying her experimental work. What's more, her father is one of my best friends; in his name, and in hers, I demand a full retraction of the slanderous statements you have just made."

"Do you know who I am?" the beefy one shouted.

"I know *what* you are," Verkan Vall shouted back. Like most ancient languages, the Akor-Neb speech included an elaborate, delicately shaded, and utterly vile vocabulary of abuse; Verkan Vall culled from it judiciously and at length. "And if I don't make myself understood verbally, we'll go down to the object level," he added, snatching a bowl of soup from in front of the monkish-looking young man and throwing it across the table.

The soup was a dark brown, almost black. It contained bits of meat, and mushrooms, and slices of hard-boiled egg, and yellow Martian rock lichen. It produced, on the light tunic, a most spectacular effect.

For a moment, Verkan Vall was afraid the fellow would have an apoplectic stroke, or an epileptic fit. Mastering himself, however, he bowed jerkily.

"Marnark of Bashad," he identified himself. "When and where can my friends consult yours?"

"Lord Virzal of Verkan," the paratimer bowed back. "Your friends can negotiate with mine here and now. I am represented by these Gentlemen-Assassins."

"I won't submit my friends to the indignity of negotiating with them," Marnark retorted. "I insist that you be represented by persons of your own quality and mine."

"Oh, you do?" Olirzon broke in. "Well, is your objection personal to me, or to Assassins as a class? In the first case, I'll remember to make a private project of you, as soon as I'm through with my present employment; if it's the latter, I'll report your attitude to the Society. I'll see what Klarnood, our President-General, thinks of your views."

A crowd had begun to accumulate around the table. Some of them were persons in evening dress, some were Assassins on the hotel payroll, and some were unattached Assassins.

"Well, you won't have far to look for him," one of the latter said, pushing through the crowd to the table.

He was a man of middle age, inclined to stoutness; he made Verkan Vall think of a chocolate figure of Tortha Karf. The red badge on his breast was surrounded with gold lace, and, instead of black wings and a silver bullet, it bore silver wings and a golden dagger. He bowed contemptuously at Marnark of Bashad.

"Klarnood, President-General of the Society of Assassins," he announced. "Marnark of Bashad, did I hear you say that you considered members of the Society as unworthy to negotiate an affair of honor with your friends, on behalf of this nobleman who has been courteous enough to accept your challenge?" he demanded.

Marnark of Bashad's arrogance suffered considerable evaporation-loss. His tone became almost servile.

"Not at all, Honorable Assassin-President," he protested. "But as I was going to ask these gentlemen to represent me, I thought it would be more fitting for the other gentleman to be represented by personal friends, also. In that way—"

"Sorry, Marnark," the gray-haired man at the table said. "I can't second you; I have a quarrel with the Lord Virzal, too."

He rose and bowed. "Sirzob of Abo. Inasmuch as the Honorable Marnark is a guest at my table, an affront to him is an affront to me. In my quality as his host, I must demand satisfaction from you, Lord Virzal."

"Why, gladly, Honorable Sirzob," Verkan Vall replied. This was getting better and better every moment. "Of course, your friend, the Honorable Marnark, enjoys priority of challenge; I'll take care of you as soon as I have, shall we say, satisfied him."

The earnest and rather consecrated-looking young man rose also, bowing to Verkan Vall.

"Yirzol of Narva. I, too, have a quarrel with you, Lord Virzal; I cannot submit to the indignity of having my food snatched from in front of me, as you just did. I also demand satisfaction."

"And quite rightly, Honorable Yirzol," Verkan Vall approved. "It looks like such good soup, too," he sorrowed, inspecting the front of Marnark's tunic. "My seconds will negotiate with yours immediately; your satisfaction, of course, must come after that of Honorable Sirzob."

"If I may intrude," Klarnood put in smoothly, "may I suggest that as the Lord Virzal is represented by his Assassins, yours can represent all three of you at the same time. I will glady offer my own good offices as impartial supervisor."

Verkan Vall turned and bowed as to royalty. "An honor, Assassin-President; I am sure no one could act in that capacity more satisfactorily."

"Well, when would it be most convenient to arrange the details?" Klarnood inquired. "I am completely at your disposal, gentlemen."

"Why, here and now, while we're all together," Verkan Vall replied.

"I object to that!" Marnark of Bashad vociferated. "We can't make arrangements here; why, all these hotel people, from the manager down, are nothing but tipsters for the newscast services!"

"Well, what's wrong with that?" Verkan Vall demanded. "You knew that when you slandered the Lady Dallona in their hearing."

"The Lord Virzal of Verkan is correct," Klarnood ruled. "And the offenses for which you have challenged him were also committed in public. By all means, let's discuss the arrangements now." He turned to Verkan Vall. "As the challenged party, you have the choice of weapons; your opponents, then, have the right to name the conditions under which they are to be used."

Marnark of Bashad raised another outcry over that. The assault upon him by the Lord Virzal of Verkan was deliberately provocative, and therefore tantamount to a challenge; he, himself, had the right to name the weapons. Klarnood upheld him.

"Do the other gentlemen make the same claim?" Verkan Vall wanted to know.

"If they do, I won't allow it," Klarnood replied. "You deliberately provoked Honorable Marnark, but the offenses of provoking him at Honorable Sirzob's table, and of throwing Honorable Yirzol's soup at him, were not given with the intent to provoke. These gentlemen have a right to challenge, but not to consider themselves provoked."

"Well, I choose knives, then," Marnark hastened to say.

Verkan Vall smiled thinly. He had learned knifeplay among the greatest masters of that art in all paratime, the Third Level Khanga pirates of the Caribbean Islands.

"And we fight barefoot, stripped to the waist, and without any parrying weapon in the left hand," Verkan Vall stipulated.

The beefy Marnark fairly licked his chops in anticipation. He outweighed Verkan Vall by forty pounds; he saw an easy victory ahead. Verkan Vall's own confidence increased at these signs of his opponent's assurance.

"And as for Honorable Sirzob and Honorable Yirzol, I chose pistols," he added.

Sirzob and Yirzol held a hasty whispered conference.

"Speaking both for Honorable Yirzol and for myself," Sirzob announced, "we stipulate that the distance shall be twenty meters, that the pistols shall be fully loaded, and that fire shall be at will after the command."

"Twenty rounds, fire at will, at twenty meters!" Olirzon hooted. "You must think our principal's as bad a shot as you are!"

The four Assassins stepped aside and held a long dicussion about something, with considerable argument and gesticulation. Klarnood, observing Verkan Vall's impatience, leaned close to him and whispered:

"This is highly irregular; we must pretend ignorance and be patient. They're laying bets on the outcome. You must do your best, Lord Virzal; you don't want your supporters to lose money."

He said it quite seriously, as though the outcome were otherwise a matter of indifference to Verkan Vall.

Marnark wanted to discuss time and place, and proposed that all three duels be fought at dawn, on the fourth landing stage of Darsh Central Hospital; that was closest to the maternity wards, and statistics showed that most births occurred just before that hour.

"Certainly not," Verkan Vall vetoed. "We'll fight here and now; I don't propose going a couple of hundred miles to meet you at any such unholy hour. We'll fight in the nearest hallway that provides twenty meters' shooting distance."

Marnark, Sirzob and Yirzol all clamored in protest. Verkan Vall shouted them down, drawing on his hypnotically acquired knowledge of Akor-Neb dueling customs. "The code explicitly states that satisfaction shall be rendered as promptly as possible, and I insist on a literal interpretation. I'm not going to inconvenience myself and Assassin-President Klarnood and these four Gentlemen-Assassins just to humor Statisticalist superstitions."

The manager of the hotel, drawn to the Martian Room by the uproar, offered a hallway connecting the kitchens with the refrigerator rooms; it was fifty meters long by five in width, was well lighted and soundproof, and had a bay in which the seconds and others could stand during the firing.

They repaired thither in a body, Klarnood gathering up several hotel servants on the way through the kitchen. Verkan Vall stripped to the waist, pulled off his ankle boots, and examined Olirzon's knife. Its tapering eight-inch blade was double-edged at the point, and its handle was covered with black velvet to afford a good grip, and wound with gold wire. He nodded approvingly, gripped it with his index finger crooked around the crossguard, and advanced to meet Marnark of Bashad.

As he had expected, the burly politician was depending upon his great brawn to overpower his antagonist. He advanced with a sidling, spread-legged gait, his knife hand against his right hip and his left hand extended in front. Verkan Vall nodded with pleased satisfaction; a wrist-grabber. Then he blinked. Why, the fellow was actually holding his knife reversed, his little finger to the guard and his thumb on the pommel! Verkan Vall went briskly to meet him, made a feint at his knife hand with his own left, and then sidestepped quickly to the right. As Marnark's left hand grabbed at his right wrist, his left hand brushed against it and closed into a fist, with Marnark's left thumb inside of it. He gave a quick downward twist with his wrist, pulling Marnark off balance.

Caught by surprise, Marnark stumbled, his knife flailing wildly away from Verkan Vall. As he stumbled forward, Verkan Vall pivoted on his left heel and drove the point of his knife into the back of Marnark's neck, twisting it as he jerked it free. At the same time, he released Marnark's thumb. The politician continued his stumble and fell forward on his face, blood spurting from his neck. He gave a twitch or so, and was still.

Verkan Vall stooped and wiped the knife on the dead man's clothes—another Khanga pirate gesture—and then returned it to Olirzon.

"Nice weapon, Olirzon," he said. "It fitted my hand as though I'd been born holding it."

"You used it as though you had, Lord Virzal," the Assassin replied. "Only eight seconds from the time you closed with him."

The function of the hotel servants whom Klarnood had gathered up now became apparent; they advanced, took the body of Marnark by the heels, and dragged it out of the way. The others watched this removal with mixed emotions. The two remaining principals were impassive and frozen-faced. Their two Assassins, who had probably bet heavily on Marnark, were chagrined. And Klarnood was looking at Verkan Vall with a considerable accretion of respect. Verkan Vall pulled on his boots and resumed his clothing.

There followed some argument about the pistols; it was finally decided that each combatant should use his own shoulder-holster weapon. All three were nearly enough alike—small weapons, rather heavier than they looked, firing a tiny ten-grain bullet at ten thousand foot-seconds. On impact, such a bullet would almost disintegrate; a man hit anywhere in the body with one would be killed instantly, his nervous system paralyzed and his heart stopped by internal pressure. Each of the pistols carried twenty rounds in the magazine.

Verkan Vall and Sirzob of Abo took their places, their pistols lowered at their sides, facing each other across a measured twenty meters.

"Are you ready, gentlemen?" Klarnood asked. "You will not raise your pistols until the command to fire; you may fire at will after it. Ready. *Fire!*"

Both pistols swung up to level. Verkan Vall found Sirzob's head in his sights and squeezed; the pistol kicked back in his hand, and he saw a lance of blue flame jump from the muzzle of Sirzob's. Both weapons barked together, and with the double report came the whip-cracking sound of Sirzob's bullet passing Verkan Vall's head. Then Sirzob's face altered its appearance unpleasantly, and he pitched forward. Verkan Vall thumbed on his safety and stood motionless, while the servants advanced, took Sirzob's body by the heels, and dragged it over beside Marnark's.

"All right; Honorable Yirzol, you're next," Verkan Vall called out.

"The Lord Virzal has fired one shot," one of the opposing seconds objected, "and Honorable Yirzol has a full magazine. The Lord Virzal should put in another magazine."

"I grant him the advantage; let's get on with it," Verkan Vall said.

Yirzol of Narva advanced to the firing point. He was not afraid of death—none of the Akor-Neb people were; their language contained no word to express the concept of total and final extinction—and discarnation by gunshot was almost entirely painless. But he was beginning to suspect that he had made a fool of himself by getting into this affair, he had work in his present reincarnation which he wanted to finish, and his political party would suffer loss, both of his services and of prestige.

"Are you ready, gentlemen?" Klarnood intoned ritualistically. "You will not raise your pistols until the command to fire; you may fire at will after it. Ready, *Fire!*"

Verkan Vall shot Yirzol of Narva through the head before the latter had his pistol half raised. Yirzol fell forward on the splash of blood Sirzob had made, and the servants came forward and dragged his body over with the others. It reminded Verkan Vall of some sort of industrial assembly-line operation. He replaced the two expended rounds in his magazine with fresh ones and slid the pistol back into its holster. The two Assassins whose principals had been so expeditiously massacred were beginning to count up their losses and pay off the winners.

Klarnood, the President-General of the Society of Assassins, came over, hooking fingers and clapping shoulders with Verkan Vall.

"Lord Virzal, I've seen quite a few duels, but nothing quite like that," he said. "You should have been an Assassin!"

That was a considerable compliment. Verkan Vall thanked him modestly.

"I'd like to talk to you privately," the Assassin-President

continued. "I think it'll be worth your while if we have a few words together."

Verkan Vall nodded. "My suite is on the fifteenth floor above; will that be all right?" He waited until the losers had finished settling their bets, then motioned to his own pair of Assassins.

As they emerged into the Martian Room again, the manager was waiting; he looked as though he were about to demand that Verkan Vall vacate his suite. However, when he saw the arm of the President-General of the Society of Assassins draped amicably over his guest's shoulder, he came forward bowing and smiling.

"Larnorm, I want you to put five of your best Assassins to guarding the approaches to the Lord Virzal's suite," Klarnood told him. "I'll send five more from Assassins' Hall to replace them at their ordinary duties. And I'll hold you responsible with your carnate existence of the Lord Virzal's safety in this hotel. Understand?"

"Oh, yes, Honorable Assassin-President; you may trust me. The Lord Virzal will be perfectly safe."

In Verkan Vall's suite, above, Klarnood sat down and got out his pipe, filling it with tobacco lightly mixed with *zerfa*. To his surprise, he saw his host light a plain tobacco cigarette.

"Don't you use *zerfa?*" he asked.

"Very little," Verkan Vall replied. "I grow it. If you'd see the bums who hang around our drying sheds, on Venus, cadging rejected leaves and smoking themselves into a stupor, you'd be frugal in using it, too."

Klarnood nodded. "You know, most men would want a pipe of fifty percent, or a straight *zerfa* cigarette, after what you've been through," he said.

"I'd need something like that, to deaden my conscience, if I had one to deaden," Verkan Vall said. "As it is, I feel like a murderer of babes. That overgrown fool Marnark handled his knife like a cow-butcher. The young fellow couldn't handle a pistol at all. I suppose the old fellow, Sirzob, was a fair shot, but dropping him wasn't any great feat of arms, either."

Klarnood looked at him curiously for a moment. "You know," he said, at length, "I believe you actually mean that. Well, until he met you, Marnark of Bashad was rated as the best knife-fighter in Darsh. Sirzob had ten dueling victories to his credit, and young Yirzol four." He puffed slowly on his pipe. "I like you, Lord Virzal; a great Assassin was lost when you decided to reincarnate as a Venusian landowner. I'd hate to see you discarnated without proper warning. I take it you're ignorant of the intricacies of Terran politics?"

"To a large extent, yes."

"Well, do you know who those three men were?" When Verkan Vall shook his head, Klarnood continued: "Marnark was the son and right-hand associate of old Mirzark of Bashad, the Statisticalist Party leader. Sirzob of Abo was their propaganda director. And Yirzol of Narva was their leading socioeconomic theorist, and their candidate for Executive Chairman. In six minutes, with one knife thrust and two shots, you did the Statisicalist Party an injury second only to that done them by the young lady in whose name you were fighting. In two weeks, there will be a planet-wide general election. As it stands, the Statisticalists have a majority of the seats in Parliament and on the Executive Council. As a result of your work and the Lady Dallona's, they'll lose that majority, and more, when the votes are tallied."

"Is that another reason why you like me?" Verkan Vall asked.

"Unofficially, yes. As President-General of the Society of Assassins, I must be nonpolitical. The Society is rigidly so; if we let ourselves become involved, as an organization, in politics, we could control the System Government inside of five years, and we'd be wiped out of existence in fifty years by the very forces we sought to control," Klarnood said. "But personally, I would like to see the Statisticalist Party destroyed. If they succeed in their program of socialization, the Society would be finished. A socialist state is, in its final development, an absolute, total state; no total state can tolerate extralegal and paragovernmental organizations. So we have adopted the policy of giving a little inconspicuous aid, here and there, to people who are dangerous to the Statisticalists. The Lady Dallona of Hadron and Dr. Harnosh of Hosh are such persons. You appear to be another. That's why I ordered that fellow Larnorm to make sure you were safe in this hotel."

"Where is the Lady Dallona?" Verkan Vall asked. "From your use of the present tense, I assume you believe her to be still carnate."

Klarnood looked at Verkan Vall keenly. "That's a pretty blunt question, Lord Virzal," he said. "I wish I knew a little more about you. When you and your Assassins started inquiring about the Lady Dallona, I tried to check up on you. I found out that you had come to Darsh from Ghamma on a ship of the family of Zorda, accompanied by Brarnend of Zorda himself. And that's all I could find out. You claim to be a Venusian planter, and you might be. Any Terran who can handle weapons as you can would have come to my notice long ago. But you have no more ascertainable history than if you'd stepped out of another dimension."

That was getting uncomfortably close to the truth. In fact, it *was* the truth. Verkan Vall laughed.

"Well, confidentially," he said, "I'm from the Arcturus System. I followed the Lady Dallona here from our home planet, and when I have rescued her from among you Solarians, I shall, according to our customs, receive her hand in marriage. As she is the daughter of the Emperor of Arcturus, that'll be quite a good thing for me."

Klarnood chuckled. "You know, you'd only have to tell me that about three or four times and I'd start believing it," he said. "And Dr. Harnosh of Hosh would believe it the first time; he's been talking to himself ever since the Lady Dallona started her experimental work here. Lord Virzal, I'm going to take a chance on you. The Lady Dallona is still carnate, or was four days ago, and the same for Dirzed. They both went into hiding after the discarnation feast of Garnon of Roxor, to escape the enmity of the Statisticalists. Two days after they disappeared, Dirzed called Assassins' Hall and reported this, but told us nothing more. I suppose, in about three or four days, I could reestablish contact with him. We want the public to think that the Statisticalists made away with the Lady Dallona, at least until the election's over."

Verkan Vall nodded. "I was pretty sure that was the situation," he said. "It may be that they will get in touch with me; if they don't, I'll need your help in reaching them."

"Why do you think the Lady Dallona will try to reach you?"

"She needs all the help she can get. She knows she can get plenty from me. Why do you think I interrupted my search for her, and risked my carnate existence, to fight those people over a matter of verbalisms and political propaganda?" Verkan Vall went to the newscast visiplate and snapped it on. "We'll see if I'm getting results yet."

The plate lighted, and a handsome young man in a gold-laced green suit was speaking out of it:

". . . where he is heavily guarded by Assassins. However, in an exclusive interview with representatives of this service, the Assassin Hirzif, one of the two who seconded the men the Lord Virzal fought, said that in his opinion all of the three were so outclassed as to have had no chance whatever, and that he had already refused an offer of ten thousand System Monetary Units to discarnate the Lord Virzal for the Statisticalist Party. 'When I want to discarnate,' Hirzif the Assassin said, 'I'll invite in my friends and do it properly; until I do, I wouldn't go up against the Lord Virzal of Verkan for ten million S.M.U.' "

Verkan Vall snapped off the visiplate. "See what I mean?" he asked. "I fought those politicians just for the advertising. If Dallona and Dirzed are anywhere near a visiplate, they'll know how to reach me."

"Hirzif shouldn't have talked about refusing that retainer," Klarnood frowned. "That isn't good Assassin ethics. Why, yes, Lord Virzal; that was cleverly planned. It ought to get results. But I wish you'd get the Lady Dallona out of Darsh, and preferably off Terra, as soon as you can. We've benefited by this, so far, but I shouldn't like to see things go much further. A real civil war could develop out of this situation, and I don't want that. Call on me for help; I'll give you a code word to use at Assassins' Hall."

A real civil war was developing even as Klarnood spoke; by midmorning of the next day, the fighting that had been partially suppressed by the Constabulary had broken out anew. The Assassins employed by the Solar Hotel—heavily reinforced during the night—had fought a pitched battle with Statisticalist partisans on the landing stage above Verkan Vall's suite, and now several Constabulary airboats were patrolling around the building. The rule on Constabulary interference seemed to be that while individuals had an unquestionable right to shoot out their differences among themselves, any fighting likely to endanger nonparticipants was taboo.

Just how successful in enforcing this rule the Constabulary were was open to some doubt. Ever since arising, Verkan Vall had heard the crash of small arms and the hammering of automatic weapons in other parts of the towering city-unit. There hadn't been a civil war on the Akor-Neb Sector for over five centuries, he knew, but then, Hadron Dalla, Doctor of Psychic Science, and intertemporal trouble-carrier extraordinary, had only been on this sector for a little under a year. If anything, he was surprised that the explosion had taken so long to occur.

One of the servants furnished to him by the hotel management approached him in the drawing room, holding a four-inch-square wafer of white plastic.

"Lord Virzal, there is a masked Assassin in the hallway who brought this under Assassin's Truce," he said.

Verkan Vall took the wafer and pared off three of the four edges, which showed black where they had been fused. Unfolding it, he found, as he had expected, that the pyrographed message within was in the alphabet and lanugage of the First Paratime Level:

Vall, darling:

Am I glad you got here; this time I really *am* in the middle, but good! The Assassin, Dirzed, who brings this, is in my service. You can trust him implicitly; he's about the only person in Darsh you can trust. He'll bring you to where I am.

Dalla

P.S. I hope you're not still angry about that musician. I told you, at the time, that he was just helping me with an experiment in telepathy.

D.

Verkan Vall grinned at the postscript. That had been twenty years ago, when he'd been eighty and she'd been seventy. He supposed she'd expect him to take up his old relationship with her again. It probably wouldn't last any longer than it had the other time; he recalled a Fourth Level proverb about the leopard and his spots. It certainly wouldn't be boring, though.

"Tell the Assassin to come in," he directed. Then he tossed the message down on a table. Outside of himself, nobody in Darsh could read it but the woman who had sent it; if, as he thought highly probable, the Statisticalists had spies among the hotel staff, it might serve to reduce some cryptanalyst to gibbering insanity.

The assassin entered, drawing off a cowlike mask. He was the man whose arm Dalla had been holding in the visiplate picture; Verkan Vall even recognized the extremely ornate pistol and knife on his belt.

"Dirzed the Assassin," he named himself. "If you wish, we can visiphone Assasins' Hall for verification of my identity."

"Lord Virzal of Verkan. And my Assassins, Marnik and

Olirzon." They all hooked fingers and clapped shoulders with the newcomer. "That won't be needed," Verkan Vall told Dirzed. "I know you from seeing you with the Lady Dallona, on the visiplate; you're 'Dirzed, her faithful Assassin.' "

Dirzed's face, normally the color of a good walnut gunstock, turned almost black. He used shockingly bad language.

"And that's why I have to wear this abomination," he finished, displaying the mask. "The Lady Dallona and I can't show our faces anywhere; if we did, every Statisticalist and his six-year-old brat would know us, and we'd be fighting off an army of them in five minutes."

"Where's the Lady Dallona now?"

"In hiding, Lord Virzal, at a private dwelling dome in the forest; she's most anxious to see you. I'm to take you to her, and I would strongly advise that you bring your Assassins along. There are other people at this dome, and they are not personally loyal to the Lady Dallona. I've no reason to suspect them of secret enmity, but their friendship is based entirely on political expediency."

"And political expediency is subject to change without notice," Verkan Vall finished for him. "Have you an airboat?"

"On the landing stage below. Shall we go now, Lord Virzal?"

"Yes." Verkan Vall made a two-handed gesture to his Assassins, as though gripping a submachine gun; they nodded, went into another room, and returned carrying light automatic weapons in their hands and pouches of spare drums slung over their shoulders. "And may I suggest, Dirzed, that one of my Assassins drives the airboat? I want you on the back seat with me, to explain the situation as we go."

Dirzed's teeth flashed white against his brown skin as he gave Verkan Vall a quick smile.

"By all means, Lord Virzal; I would much rather be distrusted than to find that my client's friends were not discreet."

There were a couple of hotel Assassins guarding Dirzed's airboat, on the landing stage. Marnik climbed in under the controls, with Olirzon beside him; Verkan Vall and Dirzed entered the rear seat. Dirzed gave Marnik the coordinate reference for their destination.

"Now, what sort of a place is this, where we're going?" Verkan Vall asked. "And who's there whom we may or may not trust?"

"Well, it's a dome house belonging to the family of Starpha; they own a five-mile radius around it, oak and beech forest and underbrush, stocked with deer and boar. A hunting lodge. Prince Jirzyn of Starpha, Lord Girzon of Roxor, and a few other top-level Volitionalists know that the Lady Dallona's hiding there. They're keeping her out of sight till after the election, for propaganda purposes. We've been hiding there since immediately after the discarnation feast of the Lord Garnon of Roxor."

"What happened, after the feast?" Verkan Vall wanted to know.

"Well, you know how the Lady Dallona and Dr. Harnosh of Hosh had this telepathic-sensitive there, in a trance and drugged with a *zerfa*-derivative alkaloid the Lady Dallona had developed. I was Lord Garnon's Assassin; I discarnated him myself. Why, I hadn't even put my pistol away before he was in control of this sensitive, in a room five stories above the banquet hall; he began communicating at once. We had visiplates to show us what was going on.

"Right away, Nirzav of Shonna, one of the Statisticalist leaders who was a personal friend of Lord Garnon's in spite of his politics, renounced Statisticalism and went over to the Volitionalists, on the strength of this communication. Prince Jirzyn and Lord Girzon, the new family-head of Roxor, decided that there would be trouble in the next few days, so they advised the Lady Dallona to come to this hunting lodge for safety. She and I came here in her airboat, directly from the feast. A good thing we did, too; if we'd gone to her apartment, we'd have walked in before that lethal gas had time to clear.

"There are four Assassins of the family of Starpha, and six menservants, and an upper-servant named Tarnod, the gamekeeper. The Starpha Assassins and I have been keeping the rest under observation. I left one of the Starpha Assassins guarding the Lady Dallona when I came for you, under brotherly oath to protect her in my name till I returned."

The airboat was skimming rapidly above the treetops, toward the northern part of the city.

"What's known about that package bomb?" Verkan Vall asked. "Who sent it?"

Dirzed shrugged. "The Statisticalists, of course. The wrapper was stolen from the Reincarnation Research Institute; so was the case. The Constabulary are working on it." Dirzed shrugged again.

The dome, about a hundred and fifty feet in width and some fifty in height, stood among the trees ahead. It was almost invisible from any distance; the concrete dome was of mottled green and gray concrete, trees grew so close as to brush it with their branches, and the little pavilion on the flattened top was roofed with translucent green plastic. As the airboat came in, a couple of men in Assassins' garb emerged from the pavilion to meet them.

"Marnik, stay at the controls," Verkan Vall directed. "I'll send Olirzon up for you if I want you. If there's any trouble, take off for Assassin's Hall and give the code word, then come back with twice as many men as you think you'll need."

Dirzed raised his eyebrows over this. "I hadn't known the Assassin-President had given you a code word, Lord Virzal," he commented. "That doesn't happen very often."

"The Assassin-President has honored me with his friendship," Verkan Vall replied noncommittally, as he, Dirzed and Olirzon climbed out of the airboat. Marnik was holding it an unobtrusive inch or so above the flat top of the dome, away from the edge of the pavilion roof.

The two Assassins greeted him, and a man in upper-servant's garb and wearing a hunting knife and a long hunting pistol approached.

"Lord Virzal of Verkan? Welcome to Starpha Dome. The Lady Dallona awaits you below."

Verkan Vall had never been in an Akor-Neb dwelling dome, but a description of such structures had been included in his hypno-mech indoctrination. Originally, they had been the standard structure for all purposes; about two thousand elapsed years ago, when nationalism had still existed on the Akor-Neb Sector, the cities had been almost entirely underground, as protection from air attack. Even now, the design had been retained by those who wished to live apart from the towering city units, to preserve the natural appearance of the landscape. The Starpha hunting lodge was typical of such domes. Under it was a circular well, eighty feet in depth and fifty in width, with a fountain and a shallow circular pool at the bottom. The storerooms, kitchens and servants' quarters were at the top, the living quarters at the bottom, in segments of a wide circle around the well, back of balconies.

"Tarnod, the gamekeeper," Dirzed performed the introductions. "And Erarno and Kirzol, Assassins."

Verkan Vall hooked fingers and clapped shoulders with them. Tarnod accompanied them to the lifter tubes—two percent positive gravitation for descent and two percent negative for ascent—and they all floated down the former, like air-filled balloons, to the bottom level.

"The Lady Dallona is in the gun room," Tarnod informed Verkan Vall, making as though to guide him.

"Thanks, Tarnod; we know the way," Dirzed told him shortly, turning his back on the upper-servant and walking toward a closed door on the other side of the fountain. Verkan Vall and Olirzon followed; for a moment, Tarnod stood looking after them, then he followed the other two Assassins into the ascent tube.

"I don't relish that fellow," Dirzed explained. "The family of Starpha use him for work they couldn't hire an Assassin to do at any price. I've been here often, when I was with the Lord Garnon; I've always thought he had something on Prince Jirzyn."

He knocked sharply on the closed door with the butt of his pistol. In a moment, it slid open, and a young Assassin with a narrow mustache and a tuft of chin-beard looked out.

"Ah, Dirzed." He stepped outside. "The Lady Dallona is within; I return her to your care."

Verkan Vall entered, followed by Dirzed and Olirzon. The big room was fitted with reclining chairs and couches and low tables; its walls were hung with the heads of deer and boar and wolves, and with racks holding rifles and hunting pistols and fowling pieces. It was filled with the soft glow of indirect cold light. At the far side of the room, a young woman was seated at a desk, speaking softly into a sound transcriber. As they entered, she snapped it off and rose.

Hadron Dalla wore the same costume Verkan Vall had seen on the visiplate; he recognized her instantly. It took her a second or two to perceive Verkan Vall under the brown skin and black hair of the Lord Virzal of Verkan. Then her face lighted with a happy smile.

"Why, Va-a-a-ll!" she whooped, running across the room and tossing herself into his not particularly reluctant arms. After all, it had been twenty years. "I didn't know you at first!"

"You mean, in these clothes?" he asked, seeing that she had forgotten, for the moment, the presence of the two Assassins. She had even called him by his First Level name, but that was unimportant—the Akor-Neb affectionate diminutive was formed by omitting the *-irz-* or *-arn-*. "Well, they're not exactly what I generally wear on the plantation." He kissed her again, then turned to his companions. "Your pardon, Gentlemen-Assassins; it's been something over a year since we've seen each other."

Olirzon was smiling at the affectionate reunion; Dirzed wore a look of amused resignation, as though he might have expected something like this to happen. Verkan Vall and Dalla sat down on a couch near the desk.

"That was really sweet of you, Vall, fighting those men for talking about me," she began. "You took an awful chance, though. But if you hadn't, I'd never have known you were in Darsh—oh, oh! That was why you did it, wasn't it?"

"Well, I had to do something. Everybody either didn't know or wasn't saying where you were. I assumed, from the circumstances, that you were hiding somewhere. Tell me, Dalla; do you really have scientific proof of reincarnation? I mean, as an established fact?"

"Oh, yes; these people on this sector have had that for over ten centuries. They have hypnotic techniques for getting back into a part of the subconscious mind that we've never been able to reach. And after I found out how they did it, I was able to adapt some of our hypno-epistemological techniques to it, and—"

"All right; that's what I wanted to know," he cut her off. "We're getting out of here, right away."

"But where?"

"Ghamma, in an airboat I have outside, and then back to the First Level. Unless there's a paratime-transposition conveyor somewhere nearer."

"But why, Vall? I'm not ready to go back; I have a lot of work to do here yet. They're getting ready to set up a series of control experiments at the Institute, and then I'm in the middle of an experiment, a two-hundred-subject memory-recall experiment. See, I distributed two hundred sets of equipment for my new technique—injection-ampoules of this *zerfa*-derivative drug, and sound records of the hypnotic suggestion formula, which can be played on an ordinary reproducer. It's just a crude variant of our hypno-mech process, except that instead of implanting information in the subconscious mind, to be brought at will to the level of consciousness, it works the other way, and draws into conscious knowledge information already in the subconscious mind. The way these people have always done has been to put the subject in a hypnotic trance and then record verbal statements made in the trance state; when the subject comes out of the trance, the record is all there is, because the memories of past reincarnations have never been in the conscious mind. But with my process, the subject can consciously remember everything about his last reincarnation, and as many reincarnations before that as he wishes to. I haven't heard from any of the people who received these auto-recall kits, and I really must—"

"Dalla, I don't want to have to pull Paratime Police authority on you, but so help me, if you don't come back voluntarily with me, I will. Security of the secret of paratime transposition."

"Oh, my eye!" Dalla exclaimed. "Don't give me that, Vall!"

"Look, Dalla. Suppose you get discarnated here," Verkan Vall said. "You say reincarnation is a scientific fact. Well, you'd reincarnate on this sector, and then you'd take a memory-recall, under hypnosis. And when you did, the paratime secret wouldn't be a secret anymore."

"Oh!" Dalla's hand went to her mouth in consternation. Like every paratimer, she was conditioned to shrink with all her being from the mere thought of revealing to any outtime dweller the secret ability of her race to pass to other time-lines, or even the existence of alternate lines of probability. "And if I took one of the old-fashioned trance-recalls, I'd blat out everything; I wouldn't be able to keep a thing back. And I even know the principles of transposition!" She looked at him, aghast.

"When I get back, I'm going to put a recommendation through department channels that this whole sector be declared out of bounds for all paratime-transposition, until you people at Rhogom Foundation work out the problem of discarnate return to the First Level," he told her. "Now, have you any notes or anything you want to take back with you?"

She rose. "Yes; just what's on the desk. Find me something to put the tape spools and notebooks in, while I'm getting them in order."

He secured a large game bag from under a rack of fowling pieces, and held it while she sorted the material rapidly, stuffing spools of record tape and notebooks into it. They had barely begun when the door slid open and Olirzon, who had gone outside, sprang into the room, his pistol drawn, swearing vilely.

"They've double-crossed us!" he cried. "The servants of Starpha have turned on us." He holstered his pistol and snatched up his submachine gun, taking cover behind the edge of the door and letting go with a burst in the direction of the lifter tubes. "Got that one!" he grunted.

"What happened, Olirzon?" Verkan Vall asked, dropping the game bag on the table and hurrying across the room.

"I went up to see how Marnik was making out. As I came

out of the lifter tube, one of the obscenities took a shot at me
with a hunting pistol. He missed me; I didn't miss him. Then a
couple more of them were coming up, with fowling pieces; I
shot one of them before they could fire, and jumped into the
descent tube and came down heels over ears. I don't know
what's happened to Marnik." He fired another burst, and swore.
"Missed him!"

"Assassins' Truce! Assassins' Truce!" a voice howled out of
the descent tube. "Hold your fire, we want to parley."

"Who is it?" Dirzed shouted, over Olirzon's shoulder. "You,
Sarnax? Come on out; we won't shoot."

The young Assassin with the mustache and chin-beard emerged
from the descent tube, his weapons sheathed and his clasped
hands extended in front of him in a peculiarly ecclesiastical-
looking manner. Dirzed and Olirzon stepped out of the gun
room, followed by Verkan Vall and Hadron Dalla. Olirzon had
left his submachine gun behind. They met the other Assassin by
the rim of the fountain pool.

"Lady Dallona of Hadron," the Starpha Assassin began. "I
and my colleagues, in the employ of the family of Starpha, have
received orders from our clients to withdraw our protection
from you, and to discarnate you, and all with you who undertake to protect or support you." That much sounded like a
recitation of some established formula; then his voice became
more conversational. "I and my colleagues, Erarno and Kirzol
and Harnif, offer our apologies for the barbarity of the servants
of the family of Starpha, in attacking without declaration of
cessation of friendship. Was anybody hurt or discarnated?"

"None of us," Olirzon said. "How about Marnik?"

"He was warned before hostilities were begun against him,"
Sarnax replied. "We will allow five minutes until—"

Olirzon, who had been looking up the well, suddenly sprang
at Dalla, knocking her flat, and at the same time jerking out his
pistol. Before he could raise it, a shot banged from above and
he fell on his face. Dirzed, Verkan Vall, and Sarnax all drew
their pistols, but whoever had fired the shot had vanished.
There was an outburst of shouting above.

"Get to cover," Sarnax told the others. "We'll let you know
when we're ready to attack; we'll have to deal with whoever
fired that shot, first." He looked at the dead body on the floor,
exclaimed angrily, and hurried to the ascent tube, springing
upward.

Verkan Vall replaced the small pistol in his shoulder holster and took Olirzon's belt, with his knife and heavier pistol.

"Well, there you see," Dirzed said, as they went back to the gun room. "So much for political expediency."

"I think I understand why your picture and the Lady Dallona's were exhibited so widely," Verkan Vall said. "Now anybody would recognize your bodies, and blame the Statisticalists for discarnating you."

"That thought had occurred to me, Lord Virzal," Dirzed said. "I suppose our bodies will be astrociously but not unidentifiably mutilated, to further enrage the public," he added placidly. "If I get out of this carnate, I'm going to pay somebody off for it."

After a few minutes, there was more shouting of "Assassins' Truce!" from the descent tube. The two Assassins, Erarno and Kirzol, emerged, dragging the gamekeeper, Tarnod, between them. The upper-servant's face was bloody, and his jaw seemed to be broken. Sarnax followed, carrying a long hunting pistol in his hand.

"Here he is!" he announced. "He fired during Assassins' Truce; he's subject to Assassins' Justice!"

He nodded to the others. They threw the gamekeeper forward on the floor, and Sarnax shot him through the head, then tossed the pistol down beside him. "Any more of these people who violate the decencies will be treated similarly," he promised.

"Thank you, Sarnax," Dirzed spoke up. "But we lost an Assassin; discarnating this lackey won't equalize that. We think you should retire one of your number."

"That at least, Dirzed; wait a moment."

The three Assassins conferred at some length. Then Sarnax hooked fingers and clapped shoulders with his companions.

"See you in the next reincarnation, brothers," he told them. walking toward the gun-room door, where Verkan Vall, Dalla and Dirzed stood. "I'm joining you people. You had two Assassins when the parley began, you'll have two when the shooting starts."

Verkan Vall looked at Dirzed in some surprise. Hadron Dalla's Assassin nodded.

"He's entitled to do that, Lord Virzal; the Assassins' code provides for such changes of allegiance."

"Welcome, Sarnax," Verkan Vall said, hooking fingers with him. "I hope we'll all be together when this is over."

"We will be," Sarnax assured him cheerfully. "Discarnate. We won't get out of this in the body, Lord Virzal."

A submachine gun hammered from above, the bullets lashing the fountain pool; the water actually steamed, so great was their velocity.

"All right!" a voice called down. "Assassins' Truce is over!"

Another burst of automatic fire smashed out the lights at the bottom of the ascent tube. Dirzed and Dalla struggled across the room, pushing a heavy steel cabinet between them; Verkan Vall who was holding Olirzon's submachine gun, moved aside to allow them to drop it on the edge in the open doorway, then wedged the door half-shut against it. Sarnax came over, bringing rifles, hunting pistols, and ammunition.

"What's the situation up there?" Verkan Vall asked him. "What force have they, and why did they turn against us?"

"Lord Virzal!" Dirzed objected, scandalized. "You have no right to ask Sarnax to betray confidences!"

Sarnax spat against the door. "In the face of Jirzyn of Starpha!" he said. "And in the face of his *zortan* mother, and of his father, whoever he was! Dirzed, do not talk foolishly; one does not speak of betraying betrayers." He turned to Verkan Vall. "They have three menservants of the family of Starpha; your Assassin, Olirzon, discarnated the other three. There is one of Prince Jirzyn's poor relations, named Girzad. There are three other men, Volitionalist precinct workers, who came with Girzad, and four Assassins, the three who were here, and one who came with Girzad. Eleven, against the three of us."

"The four of us, Sarnax," Dalla corrected. She had buckled on a hunting pistol, and had a light deer rifle under her arm.

Something moved at the bottom of the descent tube. Verkan Vall gave it a short burst, though it was probably only a dummy, dropped to draw fire.

"The four of us, Lady Dallona," Sarnax agreed. "As to your other Assassin, the one who stayed in the airboat, I don't know how he fared. You see, about twenty minutes ago, this Girzad arrived in an airboat, with an Assassin and these three Volitionist workers. Erarno and I were at the top of the dome when he came in. He told us that he had orders from Prince Jirzyn to discarnate the Lady Dallona and Dirzed at once. Tarnod, the gamekeeper"—Sarnax spat ceremoniously against the door again— "told him you were here, and that Marnik was one of your men. He was going to shoot Marnik at once, but Erarno and I and his Assassin stopped him. We warned Marnik about the change in the situation, according to the code, expecting Marnik to go down here and join you. Instead, he lifted the airboat, zoomed over Girzad's boat, and let go a rocket blast, setting Girzad's boat on fire. Well, that was a hostile act, so we all fired after him. We must have hit something, because the boat went down, trailing smoke, about ten miles away. Girzad got another airboat out of the hangar and he and his Assassin started after your man. About that time, your Assassin, Olirzon—happy reincarnation to him—came up, and the Starpha servants fired at him, and he fired back and discarnated two of them, and then jumped down the descent tube. One of the servants jumped after him; I found his body at the bottom when I came down to warn you formally. You know what happened after that."

"But why did Prince Jirzyn order our discarnation?" Dalla wanted to know. "Was it to blame the Statisticalists with it?"

Sarnax, about to answer, broke off suddenly and began firing at the opening of the ascent tube with a hunting pistol.

"I got him," he said, in a pleased tone. "That was Erarno; he was always playing tricks with the tubes, climbing down against negative gravity and up against positive gravity. His body will float up to the top. . . . Why, Lady Dallona, that was only part of it. You didn't hear about the big scandal, on the newscast, then?"

"We didn't have it on. What scandal?"

Sarnax laughed. "Oh, the very father and family-head of all scandals! You ought to know about it, because you started it; that's why Prince Jirzyn wants you out of the body. You devised a process by which people could give themselves memory-recalls of previous reincarnations, didn't you? And distributed apparatus to do it with? And gave one set to young Tarnov, the son of Lord Tirzov of Fastor?"

Dalla nodded. Sarnax continued:

"Well, last evening, Tarnov of Fastor used his recall outfit, and what do you think? It seems that thirty years ago, in his last reincarnation, he was Jirzid of Starpha, Jirzyn's older brother. Jirzid was betrothed to the Lady Annitra of Zabna. Well, his younger brother was carrying on a clandestine affair with the Lady Annitra, and he also wanted the title of Prince and family-head of Starpha. So he bribed this fellow Tarnod, whom I had the pleasure of discarnating, and who was an underservant here at the hunting lodge. Between them, they shot Jirzid during a boar hunt. An accident, of course. So Jirzyn married the Lady Annitra, and when old Prince Jarnid, his father, discarnated a year later, he succeeded to the title. And immediately, Tarnod was made head game-keeper here."

"What did I tell you, Lord Virzal? I knew that son of a *zortan* had something on Jirzyn of Starpha!" Dirzed exclaimed. "A nice family, this of Starpha!"

"Well, that's not the end of it," Sarnax continued. "This morning, Tarnov of Fastor, late Jirzid of Starpha, went before the High Court of Estates and entered suit to change his name to Jirzid of Starpha and laid claim to the title of Starpha family-head. The case has just been entered, so there's been no hearing, but there's the blazes of an argument among all the nobles about it—some are claiming that the individuality doesn't change from one reincarnation to the next, and others claiming that property and titles should pass along the line of physical descent, no matter what individuality has reincarnated into what body. They're the ones who want the Lady Dallona discarnated and her discoveries suppressed. And there's talk about revising the entire system of estate ownership and estate inheritance. Oh, it's an utter obscenity of a business!"

"This," Verkan Vall told Dalla, "is something we will not emphasize when we get home." That was as close as he dared come to it, but she caught his meaning. The working of major changes in outtime social structure was not viewed with approval by the Paratime Commission on the First Level. "*If* we get home," he added. Then an idea occurred to him.

"Dirzed, Sarnax; this place must have been used by the leaders of the Volitionists for top-level conferences. Is there a secret passage anywhere?"

Sarnax shook his head. "Not from here. There is one on the floor above, but they control it. And even if there were one down here, they would be guarding the outlet."

"That's what I was counting on. I'd hoped to simulate an escape that way, and then make a rush up the regular tubes." Verkan Vall shrugged. "I suppose Marnik's our only chance. I hope he got away safely."

"He was going for help? I was surprised that an Assassin would desert his client; I should have thought of that," Sarnax said. "Well, even if he got down carnate, and if Girzad didn't catch him, he'd still be afoot ten miles from the nearest city unit. That gives us a little chance—about one in a thousand."

"Is there any way they can get at us except by those tubes?"
Dalla asked.

"They could cut a hole in the floor, or burn one through,"
Sarnax replied. "They have plenty of thermite. They could
detonate a charge of explosives over our heads, or clear out of
the dome and drop one down the well. They could use lethal
gas or radiodust, but their Assassins wouldn't permit such illegal methods. Or they could shoot sleep-gas down at us, and
then come down and cut our throats at their leisure."

"We'll have to get out of this room, then," Verkan Vall
decided. "They know we've barricaded ourselves in here; this is
where they'll attack. So we'll patrol the perimeter of the well;
we'll be out of danger from above if we keep close to the wall.
And we'll inspect all the rooms on this floor for evidence of
cutting through from above."

Sarnax nodded. "That's sense, Lord Virzal. How about the
lifter tubes?"

"We'll have to barricade them. Sarnax, you and Dirzed know
the layout of this place better than the Lady Dallona or I;
suppose you two check the rooms, while we cover the tubes and
the well," Verkan Vall directed. "Come on, now."

They pushed the door wide open and went out past the
cabinet. Hugging the wall, they began a slow circuit of the well,
Verkan Vall in the lead with the submachine gun, then Sarnax
and Dirzed, the former with a heavy boar rifle and the latter
with a hunting pistol in each hand, and Hadron Dalla brought
up in the rear with her rifle. It was she who noticed a movement along the rim of the balcony above and snapped a shot at
it; there was a crash above, and a shower of glass and plastic
and metal fragments rattled on the pavement of the court.
Somebody had been trying to lower a scanner or a visiplate
pickup, or something of the sort; the exact nature of the instrument was not evident from the wreckage Dalla's bullet had
made of it.

The rooms Dirzed and Sarnax entered were all quiet; nobody
seemed to be attempting to cut through the ceiling, fifteen feet
above. They dragged furniture from a couple of rooms, blocking the openings of the lifter tubes, and continued around the
well until they had reached the gun room again.

Dirzed suggested that they move some of the weapons and
ammunition stored there to Prince Jirzyn's private apartment,
halfway around to the lifter tubes, so that another place of

refuge would be stocked with munitions in event of their being driven from the gun room.

Leaving him on guard outside, Verkan Vall, Dalla and Sarnax entered the gun room and began gathering weapons and boxes of ammunition. Dalla finished packing her game bag with the recorded data and notes of her experiments. Verkan Vall selected four more of the heavy hunting pistols, more accurate than his shoulder-holster weapon or the dead Olirzon's belt arm, and capable of either full- or semi-automatic fire. Sarnax chose a couple more boar rifles. Dalla slung her bag of recorded notes, and another bag of ammunition, and secured another deer rifle. They carried this accumulation of munitions to the private apartments of Prince Jirzyn, dumping everything in the middle of the drawing room, except the bag of notes, from which Dalla refused to separate herself.

"Maybe we'd better put some stuff over in one of the rooms on the other side of the well," Dirzed suggested. "They haven't really begun to come after us; when they do, we'll probably be attacked from two or three directions at once."

They returned to the gun room, casting anxious glances at the edge of the balcony above and at the barricade they had erected across the openings to the lifter tubes. Verkan Vall was not satisfied with this last; it looked to him as though they had provided a breastwork for somebody to fire on them from, more than anything else.

He was about to step around the cabinet which partially blocked the gun-room door when he glanced up and saw a six-foot circle on the ceiling turning slowly brown. There was a smell of scorched plastic. He grabbed Sarnax by the arm and pointed.

"Thermite," the Assassin whispered. "The ceiling's got six inches of spaceship insulation between it and the floor above; it'll take them a few minutes to burn through it." He stopped and pushed on the barricade, shoving it into the room. "Keep back; they'll probably drop a grenade or so through, first, before they jump down. If we're quick, we can get a couple of them."

Dirzed and Sarnax crouched, one at either side of the door, with weapons ready. Verkan Vall and Dalla had been ordered, rather peremptorily, to stay behind them; in a place of danger, an Assassin was obliged to shield his client. Verkan Vall, unable to see what was going on inside the room, kept his eyes and his gun muzzle on the barricade across the openings to the lifter tubes, the erection of which he was now regretting as a major tactical error.

Inside the gun room, there was a sudden crash, as the circle of thermite burned through and a section of ceiling dropped out and hit the floor. Instantly, Dirzed flung himself back against Verkan Vall, and there was a tremendous explosion inside, followed by another and another. A second or so passed, then Dirzed, leaping around the corner of the door, began firing rapidly into the room. From the other side of the door, Sarnax began blazing away with his rifle. Verkan Vall kept his position, covering the lifter tubes.

Suddenly, from behind the barricade, a blue-white gun flash leaped into being, and a pistol banged. He sprayed the opening between a couch and a section of bookcase from whence it had come, releasing his trigger as the gun rose with the recoil, squeezing and releasing and squeezing again. Then he jumped to his feet.

"Come on, the other place; hurry!" he ordered.

Sarnax swore in exasperation. "Help me with her, Dirzed!" he implored.

Verkan Vall turned his head, to see the two Assassins drag Dalla to her feet and hustle her away from the gun room; she was quite senseless, and they had to drag her between them. Verkan Vall gave a quick glance into the gun room; two of the Starpha servants and a man in rather flashy civil dress were lying on the floor, where they had been shot as they had jumped down from above. He saw a movement at the edge of the irregular smoking hole in the ceiling and gave it a short burst, then fired another at the exit from the descent tube. Then he took to his heels and followed the Assassins and Hadron Dalla into Prince Jirzyn's apartment.

As he ran through the open door, the Assassins were letting Dalla down into a chair; they instantly threw themselves into the work of barricading the doorway so as to provide cover and at the same time allow them to fire out into the central well.

For an instant, as he bent over her, he thought Dalla had been killed, an assumption justified by his knowledge of the deadliness of Akor-Neb bullets. Then he saw her eyelids flicker. A moment later, he had the explanation of her escape. The bullet had hit the game bag at her side; it was full of spools of metal tape, in metal cases, and notes in written form, pyrographed upon sheets of plastic ring-fastened into metal binders. Because of their extreme velocity, Akor-Neb bullets were sure killers when they struck animal tissue, but for the same reason, they had very poor penetration on hard objects. The alloy-steel tape, and the steel spools and spool cases, and the notebook binders, had been enough to shatter the little bullet into tiny splinters of magnesium-nickel alloy, and the stout leather back of the game bag had stopped all of these. But the impact, even distributed as it had been through the contents of the bag, had been enough to knock the girl unconscious.

He found a bottle of some sort of brandy and a glass on a serving table nearby and poured her a drink, holding it to her lips. She spluttered over the first mouthful, then took the glass from him and sipped the rest.

"What happened?" she asked. "I thought those bullets were sure death."

"Your notes. The bullet hit the bag. Are you all right now?"

She finished the brandy. "I think so." She put a hand into the game bag and brought out a snarled and tangled mess of steel tape. "Oh, *blast!* That stuff was important; all the records on the preliminary auto-recall experiments." She shrugged. "Well, it wouldn't have been worth much more if I'd stopped that bullet, myself." She slipped the strap over her shoulder and started to rise.

As she did, a bedlam of firing broke out, both from the two Assassins at the door and from outside. They both hit the floor and crawled out of line of the partly open door; Verkan Vall recovered his submachine gun, which he had set down beside Dalla's chair. Sarnax was firing with his rifle at some target in the direction of the lifter tubes; Dirzed lay slumped over the barricade, and one glance at his crumpled figure was enough to tell Verkan Vall that he was dead.

"You fill magazines for us," he told Dalla, then crawled to Dirzed's place at the door. "What happened, Sarnax?"

"They shoved over the barricade at the lifter tubes and came out into the well. I got a couple, they got Dirzed, and now they're holed up in rooms all around the circle. They—aah!" He fired three shots, quickly, around the edge of the door. "That stopped that." The Assassin crouched to insert a fresh magazine into his rifle.

Verkan Vall risked one eye around the corner of the doorway, and as he did, there was a red flash and a dull roar, unlike the blue flashes and sharp cracking reports of the pistols and rifles, from the doorway of the gun room. He wondered, for a split second, if it might be one of the fowling pieces he had seen there, and then something whizzed past his head and exploded with a soft *plop* behind him. Turning, he saw a pool of gray vapor beginning to spread in the middle of the room. Dalla must have got a breath of it, for she was slumped over the chair from which she had just risen.

Dropping the submachine gun and gulping a lungful of fresh air from outside, Verkan Vall rushed to her, caught her by the heels, and dragged her into Prince Jirzyn's bedroom, beyond. Leaving her in the middle of the floor, he took another deep breath and returned to the drawing room, where Sarnax was already overcome by the sleep-gas.

He saw the serving table from which he had got the brandy, and dragged it over to the bedroom door, overturning it and laying it across the doorway, its legs in the air. Like most Akor-Neb serving tables, it had a gravity-counteraction unit under it; he set this for double minus-gravitation and snapped it on. As it was now above the inverted table, the table did not rise, but a tendril of sleep-gas, curling toward it, bent upward and drifted away from the doorway. Satisfied that he had made a temporary barrier against the sleep-gas, Verkan Vall secured Dalla's hunting pistol and spare magazines and lay down at the bedroom door.

For some time, there was silence outside. Then the besiegers evidently decided that the sleep-gas attack had been a success. An Assassin wearing a gas mask and carrying a submachine gun appeared in the doorway, and behind him came a tall man in a tan tunic, similarly masked. They stepped into the room and looked around.

Knowing that he would be shooting over a two hundred percent negative gravitation field, Verkan Vall aimed for the Assassin's belt buckle and squeezed. The bullet caught him in the throat. Evidently the bullet had not only been lifted in the negative gravitation, but lifted point-first and deflected upward. He held his front sight just above the other man's knee, and hit him in the chest.

As he fired, he saw a wisp of gas come sliding around the edge of the inverted table. There was silence outside, and for an instant he was tempted to abandon his post and go to the bathroom, back of the bedroom, for wet towels to improvise a mask. Then, when he tried to crawl backward, he could not. There was an impression of distant shouting which turned to a roaring sound in his head. He tried to lift his pistol, but it slipped from his fingers.

*   *   *

When consciousness returned, he was lying on his back, and something cold and rubbery was pressing into his face. He raised his arms to fight off whatever it was, and opened his eyes, to find he was staring directly at the red oval and winged bullet of the Society of Assassins. A hand caught his wrist as he reached for the small pistol under his arm. The pressure on his face eased.

"It's all right, Lord Virzal," a voice came to him. "Assassins' Truce!"

He nodded stupidly and repeated the words. "Assassins' Truce; I won't shoot. What happened?"

Then he sat up and looked around. Prince Jirzyn's bedchamber was full of Assassins. Dalla, recovering from her touch of sleep-gas, was sitting groggily in a chair, while five or six of them fussed around her, getting in each other's way, handing her drinks, chafing her wrists, holding damp cloths on her brow. That was standard procedure, when any group of males thought Dalla needed any help. Another Assassin, beside the bed, was putting away an oxygen-mask outfit, and the Assassin who had prevented Verkan Vall from drawing his pistol was his own follower, Marnik. And Klarnood, the Assassin-President, was sitting on the foot of the bed, smoking one of Prince Jirzyn's monogrammed and crested cigarettes, critically.

Verkan Vall looked at Marnik, and then at Klarnood, and back to Marnik.

"You got through," he said. "Good work, Marnik; I thought they'd downed you."

"They did; I had to crash-land in the woods. I went about a mile on foot, and then I found a man and woman and two children, hiding in one of these little log rain shelters. They had an airboat, a good one. It seemed that rioting had broken out in the city unit where they lived, and they'd taken to the woods till things quieted down again. I offered them Assassins' protection if they'd take me to Assassins' Hall, and they did."

"By luck, I was in when Marnik arrived," Klarnood took over. "We brought three boatloads of men, and came here at once. Just as we got here, two boatloads of Starpha dependents arrived; they tried to give us an argument, and we discarnated the lot of them. Then we came down here, crying Assassins' Truce. One of the Starpha Assassins, Kirzol, was still carnate; he told us what had been going on." The President-General's face became grim. "You know, I take a rather poor view of

Prince Jirzyn's procedure in this matter, not to mention that of his underlings. I'll have to speak to him about this. Now, how about you and the Lady Dallona? What do you intend doing?"

"We're getting out of here," Verkan Vall said. "I'd like air transport and protection as far as Ghamma, to the establishment of the family of Zorda. Brarnend of Zorda has a private space yacht; he'll get us to Venus."

Klarnood gave a sigh of obvious relief. "I'll have you and the Lady Dallona airborne and off for Ghamma as soon as you wish," he promised. "I will, frankly, be delighted to see the last of both of you. The Lady Dallona has started a fire here at Darsh that won't burn out in a half-century, and who knows what it may consume." He was interrupted by a heaving shock that made the underground dome dwelling shake like a light airboat in turbulence. Even eighty feet under the ground, they could hear a continued crashing roar. It was an appreciable interval before the sound and the shock ceased.

For an instant, there was silence, and then an excited bedlam of shouting broke from the Assassins in the room. Klarnood's face was frozen in horror.

"That was a fission bomb!" he exclaimed. "The first one that has been exploded on this planet in hostility in a thousand years!" He turned to Verkan Vall. "If you feel well enough to walk, Lord Virzal, come with us. I must see what's happened."

They hurried from the room and went streaming up the ascent tube to the top of the dome. About forty miles away, to the south, Verkan Vall saw the sinister thing that he had seen on so many other time-lines, in so many other paratime sectors—a great pillar of varicolored fire-shot smoke, rising to a mushroom head fifty thousand feet away.

"Well, that's it," Klarnood said sadly. "That is civil war."

"May I make a suggestion, Assassin-President?" Verkan Vall asked. "I understand that Assassins' Truce is binding even upon non-Assassins; is that correct?"

"Well, not exactly; it's generally kept by such non-Assassins as want to remain in their present reincarnations, though."

"That's what I meant. Well, suppose you declare a general, plant-wide Assassin's Truce in this political war, and make the leaders of both parties responsible for keeping it. Publish lists of the top two or three thousand Statisticalists and Volitionalists, starting with Mirzark of Bashad and Prince Jirzyn of Starpha, and inform them that they will be assassinated, in order, if the fighting doesn't cease."

"Well!" A smile grew on Klarnood's face. "Lord Virzal, my thanks; a good suggestion. I'll try it. And furthermore, I'll withdraw all Assassin protection permanently from anybody involved in political activity, and forbid any Assassin to accept any retainer connected with political factionalism. It's about time our members stopped discarnating each other in these political squabbles." He pointed to the three airboats drawn up on the top of the dome; speedy black craft, bearing the red oval and winged bullet. "Take your choice, Lord Virzal. I'll lend you a couple of my men, and you'll be in Ghamma ·in three hours." He hooked fingers and clapped shoulders with Verkan Vall, bent over Dalla's hand. "I still like you, Lord Virzal, and I have seldom met a more charming lady than you, Lady Dallona. But I sincerely hope I never see either of you again."

The ship for Dhergabar was driving north and west; at seventy thousand feet, it was still daylight, but the world below was wrapping itself in darkness. In the big visiscreens, which served in lieu of the windows which could never have withstood the pressure and friction heat of the ship's speed, the sun was sliding out of sight over the horizon to port. Verkan Vall and Dalla sat together, watching the blazing western sky—the sky of their own First Level time-line.

"I blame myself terribly, Vall," Dalla was saying. "And I don't mean any of them the least harm. All I was interested in was learning the facts. I know, that sounds like 'I didn't know it was loaded,' but—"

"It sounds to me like those Fourth Level Europo-American Sector physicists who are giving themselves guilt complexes because they designed an atomic bomb," Verkan Vall replied. "All you were interested in was learning the facts. Well, as a scientist, that's all you're supposed to be interested in. You don't have to worry about any special or political implications. People have to learn to live with newly discovered facts; if they don't, they die of them."

"But, Vall; that sounds dreadfully irresponsible—"

"Does it? You're worrying about the results of your reincarnation memory-recall discoveries, the shootings and riotings and the bombing we saw." He touched the pommel of Olirzon's knife, which he still wore. "You're no more guilty of that than the man who forged this blade is guilty of the death of Marnark of Bashad; if he'd never lived, I'd have killed Marnark with some other knife somebody else made. And what's more, you can't know the results of your discoveries. All you can see is a thin film of events on the surface of an immediate situation, so you can't say whether the long-term results will be beneficial or calamitous.

"Take this Fourth Level Europo-American atomic bomb, for example. I choose that because we both know that sector, but I could think of a hundred other examples in other paratime areas. Those people, because of deforestation, bad agricultural methods and general mismanagement, are eroding away their arable soil at an alarming rate. At the same time, they are breeding like rabbits. In other words, each successive generation has less and less food to divide among more and more people, and, for inherited traditional and superstitious reasons, they refuse to adopt any rational program of birth control and population limitation.

"But, fortunately, they now have the atomic bomb, and they are developing radioactive poisons, weapons of mass effect. And their racial, nationalistic and ideological conflicts are rapidly reaching the explosion point. A series of all-out atomic wars is just what that sector needs, to bring their population down to their world's carrying capacity; in a century or so, the inventors of the atomic bomb will be hailed as the saviors of their species."

"But how about my work on the Akor-Neb Sector?" Dalla asked. "It seems that my memory-recall technique is more explosive than any fission bomb. I've laid the train for a century-long reign of anarchy!"

"I doubt that; I think Klarnood will take hold, now that he has committed himself to it. You know, in spite of his sanguinary profession, he's the nearest thing to a real man of goodwill I've found on that sector. And here's something else you haven't considered. Our own First Level life expectancy is from four to five hundred years. That's the main reason why we've accomplished as much as we have. We have, individually, time to accomplish things. On the Akor-Neb Sector, a scientist or artist or scholar or statesman will grow senile and die before he's as old as either of us. But now, a young student of twenty or so can take one of your auto-recall treatments and immediately have available all the knowledge and experience gained in four or five previous lives. He can start where he left off in his last reincarnation. In other words, you've made those people time-binders, individually as well as racially. Isn't that worth the temporary discarnation of a lot of ward-heelers and plug-uglies, or even a few decent types like Dirzed and Olirzon? If it isn't, I don't know what scales of values you're using."

"Vall!" Dalla's eyes glowed with enthusiasm. "I never thought of that! And you said 'temporary discarnation.' That's just what it is. Dirzed and Olirzon and the others aren't dead; they're just waiting, discarnate, between physical lives. You know, in the sacred writings of one of the Fourth Level peoples it is stated: 'Death is the last enemy.' By proving that death is just a cyclic condition of continued individual existence, these people have conquered their last enemy."

"Last enemy but one," Verkan Vall corrected. "They still have one enemy to go, an enemy within themselves. Call it semantic confusion, or illogic, or incomprehension, or just plain stupidity. Like Klarnood, stymied by verbal objections to something labeled 'political intervention.' He'd never have consented to use the power of his Society if he hadn't been shocked out of his inhibitions by that nuclear bomb. Or the Statisticalists, trying to create a classless order of society through a political program which would only result in universal servitude to an omnipotent government. Or the Volitionalist nobles, trying to preserve their hereditary feudal privileges, and now they can't even agree on a definition of the term 'hereditary.' Might they not recover all the silly prejudices of their past lives, along with the knowledge and wisdom?"

"But . . . I thought you said—" Dalla was puzzled, a little hurt.

Verkan Vall's arm squeezed around her waist, and he laughed comfortingly.

"You see? Any sort of result is possible, good or bad. So don't blame yourself in advance for something you can't possibly estimate." An idea occurred to him, and he straightened in the seat. "Tell you what. If you people at Rhogom Foundation get the problem of discarnate paratime transposition licked by then, let's you and I go back to the Akor-Neb Sector in about a hundred years and see what sort of a mess those people have made of things."

"A hundred years; that would be Year Twenty-two of the next millennium. It's a date, Vall; we'll do it."

They bent to light their cigarettes together at his lighter.

When they raised their heads again and got the flame glare out of their eyes, the sky was purple-black, dusted with stars, and dead ahead, spilling up over the horizon, was a golden glow— the lights of Dhergabar and home.

ARISTOTLE AND THE GUN

by L. Sprague de Camp

Now one of science fiction's elder statesmen, L. Sprague de Camp (1907–) is as distinguished as his name. His sf career began in 1938, and since that date he has produced dozens of solid novels and story collections of fantasy and science fiction, in addition to dozens of notable nonfiction books for adults and children. He is also the biographer of two of the most important figures in the fantasy/horror field, H. P. Lovecraft (Lovecraft: A Biography, 1975) and Robert E. Howard (Dark Valley Destiny: The Life of Robert E. Howard, 1983). Novels like Lest Darkness Fall (1941) Rogue Queen (1951), and Divide and Rule (1948) belong on the shelf of every sf reader, as does The Best of L. Sprague de Camp (1977). Among his honors are the International Fantasy Award, the Gandalf Award, a Grand Master Nebula, and a World Fantasy Life Achievement Award.

From:

> Sherman Weaver, Librarian
> The Palace
> Paumanok, Sewanhaki
> Sachimate of Lenape
> Flower Moon 3, 3097

To:

Messire Markos Koukidas
Consulate of the Balkan Commonwealth
Kataapa, Muskhogian Federation

My dear Consul:

You have no doubt heard of our glorious victory at Ptaksit, when our noble Sachim destroyed the armored chivalry of the Mengwe by the brilliant use of pikemen and archery. (I suggested it to him years ago, but never mind.) Sagoyewatha and most of his Senecas fell, and the Oneidas broke before our countercharge. The envoys from the Grand Council of the Long House arrive tomorrow for a peace-pauwau. The roads to the South are open again, so I send you my long-promised account of the events that brought me from my own world into this one.

If you could have stayed longer on your last visit, I think I could have made the matter clear, despite the language difficulty and my hardness of hearing. But perhaps, if I give you a simple narrative, in the order in which things happened to me, truth will transpire.

Know, then, that I was born into a world that looks like this one on the map, but is very different as regards human affairs. I tried to tell you some of the triumphs of our natural philosophers, of our machines and discoveries. No doubt you thought me a first-class liar, though you were too polite to say so.

Nonetheless, my tale is true, though for reasons that will appear I cannot prove it. I was one of those natural philosophers. I commanded a group of younger philosophers, engaged in a task called a *project*, at a center of learning named Brookhaven, on the south shore of Sewanhaki twenty parasangs east of Paumanok. Paumanok itself was known as Brooklyn, and formed part of an even larger city called New York.

My project had to do with the study of space-time. (Never mind what that means but read on.) At this center we had learned to get vast amounts of power from seawater by what we called a fusion process. By this process we could concentrate so much power in a small space that we could warp the entity called space-time and cause things to travel in time as our other machines traveled in space.

When our calculations showed that we could theoretically hurl an object back in time, we began to build a machine for testing this hypothesis. First we built a small pilot model. In this we sent small objects back in time for short periods.

We began with inanimate objects. Then we found that a rabbit or rat could also be projected without harm. The time-translation would not be permanent; rather, it acted like one of these rubber balls the Hesperians play games with. The object would stay in the desired time for a period determined by the power used to project it and its own mass, and would then return spontaneously to the time and place from which it started.

We had reported our progress regularly, but my chief had other matters on his mind and did not read our reports for many months. When he got a report saying that we were completing a machine to hurl human beings back in time, however, he awoke to what was going on, read our previous reports, and called me in.

"Sherm," he said, "I've been discussing this project with Washington, and I'm afraid they take a dim view of it."

"Why?" said I, astonished.

"Two reasons. For one thing, they think you've gone off the reservation. They're much more interested in the Antarctic Reclamation Project and want to concentrate all our appropriations and brain power on it.

"For another, they're frankly scared of this time machine of yours. Suppose you went back, say, to the time of Alexander the Great and shot Alexander before he got started? That would change all later history, and we'd go like candles."

"Ridiculous," I said.

"What, what *would* happen?"

"Our equations are not conclusive, but there are several possibilities. As you will see if you read Report No. 9, it depends on whether space-time has a positive or negative curvature. If positive, any disturbance in the past tends to be ironed out in subsequent history, so that things become more and more nearly identical with what they would have been anyway. If negative, then events will diverge more and more from their original pattern with time.

"Now, as I showed in this report, the chances are overwhelmingly in favor of a positive curvature. However, we intend to take every precaution and make our first tests for short periods, with a minimum—"

"That's enough," said my superior, holding up a hand. "It's very interesting, but the decision has already been made.'

"What do you mean?"

"I mean Project A-257 is to be closed down and a final report written at once. The machines are to be dismantled, and the group will be put to work on another project."

"What?" I shouted. "But you can't stop us just when we're on the verge—"

"I'm sorry, Sherm, but I can. That's what the AEC decided at yesterday's meeting. It hasn't been officially announced, but they gave me positive orders to kill the project as soon as I got back here."

"Of all the lousy, arbitrary, benighted—"

"I know how you feel, but I have no choice."

I lost my temper and defied him, threatening to go ahead with the project anyway. It was ridiculous, because he could easily dismiss me for insubordination. However, I knew he valued my ability and counted on his wanting to keep me for that reason. But he was clever enough to have his cake and eat it.

"If that's how you feel," he said, "the section is abolished here and now. Your group will be broken up and assigned to other projects. You'll be kept at your present rating with the title of consultant. Then when you're willing to talk sense, perhaps we can find you a suitable job."

I stamped out his office and went home to brood. I ought now to tell you something of myself. I am old enough to be objective, I hope. And, as I have but a few years left, there is no point in pretense.

I have always bheen a solitary, misanthropic man. I had little interest in or liking of my fellow man, who naturally paid me back in the same coin. I was awkward and ill at ease in company. I had a genius for saying the wrong thing and making a fool of myself.

I never understood people. Even when I watched and planned my own actions with the greatest care, I never could tell how others would react to them. To me men were and are an unpredictable, irrational, and dangerous species of hairless ape. While I could avoid some of my worst gaffes by keeping my own counsel and watching my every word, they did not like that either. They considered me a cold, stiff, unfriendly sort of person when I was only trying to be polite and avoid offending them.

I never married. At the time of which I speak, I was verging on middle age without a single close friend and no more acquaintances than my professional work required.

My only interest, outside my work, was a hobby of the history of science. Unlike most of my fellow philosophers, I was historically minded, with a good smattering of a classical education. I belonged to the History of Science Society and wrote papers on the history of science for its periodical *Isis*.

I went back to my little rented house, feeling like Galileo. He was a scientist persecuted for his astronomical theories by the religious authorities of my world several centuries before my time, as Georg Schwartzhorn was a few years ago in this world's Europe.

I felt I had been born too soon. If only the world were scientifically more advanced, my genius would be appreciated and my personal difficulties solved.

Well, I thought, why is the world not scientifically more advanced? I reviewed the early growth of science. Why had not your fellow countrymen, when they made a start towards a scientific age two thousand to twenty-five hundred years ago, kept at it until they made science the self-supporting, self-accelerating thing it at last became—in my world, that is?

I knew the answers that historians of science had worked out. One was the effect of slavery, which made work disgraceful to a free man and therefore made experiment and invention unattractive because they looked like work. Another was the primitive state of the mechanical arts: things like making clear glass and accurate measuring devices. Another was the Hellenes' fondness for spinning cosmic theories without enough facts to go on, the result of which was that most of their theories were wildly wrong.

Well, thought I, could a man go back to this period and, by applying a stimulus at the right time and place, give the necessary push to set the whole trend rolling off in the right direction?

People had written fantastic stories about a man's going back in time and overawing the natives by a display of the discoveries of his own later era. More often than not, such a time-traveling hero came to a bad end. The people of the earlier time killed him as a witch, or he met with an accident, or something happened to keep him from changing history. But, knowing these dangers, I could forestall them by careful planning.

It would do little or no good to take back some major invention, like a printing press or an automobile, and turn it over to the ancients in the hope of grafting it on their culture. I could not teach them to work it in a reasonable time; and if it broke down or ran out of supplies, there would be no way to get it running again.

What I had to do was to find a key mind and implant in it an appreciation of sound scientific method. He would have to be somebody who would have been important in any event, or I could not count on his influence's spreading far and wide.

After study of Sarton and other historians of science, I picked Aristotle. You have heard of him, have you not? He existed in your world just as he did in mine. In fact, up to Aristotle's time our worlds were one and the same.

Aristotle was one of the greatest minds of all time. In my world, he was the first encyclopedist; the first man who tried to know everything, write down everything, and explain everything. He did much good original scientific work, too, mostly in biology.

However, Aristotle tried to cover so much ground, and accepted so many fables as facts, that he did much harm to science as well as good. For, when a man of such colossal intellect goes wrong, he carries with him whole generations of weaker minds who cite him as an infallible authority. Like his colleagues, Aristotle never appreciated the need for constant verification. Thus, though he was married twice, he said that men have more teeth than women. He never thought to ask either of his wives to open her mouth for a count. He never grasped the need for invention and experiment.

Now, if I could catch Aristotle at the right period of his career, perhaps I could give him a push in the right direction.

When would that be? Normally, one would take him as a young man. But Aristotle's entire youth, from seventeen to thirty-seven, was spent in Athens listening to Plato's lectures. I did not wish to compete with Plato, an overpowering personality who could argue rings around anybody. His viewpoint was mystical and antiscientific, the very thing I wanted to steer Aristotle away from. Many of Aristotle's intellectual vices can be traced back to Plato's influence.

I did not think it wise to present myself in Athens either during Aristotle's early period, when he was a student under Plato, or later, when he headed his own school. I could not pass myself off as a Hellene, and the Hellenes of that time had a contempt for all non-Hellenes, who they called "barbarians." Aristotle was one of the worst offenders in this respect. Of course this is a universal human failing, but it was particularly virulent among Athenian intellectuals. In his later Athenian period, too, Aristotle's ideas would probably be too set with age to change.

I concluded that my best chance would be to catch Aristotle while he was tutoring young Alexander the Great at the court of Philip the Second of Macedon. He would have regarded Macedon as a backward country, even though the court spoke

Attic Greek. Perhaps he would be bored with bluff Macedonian stag-hunting squires and lonesome for intellectual company. As he would regard the Macedonians as the next thing to *barbaroi,* another barbarian would not appear at such a disadvantage there as at Athens.

Of course, whatever I accomplished with Aristotle, the results would depend on the curvature of space-time. I had not been wholly frank with my superior. While the equations tended to favor the hypothesis of a positive curvature, the probability was not overwhelming as I claimed. Perhaps my efforts would have little effect on history, or perhaps the effect would grow and widen like ripples in a pool. In the latter case the existing world would, as my superior said, be snuffed out.

Well, at that moment I hated the existing world and would not give a snap of my fingers for its destruction. I was going to create a much better one and come back from ancient times to enjoy it.

Our previous experiments showed that I could project myself back to ancient Macedon with an accuracy of about two months temporally and a half-parasang spatially. The machine included controls for positioning the time traveler anywhere on the globe, and safety devices for locating him above the surface of the earth, not in a place already occupied by a solid object. The equations showed that I should stay in Macedon about nine weeks before being snapped back to the present.

Once I had made up my mind, I worked as fast as I could. I telephoned my superior (you remember what a telephone is?) and made my peace. I said:

"I know I was a damned fool, Fred, but this thing was my baby; my one chance to be a great and famous scientist. I might have got a Nobel prize out of it."

"Sure, I know, Sherm," he said. "When are you coming back to the lab?"

"Well—uh—what about my group?"

"I held up the papers on that, in case you might change your mind. So if you come back, all will go on organization-wise as before."

"You want that final report on A-257, don't you?" I said, trying to keep my voice level.

"Sure."

"Then don't let the mechanics start to dismantle the machines until I've written the report."

"No; I've had the place locked up since yesterday."

"Okay. I want to shut myself in with the apparatus and the data sheets for a while and bat out the report without being bothered."

"That'll be fine," he said.

My first step in getting ready for my journey was to buy a suit of classical traveler's clothing from a theatrical costume company. This comprised a knee-length pullover tunic or chiton, a short horseman's cloak or chlamys, knitted buskins, sandals, a broad-brimmed black felt hat, and a staff. I stopped shaving, though I did not have time to raise a respectable beard.

My auxiliary equipment included a purse of coinage of the time, mostly golden Macedonian staters. Some of these coins were genuine, bought from a numismatic supply house, but most were copies I cast myself in the laboratory at night. I made sure of being rich enough to live decently for longer than my nine weeks' stay. This was not hard, as the purchasing power of precious metals was more than fifty times greater in the classical world than in mine.

I wore the purse attached to a heavy belt next to my skin. From this belt also hung a missle-weapon called a *gun*, which I have told you about. This was a small gun, called a pistol or revolver. I did not mean to shoot anybody, or expose the gun at all if I could help it. It was there as a last resort.

I also took several devices of our science to impress Aristotle: a pocket microscope and a magnifying glass, a small telescope, a compass, my timepiece, a flashlight, a small camera, and some medicines. I intended to show these things to people of ancient times only with the greatest caution. By the time I had slung all these objects in their pouches and cases from my belt, I had a heavy load. Another belt over the tunic supported a small purse for day-to-day buying and an all-purpose knife.

I already had a good reading knowledge of classical Greek, which I tried to polish by practice with the spoken language and listening to it on my talking machine. I knew I should arrive speaking with an accent, for we had no way of knowing exactly what Attic Greek sounded like.

I decided, therefore, to pass myself off as a traveler from India. Nobody would believe I was a Hellene. If I said I came from the north or wast, no Hellene would listen to me, as they regarded Europeans as warlike but half-witted savages. If I said I was from some well-known civilized country like Carthage, Egypt, Babylonia, or Persia, I should be in danger of meeting someone who knew those countries and of being exposed as a fraud.

To tell the truth of my origin, save under extraordinary circumstances, would be most imprudent. It would lead to my being considered a lunatic or a liar, as I can guess that your good self has more than once suspected me of being.

An Indian, however, should be acceptable. At this time, the Hellenes knew about that land only a few wild rumors and the account of Ktesias of Knidos, who made a book of the tales he picked up about India at the Persian court. The Hellenes had heard that India harbored philosophers. Therefore, thinking Greeks might be willing to consider Indians as almost as civilized as themselves.

What should I call myself? I took a common Indian name, Chandra, and Hellenized it to Zandras. That, I knew, was what the Hellenes would do anyway, as they had no "tch" sound and insisted on putting Greek inflectional endings on foreign names. I would not try to use my own name, which is not even remotely Greek or Indian-sounding. (Someday I must explain the blunders in my world that led to Hesperians' being called "Indians.")

The newness and cleanliness of my costume bothered me. It did not look worn, and I could hardly break it in around Brookhaven without attracting attention. I decided that if the question came up, I should say: yes, I bought it when I entered Greece, so as not to be conspicuous in my native garb.

During the day, when not scouring New York for equipment, I was locked in the room with the machine. While my colleagues thought I was either writing my report or dismantling the apparatus, I was getting ready for my trip.

Two weeks went by thus. One day a memorandum came down from my superior, saying: "How is that final report coming?"

I knew then I had better put my plan into execution at once. I sent back a memorandum: "Almost ready for the writing machine."

That night I came back to the laboratory. As I had been doing this often, the guards took no notice. I went to the time-machine room, locked the door from the inside, and got out my equipment and costume.

I adjusted the machine to set me down near Pella, the capital of Macedon, in the spring of the year 340 before Christ in our system of reckoning (976 Algonkian). I set the auto-actuator, climbed inside, and closed the door.

* * *

The feeling of being projected through time cannot really be described. There is a sharp pain, agonizing but too short to let the victim even cry out. At the same time there is the feeling of terrific acceleration, as if one were being shot from a catapult, but in no particular direction.

Then the seat in the passenger compartment dropped away from under me. There was a crunch, and a lot of sharp things jabbed me. I had fallen into the top of a tree.

I grabbed a couple of branches to save myself. The mechanism that positioned me in Macedon, detecting solid matter at the point where I was going to materialize, had raised me up above the treetops and then let go. It was an old oak, just putting out its spring leaves.

In clutching for branches I dropped my staff, which slithered down through the foliage and thumped the ground below. At least it thumped something. There was a startled yell.

Classical costume is impractical for tree-climbing. Branches kept knocking off my hat, or snagging my cloak, or poking me in tender places not protected by trousers. I ended my climb with a slide and a fall of several feet, tumbling into the dirt.

As I looked up, the first thing I saw was a burly, black-bearded man in a dirty tunic, standing with a knife in his hand. Near him stood a pair of oxen yoked to a wooden plow. At his feet rested a water jug.

The plowman had evidently finished a furrow and lain down to rest himself and his beasts when the fall of my staff on him and then my arrival in person aroused him.

Around me stretched the broad Emathian Plain, ringed by ranges of stony hills and craggy mountains. As the sky was overcast, and I did not dare consult my compass, I had no sure way of orienting myself, or even telling what time of day it was. I assumed that the biggest mountain in sight was Mount Bermion, which ought to be to the west. To the north I could see a trace of water. This would be Lake Loudias. Beyond the lake rose a range of low hills. A discoloration on the nearest spur of these hills might be a city, though my sight was not keen enough to make out details, and I had to do without my eyeglasses. The gently rolling plain was cut up into fields and pastures with occasional trees and patches of marsh. Dry brown grasses left over from winter nodded in the wind.

My realization of all this took but a flash. Then my attention was brought back to the plowman, who spoke.

I could not understand a word. But then, he would speak Macedonian. Though this can be deemed a Greek dialect, it differed so from Attic Greek as to be unintelligible.

No doubt the man wanted to know what I was doing in his tree. I put on my best smile and said in my slow fumbling Attic: "Rejoice! I am lost, and climbed your tree to find my way."

He spoke again. When I did not respond, he repeated his words more loudly, waving his knife.

We exchanged more words and gestures, but it was evident that neither had the faintest notion of what the other was trying to say. The plowman began shouting, as ignorant people will when faced by the linguistic barrier.

At last I pointed to the distant headland overlooking the lake, on which there appeared a discoloration that might be the city. Slowly and carefully I said:

"Is that Pella?"

"Nai, Pella!" The man's mien became less threatening.

"I am going to Pella. Where can I find the philosopher Aristoteles?" I repeated the name.

He was off again with more gibberish, but I gathered from his expression that he had never heard of any Aristoteles. So, I picked up my hat and stick, felt through my tunic to make sure my gear was all in place, tossed the rustic a final *"Chaire!"* and set off.

By the time I had crossed the muddy field and come out on a cart track, the problem of looking like a seasoned traveler had solved itself. There were green and brown stains on my clothes from the scramble down the tree; the cloak was torn; the branches had scratched my limbs and face; my feet and lower legs were covered with mud. I also became aware that, to one who has lived all his life with his loins decently swathed in trousers and underdrawers, classical costume is excessively drafty.

I glanced back to see the plowman still standing with one hand on his plow, looking at me in puzzled fashion. The poor fellow had never been able to decide what, if anything, to do about me.

When I found a road, it was hardly more than a heavily used cart track, with a pair of deep ruts and the space between them alternating stones, mud, and long grass.

I walked towards the lake and passed a few people on the road. To one used to the teeming traffic of my world, Macedon seemed dead and deserted. I spoke to some of the people, but ran into the same barrier of language as with the plowman.

Finally a two-horse chariot came along, driven by a stout man wearing a headband, a kind of kilt, and high-laced boots. He pulled up at my hail.

"What is it?" he said, in Attic not much better than mine.

"I seek the philosopher Aristoteles of Stageira. Where can I find him?"

"He lives in Mieza."

"Where is that?"

The man waved. "You are going the wrong way. Follow this road back the way you came. At the ford across the Bottiais, take the right-hand fork, which will bring you to Mieza and Kition. Do you understand?"

"I think so," I said. "How far is it?"

"About two hundred stadia."

My heart sank to my sandals. This meant five parasangs, or a good two days' walk. I thought of trying to buy a horse or a chariot, but I had never ridden or driven a horse and saw no prospect of learning how soon enough to do any good. I had read about Mieza as Aristotle's home in Macedon but, as none of my maps had shown it, I had assumed it to be a suburb of Pella.

I thanked the man, who trotted off, and set out after him. The details of my journey need not detain you. I was benighted far from shelter through not knowing where the villages were, attacked by watchdogs, eaten alive by mosquitoes, and invaded by vermin when I did find a place to sleep the second night. The road skirted the huge marshes that spread over the Emathian Plain west of Lake Loudias. Several small streams came down from Mount Bermion and lost themselves in this marsh.

At last I neared Mieza, which stands on one of the spurs of Mount Bermion. I was trudging wearily up the long rise to the village when six youths on little Greek horses clattered down the road. I stepped to one side, but instead of cantering past they pulled up and faced me in a semicircle.

"Who are you?" asked one, a smallish youth of about fifteen, in fluent Attic. He was blond and would have been noticeably handsome without his pimples.

"I am Zandras of Pataliputra," I said, giving the ancient name for Patna on the Ganges. "I seek the philosopher Aristoteles."

"Oh, a barbarian!" cried Pimples. "We know what the Aristoteles thinks of these, eh, boys?"

The others joined in, shouting noncompliments and bragging about all the barbarians they would someday kill or enslave.

I made the mistake of letting them see I was getting angry. I knew it was unwise, but I could not help myself. "If you do not wish to help me, then let me pass," I said.

"Not only a barbarian, but an insolent one!" cried one of the group, making his horse dance uncomfortably close to me.

"Stand aside, children!" I demanded.

"We must teach you a lesson," said Pimples. The others giggled.

"You had better let me alone," I said, gripping my staff in both hands.

A tall handsome adolescent reached over and knocked my hat off. "That for you, cowardly Asiatic!" he yelled.

Without stopping to think, I shouted an English epithet and swung my staff. Either the young man leaned out of the way or his horse shied, for my blow missed him. The momentum carried the staff past my target and the end struck the nose of one of the other horses.

The pony squealed and reared. Having no stirrups, the rider slid off the animal's rump into the dirt. The horse galloped off.

All six youths began screaming. The blond one, who had a particularly piercing voice, mouthed some threat. The next thing I knew, his horse bounded directly at me. Before I could dodge, the animal's shoulder knocked me head over heels and the beast leaped over me as I rolled. Luckily, horses' dislike of stepping on anything squashy saved me from being trampled.

I scrambled up as another horse bore down upon me. By a frantic leap, I got out of its way, but I saw that the other boys were jockeying their mounts to do likewise.

A few paces away rose a big pine. I dodged in among its lower branches as the other horses ran at me. The youths could not force their mounts in among these branches, so they galloped round and round and yelled. Most of their talk I could not understand, but I caught a sentence from Pimples:

"Ptolemaios! Ride back to the house and fetch bows or javelins!"

Hooves receded. While I could not see clearly through the pine needles, I inferred what was happening. The youths would not try to rush me on foot, first because they liked being on horseback, and if they dismounted they might lose their horses or have trouble remounting; second, because, as long as I kept my back to the tree, they would have a hard time getting at me through the tangle of branches, and I could hit and poke them with my stick as they came. Though not an unusually tall man in my own world, I was much bigger than any of these boys.

This, however, was a minor consideration. I recognized the name "Ptolemaios" as that of one of Alexander's companions, who in my world became King Ptolemy of Egypt and founded a famous dynasty. Young Pimples, then, must be Alexander himself.

I was in a real predicament. If I stayed where I was, Ptolemaios would bring back missiles for target practice with me as the target. I could of course shoot some of the boys with my gun, which would save me for the time being. But, in an absolute monarchy, killing the crown prince's friends, let alone the crown prince himself, is no way to achieve a peaceful old age, regardless of the provocation.

While I was thinking of these matters and listening to my attackers, a stone swished through the branches and bounced off the trunk. The small dark youth who had fallen off his horse had thrown the rock and was urging his friends to do likewise. I caught glimpses of Pimples and the rest dismounting and scurrying around for stones, a commodity with which Greece and Macedon are notoriously well supplied.

More stones came through the needles, caroming from the branches. One the size of my fist struck me lightly in the shin.

The boys came closer so that their aim got better. I wormed my way around the trunk to put it between me and them, but they saw the movement and spread out around the tree. A stone grazed my scalp, dizzying me and drawing blood. I thought of climbing, but, as the tree became more slender with height, I should be more exposed the higher I got. I should also be less able to dodge while perched in the branches.

That is how things stood when I heard hoofbeats again. This is the moment of decision, I thought. Ptolemaios is coming back with missile weapons. If I used my gun, I might doom myself in the long run, but it would be ridiculous to stand there and let them riddle me while I had an unused weapon.

I fumbled under my tunic and unsnapped the safety strap that kept the pistol in its holster. I pulled the weapon out and checked its projectiles.

A deep voice broke into the bickering. I caught phrases: ". . . insulting an unoffending traveler . . . how know you he is not a prince in his own country? . . . the king shall hear of this . . . like newly freed slaves, not like princes and gentlemen . . ."

I pushed towards the outer limits of the screen of pine needles. A heavy-set, brown-bearded man on a horse was haranguing the youths, who had dropped their stones. Pimples said:

"We were only having a little sport."

I stepped out from the branches, walked over to where my battered hat lay, and put it on. Then I said to the newcomer: "Rejoice! I am glad you came before your boys' play got too rough." I grinned, determined to act cheerful if it killed me. Only iron self-control would get me through this difficulty.

The man grunted. "Who are you?"

"Zandras of Pataliputra, a city in India. I seek Aristoteles the philosopher."

"He insulted us—" began one of the youths, but Brownbeard ignored him. He said:

"I am sorry you have had so rude an introduction to our royal house. This mass of youthful insolence"—(he indicated Pimples)—"is the Alexandros Philippou, heir to the throne of Makedonia." He introduced the others: Hepaistion, who had knocked my hat off and was now holding the others' horses; Nearchos, who had lost his horse; Ptolemaios, who had gone for weapons; and Harpalos and Philotas. He continued:

"When the Ptolemaios dashed into the house, I inquired the reason for his haste, learned of their quarrel with you, and came out forthwith. They have misapplied their master's teachings. They should not behave thus even to a barbarian like yourself, for in so doing they lower themselves to the barbarian's level. I am returning to the house of Aristoteles. You may follow."

The man turned his horse and started walking it back towards Mieza. The six boys busied themselves with catching Nearchos' horse.

I walked after him, though I had to dog-trot now and then to keep up. As it was uphill, I was soon breathing hard. I panted: "Who—my lord—are you?"

The man's beard came round and he raised an eyebrow. "I thought you would know. I am Antipatros, regent of Makedonia."

Before we reached the village proper, Antipatros turned off through a kind of park, with statues and benches. This, I supposed, was the Precinct of the Nymphs, which Aristotle used as a school ground. We went through the park and stopped at a mansion on the other side. Antipatros tossed the reins to a groom and slid off his horse.

"Aristoteles!" roared Antipatros. "A man wishes to see you."

A man of about my own age—the early forties—came out. He was of medium height and slender build, with a thin-lipped, severe-looking face and a pepper-and-salt beard cut short. He was wrapped in a billowing himation or large cloak, with a colorful scroll-patterned border. He wore golden rings on several fingers.

Antipatros made a fumbling introduction: "Old fellow, this is—ah—what's-his-name from—ah—some place in India." He told of rescuing me from Alexander and his fellow delinquents, adding: "If you do not beat some manners into your pack of cubs soon, it will be too late."

Aristotle looked at me sharply and lisped: "It ith always a pleasure to meet men from afar. What brings you here, my friend?"

I gave my name and said: "Being accounted something of a philosopher in my own land, I thought my visit to the West would be incomplete without speaking to the greatest Western philosopher. And when I asked who he was, everyone told me to seek out Aristoteles Nikomachou."

Aristotle purred. "It is good of them to thay tho. Ahem. Come in and join me in a drop of wine. Can you tell me of the wonders of India?"

"Yes indeed, but you must tell me in turn of your discoveries, which to me are much more wonderful."

"Come, come, then. Perhaps you could stay over a few days. I shall have many, many things to athk you."

That is how I met Aristotle. He and I hit it off, as we said in my world, from the start. We had much in common. Some people would not like Aristotle's lisp, or his fussy, pedantic ways, or his fondness for worrying any topic of conversation to death. But he and I got along fine.

That afternoon, in the house that King Philip had built for Aristotle to use as the royal school, he handed me a cup of wine flavored with turpentine and asked:

"Tell me about the elephant, that great beast we have heard of with a tail at both ends. Does it truly exist?"

"Indeed it does," I said, and went on to tell what I knew of elephants, while Aristotle scribbled notes on a piece of papyrus.

"What do they call the elephant in India?" he asked.

The question caught me by surprise, for it had never occured to me to learn ancient Hindustani along with all the other things I had to know for this expedition. I sipped the wine to give me time to think. I have never cared for alcoholic liquors, and this stuff tasted awful to me. But, for the sake of my objective, I had to pretend to like it. No doubt I should have to make up some kind of gibberish—but then a mental broad-jump carried me back to the stories of Kipling I had read as a boy.

"We call it a *hathi*," I said. "Though of course there are many languages in India."

"How about that Indian wild ath of which Ktesias thpeakth, with a horn in the middle of its forehead?"

"You had better call it a nose-horn"—*rhinokerōs*—"for that is where its horn really is, and it is more like a gigantic pig than an ass. . . ."

As dinner time neared, I made some artful remarks about going out to find accommodations in Mieza, but Aristotle (to my joy) would have none of it. I should stay right there at the school; my polite protestations of unworthiness he waved aside.

"You mutht plan to stop here for months," he said. "I shall never, never have such a chance to collect data on India again. Do not worry about expense; the king pays all. You are—ahem—the first barbarian I have known with a decent intellect, and I get lonethome for good tholid talk. Theophrastos has gone to Athens, and my other friends come to these backlands but seldom."

"How about the Macedonians?"

"*Aiboi!* Thome like my friend Antipatros are good fellows, but most are as lackwitted as a Persian grandee. And now tell me of Patal—what is your city's name?"

Presently Alexander and his friends came in. They seemed taken aback at seeing me closeted with their master. I put on a brisk smile and said: "Rejoice, my friends!" as if nothing untoward had happened. The boys glowered and whispered among themselves, but did not attempt any more disturbance at that time.

When they gathered for their lecture next morning, Aristotle told them: "I am too busy with the gentleman from India to waste time pounding unwanted wisdom into your miserable little thouls. Go shoot some rabbits or catch some fish for dinner, but in any case begone!"

The boys grinned. Alexander said: "It seems the barbarian has his uses after all. I hope you stay with us forever, good barbarian!"

After they had gone, Antipatros came in to say goodbye to Aristotle. He asked me with gruff goodwill how I was doing and went out to ride back to Pella.

The weeks passed unnoticed and the flowers of spring came out while I visited Aristotle. Day after day we strolled about the Precinct of the Nymphs, talking, or sat indoors when it rained. Sometimes the boys followed us, listening; at other times we talked alone. They played a couple of practical jokes on me, but, by pretending to be amused when I was really furious, I avoided serious trouble with them.

I learned that Aristotle had a wife and a little daughter in another part of the big house, but he never let me meet the lady. I only caught glimpses of them from a distance.

I carefully shifted the subject of our daily discourse from the marvels of India to the more basic questions of science. We argued over the nature of matter and the shape of the solar system. I gave out that the Indians were well on the road to the modern concepts—modern in my world, that is—of astronomy, physics, and so forth. I told of the discoveries of those eminent Pataliputran philosophers: Kopernikos in astronomy, Neuton in physics, Darben in evolution, and Mendeles in genetics. (I forgot; these names mean nothing to you, though an educated man of my world would recognize them at once through their Greek disguise.)

Always I stressed *method:* the need for experiment and invention and for checking each theory back against the facts. Though an opinionated and argumentative man, Aristotle had a mind like a sponge, eagerly absorbing any new fact, surmise, or opinion, whether he agreed with it or not.

I tried to find a workable compromise between what I knew science could do on one hand and the limits of Aristotle's credulity on the other. Therefore I said nothing about flying machines, guns, buildings a thousand feet high, and other technical wonders of my world. Nevertheless, I caught Aristotle looking at me sharply out of those small black eyes one day.

"Do you doubt me, Aristoteles?" I said.

"N-no, no," he said thoughtfully. "But it does theem to me that, were your Indian inventors as wonderful as you make out, they would have fabricated you wings like those of Daidalos in the legend. Then you could have flown to Makedonia directly, without the trials of crossing Persia by camel."

"That has been tried, but men's muscles do not have enough strength in proportion to their weight."

"Ahem. Did you bring anything from India to show the skills of your people?"

I grinned, for I had been hoping for such a question. "I did fetch a few small devices," said I, reaching into my tunic and bringing out the magnifying glass. I demonstrated its use.

Aristotle shook his head. "Why did you not show me this before? It would have quieted my doubts."

"People have met with misfortune by trying too suddenly to change the ideas of those around them. Like your teacher's teacher, Sokrates."

"That is true, true. What other devices did you bring?"

I had intended to show my devices at intervals, gradually, but Aristotle was so insistent on seeing them all that I gave in to him before he got angry. The little telescope was not powerful enough to show the moons of Jupiter or the rings of Saturn, but it showed enough to convince Aristotle of its power. If he could not see these astronomical phenomena himself, he was almost willing to take my word that they could be seen with the larger telescopes we had in India.

One day a light-armed soldier galloped up to us in the midst of our discussions in the Precinct of Nymphs. Ignoring the rest of us, the fellow said to Alexander: "Hail, O Prince! The king, your father, will be here before sunset."

Everybody rushed around cleaning up the place. We were all lined up in front of the big house when King Philip and his entourage arrived on horseback with a jingle and a clatter, in crested helmets and flowing mantles. I knew Philip by his one eye. He was a big powerful man, much scarred, with a thick curly black beard going gray. He dismounted, embraced his son, gave Aristotle a brief greeting, and said to Alexander:

"How would you like to attend a siege?"

Alexander whooped.

"Thrace is subdued," said the king, "but Byzantion and Perinthos have declared against me, thanks to Athenian intrigue. I shall give the Perintheans something to think about besides the bribes of the Great King. It is time you smelled blood, youngster; would you like to come?"

"Yes, yes! Can my friends come too?"

"If they like and their fathers let them."

"O King!" said Aristotle.

"What is it, spindle-shanks?"

"I trust thith is not the end of the prince's education. He has much yet to learn."

"No, no; I will send him back when the town falls. But he nears the age when he must learn by doing, not merely by listening to your rarefied wisdom. Who is this?" Philip turned his one eye on me.

"Zandras of India, a barbarian philothopher."

Philip grinned in a friendly way and clapped me on the shoulder. "Rejoice! Come to Pella and tell my generals about India. Who knows? A Macedonian foot may tread there yet."

"It would be more to the point to find out about Persia," said one of Philip's officers, a handsome fellow with a reddish-brown beard. "This man must have just come through there. How about it, man? Is the bloody Artaxerxes still solid on his throne?"

"I know little of such matters," I said, my heart beginning to pound at the threat of exposure. "I skirted the northernmost parts of the Great King's dominions and saw little of the big cities. I know nothing of their politics."

"Is that so?" said Redbeard, giving me a queer look. "We must talk of this again."

They all trooped into the big house, where the cook and the serving wenches were scurrying about. During dinner I found myself between Nearchos, Alexander's little Cretan friend, and a man-at-arms who spoke no Attic. So I did not get much conversation, nor could I follow much of the chatter that went on among the group at the head of the tables. I gathered that they were discussing politics. I asked Nearchos who the generals were.

"The big one at the king's right is the Parmenion," he said, "and the one with the red beard is the Attalos."

When the food was taken away and the drinking had begun, Attalos came over to me. The man-at-arms gave him his place. Attalos had drunk a lot of wine already; but, if it made him a little unsteady, it did not divert him.

"How did you come through the Great King's domain?" he asked. "What route did you follow?"

"I told you, to the north," I said.

"Then you must have gone through Orchoê."

"I—" I began, then stopped. Attalos might be laying a trap for me. What if I said yes and Orchoê was really in the south? Or suppose he had been there and knew all about the place? Many Greeks and Macedonians served the Great King as mercenaries.

"I passed through many places whose names I never got straight," I said. "I do not remember if Orchoê was among them."

Attalos gave me a sinister smile through his beard. "Your journey will profit you little, if you cannot remember where you have been. Come, tell me if you heard of unrest among the northern provinces."

I evaded the question, taking a long pull on my wine to cover my hesitation. I did this again and again until Attalos said: "Very well, perhaps you are really as ignorant of Persia as you profess. Then tell me about India."

"What about it?" I hiccupped; the wine was beginning to affect me, too.

"As a soldier, I should like to know of the Indian art of war. What is this about training elephants to fight?"

"Oh, we do much better than that."

"How so?"

"We have found that the flesh-and-blood elephant, despite its size, is an untrustworthy war beast because it often takes fright and stampedes back through its own troops. So, the philosophers of Pataliputra make artificial elephants of steel with rapid-fire catapults on their backs."

I was thinking in a confused way of the armored war vehicles of my own world. I do not know what made me tell Attalos such ridiculous lies. Partly, I suppose, it was to keep him off the subject of Persia.

Partly it was a natural antipathy between us. According to history, Attalos was not a bad man, though at times a reckless and foolish one. But it annoyed me that he thought he could pump me by subtle questions, when he was about as subtle as a ton of bricks. His voice and manner said as plainly as words: I am a shrewd, sharp fellow; watch out for me, everybody. He was the kind of man who, if told to spy on the enemy, would don an obviously false beard, wrap himself in a long black cloak, and go slinking about the enemy's places in broad daylight, leering and winking and attracting as much attention as possible. No doubt, too, he had prejudiced me against him by his alarming curiosity about my past.

But the main cause for my rash behavior was the strong wine I had drunk. In my own world, I drank very little and so was not used to these carousals.

Attalos was all eyes and ears at my tale of mechanical elephants. "You do not say!"

"Yes, and we do even better than that. If the enemy's ground forces resist the charge of our iron elephants, we send flying chariots, drawn by gryphons, to drop darts on the foe from

above." It seemed to me that never had any imagination been
so brilliant.

Attalos gave an audible gasp. "What else?"

"Well—ah—we also have a powerful navy, you know, which
controls the lower Ganges and the adjacent ocean. Our ships
move by machinery, without oars or sails."

"Do the other Indians have these marvels too?"

"Some, but none is so advanced as the Pataliputrans. When
we are outnumbered on the sea, we have a force of tame
Tritons who swim under the enemy's ships and bore holes in
their bottoms."

Attalos frowned. "Tell me, barbarian, how it is that, with
such mighty instruments of war, the Palalal—the Patapata—the
people of your city have not conquered the whole world?"

I gave a shout of drunken laughter and slapped Attalos on
the back. "We *have,* old boy, we have! You Macedonians have
just not yet found out that you are our subjects!"

Attalos digested this, then scowled blackly. "You temple-
thief! I think you have been making a fool of me! Of *me!* By
Herakles, I ought—"

He rose and swung a fist back to clout me. I jerked an arm
up to guard my face.

There came a roar of "Attalos!" from the head of the table.
King Philip had been watching us.

Attalos dropped his fist, muttered something like "Flying
chariots and tame Tritons, forsooth!" and stumbled back to his
own crowd.

This man, I remembered, did not have a happy future in
store. He was destined to marry his niece to Philip, whose first
wife, Olympias, woud have the girl and her baby killed after
Philip's assassination. Soon afterwards, Attalos would be murdered by Alexander's orders. It was on the tip of my tongue to
give him a veiled warning, but I forebore. I had attracted
enough hostile attention already.

Later, when the drinking got heavy, Aristotle came over and
shooed his boys off to bed. He said to me: "Let uth walk
outside to clear our heads, Zandras, and then go to bed, too.
The Makedones drink like sponges. I cannot keep up with
them."

Outside, he said: "The Attalos thinks you are a Persian thpy."

"A spy? Me? In Hera's name, why?" silently I cursed my
folly in making an enemy without any need. Would I never
learn to deal with this damned human species?

Aristotle said: "He thays nobody could pass through a country and remain as ignorant of it as you theem to be. *Ergo,* you know more of the Persian Empire than you pretend, but wish us to think you have nothing to do with it. And why should you do that, unleth you are yourself a Persian? And being a Persian, why should you hide the fact unleth you are on some hostile mission?"

"A Persian might fear anti-Persian prejudice among the Hellenes. Not that I am one," I hastily added.

"He need not. Many Persians live in Hellas without molestation. Take Artabazos and his sons, who live in Pella, refugees from their own king."

Then the obvious alibi came to me, long after it should have. "The fact is I went even farther north than I said. I went around the northern ends of the Caspian and Euxine seas and so did not cross the Great King's domains save through the Bactrian deserts."

"You did? Then why did you not thay tho? If that is true, you have settled one of our hottest geographical disputes: whether the Caspian is a closed thea or a bay of the Northern Ocean."

"I feared nobody would believe me."

"I am not sure what to believe, Zandras. You are a strange man. I do not think you are a Persian, for no Persian was ever a philothoper. It is good for you that you are not."

"Why?"

"Because I *hate* Persia!" he hissed.

"You do?"

"Yeth. I could list the wrongs done by the Great Kings, but it is enough that they seized my beloved father-in-law by treachery and tortured and crucified him. People like Isokrates talk of uniting the Hellenes to conquer Persia, and Philippos may try it if he lives. I hope he does. However," he went on in a different tone, "I hope he does it without dragging the cities of Hellas into it, for the repositories of civilization have not busineth getting into a brawl between tyrants."

"In India," said I sententiously, "we are taught that a man's nationality means nothing and his personal qualities everything. Men of all nations come good, bad, and indifferent."

Aristotle shrugged. "I have known virtuouth Persians too, but that monstrouth, bloated empire . . . No state can be truly civilized with more than a few thousand citizens."

There was no use telling him that large states, however monstrous and bloated he thought them, would be a permanent feature of the landscape from then on. I was trying to reform, not Aristotle's narrow view of international affairs, but his scientific methodology.

Next morning King Philip and his men and Aristotle's six pupils galloped off toward Pella, followed by a train of baggage mules and the boys' personal slaves. Aristotle said:

"Let us hope no chance sling-thtone dashes out Alexandros' brains before he has a chance to show his mettle. The boy has talent and may go far, though managing him is like trying to plow with a wild bull. Now, let us take up the question of atoms again, my dear Zandras, about which you have been talking thuch utter rubbish. First, you must admit that if a thing exists, parts of it must also exist. Therefore there is no thuch thing as an indivisible particle. . . ."

Three days later, while we were still hammering at the question of atoms, we looked up at the clatter of hooves. Here came Attalos and a whole troop of horsemen. Beside Attalos rode a tall swarthy man with a long gray beard. This man's appearance startled me into thinking he must be another time traveler from my own time, for he wore a hat, coat, and pants. The mere sight of these familiar garments filled me with homesickness for my own world, however much I hated it when I lived in it.

Actually, the man's garb was not that of one from my world. The hat was a cylindrical felt cap with ear flaps. The coat was a brown knee-length garment, embroidered with faded red and blue flowers, with trousers to match. The whole outfit looked old and threadbare, with patches showing. He was a big craggy-looking fellow, with a great hooked nose, wide cheekbones, and deep-set eyes under bushy, beetling brows.

They all dismounted, and a couple of grooms went around collecting the bridles to keep the horses from running off. The soldiers leaned on their spears in a circle around us.

Attalos said: "I should like to ask your guest some more philosophical questions, O Aristoteles."

"Ask away."

Attalos turned, not to me, but to the tall graybeard. He said something I did not catch, and then the man in trousers spoke to me in a language I did not know.

"I do not understand," I said.

The graybeard spoke again, in what sounded like a different tongue. He did this several times, using a different-sounding speech each time, but each time I had to confess ignorance.

"Now you see," said Attalos. "He pretends not to know

Persian, Median, Armenian, or Aramaic. He could not have traversed the Great King's dominions from east to west without learning at least one of these."

"Who are you, my dear sir?" I asked Graybeard.

The old man gave me a small dignified smile and spoke in Attic with a guttural accent. "I am Artavazda, or Artabazos as the Hellenes say, once governor of Phrygia but now a poor pensioner of King Philippos."

This, then, was the eminent Persian refugee of whom Aristotle had spoken.

"I warrant he does not even speak Indian," said Attalos.

"Certainly," I said, and started off in English. *"Now is the time for all good men to come to the aid of the party. Four score and seven years ago our fathers brought forth—"*

"What would you call that?" Attalos asked Artavazda.

The Persian spread his hands. "I have never heard the like. But then, India is a vast country of many tongues."

"I was not—" I began, but Attalos kept on:

"What race would you say he belonged to?"

"I know not. The Indians I have seen were much darker, but there might be lightskinned Indians for aught I know."

"If you will listen, General, I will explain," I said. "For most of the journey I was not even in the Persian Empire. I crossed through Bactria and went around the north of the Caspian and Euxine seas."

"Oh, so now you tell another story?" said Attalos. "Any educated man knows the Caspian is but a deep bay opening into the Ocean River to the north. Therefore you could not go around it. So, in trying to escape, you do but mire yourself deeper in your own lies."

"Look here," said Aristotle. "You have proved nothing of the sort, O Attalos. Ever thince Herodotos there have been those who think the Caspian a closed thea—"

"Hold your tongue, Professor," said Attalos. "This is a matter of national security. There is something queer about this alleged Indian, and I mean to find out what it is."

"It is not queer that one who comes from unknown distant lands should tell a singular tale of his journey."

"No, there is more to it than that. I have learned that he first appeared in a treetop on the farm of the freeholder Diktys Pisandrou. Diktys remembers looking up into the tree for crows before he cast himself down under it to rest. If the Zandras had been in the tree, Diktys would have seen him, as it was not yet fully in leaf. The next instant there was a crash of a body falling into the branches, and Zandras' staff smote Diktys on the head. Normal mortal men fall not out of the sky into trees."

"Perhaps he flew from India. They have marvelous mechanisms there, he tells me," said Aristotle.

"If he survives our interrogation in Pella, perhaps he can make me a pair of wings," said Attalos. "Or better yet, a pair for my horse, so he shall emulate Pegasos. Meanwhile, seize and bind him, men!"

The soldiers moved. I did not dare submit for fear they would take my gun and leave me defenseless. I snatched up the hem of my tunic to get at my pistol. It took precious seconds to unsnap the safety strap, but I got the gun out before anybody laid hand on me.

"Stand back or I will blast you with lightning!" I shouted, raising the gun.

Men of my own world, knowing how deadly such a weapon can be, would have given ground at the sight of it. But the Macedonians, never having seen one, merely stared at the device and came on. Attalos was one of the nearest.

I fired at him, then whirled and shot another soldier who was reaching out to seize me. The discharge of the gun produces a lightning-like flash and a sharp sound like a close clap of thunder. The Macedonians cried out, and Attalos fell with a wound in his thigh.

I turned again, looking for a way out of the circle of soldiers, while confused thoughts of taking one of their horses flashed through my head. A heavy blow in the flank staggered me. One of the soldiers had jabbed me with his spear, but my belt kept the weapon from piercing me. I shot at the man but missed him in my haste.

"Do not kill him!" screamed Aristotle.

Some of the soldiers backed up as if to flee; others poised their spears. They hesitated for the wink of an eye, either for fear of me or because Aristotle's command confused them. Ordinarily they would have ignored the philosopher and listened for their general's orders, but Attalos was down on the grass and looking in amazement at the hole in his leg.

As one soldier dropped his spear and started to run, a blow on the head sent a flash of light through my skull and hurled me to the ground, nearly unconscious. A man behind me had swung his spear like a club and struck me on the pate with the shaft.

Before I could recover, they were all over me, raining kicks and blows. One wrenched the gun from my hand. I must have lost consciousness, for the next thing I remember is lying in the dirt while the soldiers tore off my tunic. Attalos stood over me with a bloody bandage around his leg, leaning on a soldier. He looked pale and frightened but resolute. The second man I had shot lay still.

"So that is where he keeps his infernal devices!" said Attalos, indicating my belt. "Take it off, men."

The soldiers struggled with the clasp of the belt until one impatiently sawed through the straps with his dagger. The gold in my money pouch brought cries of delight.

I struggled to get up, but a pair of soldiers knelt on my arms to keep me down. There was a continuous mumble of talk. Attalos, looking over the belt, said:

"He is too dangerous to live. Even stripped as he is, who knows but what he will soar into the air and escape by magic?"

"Do not kill him!" said Aristotle. "He has much valuable knowledge to impart."

"No knowledge is worth the safety of the kingdom."

"But the kingdom can benefit from his knowledge. Do you not agree?" Aristotle asked the Persian.

"Drag me not into this, pray," said Artavazda. "It is no concern of mine."

"If he is a danger to Makedonia, he should be destroyed at once," said Attalos.

"There is but little chance of his doing harm now," said Aristotle, "and an excellent chance of his doing us good."

"Any chance of his doing harm is too much," said Attalos. "You philosophers can afford to be tolerant of interesting strangers. But if they carry disaster in their baggage, it is on us poor soldiers that the brunt will fall. Is it not so, Artabazos?"

"I have done what you asked and will say no more," said Artavazda. "I am but a simple-minded Persian nobleman who does not understand your Greek subtleties."

"I can increase the might of your armies, General!" I cried to Attalos.

"No doubt, and no doubt you can also turn men to stone with an incantation, as the Gorgons did with their glance." He drew his sword and felt the edge with his thumb.

"You will slay him for mere thuperstition!" wailed Aristotle, wringing his hands. "At least, let the king judge the matter."

"Not superstition," said Attalos; "murder." He pointed to the dead soldier.

"I come from another world! Another age!" I yelled, but Attalos was not to be diverted.

"Let us get this over with," he said. "Set him on his knees, men. Take my sword, Glaukos; I am too unsteady to wield it. Now bow your head, my dear barbarian, and—"

In the middle of Attalos' sentence, he and the others and all my surroundings vanished. Again there came that sharp pain and sense of being jerked by a monstrous catapult. . . .

I found myself lying in leaf mold with the pearl-gray trunks of poplars all around me. A brisk breeze was making the poplar leaves flutter and show their silvery bottoms. It was too cool for a man who was naked save for sandals and socks.

I had snapped back to the year 1981 of the calendar of my world, which I had set out from. But where was I? I should be near the site of the Brookhaven National Laboratories in a vastly improved superscientific world. There was, however, no sign of superscience here; nothing but poplar trees.

I got up, groaning, and looked around. I was covered with bruises and bleeding from nose and mouth.

The only way I had of orienting myself was the boom of a distant surf. Shivering, I hobbled towards the sound. After a few hundred paces, I came out of the forest on a beach. This beach could be the shore of Sewanhaki, or Long Island as we called it, but there was no good way of telling. There was no sign of human life; just the beach curving into the distance and disappearing around headlands, with the poplar forest on one side and the ocean on the other.

What, I wondered, had happened? Had science advanced so fast as a result of my intervention that man had already exterminated himself by scientific warfare? Thinkers of my world had concerned themselves with this possibility, but I had never taken it seriously.

It began to rain. In despair I cast myself down on the sand and beat it with my fists. I may have lost consciousness again.

At any rate, the next thing I knew was the now-familiar sound of hooves. When I looked up, the horseman was almost upon me, for the sand had muffled the animal's footsteps until it was quite close.

I blinked with incredulity. For an instant I thought I must be back in the classical era still. The man was a warrior armed and armored in a style much like that of ancient times. At first he seemed to be wearing a helmet of classical Hellenic type. When he came closer I saw that this was not quite true, for the crest was made of feathers instead of horsehair. The nasal and cheek plates hid most of his face, but he seemed dark and beardless. He wore a shirt of scale mail, long leather trousers, and low shoes. He had a bow and a small shield hung from his saddle and a slender lance slung across his back by a strap. I saw that this could not be ancient times because the horse was fitted with a large, well-molded saddle and stirrups.

As I watched the man stupidly, he whisked the lance out of its boot and couched it. He spoke in an unknown language.

I got up, holding my hands over my head in surrender. The man kept repeating his question, louder and louder, and making jabbing motions. All I could say was "I don't understand" in the languages I knew, none of which seemed familiar to him.

Finally he maneuvered his horse around to the other side of me, barked a command, pointed along the beach the way he had come, and prodded me with the butt of the lance. Off I limped, with rain, blood, and tears running down my hide.

You know the rest, more or less. Since I could not give an intelligible account of myself, the Sachim of Lenape, Wayotan the Fat, claimed me as a slave. For fourteen years I labored on his estate at such occupations as feeding hogs and chopping kindling. When Wayotan died and the present Sachim was elected, he decided I was too old for that kind of work, especially as I was half crippled from the beatings of Wayotan and his overseers. Learning that I had some knowledge of letters (for I had picked up spoken and written Algonkian in spite of my wretched lot) he freed me and made me official librarian.

In theory I can travel about as I like, but I have done little of it. I am too old and weak for the rigors of travel in this world, and most other places are, as nearly as I can determine, about as barbarous as this one. Besides, a few Lenapes come to hear me lecture on the nature of man and the universe and the virtues of the scientific method. Perhaps I can light a small spark after I failed in the year 340 B.C.

When I went to work in the library, my first thought was to find out what had happened to bring the world to its present pass.

Wayotan's predecessor had collected a considerable library which Wayotan had neglected, so that some of the books had been chewed by rats and others ruined by dampness. Still, there was enough to give me a good sampling of the literature of this world, from ancient to modern times. There were even Herodotos' history and Plato's dialogues, identical with the versions that existed in my own world.

I had to struggle against more language barriers, as the European languages of this world are different from, though related to, those of my own world. The English of today, for instance, is more like the Dutch of my own world, as a result of England's never having been conquered by the Normans.

I also had the difficulty of reading without eyeglasses. Luckily, most of these manuscript books are written in a large, clear hand. A couple of years ago I did get a pair of glasses, imported from China, where the invention of the printing press has stimulated their manufacture. But, as they are a recent invention in this world, they are not so effective as those of mine.

I rushed through all the history books to find out when and how your history diverged from mine. I found that differences appeared quite early. Alexander still marched to the Indus but failed to die at thirty-two on his return. In fact he lived fifteen years longer and fell at last in battle with the Sarmatians in the Caucasus Mountains.

I do not know why that brief contact with me enabled him to avoid the malaria mosquito that slew him in my world. Maybe I aroused in him a keener interest in India than he would otherwise have had, leading him to stay there longer so that all his subsequent schedules were changed. His empire held together for most of a century instead of breaking up right after his death as it did in my world.

The Romans still conquered the whole Mediteranean, but the course of their conquests and the names of the prominent Romans were all different. Two of the chief religions of my world, Christianity and Islam, never appeared at all. Instead we have Mithraism, Odinism, and Soterism, the last an Egypto-Hellenic synthesis founded by that Egyptian prophet whose followers call him by the Greek word for "savior."

Still, classical history followed the same *general* course that it had in my world, even though the actors bore other names. The Roman Empire broke up, as it did in my world, though the details are all different, with a Hunnish emperor ruling in Rome and a Gothic one in Antioch.

It is after the fall of the Roman Empire that profound differences appear. In my world there was a revival of learning that began about nine hundred years ago, followed by a scientific revolution beginning four centuries later. In your history the revival of learning was centuries later, and the scientific revolution has hardly begun. Failure to develop the compass and the full-rigged ship resulted in North America's (I mean Hesperia's) being discovered and settled via the northern route, by way of Iceland, and more slowly than in my world. Failure to invent the gun meant that the natives of Hesperia were not swept aside by the invading Europeans, but held their own against them and gradually learned their arts of iron-working, weaving, cereal-growing, and the like. Now most of the European settlements have been assimilated, though the ruling families of the Abnakis and Mohegans frequently have blue eyes and still call themselves by names like "Sven" and "Eric."

I was eager to get hold of a work by Aristotle, to see what effect I had had on him and try to relate this effect to the subsequent course of history. From allusions in some of the works in this library I gathered that many of his writings had come down to modern times, though the titles all seemed different from those of his surviving works in my world. The only actual samples of his writings in the library were three essays, *Of Justice, On Education* and *Of Passions and Anger.* None of these showed my influence.

I had struggled through most of the Sachim's collection when I found the key I was looking for. This was an Iberic translation of *Lives of the Great Philosophers,* by one Diomedes of Mazaka. I never heard of Diomedes in the literary history of my own world, and perhaps he never existed. Anyway, he had a long chapter on Aristotle, in which appears the following section:

> Now Aristotle, during his sojourn at Mytilene, had been an assiduous student of natural sciences. He had planned, according to Timotheus, a series of works which should correct the errors of Empedokles, Demokritos, and others of his predecessors. But, after he had removed to Macedonia and busied himself with the education of Alexander, there one day appeared before him a traveler, Sandos of Palibothra, a mighty philosopher of India.
>
> The Indian ridiculed Aristotle's attempts at scientific research, saying that in his land these investigations had gone far beyond anything the Hellenes had attempted, and the Indians were still a long way from arriving at satisfactory explanations of the universe. Moreover, he asserted that no real progress could be made in natural philosophy

unless the Hellenes abandoned their disdain for physical labor and undertook exhaustive experiments with mechanical devices of the sort which cunning Egyptian and Asiatic craftsmen make.

King Philip, hearing of the presence of this stranger in his land and fearing lest he be a spy sent by some foreign power to harm or corrupt the young prince, came with soldiers to arrest him. But, when he demanded that Sandos accompany him back to Pella, the latter struck dead with thunderbolts all the king's soldiers that were with him. Then, it is said, mounting into his chariot drawn by winged gryphons, he flew off in the direction of India. But other authorities say that the man who came to arrest Sandos was Antipatros, the regent, and that Sandos cast darkness before the eyes of Antipatros and Aristotle, and when they recovered from their swoon he had vanished.

Aristotle, reproached by the king for harboring so dangerous a visitor and shocked by the sanguinary ending of the Indian's visit, resolved to have no more to do with the sciences. For, as he explains in his celebrated treatise *On the Folly of Natural Science,* there are three reasons why no good Hellene should trouble his mind with such matters.

One is that the number of facts which must be mastered before sound theories become possible is so vast that if all the Hellenes did nothing else for centuries, they would still not gather the amount of data required. The task is therefore futile.

Secondly, experiments and mechanical inventions are necessary to progress in science, and such work, though all very well for slavish Asiatics, who have a natural bent for it, is beneath the dignity of a Hellenic gentleman.

And, lastly, some of the barbarians have already surpassed the Hellenes in this activity, wherefore it ill becomes the Hellenes to compete with their inferiors in skills at which the latter have an inborn advantage. They should rather cultivate personal rectitude, patriotic valor, political rationality, and aesthetic sensitivity, leaving to the barbarians such artificial aids to the good and virtuous life as are provided by scientific discoveries.

This was it, all right. The author had gotten some of his facts wrong, but that was to be expected from an ancient historian.
So! My teachings had been too successful. I had so well

shattered the naïve self-confidence of the Hellenic philosophers as to discourage them from going on with science at all.

I should have remembered that glittering theories and sweeping generalizations, even when wrong, are the frosting on the cake; they are the carrot that makes the donkey go. The possibility of pronouncing such universals is the stimulus that keeps many scientists grinding away, year after year, at the accumulation of facts, even seemingly dull and trivial facts. If ancient scientists had realized how much laborious fast-finding lay ahead of them before sound theories would become possible, they would have been so appalled as to drop science altogether. And that is just what happened.

The sharpest irony of all was that I had placed myself where I could not undo my handiwork. If I had ended up in a scientifically advanced world, and did not like what I found, I might have built another time machine, gone back, and somehow warned myself of the mistake lying in wait for me. But such a project is out of the question in a backward world like this one, where seamless columbium tubing, for instance, is not even thought of. All I proved by my disastrous adventure is that space-time has a negative curvature, and who in this world cares about that?

You recall, when you were last here, asking me the meaning of a motto in my native language on the wall of my cell. I said I would tell you in connection with my whole fantastic story. The motto says: "Leave Well Enough Alone," and I wish I had.

Cordially yours,
Sherman Weaver

THERE'S A WOLF
IN MY TIME MACHINE

by Larry Niven

Larry Niven (1938-   ) has never held any other job besides that of full-time writer. The son of wealthy parents, he nevertheless made his own fortune through talent and hard work. He has won four Hugo Awards and one Nebula Award in a career that is still going strong. Among his most famous works are Ringworld, *(1970)* The Ringworld Engineers *(1980), and* The Integral Trees *(1984); and in collaboration with Jerry Pournelle,* The Mote in God's Eye *(1974),* Lucifer's Hammer *(1977), and the bestselling* Footfall *(1985). Although not a trained scientist, he has excelled in the "hard science" corner of science fiction, notwithstanding a real feel for fantasy. Much of his fiction takes place within a consistent universe called "Known Space."*

The old extension cage had no fine controls; but that hardly mattered. It wasn't as if Svetz were chasing some particular extinct animal. Ra Chen had told him to take whatever came to hand.

Svetz guided the cage back to preindustrial America, somewhere in mid-continent, around 1000 Ante Atomic Era. Few humans, many animals. Perhaps he'd find a bison.

And when he pulled himself to the window, he looked out upon a vast white land.

Svetz had not planned to arrive in midwinter.

Briefly he considered moving into the time stream again and using the interrupter circuit. Try another date, try luck again. But the interrupter circuit was new, untried, and Svetz wasn't about to be the first man to test it.

Besides which, a trip into the past cost over a million commercials. Using the interrupter circuit would nearly double that. Ra Chen would be displeased.

Svetz began freezing to death the moment he opened the door. From the doorway the view was all white, with one white bounding shape far away.

Svetz shot it with a crystal of soluble anesthetic.

He used the flight stick to reach the spot. Now that it was no longer moving, the beast was hard to find. It was just the color of the snow, but for its open red mouth and the black pads on its feet. Svetz tentatively identified it as an arctic wolf.

It would fit the Vivarium well enough. Svetz would have settled for anything that would let him leave this frozen wilderness. He felt uncommonly pleased with himself. A quick, easy mission.

Inside the cage, he rolled the sleeping beast into what might have been a clear plastic bag, and sealed it. He strapped the wolf against one curved wall of the extension cage. He relaxed into the curve of the opposite wall as the cage surged in a direction vertical to all directions.

Gravity shifted oddly.

A transparent sac covered Svetz's own head. Its lip was fixed to the skin of his neck. Now Svetz pulled it loose and dropped it. The air system was on; he would not need the filter sac.

The wolf would. It could not breathe industrial-age air. Without the filter sac to remove the poisons, the wolf would choke to death. Wolves were extinct in Svetz's time.

Outside, time passed at a furious rate. Inside, time crawled. Nestled in the spherical curve of the extension cage, Svetz stared up at the wolf, who now seemed fitted into the curve of the ceiling.

Svetz had never met a wolf in the flesh. He had seen pictures in children's books . . . and even the children's books had been stolen from the deep past. Why should the wolf look so familiar?

It was a big beast, possibly as big as Hanville Svetz, who was a slender, small-boned man. Its sides heaved with its panting. Its tongue was long and red and its teeth were white and sharp.

Like the dogs, Svetz remembered. The dogs in the Vivarium, in the glass case labeled:

DOG
CONTEMPORARY

Alone of the beasts in the Vivarium, the dogs were not sealed in glass for their own protection. The others could not breathe the air outside. The dogs could.

In a very real sense, they were the work of one man. Lawrence Wash Porter had lived near the end of the Industrial Period, between 50 and 100 Post Atomic Era, when billions of human beings were dying of lung diseases while scant millions adapted. Porter had decided to save the dogs.

Why the dogs? His motives were obscure, but his methods smacked of genius. He had acquired members of each of the breeds of dog in the world, and bred them together, over many generations of dogs and most of his own lifetime.

There would never be another dog show. Not a purebred dog was left in the world. But hybrid vigor had produced a new breed. These, the ultimate mongrels, could breathe industrial-age air, rich in oxides of carbon and nitrogen, scented with raw gasoline and sulfuric acid.

The dogs were behind glass because people were afraid of them. Too many species had died. The people of 1100 Post Atomic were not used to animals.

Wolves and dogs . . . could one have sired the other?

Svetz looked up at the sleeping wolf and wondered. He was both like and unlike the dogs. The dogs had grinned out through the glass and wagged their tails when children waved. Dogs liked people. But the wolf, even in sleep . . .

Svetz shuddered. Of all the things he hated about his profession, this was the worst: the ride home, staring up at a strange and dangerous extinct animal. The first time he'd done it, a captured horse had seriously damaged the control panel. On his last mission an ostrich had kicked him and broken three ribs.

The wolf was stirring restlessly . . . and something about it had changed.

Something was changing now. The beast's snout was shorter, wasn't it? Its forelegs lenghtened peculiarly; its paws seemed to grow and spread. Svetz caught his breath.

Svetz caught his breath, and instantly forgot the wolf. Svetz was choking, dying. He snatched up his filter sac and threw himself at the controls.

Svetz stumbled out of the extension cage, took three steps and collapsed. Behind him invisible contaminants poured into the open air.

The sun was setting in banks of orange cloud.

Svetz lay where he had fallen, retching, fighting for air. There was an outdoor carpet beneath him, green and damp, smelling of plants. Svetz did not recognize the smell, did not at once realize that the carpet was alive. He would not have cared at that point. He knew only that the cage's air system had tried to kill him. The way he felt, it had probably succeeded.

It had been a near thing. He had been passing 30 Post Atomic when the air went bad. He remembered clutching the interrupter switch, then waiting, waiting. The foul air stank in his nostrils and caught in his throat and tore at his larynx. He had waited through twenty years, feeling every second of them. At 50 Post Atomic he had pulled the interrupter switch and run choking from the cage.

50 PA. At least he had reached industrial times. He could breathe the air.

It was the horse, he thought without surprise. The horse had pushed its wickedly pointed horn through Svetz's control panel, three years ago. Maintenance was supposed to fix it. They *had* fixed it.

Something must have worn through.

The way he looked at me every time I passed his cage. I always knew the horse would get me, Svetz thought.

He noticed the filter sac still in his hand. Not that he'd be— Svetz sat up suddenly.

There was green all about him. The damp green carpet beneath him was alive; it grew from the black ground. A rough, twisted pillar thrust from the ground, branched into an explosion of red and yellow papery things. More of the crumpled colored paper lay about the pillar's base. Something that was not an aircraft moved erratically overhead, a tiny thing that fluttered and warbled.

Living, all of it. A preindustrial wilderness.

Svetz pulled the filter sac over his head and hurriedly smoothed the edges around his neck to form a seal. Blind luck that he hadn't fainted yet. He waited for it to puff up around his head. A selectively permeable membrane, it would pass the right gases in and out until the composition of the air was—was—

Svetz was choking, tearing at the sac.

He wadded it up and threw it, sobbing. First the air plant, now the filter sac! Had someone wrecked them both? The inertial calendar too; he was at least a hundred years previous to 50 Post Atomic.

Someone had tried to kill him.

Svetz looked wildly about him. Uphill across a wide green carpet, he saw an angular vertical-sided formation painted in shades of faded green. It had to be artificial. There might be people there. He could—

No, he couldn't ask for help either. Who would believe him? How could they help him anyway? His only hope was the extension cage. And his time must be very short.

The extension cage rested a few yards away, the door a black circle on one curved side. The other side seemed to fade away into nothing. It was still attached to the rest of the time machine, in 1103 PA, along a direction eyes could not follow.

Svetz hesitated near the door. His only hope was to disable the air plant somehow. Hold his breath, then—

The smell of contaminants was gone.

Svetz sniffed at the air. Yes, gone. The air plant had exhausted itself, drained its contaminants into the open air. No need to wreck it now, Svetz was sick with relief.

He climbed in.

He remembered the wolf when he saw the filter sac, torn and empty. Then he saw the intruder towering over him, the coarse thick hair, the yellow eyes glaring, the taloned hands spread wide to kill.

The land was dark. In the east a few stars showed, though the west was still deep red. Perfumes tinged the air. A full moon was rising.

Svetz staggered uphill, bleeding.

The house on the hill was big and old. Big as a city block, and two floors high. It sprawled out in all directions, as though a mad architect had built to a whim that changed moment by moment. There were wrought-iron railings on the upper windows, and wrought-iron handles on the screens on both floors, all painted the same dusty shade of green. The screens were wood, painted a different shade of green. They were closed across every window. No light leaked through anywhere.

The door was built for someone twelve feet tall. The knob was huge. Svetz used both hands and put all his weight into it, and still it would not turn. He moaned. He looked for the lens of a peeper camera and could not find it. How would anyone know he was here? He couldn't find a doorbell either.

Perhaps there was nobody inside. No telling what this building was. It was far too big to be a family dwelling, too spread-out to be a hotel or apartment house. Might it be a warehouse or a factory? Making or storing what?

Svetz looked back toward the extension cage. Dimly he caught the glow of the interior lights. He also saw something moving on the living green that carpeted the hill.

Pale forms, more than one.

Moving this way?

Svetz pounded on the door with his fists. Nothing. He noticed a golden metal thing, very ornate, high on the door. He touched it, pulled at it, let it go. It clanked.

He took it in both hands and slammed the knob against its base again and again. Rhythmic clanking sounds. Someone should hear it.

Something zipped past his ear and hit the door hard. Svetz spun around, eyes wild, and dodged a rock the size of his fist. The white shapes were nearer now. Bipeds, walking hunched.

They looked too human—or not human enough.

The door opened.

She was young, perhaps sixteen. Her skin was very pale, and her hair and brows were pure white, quite beautiful. Her garment covered her from neck to ankles, but left her arms bare. She seemed sleepy and angry as she pulled the door open— manually, and it was heavy, too. Then she saw Svetz.

"Help me," said Svetz.

Her eyes went wide. Her ears moved too. She said something Svetz had trouble interpreting, for she spoke in ancient american.

"What *are* you?"

Svetz couldn't blame her. Even in good condition his clothes would not fit the period. But his blouse was ripped to the navel, and so was his skin. Four vertical parallel lines of blood ran down his face and chest.

Zeera had been coaching him in the american speech. Now he said carefully, "I am a traveler. An animal, a monster, has taken my vehicle away from me."

Evidently the sense came through. "You poor man! What kind of animal?"

"Like a man, but hairy all over, with a horrible face—and claws—claws—"

"I see the mark they made."

"I don't know how he got in. I—" Svetz shuddered. No, he couldn't tell her that. It was insane, utterly insane, this conviction that Svetz's wolf had become a bloodthirsty humanoid monster. "He only hit me once. On the face. I could get him out with a weapon, I think. Have you a bazooka?"

"What a funny word! I don't think so. Come inside. Did the

trolls bother you?" She took his arm and pulled him in and shut the door.

Trolls?

"You're a strange person," the girl said, looking him over. "You look strange, you smell strange, you move strangely. I did not know that there were people like you in the world. You must come from very far away."

"Very," said Svetz. He felt himself close to collapse. He was safe at last, safe inside. But why were the hairs on the back of his neck trying to stand upright?

He said, "My name is Svetz. What's yours?"

"Wrona." She smiled up at him, not afraid despite his strangeness . . . and he must look strange to her, for she surely looked strange to Hanville Svetz. Her skin was sheet-white, and her rich white hair would better have fit a centenarian. Her nose, very broad and flat, would have disfigured an ordinary girl. Somehow it fit Wrona's face well enough; but her face was most odd, and her ears were too large, almost pointed, and her eyes were too far apart, and her grin stretched *way* back . . . and Svetz liked it. Her grin was curiosity and enjoyment, and was not a bit too wide. The firm pressure of her hand was friendly, reassuring. Though her fingernails were uncomfortably long and sharp.

"You should rest, Svetz," she said. "My parents will not be up for another hour, at least. Then they can decide how to help you. Come with me, I'll take you to a spare room."

He followed her through a room dominated by a great rectangular table and a double row of high-backed chairs. There was a large microwave oven at one end, and beside it a platter of . . . red things. Roughly conical they were, each about the size of a strong man's upper arm, each with a dot of white in the big end. Svetz had no idea what they were; but he didn't like their color. They seemed to be bleeding.

"Oh," Wrona exclaimed. "I should have asked. Are you hungry?"

Svetz was, suddenly. "Have you dole yeast?"

"Why, I don't know the word. Are those dole yeast? They are all we have."

"We'd better forget it." Svetz's stomach lurched at the thought of eating something that color. Even if it turned out to be a plant.

Wrona was half supporting him by the time they reached the room. It was rectangular and luxuriously large. The bed was wide enough, but only six inches off the floor, and without coverings. She helped him down to it. "There's a washbasin behind that door, if you find the strength. Best you rest, Svetz. In perhaps two hours I will call you."

Svetz eased himself back. The room seemed to rotate. He heard her go out.

How strange she was. How odd he must look to her. A good thing she hadn't called anyone to tend him. A doctor would notice the differences.

Svetz had never dreamed that primitives would be so different from his own people. During the thousand years between now and the present, there must have been massive adaptation to changes in air and water, to DDT and other compounds in foods, to extinction of food plants and meat animals until only dole yeast was left, to higher noise levels, less room for exercise, greater dependence on medicines . . . Well, why shouldn't they be different? It was a wonder humanity had survived at all.

Wrona had not feared his strangeness, nor cringed from the scratches on his face and chest. She was only amused and interested. She had helped him without asking too many questions. He liked her for that.

He dozed.

Pain from deep scratches, stickiness in his clothes made his sleep restless. There were nightmares. Something big and shadowy, half man and half beast, reached far out to slash his face. Over and over. At some indeterminate time he woke completely, already trying to identify a musky, unfamiliar scent.

No use. He looked about him, at a strange room that seemed even stranger from floor level. High ceiling. One frosted globe, no brighter than a full moon, glowed so faintly that the room was all shadow. Wrought-iron bars across the windows; black night beyond.

A wonder he'd wakened at all. The preindustrial air should have killed him hours ago.

It had been a futz of a day, he thought. And he shied from the memory of the thing in the extension cage. The snarling face, pointed ears, double row of pointed white teeth. The clawed hand reaching out, swiping down. The nightmare conviction that a wolf had turned into *that*.

It could not be. Animals did not change shape like that. Something must have gotten in while Svetz was fighting for air. Chased the wolf out, or killed it.

But there were legends of such things, weren't there? Two

and three thousand years old and more, everywhere in the world, were the tales of men who could become beasts and vice versa.

Svetz sat up. Pain gripped his chest, then relaxed. He stood up carefully and made his way to the bathroom.

The spigots were not hard to solve. Svetz wet a cloth with warm water. He watched himself in the mirror, emerging from under the crusted blood. A pale, slender young man topped with thin blond hair . . . and an odd distortion of chin and forehead. That must be the mirror, he decided. Primitive workmanship. It might have been worse. Hadn't the first mirrors been two-dimensional?

A shrill whistle sounded outside his door. Svetz went to look and found Wrona. "Good, you're up," she said. "Father and Uncle Wrocky would like to see you."

Svetz stepped into the hall, and again noticed the elusive musky scent. He followed Wrona down the dark hallway. Like his room, it was lit only by a single white frosted globe. Why would Wrona's people keep the house so dark? They had electricity.

And why were they all sleeping at sunset? With breakfast laid out and waiting . . .

Wrona opened a door, gestured him in.

Svetz hesitated a step beyond the threshold. The room was as dark as the hallway. The musky scent was stronger here. He jumped when a hand closed on his upper arm—it felt wrong, there was hair on the palm, the hard nails made a circlet of pressure points—and a gravelly male voice boomed, "Come in, Mister Svetz. My daughter tells me you're a traveler in need of help."

In the dim light Svetz made out a man and a woman seated on backless chairs. Both had hair as white as Wrona's, but the woman's hair bore a broad black stripe. A second man urged Svetz toward another backless chair. He too bore black markings: a single black eyebrow, a black crescent around one ear.

And Wrona was just behind him. Sveta looked around at them all, seeing how like they were, how different from Hanville Svetz.

The fear rose up in him like a strong drug. Svetz was a xenophobe.

They were all alike. Rich white hair and eyebrows, black markings. Narrow black fingernails. The broad flat noses and the wide, wide mouths, the sharp white conical teeth, the high, pointed ears that moved, the yellow eyes, the hairy palms.

Svetz dropped heavily onto the padded footstool.

One of the males noticed: the larger one, who was still standing. "It must be the heavier gravity," he guessed. "It's true, isn't it, Svetz? You're from another world. Obviously you're not quite a man. You told Wrona you were a traveler, but you didn't say how far away."

"Very far," Svetz said weakly. "From the future."

The smaller male was jolted. "The future? You're a time traveler?" His voice became a snarl. "You're saying that we will evolve into something like you!"

Svetz cringed. "No. Really."

"I hope not. What, then?"

"I think I must have gone sidewise in time. You're descended from wolves, aren't you? Not apes. Wolves."

"Yes, of course."

The seated male was looking him over. "Now that he mentions it, he does look much more like a troll than any man has a right to. No offense intended, Svetz."

Svetz, surrounded by wolf men, tried to relax. And failed. "What is a troll?"

Wrona perched on the edge of his stool. "You must have seen them on the lawn. We keep about thirty."

"Plains apes," the smaller male supplied. "Imported from Africa, sometime in the last century. They make good watchbeasts and meat animals. You have to be careful with them, though. They throw things."

"Introductions," the other said suddenly. "Excuse our manners, Svetz. I'm Flakee Wrocky. This is my brother Flakee Worrel, and Brenda, his wife. My niece you know."

"Pleased to meet you," Svetz said hollowly.

"You say you slipped sideways in time?"

"I think so. A futz of a long way, too," said Svetz. "Marooned. Gods protect me. It must have been the horse—"

Wrocky broke in. "Horse?"

"The horse. Three years ago, a horse damaged my extension cage. It was supposed to be fixed. I suppose the repairs just wore through, and the cage slipped sideways in time instead of forward. Into a world where wolves evolved instead of *Homo habilis.* Gods know where I'm likely to wind up if I try to go back."

Then he remembered. "At least you can help me there. Some kind of monster has taken over my extension cage."

"Extension cage?"

"The part of the time machine that does the moving. You'll help me evict the monster?"

"Of course," said Worrel, at the same time the other was saying, "I don't think so. Bear with me, please, Worrel. Svetz, it would be a disservice to you if we chased the monster out of your extension cage. You would try to reach your own time, would you not?"

"Futz, yes!"

"But you would only get more and more lost. At least in our world you can eat the food and breathe the air. Yes, we grow food plants for the trolls; you can learn to eat them."

"You don't understand. I can't stay here. I'm a xenophobe!"

Wrocky frowned. His ears flicked forward inquiringly. "What?"

"I'm afraid of intelligent beings who aren't human. I can't help it. It's in my bones."

"Oh, I'm sure you'll get used to us, Svetz."

Svetz looked from one male to the other. It was obvious enough who was in charge. Wrocky's voice was much louder and deeper than Worrel's; he was bigger than the other man, and his white fur fell about his neck in a mane like a lion's. Worrel was making no attempt to assert himself. As for the women, neither had spoken a word since Svetz entered the room.

Wrocky was emphatically the boss. And Wrocky didn't want Svetz to leave.

"You don't understand," Svetz said desperately. "The air—" He stopped.

"What about the air?"

"It should have killed me by now. A dozen times over. In fact, why hasn't it?" Odd enough that he'd ever stopped wondering about that. "I must have adapted," Svetz said half to himself. "That's it. The cage passed too close to this line of history. My heredity changed. My lungs adapted to preindustrial air. Futz it! If I hadn't pulled the interrupter switch I'd have adapted back!"

"Then you can breathe our air," said Wrocky.

"I still don't understand it. Don't you have any industries?"

"Of course," Worrel said in surprise.

"Internal combustion cars and aircraft? Diesel trucks and ships? Chemical fertilizers, insect repellents—"

"No, none of that. Chemical fertilizers wash away, ruin the water. The only insect repellents I ever heard of smelled to high heaven. They never got beyond the experimental stage. Most of our vehicles are battery-powered."

"There *was* a fad for internal combustion once," said Wrocky. "It didn't spread very far. They stank. The people inside didn't care, of course, because they were leaving the stink behind. At its peak there were over two hundred cars tootling around the city of Detroit, poisoning the air. Then one night the citizenry rose in a pack and tore all the cars to pieces. The owners too."

Worrel said, "I've always thought that men have more sensitive noses than trolls."

"Wrona noticed my smell long before I noticed hers. Wrocky, this is getting us nowhere. I've *got* to go home. I seem to have adapted to the air, but there are other things. Foods: I've never eaten anything but dole yeast; everything else died out long ago. Bacteria."

Wrocky shook his head. "Anywhere you go, Svetz, your broken time machine will only take you to more and more exotic environments. There must be a thousand ways the world could end. Suppose you stepped out into one of them? Or just passed near one?"

"But—"

"Here, on the other paw, you will be an honored guest. Think of all the things you can teach us! You, who were born into a culture that builds time-traveling vehicles!"

So that was it. "Oh, no. You couldn't use what I know," said Svetz. "I'm no mechanic. I couldn't show you how to do anything. Besides, you'd hate the side effects. Too much of past civilizations was built on petrochemicals. And plastics. Burning plastics produces some of the strangest—"

"But even the most extensive oil reserves could not last forever. You must have developed other power sources by your own time." Wrocky's yellow eyes seemed to bore right through him. "Controlled hydrogen fusion?"

"But I can't tell you how it's done!" Svetz cried desperately. "I know nothing of plasma physics!"

"Plasma physics? What are plasma physics?"

"Using electromagnetic fields to manipulate ionized gases. You *must* have plasma physics."

"No, but I'm sure you can give us some valuable hints. Already we have fusion bombs. And so do the Europeans . . . but we can discuss that later." Wrocky stood up. His black nails made pressure points on Svetz's arm. "Think it over, Svetz.

Oh, and make yourself free of the house, but don't go outside without an escort. The trolls, you know."

Svetz left the room with his head whirling. The wolves would not let him leave.

"Svetz, I'm glad you're staying," Wrona chattered. "I like you. I'm sure you'll like it here. Let me show you the house."

Down the length of the hallway, one frosted globe burned dimly in the gloom, like a full moon transported indoors. Nocturnal, they were nocturnal.

Wolves.

"I'm a xenophobe," he said. "I can't help it. I was born that way."

"Oh, you'll learn to like us. You like me a little already, don't you, Svetz?" She reached up to scratch him behind the ear. A thrill of pleasure ran through him, unexpectedly sharp, so that he half closed his eyes.

"This way," she said.

"Where are we going?"

"I thought I'd show you some trolls. Svetz, are you really descended from trolls? I can't believe it!"

"I'll tell you when I see them," said Svetz. He remembered the *Homo habilis* in the Vivarium. It had been a man, an Advisor, until the Secretary-General ordered him regressed.

They went through the dining room, and Svetz saw unmistakable bones on the plates. He shivered. His forebears had eaten meat; the trolls were brute animals here, whatever they might be in Svetz's world—but Svetz shuddered. His thinking seemed turgid, his head felt thick. He had to get out of here.

"If you think Uncle Wrocky's tough, you should meet the European ambassador," said Wrona. "Perhaps you will."

"Does he come here?"

"Sometimes." Wrona growled low in her throat. "I don't like him. He's a different species, Svetz. Here it was the wolves that evolved into men; at least that's what our teacher tells us. In Europe it was something else."

"I don't think Uncle Wrocky will let me meet him. Or even tell him about me." Svetz rubbed at his eyes.

"You're lucky. Herr Dracula smiles a lot and says nasty things in a polite voice. It takes you a minute to—Svetz! What's wrong?"

Svetz groaned like a man in agony. "My eyes!" He felt higher. "My forehead! I don't have a forehead any more!"

"I don't understand."

Svetz felt his face with his fingertips. His eyebrows were a caterpillar of hair on a thick, solid ridge of bone. From the brow ridge his forehead sloped back at forty-five degrees. And his chin, his chin was gone too. There was only a regular curve of jaw into neck.

"I'm regressing. I'm turning into a troll," said Svetz. "Wrona, if I turn into a troll, will they eat me?"

"I don't know. I'll stop them, Svetz!"

"No. Take me down to the extension cage. If you're not with me the trolls will kill me."

"All right. But Svetz, what about the monster?"

"He should be easier to handle by now. It'll be all right. Just take me there. Please."

"All right, Svetz." She took his hand and led him.

The mirror hadn't lied. He'd been changing even then, adapting to this line of history. First his lungs had lost their adaptation to normal air. There had been no industrial age here. But there had been no *Homo sapiens* either. . . .

Wrona opened the door. Svetz sniffed at the night. His sense of smell had become preternaturally acute. He smelled the trolls before he saw them, coming uphill toward him across the living green carpet. Svetz's fingers curled, wishing for a weapon.

Three of them. They formed a ring around Svetz and Wrona. One of them carried a length of white bone. They all walked upright on two legs, but they walked as if their feet hurt them. They were as hairless as men. Apes' heads mounted on men's bodies.

Homo habilis, the killer plains ape. Man's ancestor.

"Pay them no attention," Wrona said offhandedly. "They won't hurt us." She started down the hill. Svetz followed closely.

"He really shouldn't have that bone," she called back. "We try to keep bones away from them. They use them as weapons. Sometimes they hurt each other. Once one of them got hold of the iron handle for the lawn sprinkler and killed a gardener with it."

"I'm not going to take it away from him."

"That glaring light, is that your extension cage?"

"Yes."

"I'm not sure about this, Svetz." She stopped suddenly. "Uncle Wrocky's right. You'll only get more lost. Here you'll at least be taken care of."

"No. Uncle Wrocky was wrong. See the dark side of the

extension cage, how it fades away to nothing? It's still attached to the rest of the time machine. It'll just reel me in."

"Oh."

"No telling how long it's been veering across the time lines. Maybe ever since that futzy horse poked his futzy horn through the controls. Nobody ever noticed before. Why should they? Nobody ever stopped a time machine halfway before."

"Svetz, horses don't have horns."

"Mine does."

There was noise behind them. Wrona looked back into a darkness Svetz's eyes could not pierce. "Somebody must have noticed us! Come on, Svetz!"

She pulled him toward the lighted cage. They stopped just outside.

"My head feels thick," Svetz mumbled. "My tongue too."

"What are we going to do about the monster? I can't hear anything—"

"No monster. Just a man with amnesia, now. He was only dangerous in the transition stage."

She looked in. "Why, you're right! Sir, would you mind— Svetz, he doesn't seem to understand me."

"Sure not. Why should he? He thinks he's a white arctic wolf." Svetz stepped inside. The white-haired wolf man was backed into a corner, warily watching. He looked a lot like Wrona.

Svetz became aware that he had picked up a tree branch. His hand must have done it without telling his brain. He circled, the weapon ready. An unreasoning rage built up and up in him. Invader! The man had no business here in Svetz's territory.

The wolf man backed away, his slant eyes mad and frightened. Suddenly he was out the door and running, the trolls close behind.

"Your father can teach him, maybe," said Svetz.

Wrona was studying the controls. "How do you work it?"

"Let me see. I'm not sure I remember." Svetz rubbed at his drastically sloping forehead. "That one closes the door—"

Wrona pushed it. The door closed.

"Shouldn't you be outside?"

"I want to come with you," said Wrona.

"Oh." It was getting terribly difficult to think. Svetz looked over the control panel. Eeny, meeny—that one? Svetz pulled it.

Free fall. Wrona yipped. Gravity came, vectored radially

outward from the center of the extension cage. It pulled them against the walls.

"When my lungs go back to normal, I'll probably go to sleep,"said Svetz. "Don't worry about it." Was there something else he ought to tell Wrona? He tried to remember.

Oh, yes. "You can't go home again," said Svetz. "We'd never find this line of history again."

"I want to stay with you," said Wrona.

"All right."

Within a deep recess in the bulk of the time machine, a fog formed. It congealed abruptly—and Svetz's extension cage was back, hours late. The door popped open automatically. But Svetz didn't come out.

They had to pull him out by the shoulders, out of air that smelled of beast and honeysuckle.

"He'll be all right in a minute. Get a filter tent over that other thing," Ra Chen ordered. He stood over Svetz with his arms folded, waiting.

Svetz began breathing.

He opened his eyes.

"All right," said Ra Chen. "What happened?"

Svetz sat up. "Let me think. I went back to preindustrial America. It was all snowed in. I . . . shot a wolf."

"We've got it in a tent. Then what?"

"No. The wolf left. We chased him out." Svetz's eyes went wide. "Wrona!"

Wrona lay on her her side in the filter tent. Her fur was thick and rich, white with black markings. She was built something like a wolf, but more compactly, with a big head and a short muzzle and a tightly curled tail. Her eyes were closed. She did not seem to be breathing.

Svetz knelt. "Help me get her out of there! Can't you tell the difference between a wolf and a dog?"

"No. Why would you bring back a dog, Svetz. We've got dozens of dogs."

Svetz wasn't listening. He pulled away the filter tent and bent over Wrona. "I think she's a dog. More dog than wolf, anyway. People tend to domesticate each other. She's adapted to our line of history. And our brand of air." Svetz looked up at his boss. "Sir, we'll have to junk the old extension cage. It's been veering sideways in time."

"Have you been eating gunchy pills on the job?"

"I'll tell you all about it—"

Wrona opened her eyes. She looked about her in rising panic until she found Svetz. She looked up at him, her golden eyes questioning.

"I'll take care of you. Don't worry," Svetz told her. He scratched her behind the ear, his fingertips deep in soft fur. To Ra Chen he said, "The Vivarium doesn't need any more dogs. She can stay with me."

"Are you crazy, Svetz? You, live with an animal? You hate animals!"

"She saved my life. I won't let anyone put her in a cage."

"Sure, keep it! Live with it! I don't suppose you plan to pay back the two million commercials she cost us? I thought not." Ra Chen made a disgusted sound. "All right, let's have your report. And keep that thing under control, will you?"

Wrona raised her nose and sniffed at the air. Then she howled. The sound echoed within the Institute, and heads turned in questioning and fear.

Puzzled, Svetz imitated the gesture, and understood.

The air was rich with petrochemicals and oxides of carbon and nitrogen and sulfur. Industrial air, the air Svetz had breathed all his life.

And Svetz hated it.

MANY MANSIONS

by Robert Silverberg

*Robert Silverberg (1935–   ) has had two very differ-
ent careers in science fiction. From his debut in 1955 until
the mid-1960s, he produced a huge amount of generally
(there were of course exceptions) undistinguished but commercial science fiction. Then, after several years in which
he wrote a large number of excellent nonfiction books, he
returned to the field with some of the most striking and
powerful sf ever written—novels like* Hawksbill Station
(1968), Up the Line *(1969),* Tower of Glass *(1970),* Dying
Inside *(1972), and* The Stochastic Man *(1975) among
many others, including many fine short stories. After another retirement from the field, he returned again in 1980
with* Lord Valentine's Castle *and has continued to produce outstanding novels on a regular basis since then. His
most recent book is* Star of Gypsies *(1986).*

It's been a rough day. Everything gone wrong. A tremendous tie-up on the freeway going to work, two accounts
canceled before lunch, now some inconceivable botch by the
weather programmers. It's snowing outside. Actually snowing.
He'll have to go out and clear the driveway in the morning. He
can't remember when it last snowed. And of course a fight with
Alice again. She never lets him alone. She's at her most deadly
when she sees him come home exhausted from the office. Ted,
why don't you this; Ted, get me that. Now, waiting for dinner,
working on his third drink in forty minutes, he feels one of his
headaches coming on. Those miserable killer headaches that
can destroy a whole evening. What a life! He toys with murderous fantasies. Take her out by the reservoir for a friendly little
stroll, give her a quick hard shove with his shoulder. She can't
swim. Down, down, down. Glub. Goodbye, Alice. Free at last.

*   *   *

In the kitchen she furiously taps the keys of the console, programming dinner just the way he likes it. Cold vichyssoise, baked potato with sour cream and chives, sirloin steak blood-rare inside and charcoal-charred outside. Don't think it isn't work to get the meal just right, even with the autochef. All for him. The bastard. Tell me, why do I sweat so hard to please him? Has he made me happy? What's he ever done for me except waste the best years of my life? And he thinks I don't know about his other women. Those lunchtime quickies. Oh, I wouldn't mind at all if he dropped dead tomorrow. I'd be a great widow—so dignified at the funeral, so strong, hardly crying at all. And everybody thinks we're such a close couple. "Married eleven years and they're still in love." I heard some-one say that only last week. If they only knew the truth about us. If they only knew.

Martin peers out the window of his third-floor apartment in Sunset Village. Snow. I'll be damned. He can't remember the last time he saw snow. Thirty, forty years back, maybe, when Ted was a baby. He absolutely can't remember. White stuff on the ground—when? The mind gets wobbly when you're past eighty. He still can't believe he's an old man. It rocks him to realize that his grandson Ted, Martha's boy, is almost forty. I bounced that kid on my knee and he threw up all over my suit. Four years old then. Nixon was President. Nobody talks much about Tricky Dick these days. Ancient history. McKinley, Coolidge, Nixon. Time flies. Martin thinks of Ted's wife Alice. What a nice tight little ass she has. What a cute pair of jugs. I'd like to get my hands on them. I really would. You know something, Martin? You're not such an old ruin yet. Not if you can get it up for your grandson's wife.

His dreams of drowning her fade as quickly as they came. He is not a violent man by nature. He knows he could never do it. He can't even bring himself to step on a spider; how then could he kill his wife? If she'd die some other way of course, without the need of his taking direct action, that would solve every-thing. She's driving to the hairdresser on one of those manual-access roads she likes to use and her car swerves on an icy spot, and she goes into a tree at eighty kilometers an hour. Good. She's shopping on Union Boulevard and the bank is blown up by an activist; she's nailed by flying debris. Good. The dentist

gives her a new anesthetic and it turns out she's fatally allergic
to it. Puffs up like a blowfish and dies in five minutes. Good.
The police come—long faces, snuffy noses. Terribly sorry, Mr.
Porter. There's been an awful accident. Don't tell me it's my
wife, he cries. They nod lugubriously. He bears up bravely
under the loss, though.

"You can come in for dinner now," she says. He's sitting
slouched on the sofa with another drink in his hand. He drinks
more than any man she knows—not that she knows all that
many. Maybe he'll get cirrhosis and die. Do people still die of
cirrhosis, she wonders, or do they give them liver transplants
now? The funny thing is that he still turns her on, after eleven
years. His eyes, his face, his hands. She despises him, but he
still turns her on.

The snow reminds him of his young manhood, of his days
long ago in the East. He was quite the ladies' man then. And it
wasn't so easy to get some action back in those days, either.
The girls were always worried about what people would say if
anyone found out. *What people would say!* As if doing it with a
boy you liked was something shameful. Or they'd worry about
getting knocked up. They made you wear a rubber. How awful
that was: like wearing a sock. The pill was just starting to come
in, the original pill, the old one-a-day kind. Imagine a world
without the pill! ("Did they have dinosaurs when you were a
boy, Grandpa?") Still, Martin had made out all right. Big
muscular frame, strong earnest features, warm inquisitive eyes.
You'd never know it to look at me now. I wonder if Alice
realizes what kind of stud I used to be. If I had the money I'd
rent one of those time machines they've got now and send her
back to visit myself around 1950 or so. A little gift to my
younger self. He'd really rip into her. It gives Martin a quick
riffle of excitement to think of his younger self ripping into
Alice. But of course he can't afford any such thing.

As he forks down his steak he imagines being single again.
Would I get married again? Not on your life. Not until I'm
good and ready, anyway; maybe when I'm fifty-five or sixty.
Me for bachelorhood for the time being, just screwing around
like a kid. To hell with responsibilities. I'll wait two, three
weeks after the funeral, a decent interval, and then I'll go off
for some fun. Hawaii, Tahiti, Fiji, someplace out there. With

Nolie. Or Maria. Or Ellie. Yes, with Ellie. He thinks of Ellie's
pink thighs, her soft heavy breasts, her long, radiant, auburn
hair. Two weeks in Fiji with Ellie. Two weeks in Ellie with Fiji.
Yes. Yes. Yes. "Is the steak rare enough for you, Ted?" Alice
asks. "It's fine," he says.

She goes upstairs to check the children's bedroom. They're
both asleep, finally. Or else faking it so well that it makes no
difference. She stands by their beds a moment, thinking, I love
you, Bobby, I love you, Tink. Tink and Bobby, Bobby and
Tink. I love you even though you drive me crazy sometimes.
She tiptoes out. Now for a quiet evening of television. And
then to bed. The same old routine. Christ, I don't know why I
go on like this. There are times when I'm ready to explode. I
stay with him for the children's sake, I guess. Is that enough of
a reason?

He envisions himself running hand in hand along the beach
with Ellie. Both of them naked, their skins bronzed and gleaming in the tropical sunlight. Palm trees everywhere. Grains of
pink sand under foot. Soft, transparent wavelets lapping the
shore. A quiet cove. "No one can see us here," Ellie murmurs.
He sinks down on her firm, sleek body and enters her.

A blazing band of pain tightens like a strip of hot metal
across Martin's chest. He staggers away from the window,
dropping into a low crouch as he stumbles toward a chair. The
heart. Oh, the heart! That's what you get for drooling over
Alice. Dirty old man. "Help," he calls feebly. "Come on, you
filthy machine, help me!" The medic, activated by the key
phrase, rolls silently toward him. Its sensors are already at work
scanning him, searching for the cause of the discomfort. A
telescoping steel-jacketed arm slides out of the medic's chest
and, hovering above Martin, extrudes an ultrasonic injection
snout. "Yes," Martin murmurs, "that's right, damn you, hurry
up and give me the drug!" Calm. I must try to remain calm.
The snout makes a gentle whirring noise as it forces the relax-
ant into Martin's vein. He slumps in relief. The pain slowly
ebbs. Oh, that's much better. Saved again. Oh. Oh. Oh. Dirty
old man. Ought to be ashamed of yourself.

Ted knows he won't get to Fiji with Ellie or anybody else.
Any realistic assessment of the situation brings him inevitably

to the same conclusion. Alice isn't going to die in an accident, any more than he's likely to murder her. She'll live forever. Unwanted wives always do. He could ask for a divorce, of course. He'd probably lose everything he owned, but he'd win his freedom. Or he could simply do away with himself. That was always a temptation for him. The easy way out; no lawyers, no hassles. So it's that time of the evening again. It's the same every night. Pretending to watch television, he secretly indulges in suicidal fantasies.

Bare-bodied dancers in gaudy luminous paint gyrate lasciviously on the screen, nearly large as life. Alice scowls. The things they show on TV nowadays! It used to be that you got this stuff only on the X-rated channels, but now it's everywhere. And look at him, just lapping it up! Actually she knows she wouldn't be so stuffy about the sex shows except that Ted's fascination with them is a measure of his lack of interest in her. Let them show screwing and all the rest on TV, if that's what people want. I just wish Ted had as much enthusiasm for me as he does for the television stuff. So far as sexual permissiveness in general goes, she's no prude. She used to wear nothing but trunks at the beach until Tink was born and she started to feel a little less proud of her figure. But she still dresses as revealingly as anyone in their crowd. And gets stared at by everyone but her own husband. *He* watches the TV cuties. His other women must use him up. Maybe I ought to step out a bit myself, Alice thinks. She's had her little affairs along the way. Not many, nothing very serious, but she's had some. Three lovers in eleven years: that's not a great many, but it's a sign that she's no puritan. She wonders if she ought to get involved with somebody now. It might move her life off dead center while she still has the chance, before boredom destroys her entirely. "I'm going up to wash my hair," she announces. "Will you be staying down here till bedtime?"

There are so many ways he could do it. Slit his wrists. Drive his car off the bridge. Swallow Alice's whole box of sleeping tabs. Of course, those are all old-fashioned ways of killing yourself. Something more modern would be appropriate. Go into one of the black taverns and start making loud racial insults? No, nothing modern about that. It's very 1975. But something genuinely contemporary does occur to him. Those time machines they've got now: suppose he rented one and went back, say, sixty years, to a time when one of his parents hadn't yet been born. And killed his grandfather. Find old Martin as a young man and slip a knife into him. If I do that, Ted figured, I should instantly and painlessly cease to exist. I would never have existed, because my mother wouldn't ever have existed. Poof. Out like a light. Then he realizes he's fantasizing a murder again. Stupid—if he could ever murder anyone, he'd murder Alice and be done with it. So the whole fantasy is foolish. Back to the starting point is where he is.

She is sitting under the hair dryer when he comes upstairs. He has a peculiarly smug expression on his face, and as soon as she turns the drier off she asks him what he's thinking about. "I may have just invented a perfect murder method," he tells her. "Oh?" she says. He says, "You rent a time machine. Then you go back a couple of generations and murder one of the ancestors of your intended victim. That way you're murdering the victim too, because he won't ever have been born if you kill off one of his immediate progenitors. Then you return to your own time. Nobody can trace you because you don't have fingerprints on file in an era before your own birth. What do you think of it?" Alice shrugs. "It's an old one," she says. "It's been done on television a dozen times. Anyway, I don't like it. Why should an innocent person have to die just because he's the grandparent of somebody you want to kill?"

They're probably in bed together right now, Martin thinks gloomily. Stark naked side by side. The lights are out. The house is quiet. Maybe they're smoking a little grass. Do they still call it grass, he wonders, or is there some new nickname now? Anyway, the two of them turn on. Yes. And then he reaches for her. His hands slide over her cool smooth skin. He cups her breasts. Plays with the hard little nipples. Sucks on them. The other hand wandering down to her parted thighs. And then she. And then he. And then they. And then they. Oh, Alice, he murmurs. Oh, Ted, *Ted,* she cries. And then they. Go to it. Up and down, in and out. Oh. Oh. Oh. She claws his back. She pumps her hips. Ted! Ted! Ted! The big moment is arriving now. For her, for him. Jackpot! Afterward they lie close for a few minutes, basking in the afterglow. And then they roll apart. Good night, Ted. Good night, Alice. Oh, Jesus. They do it every night, I bet. They're so young and full of juice. And I'm all dried up. Christ, I hate being old. When I think of the man I once was. When I think of the women I once had. Jesus. Jesus. God, let me have the strength to do it just once more before I die. And leave me alone for two hours with Alice.

She has trouble falling asleep. A strange scene keeps playing itself out obsessively in her mind. She sees herself stepping out of an upright coffin-sized box of dark gray metal, festooned with dials and levers. The time machine. It delivers her into a dark, dirty alleyway, and when she walks forward to the street she sees scores of little antique automobiles buzzing around. Only they aren't antiques: they're the current models. This is the year 1947. New York City. Will she be conspicuous in her futuristic clothes? She has her breasts covered, at any rate. That's essential back here. She hurries to the proper address, resisting the temptation to browse in shop windows along the way. How quaint and ancient everything looks. And how dirty the streets are. She comes to a tall building of red brick. This is the place. No scanners study her as she enters. They don't have annunciators yet or any other automatic home-protection equipment. She goes upstairs in an elevator so creaky and unstable that she fears for her life. Fifth floor. Apartment 5-J. She rings the doorbell. *He* answers. He's terribly young, only twenty-four, but she can pick out signs of the Martin of the future in his face, the strong cheekbones, the searching blue eyes. "Are you Martin Jamieson?" she asks. "That's right," he says. She smiles. "May I come in?" "Of course," he says. He bows her into the apartment. As he momentarily turns his back on her to open the coat closet she takes the heavy steel pipe from her purse and lifts it high and brings it down on the back of his head. *Thwock.* She takes the heavy steel pipe from her purse and lifts it high and brings it down on the back of his head. *Thwock.* She takes the heavy steel pipe from her purse and lifts it high and brings it down on the back of his head. *Thwock.*

Ted and Alice visit him at Sunset Village two or three times a month. He can't complain about that; it's as much as he can expect. He's an old, old man and no doubt a boring one, but they come dutifully, sometimes with the kids, sometimes without. He's never gotten used to the idea that he's a great-grandfather. Alice always gives him a kiss when she arrives and another when she leaves. He plays a private little game with her, copping a feel at each kiss. His hand quickly stroking her butt. Or sometimes when he's really rambunctious his hand travels lightly over her breasts. Does she notice? Probably. She never lets on, though. Pretends it's an accidental touch. Most likely she thinks it's charming that a man of his age would still have at least a vestige of sexual desire left. Unless she thinks it's disgusting, that is.

The time-machine gimmick, Ted tells himself, can be used in ways that don't quite amount to murder. For instance. "What's that box?" Alice asks. He smiled cunningly. "It's called a panchronicon," he says. "It gives you a kind of televised recon-struction of ancient times. The salesman loaned me a demon-stration sample." She says, "How does it work?" "Just step inside," he tells her. "It's all ready for you." She starts to enter the machine, but then, suddenly suspicious, she hesitates on the threshold. He pushes her in and slams the door shut behind her. *Wham!* The controls are set. Off goes Alice on a one-way journey to the Pleistocene. The machine is primed to return as soon as it drops her off. That isn't murder, is it? She's still alive, wherever she may be, unless the saber-toothed tigers have caught up with her. So long, Alice.

In the morning she drives Bobby and Tink to school. Then she stops at the bank and the post office. From ten to eleven she has her regular session at the identity-reinforcement parlor. Ordinarily she would go right home after that, but this morning she strolls across the shopping-center plaza to the office that the time-machine people have just opened. TEMPONAUTICS, LTD., the sign over the door says. The place is empty except for two machines, no doubt demonstration models, and a bland-faced, smiling salesman. "Hello," Alice says nervously. "I just wanted to pick up some information about the rental costs of one of your machines."

Martin likes to imagine Alice coming to visit him by herself some rainy Saturday afternoon. "Ted isn't able to make it today," she explains. "Something came up at the office. But I knew you were expecting us, and I didn't want you to be disappointed. Poor Martin, you must lead such a lonely life." She comes close to him. She is trembling. So is he. Her face is flushed and her eyes are bright with the unmistakable glossiness of desire. He feels a sense of sexual excitement too, for the first time in ten or twenty years, that tension in the loins, that throbbing of the pulse. Electricity. Chemistry. His eyes lock on hers. Her nostrils flare, her mouth goes taut. "Martin," she whispers huskily. "Do you feel what I feel?" "You know I do," he tells her. She says, "If only I could have known you when you were in your prime!" He chuckles. "I'm not altogether senile yet," he cries exultantly. Then she is in his arms and his lips are seeking her fragrant breasts.

"Yes, it came as a terrible shock to me," Ted tells Ellie. "Having her disappear like that. She simply vanished from the face of the earth, as far as anyone can determine. They've tried every possible way of tracing her and there hasn't been a clue." Ellie's flawless forehead furrows in a fitful frown. "Was she unhappy?" she asks. "Do you think she may have done away with herself?" Ted shakes his head. "I don't know. You live with a person for eleven years and you think you know her pretty well, and then one day something absolutely incomprehensible occurs and you realize how impossible it is ever to know another human being at all. Don't you agree?" Ellie nods gravely. "Yes, oh, yes, certainly!" she says. He smiles down at her and takes her hands in his. Softly he says, "Let's not talk about Alice anymore, shall we? She's gone and that's all I'll ever know." He hears a pulsing symphonic crescendo of shimmering angelic choirs as he embraces her and murmurs, "I love you, Ellie. I love you."

She takes the heavy steel pipe from her purse and lifts it high and brings it down on the back of his head. *Thwock.* Young Martin drops instantly, twitches once, lies still. Dark blood begins to seep through the dense blond curls of his hair. How strange to see Martin with golden hair, she thinks as she kneels beside his body. She puts her hand to the bloody place, probes timidly, feels the deep indentation. Is he dead? She isn't sure how to tell. He isn't moving. He doesn't seem to be breathing. She wonders if she ought to hit him again, just to make certain. Then she remembers something she's seen on television, and takes her mirror from her purse. Holds it in front of his face. No cloud forms. That's pretty conclusive: you're dead, Martin. R.I.P. Martin Jamieson, 1923-1947. Which means that Martha Jamieson Porter (1948-   ) will never now be conceived, and that automatically obliterates the existence of her son Theodore Porter (1968-   ). Not bad going, Alice, getting rid of unloved husband and miserable shrewish mother-in-law all in one shot.

Sorry, Martin. Bye-bye, Ted. (R.I.P. Theodore Porter, 1968-1947. Eh?) She rises, goes into the bathroom with the steel pipe, and carefully rinses it off. Then she puts it back into her purse. Now to go back to the machine and return to 2006, she thinks. To start my new life. But as she leaves the apartment, a tall, lean man steps out of the hallway shadows and clamps his hand powerfully around her wrist. "Time Patrol," he says crisply, flashing an identification badge. "You're under arrest for temponautic murder, Mrs. Porter."

Today has been a better day than yesterday, low on crises and depressions, but he still feels a headache coming on as he lets himself into the house. He is braced for whatever bitchiness Alice may have in store for him this evening. But she seems oddly relaxed and amiable. "Can I get you a drink, Ted?" she asks. "How did your day go?" He smiles and says, "Well, I think we may have salvaged the Hammond account after all. Otherwise nothing special happened. And you? What did you do today, love?" She shrugs. "Oh, the usual stuff," she says. "The bank, the post office, my identity-reinforcement session."

If you had the money, Martin asks himself, how far back would you send her? 1947, that would be the year, I guess. My last year as a single man. No sense complicating things. Off you go, Alice baby, to 1947. Let's make it March. By June I was engaged and by September Martha was on the way, though I didn't find that out until later. Yes: March, 1947. So. Young Martin answers the doorbell and sees an attractive girl in the hall—a woman, really, older than he is, maybe thirty or thirty-two. Slender, dark-haired, nicely constructed. Odd clothing: a clinging gray tunic, very short, made of some strange fabric that flows over her body like a stream. How it achieves that liquid effect around the pleats is beyond him. "Are you Martin Jamieson?" she asks. And quickly answers herself. "Yes, of course, you must be. I recognize you. How handsome you were!" He is baffled. He knows nothing, naturally, about this gift from his aged future self. "Who are you?" he asks. "May I come in first?" she says. He is embarrassed by his lack of courtesy and waves her inside. Her eyes glitter with mischief. "You aren't going to believe this," she tells him, "but I'm your grandson's wife."

* * *

"Would you like to try out one of our demonstration models?" the salesman asks pleasantly. "There's absolutely no cost or obligation." Ted looks at Alice. Alice looks at Ted. Her frown mirrors his inner uncertainty. She too must be wishing that they had never come to the Temponautics showroom. The salesman, pattering smoothly onward, says, "In these demonstrations we usually send our potential customers fifteen or twenty minutes into the past. I'm sure you'll find it fascinating. While remaining in the machine, you'll be able to look through a viewer and observe your own selves actually entering this very showroom a short while ago. Well? Will you give it a try? You go first, Mrs. Porter. I assure you it's going to be the most unique experience you've ever had." Alice, uneasy, tries to back off, but the salesman prods her in a way that is at once gentle and unyielding, and she steps reluctantly into the time machine. He closes the door. A great business of adjusting fine controls ensues. Then the salesman throws a master switch. A green glow envelopes the machine and it disappears, although something transparent and vague—a retinal afterimage? the ghost of the machine?—remains dimly visible. The salesman says, "She's now gone a short distance into her own past. I've programmed the machine to take her back eighteen minutes and keep her there for a total elapsed interval of six minutes, so she can see the entire opening moments of your visit here. But when I return her to Now Level, there's no need to match the amount of elapsed time in the past, so that from our point of view she'll have been absent only some thirty seconds. Isn't that remarkable, Mr. Porter? It's one of the many extraordinary paradoxes we encounter in the strange new realm of time travel." He throws another switch. The time machine once more assumes solid form. "*Voilà!*" cries the salesman. "Here is Mrs. Porter, returned safe and sound from her voyage into the past." He flings open the door of the time machine. The passenger compartment is empty. The salesman's face crumbles. "Mrs. Porter?" he shrieks in consternation. "Mrs. Porter? I don't understand! How could there have been a malfunction? This is impossible! Mrs. Porter? *Mrs. Porter?*"

She hurries down the dirty street toward the tall brick building. This is the place. Upstairs. Fifth floor, Apartment 5-J. As she starts to ring the doorbell, a tall, lean man steps out of the shadows and clamps his hand powerfully around her wrist. "Time Patrol," he says crisply, flashing an identification badge.

"You're under arrest for contemplated temponautic murder, Mrs. Porter."

"But I haven't any grandson," he sputters. "I'm not even mar—" She laughs. "Don't worry about it!" she tells him. "You're going to have a daughter named Martha and she'll have a son named Ted and I'm going to marry Ted and we'll have two children named Bobby and Tink. And you're going to live to be an old, old man. And that's all you need to know. Now let's have a little fun." She touches a catch at the side of her tunic and the garment falls away in a single fluid cascade. Beneath it she is naked. Her nipples stare up at him like blind pink eyes. She beckons to him. "Come on!" she says hoarsely. "Get undressed, Martin! You're wasting time!"

Alice giggles nervously. "Well, as a matter of fact," she says to the salesman, "I think I'm willing to let my husband be the guinea pig. How about it, Ted?" She turns towards him. So does the salesman. "Certainly, Mr. Porter. I know you're eager to give our machine a test run, yes?" No, Ted thinks, but he feels the pressure of events propelling him willy-nilly. He gets into the machine. As the door closes on him he fears that claustrophobic panic will overwhelm him; he is reassured by the sight of a handle on the door's inner face. He pushes on it and the door opens, and he steps out of the machine just in time to see his earlier self coming into the Temponautics showroom with Alice. The salesman is going forward to greet them. Ted is now eighteen minutes into his own past. Alice and the other Ted stare at him, aghast. The salesman whirls and exclaims. "Wait a second, you aren't supposed to get out of—" How stupid they all look! How bewildered! Ted laughs in their faces. Then he rushes past them, nearly knocking his other self down, and erupts into the shopping-center plaza. He sprints in a wild frenzy of exhilaration toward the parking area. Free, he thinks. I'm free at last. And I didn't have to kill anybody.

Suppose I rent a machine, Alice thinks, and go back to 1947 and kill Martin. Suppose I really do it. What if there's some way of tracing the crime to me? After all, a crime committed by a person from 2006 who goes back to 1947 will have consequences in our present day. It might change all sorts of things. So they'd want to catch the criminal and punish him, or better yet prevent the crime from being committed in the first place. And the time-machine company is bound to know what year I asked them to send me to. So maybe it isn't such an easy way of committing a perfect crime. I don't know. God, I can't understand any of this. But perhaps I can get away with it. Anyway, I'm going to give it a try. I'll show Ted he can't go on treating me like dirt.

They lie peacefully side by side, sweaty, drowsy, exhausted in the good exhaustion that comes after a first-rate screw. Martin tenderly strokes her belly and thighs. How smooth her skin is, how pale, how transparent! The little blue veins so clearly visible. "Hey," he says suddenly. "I just thought of something. I wasn't wearing a rubber or anything. What if I made you pregnant? And if you're really who you say you are, then you'll go back to the year 2006 and you'll have a kid and he'll be his own grandfather, won't he?" She laughs. "Don't worry much about it," she says.

A wave of timidity comes over her as she enters the Temponautics office. This is crazy, she tells herself. I'm getting out of here. But before she can turn around, the salesman she spoke to the day before materializes from a side room and gives her a big hello. Mr. Friesling. He's practically rubbing his hands together in anticipation of landing a contract. "So nice to see you again, Mrs. Porter." She nods and glances worriedly at the demonstration models. "How much would it cost," she asks, "to spend a few hours in the spring of 1947?"

Sunday is a big family day. Four generations sitting down to dinner together: Martin, Martha, Ted and Alice, Bobby and Tink. Ted rather enjoys these reunions, but he knows Alice loathes them, mainly because of Martha. Alice hates her mother-in-law. Martha has never cared much for Alice, either. He watches them glaring at each other across the table. Meanwhile, old Martin stares lecherously at the gulf between Alice's breasts. You have to hand it to the old man, Ted thinks. He's never lost the old urge. Even though there's not a hell of a lot he can do about gratifying it, not at his age. Martha says sweetly, "You'd look ever so much better, Alice dear, if you'd let your hair grow out to its natural color." A sugary smile from Martha. A sour scowl from Alice. She glowers at the older woman. "This *is* its natural color," she snaps.

*   *   *

Mr. Friesling hands her the standard contract form. Eight pages of densely packed type. "Don't be frightened by it, Mrs. Porter. It looks formidable, but actually it's just a lot of empty legal rhetoric. You can show it to your lawyer, if you like. I can tell you, though, that most of our customers find no need for that." She leafs through it. So far as she can tell, the contract is mainly a disclaimer of responsibility. Temponautics, Ltd., agrees to bear the brunt of any malfunction caused by its own demonstrable negligence, but wants no truck with acts of God or with accidents brought about by clients who won't obey the safety regulations. On the fourth page Alice finds a clause warning the prospective renter that the company cannot be held liable for any consequences of actions by the renter which wantonly or willfully interfere with the already determined course of history. She translates that for herself: *If you kill your husband's grandfather, don't blame us if you get in trouble.* She skims the remaining pages. "It looks harmless enough," she says. "Where do I sign?"

As Martin comes out of the bathroom he finds Martha blocking his way. "Excuse me," he says mildly, but she remains in his path. She is a big fleshy woman. At fifty-eight she affects the fashions of the very young, with grotesque results; he hates that aspect of her. He can see why Alice dislikes her so much. "Just a moment," Martha says. "I want to talk to you, Father." "About what?" he asks. "About those looks you give Alice. Don't you think that's a little too much? How tasteless can you get?" "Tasteless?" "Are you anybody to talk about taste with your face painted green like a fifteen-year-old?" She looks angry: he's scored a direct hit. She replies, "I just think that at the age of eighty-two you ought to have a greater regard for decency than to go staring down your own grandson's wife's front." Martin sighs. "Let me have the staring, Martha. It's all I've got left."

He is at the office, deep in complicated negotiations, when his autosecretary bleeps him and announces that a call has come in from a Mr. Friesling, of the Union Boulevard Plaza office of Temponautics, Ltd. Ted is puzzled by that: What do the time-machine people want with him? Trying to line him up as a customer? "Tell him I'm not interested in time trips," Ted says. But the autosecretary bleeps again a few moments later.

Mr. Friesling, it declares, is calling in reference to Mr. Porter's credit standing. More baffled than before, Ted orders the call switched over to him. Mr. Friesling appears on the desk screen. He is small-featured and bright-eyed, rather like a chipmunk. "I apologize for troubling you, Mr. Porter," he begins. "This is strictly a routine credit check, but it's altogether necessary. As you surely know, your wife has requested rental of our equipment for a fifty-nine-year time jaunt, and inasmuch as the service fee for such a trip exceeds the level at which we extend automatic credit, our policy requires me to ask you if you'll confirm the payment schedule that she has requested us to—" Ted coughs violently. "Hold on," he says. "My wife's going on a time jaunt? What the hell, this is the first time I've heard of that!"

She is surprised by the extensiveness of the preparations. No wonder they charge so much. Getting her ready for the jaunt takes hours. They inoculate her to protect her against certain extinct diseases. They provide her with clothing in the style of the mid-twentieth century, ill-fitting and uncomfortable. They give her contemporary currency, but warn her that she would do well not to spend any except in an emergency, since she will be billed for it at its present-day numismatic value, which is high. They make her study a pamphlet describing the customs and historical background of the era and quiz her in detail. She learns that she is not under any circumstances to expose her breasts or genitals in public while she is in 1947. She must not attempt to obtain any mind-stimulating drugs other than alcohol. She should not say anything that might be construed as praise of the Soviet Union or of Marxist philosophy. She must bear in mind that she is entering the past solely as an observer, and should engage in minimal social interaction with the citizens of the era she is visiting. And so forth. At last they decide it's safe to let her go. "Please come this way, Mrs. Porter," Friesling says.

After staring at the telephone a long while, Martin punches out Alice's number. Before the second ring he loses his nerve and disconnects. Immediately he calls her again. His heart pounds so furiously that the medic, registering alarm on its delicate sensing apparatus, starts toward him. He waves the robot away and clings to the phone. Two rings. Three. Ah.

"Hello?" Alice says. Her voice is warm and rich and feminine. He has his screen switched off. "Hello? Who's there?" Martin breathes heavily into the mouthpiece. Ah. Ah. Ah. Ah. "Hello? Hello? Hello? Listen, you pervert, if you phone me once more—" *Ah. Ah. Ah.* A smile of bliss appears on Martin's withered features. Alice hangs up. Trembling, Martin sags in his chair. Oh, that was good! He signals fiercely to the medic. "Let's have the injection now, you metal monster!" He laughs. Dirty old man.

Ted realizes that it isn't necessary to kill a person's grandfather in order to get rid of that person. Just interfere with some crucial event in that person's past, is all. Go back and break up the marriage of Alice's grandparents, for example. (How? Seduce the grandmother when she's eighteen? "I'm terribly sorry to inform you that your intended bride is no virgin, and here's the documentary evidence." They were very grim about virginity back then, weren't they?) Nobody would have to die. But Alice wouldn't ever be born.

Martin still can't believe any of this, even after she's slept with him. It's some crazy practical joke, most likely. Although he wishes all practical jokes were as sexy as this one. "Are you really from the year 2006?" he asks her. She laughs prettily. "How can I prove it to you?" Then she leaps from the bed. He tracks her with his eyes as she crosses the room, breasts jiggling gaily. What a sweet little body. How thoughtful of my older self to ship her back here to me. If that's what really happened. She fumbles in her purse and extracts a handful of coins. "Look here," she says. "Money from the future. Here's a dime from 1993. And this is a two-dollar piece from 2001. And here's an old one, a 1979 Kennedy half dollar." He studies the unfamiliar coins. They have a greasy look, not silvery at all. Counterfeits? They won't necessarily be striking coins out of silver forever. And the engraving job is very professional. A two-dollar piece, eh? Well, you never can tell. And this. The half dollar. A handsome young man in profile. "Kennedy?" he says. "Who's Kennedy?"

So this is it at last. Two technicians in gray smocks watch her, sober-faced, as she clambers into the machine. It's very much like a coffin, just as she imagined it would be. She can't sit down in it; it's too narrow. Gives her the creeps, shut up in here. Of course, they've told her the trip won't take any apparent subjective time, only a couple of seconds. *Woosh!* and she'll be there. All right. They close the door. She hears the lock clicking shut. Mr. Friesling's voice comes to her over a loudspeaker. "We wish you a happy voyage, Mrs. Porter. Keep calm and you won't get into any difficulties." Suddenly the red light over the door is glowing. That means the jaunt has begun: she's traveling backward in time. No sense of acceleration, no sense of motion. One, two, three. The light goes off. That's it. I'm in 1947, she tells herself. Before she opens the door, she closes her eyes and runs through her history lessons. World War II has just ended. Europe is in ruins. There are forty-eight states. Nobody has been to the moon yet or even thinks much about going there. Harry Truman is President. Stalin runs Russia and Churchill—is Churchill still Prime Minister of England? She isn't sure. Well, no matter. I didn't come here to talk about prime ministers. She touches the latch, and the door of the time machine swings outward.

He steps from the machine into the year 2006. Nothing has changed in the showroom. Friesling, the two poker-faced technicians, the sleek desks, the thick carpeting—all the same as before. He moves bouncily. His mind is still back there with Alice's grandmother. The taste of her lips, the soft urgent cries of her fulfillment. Who ever said all women were frigid in the old days? They ought to go back and find out. Friesling smiles at him. "I hope you had a very enjoyable journey, Mr. . . . ah—" Ted nods. "Enjoyable and useful," he says. He goes out. Never to see Alice again—how beautiful! The car isn't where he remembers leaving it in the parking area. You have to expect certain small peripheral changes, I guess. He hails a cab, gives the driver his address. His key does not fit the front door. Troubled, he thumbs the annunciator. A woman's voice, not Alice's, asks him what he wants. 'Is this the Ted Porter residence?" he asks. "No, it isn't," the woman says, suspicious and irritated. The name on the doorplate, he notices now, is McKenzie. So the changes are not all so small. Where do I go now? If I don't live here, then where? "Wait!" he yells to the taxi, just pulling away. It takes him to a downtown cafe, where he phones Ellie. Her face, peering out of the tiny screen, wears an odd frowning expression. "Listen, something very strange has happened," he begins, "and I need to see you as soon as—" "I don't think I know you," she says. "I'm Ted," he tells her. "Ted who?" she asks.

How peculiar this is, Alice thinks. Like walking into a museum diorama and having it come to life. The noisy little automobiles. The ugly clothing. The squat, dilapidated twentieth-century buildings. The chaos. The oily, smoky smell of the polluted air. Wisps of dirty snow in the streets. Cans of garbage just sitting around as if nobody's ever heard of the plague. Well, I won't stay here long. In her purse she carries her kitchen carver, a tiny nickel-jacketed laser-powered implement. Steel pipes are all right for dream fantasies, but this is the real thing, and she wants the killing to be quick and efficient. Criss, cross, with the laser beam, and Martin goes. At the street corner she pauses to check the address. There's no central info number to ring for all sorts of useful data, not in these primitive times; she must use a printed telephone directory, a thick tattered book with small smeary type. Here he is: Martin Jamieson, 504 West 45th. That's not far. In ten minutes she's there. A dark brick structure, five or six stories high, with spidery metal fire escapes running down its face. Even for its day it appears unusually run-down. She goes inside. A list of tenants is posted just within the front door. JAMIESON, 3-A. There's no elevator and of course no liftshaft. Up the stairs. A musty hallway lit by a single dim incandescent bulb. This is Apartment 3-A. Jamieson. She rings the bell.

Ten minutes later Friesling calls back, sounding abashed and looking dismayed: "I'm sorry to have to tell you that there's been some sort of error, Mr. Porter. The technicians were apparently unaware that a credit check was in process and they sent Mrs. Porter off on her trip while we were still talking." Ted is shaken. He clutches the edge of the desk. Controlling himself with an effort, he says, "How far back was it that she wanted to go?" Friesling says, "It was fifty-nine years. To 1947." Ted nods grimly. A horrible idea has occurred to him. 1947 was the year that his mother's parents met and got married. What is Alice up to?

The doorbell rings. Martin, freshly showered, is sprawled out naked on his bed, leafing through the new issue of *Esquire* and thinking vaguely of going out for dinner. He isn't expecting any company. Slipping into his bathrobe, he goes toward the door.

"Who's there?" he calls. A youthful, pleasant female voice replies, "I'm looking for Martin Jamieson." Well, okay. He opens the door. She's perhaps twenty-seven, twenty-eight years old, *very* sexy, on the slender side but well-built. Dark hair, worn in a strangely boyish short cut. He's never seen her before. "Hi," he says tentatively. She grins warmly at him. "You don't know me," she tells him, "but I'm a friend of an old friend of yours. Mary Chambers? Mary and I grew up together in, ah, Ohio. I'm visiting New York for the first time, and Mary once told me that if I ever come to New York I should be sure to look up Martin Jamieson, and so—may I come in?" "You bet," he says. He doesn't remember any Mary Chambers from Ohio. But what the hell, sometimes you forget a few. What the hell.

He's much more attractive than she expected him to be. She has always known Martin only as an old man, made unattractive as much by his coarse lechery as by what age has done to him. Hollow-chested, stoop-shouldered, pleated, jowly face, sparse strands of white hair, beady eyes of faded blue—a wreck of a man. But this Martin in the doorway is sturdy, handsome, untouched by time, brimming with life and vigor and virility. She thinks of the carver in her purse and feels a genuine pang of regret at having to cut this robust boy off in his prime. But there isn't such a great hurry, is there? First we can enjoy each other, Martin. And then the laser.

"When is she due back?" Ted demands. Friesling explains that all concepts of time are relative and flexible; so far as elapsed time at Now Level goes, she's already returned. "What?" Ted yells. "Where is she?" Friesling does not know. She stepped out of the machine, bade the Temponautics staff a pleasant goodbye, and left the showroom. Ted puts his hand to his throat. What if she's already killed Martin? Will I just wink out of existence? Or is there some sort of lag, so that I'll fade gradually into unreality over the next few days? "Listen," he says raggedly, "I'm leaving my office right now and I'll be down at your place in less than an hour. I want you to have your machinery set up so that you can transport me to the exact point in space and time where you just sent my wife." "But that won't be possible," Friesling protests. "It takes hours to prepare a client properly for—" Ted cuts him off. "Get everything set up, and to hell with preparing me properly," he snaps. "Unless you feel like getting slammed with the biggest negligence suit since this time-machine thing got started, you'd better have everything ready when I get there."

He opens the door. The girl in the hallway is young and good-looking, with close-cropped dark hair and full lips. Thank you, Mary Chambers, whoever you may be. "Pardon the bathrobe," he says, "but I wasn't expecting company." She steps into his apartment. Suddenly he notices how strained and tense her face is. Country girl from Ohio, suddenly having second thoughts about visiting a strange man in a strange city? He tries to put her at her ease. "Can I get you a drink?" he asks. "Not much of a selection, I'm afraid, but I have scotch, gin, some blackberry cordial—" She reaches into her purse and takes something out. He frowns. Not a gun, exactly, but it does seem like a weapon of some sort, a little glittering metal device that fits neatly in her hand. "Hey," he says, "what's—" "I'm so terribly sorry, Martin," she whispers, and a bolt of terrible fire slams into his chest.

She sips the drink. It relaxes her. The glass isn't very clean, but she isn't worried about picking up a disease, not after all the injections Friesling gave her. Martin looks as if he can stand some relaxing too. "Aren't you drinking?" she asks. "I suppose I will," he says. He pours himself some gin. She comes up behind him and slips her hand into the front of his bathrobe. His body is cool, smooth, hard. "Oh, Martin," she murmurs. "Oh! Martin!"

Ted takes a room in one of the commercial hotels downtown. The first thing he does is try to put a call through to Alice's mother in Chillicothe. He still isn't really convinced that his little time-jaunt flirtation has retroactively eliminated Alice from existence. But the call convinces him, all right. The middle-aged woman who answers is definitely not Alice's mother. Right phone number, right address—he badgers her for the information—but wrong woman. "You don't have a daughter named Alice Porter?" he asks three or four times. "You don't know anyone in the neighborhood who does? It's important." All right. Cancel the old lady, ergo cancel Alice. But now he has a different problem. How much of the universe has he altered by removing Alice and her mother? Does he live in some other city, now, and hold some other job? What has happened to Bobby and Tink? Frantically he begins phoning people. Friends, fellow workers, the man at the bank. The same response from all of them: blank stares, shakings of the head. We don't know you, fellow. He looks at himself in the mirror. Okay, he asks himself. Who am I?

Martin moves swiftly and purposefully, the way they taught him to do in the army when it's necessary to disarm a dangerous opponent. He lunges forward and catches the girl's arm, pushing it upward before she can fire the shiny whatzis she's aiming at him. She turns out to be stronger than he anticipated, and they struggle fiercely for the weapon. Suddenly it fires. Something like a lightning bolt explodes between them and knocks him to the floor, stunned. When he picks himself up, he sees her lying near the door with a charred hole in her throat.

The telephone's jangling clatter brings Martin up out of the dream in which he is ravishing Alice's luscious young body. Dry-throated, gummy-eyed, he reaches a palsied hand toward the receiver. "Yes?" he says. Ted's face blossoms on the screen. "Grandfather!" he blurts. "Are you all right?" "Of course I'm all right," Martin says testily. "Can't you tell? What's the matter with you, boy?" Ted shakes his head. "I don't know," he mutters. "Maybe it was only a bad dream. I imagined that Alice rented one of those time machines and went back to 1947. And tried to kill you so that I wouldn't ever have existed." Martin snorts. "What idiotic nonsense! How can she have killed me in 1947 when I'm here alive in 2006?"

Naked, Alice sinks into Martin's arms. His strong hands sweep eagerly over her breasts and shoulders and his mouth descends to hers. She shivers with desire. "Yes," she murmurs tenderly, pressing herself against him. "Oh, yes, yes, yes!" They'll do it and it'll be fantastic. And afterward she'll kill him with the kitchen carver while he's lying there savoring the event. But a troublesome thought occurs. If Martin dies in 1947, Ted doesn't get to be born in 1968. Okay. But what about Tink and Bobby? They won't get born either, not if I don't marry Ted. I'll be married to someone else when I get back to 2006, and I suppose I'll have different children. Bobby? Tink? What am I doing to you? Sudden fear congeals her, and she pulls back from the vigorous young man nuzzling her throat.

"Wait," she says. "Listen, I'm sorry. It's all a big mistake. I'm sorry, but I've got to get out of here right away!"

So this is the year 1947. Well, well, well. Everything looks so cluttered and grimy and ancient. He hurries through the chilly streets toward his grandfather's place. If his luck is good, and if Friesling's technicians have calculated things accurately, he'll be able to head Alice off. That might even be her now, that slender woman walking briskly half a block ahead of him. He steps up his pace. Yes, it's Alice, on her way to Martin's. Well done, Friesling! Ted approaches her warily, suspecting that she's armed. If she's capable of coming back to 1947 to kill Martin, she'd kill him just as readily. Especially back here where neither one of them has any legal existence. When he's close to her he says in a low, hard, intense voice, "Don't turn around, Alice. Just keep walking as if everything's perfectly normal." She stiffens. "Ted?" she cries, astonished. "Is that you, Ted?" "Damned right it is." He laughs harshly. "Come on. Walk to the corner and turn to your left around the block. You're going back to your machine and you're going to get the hell out of the twentieth century without harming anybody. I know what you were trying to do, Alice. But I caught you in time, didn't I?"

Martin is just getting down to real business when the door of his apartment bursts open and a man rushes in. He's middle-aged, stocky, with weird clothes—the ultimate in zoot suits, a maze of vividly contrasting colors and conflicting patterns, shoulders padded to resemble shelves—and a wild look in his eyes. Alice leaps up from the bed. "Ted!" she screams. "My God, what are you doing here?" "You murderous bitch," the intruder yells. Martin, naked and feeling vulnerable, his nervous system stunned by the interruption, looks on in amazement as the stranger grabs her and begins throttling her. "Bitch! Bitch! Bitch!" he roars, shaking her in a mad frenzy. The girl's face is turning black. Her eyes are bugging. After a long moment Martin breaks finally from his freeze. He stumbles forward, seizes the man's fingers, peels them away from the girl's throat. Too late. She falls limply and lies motionless. "Alice!" the intruder moans. "Alice, Alice, what have I done?" He drops to his knees beside her body, sobbing. Martin blinks. "You killed her," he says, not believing that any of this can really be happening. "You actually killed her!"

*   *   *

Alice's face appears on the telephone screen. Christ, how beautiful she is, Martin thinks, and his decrepit body quivers with lust. "There you are," he says. "I've been trying to reach you for hours. I had such a strange dream—that something awful had happened to Ted—and then your phone didn't answer, and I began to think maybe the dream was a premonition of some kind, an omen, you know—" Alice looks puzzled. "I'm afraid you have the wrong number, sir," she says sweetly, and hangs up.

She draws the laser, and the naked man cowers back against the wall in bewilderment. "What the hell is this?" he asks, trembling. "Put that thing down, lady. You've got the wrong guy." "No," she says. "You're the one I'm after. I hate to do this to you, Martin, but I've got no choice. You have to die." "Why?" he demands. "*Why?*" "You wouldn't understand it even if I told you," she says. She moves her finger toward the discharge stud. Abruptly there is a frightening sound of cracking wood and collapsing plaster behind her, as though an earthquake has struck. She whirls and is appalled to see her husband breaking down the door of Martin's apartment. "I'm just in time!" Ted exclaims. "Don't move, Alice!" He reaches for her. In panic she fires without thinking. The dazzling beam catches Ted in the pit of the stomach and he goes down, gurgling in agony, clutching at his belly as he dies.

The door falls with a crash, and this character in peculiar clothing materializes in a cloud of debris, looking crazier than Napoleon. It's incredible, Martin thinks. First an unknown broad rings his bell and invites herself in and takes her clothes off, and then, just as he's about to screw her, this happens. It's pure Marx Brothers, only dirty. But Martin's not going to take any crap. He pulls himself away from the panting, gasping girl on the bed, crosses the room in three quick strides, and seizes the newcomer. "Who the hell are you?" Martin demands, slamming him hard against the wall. The girl is dancing around behind him. "Don't hurt him!" she wails. "Oh, please don't hurt him!"

Ted certainly hadn't expected to find them in bed together. He understood why she might have wanted to go back in time to murder Martin, but simply to have an affair with him—no, it didn't make sense. Of course, it was altogether likely that she had come here to kill and had paused for a little dalliance first. You never could tell about women, even your own wife. Alley cats, all of them. Well, a lucky thing for him that she had given him these few extra minutes to get here. "Okay," he says. "Get your clothes on, Alice. You're coming with me." "Just a second, mister," Martin growls. "You've got your goddamned nerve, busting in like this." Ted tries to explain, but the words won't come. It's all too complicated. He gestures mutely at Alice, at himself, at Martin. The next moment Martin jumps him and they go tumbling together to the floor.

"Who are you?" Martin yells, banging the intruder repeatedly against the wall. "You some kind of detective? You trying to work a badger game on me?" Slam. Slam. Slam. He feels the girls' small fist pounding on his own back. "Stop it!" she screams. "Let him alone, will you? He's my husband!" "*Husband!*" Martin cries. Astounded, he lets go of the stranger and swings around to face the girl. A moment later he realizes his mistake. Out of the corner of his eye he sees that the intruder has raised his fists high above his head like clubs. Martin tries to get out of the way, but no time, no time, and the fists descend with awful force against his skull.

Alice doesn't know what to do. They're rolling around on the floor, fighting like wildcats, now Martin on top, now Ted. Martin is younger and bigger and stronger, but Ted seems possessed by the strength of the insane; he's gone berserk. Both men are bloody-faced and furniture is crashing over everywhere. Her first impulse is to get between them and stop this crazy fight somehow. But then she remembers that she has come here as a killer, not as a peacemaker. She gets the laser from her purse and aims it at Martin, but then the combatants do a flip-flop and it is Ted who is in the line of fire. She hesitates. It doesn't matter which one she shoots, she realizes after a moment. They both have to die, one way or another. She takes aim. Maybe she can get them both with one bolt. But as her finger starts to tighten on the discharge stud Martin suddenly gets Ted in a bear hug and, half lifting him, throws him five feet across the room. The back of Ted's neck hits the wall and there is a loud *crack*. Ted slumps and is still. Martin gets shakily to his feet. "I think I killed him," he says. "Christ, who the hell was he?" "He was your grandson," Alice says, and begins to shriek hysterically.

* * *

Ted stares in horror at the crumpled body at his feet. His hands still tingle from the impact. The left side of Martin's head looks as though a pile driver has crushed it. "Good God in heaven," Ted says thickly, "what have I done? I came here to protect him and I've killed him! I've killed my own grandfather!" Alice, wide-eyed, futilely trying to cover her nakedness by folding one arm across her breasts and spreading her other hand over her loins, says, "If he's dead, why are you still here? Shouldn't you have disappeared?" Ted shrugs. "Maybe I'm safe as long as I remain here in the past. But the moment I try to go back to 2006, I'll vanish as though I've never been. I don't know. I don't understand any of this. What do you think?"

Alice steps uncertainly from the machine into the Temponautics showroom. There's Friesling. There are the technicians. Friesling says, smiling, "I hope you had a very enjoyable journey, Mrs. . . . ah . . . uh . . ." He falters. "I'm sorry," he says, reddening, "but your name seems to have escaped me." Alice says, "It's . . . ah . . . Alice . . . uh . . . do you know, the second name escapes me too?"

The whole clan has gathered to celebrate Martin's eigthy-third birthday. He cuts the cake, and then one by one they go to him to kiss him. When it's Alice's turn, he deftly spins her around so that he screens her from the others, and gives her rump a good hearty pinch. "Oh, if I were only fifty years younger!" he sighs.

It's a warm springlike day. Everything has been lovely at the office—three new accounts all at once—and the trip home on the freeway was a breeze. Alice is waiting for him, dressed in her finest and sexiest outfit, all ready to go out. It's a special day. Their eleventh anniversary. How beautiful she looks! He kisses her, she kisses him, he takes the tickets from his pocket with a grand flourish. "Surprise," he says. "Two weeks in Hawaii, starting next Tuesday! Happy anniversary!" "Oh, Ted!" she cries. "How marvelous! I love you, Ted darling!" He pulls her close to him again. "I love you, Alice dear."

REMEMBER THE ALAMO!

by T. F. Fehrenbach

T. F. Fehrenbach (1925–   ) is a noted mlitary historian and nonfiction writer, the author of such books as Battle of Anzio *(1962),* Crossroads in Korea *(1966),* F. D. R.'s Undeclared War *(1967),* Fire and Blood *(1973),* The San Antonio Story, *and many others. His articles and stories have appeared in the science fiction magazines and orginal anthologies since the early 1960s. "Remember the Alamo,"* *which first appeared in the December, 1961 issue of* Analog, *is by far his most famous work in the sf field, but "From the Tower of Eridu" (from* Lone Star Universe, *1976) is also outstanding.*

Toward sundown, in the murky drizzle, the man who called himself Ord brought Lieutenant Colonel William Barrett Travis word that the Mexican light cavalry had completely invaded Bexar, and that some light guns were being set up across the San Antonio River. Even as he spoke, there was a flash and bang from the west, and a shell screamed over the old mission walls. Travis looked worried.

"What kind of gun?" he asked.

"Nothing to worry about, sir," Ord said. "Only a few one-pounders, nothing of respectable siege caliber. General Santa Anna has had to move too fast for any big stuff to keep up." Ord spoke in his odd accent. After all, he was a Britainer, or some other kind of foreigner. But he spoke good Spanish, and he seemed to know everything. In the four or five days since he had appeared he had become very useful to Travis.

Frowning, Travis asked, "How many Mexicans, do you think, Ord?"

"Not more than a thousand, now," the dark-haired, blue-eyed young man said confidently. "But when the main body arrives, there'll be four, five thousand."

Travis shook his head. "How do you get all this information, Ord? You recite it like you had read it all someplace—like it were history."

Ord merely smiled. "Oh, I don't know *everything*, colonel. That is why I had to come here. There is so much we don't know about what happened . . . I mean, sir, what will happen—in the Alamo." His sharp eyes grew puzzled for an instant. "And some things don't seem to match up, somehow—"

Travis looked at him sympathetically. Ord talked queerly at times, and Travis suspected he was a bit deranged. This was understandable, for the man was undoubtedly a Britainer aristocrat, a refugee from Napoleon's thousand-year Empire. Travis had heard about the detention camps and the charcoal ovens . . . but once, when he had mentioned the *Empereur*'s sack of London in '06, Ord had gotten a very queer look in his eyes, as if he had forgotten completely.

But John Ord, or whatever his name was, seemed to be the only man in the Texas forces who understood what William Barrett Travis was trying to do. Now Travis looked around at the thick adobe wall surrounding the old mission in which they stood. In the cold, yellowish twilight even the flaring cook fires of his hundred and eighty-two men could not dispel the ghostly air that clung to the old place. Travis shivered involuntarily. But the walls were thick, and they could turn one-pounders. He asked, "What was it you called this place, Ord . . . the Mexican name?"

"The Alamo, sir." A slow, steady excitement seemed to burn in the Britainer's bright eyes. "Santa Anna won't forget that name, you can be sure. You'll want to talk to the other officers now, sir? About the message we drew up for Sam Houston?"

"Yes, of course," Travis said absently. He watched Ord head for the walls. No doubt about it, Ord understood what William Barrett Travis was trying to do here. So few of the others seemed to care.

Travis was suddenly very glad that John Ord had shown up when he did.

On the walls, Ord found the man he sought, broad-shouldered and tall in a fancy Mexican jacket. "The commandant's compliments, sir, and he desires your presence in the chapel."

The big man put away the knife with which he had been

whittling. The switchblade snicked back and disappeared into a side pocket of the jacket, while Ord watched it with fascinated eyes. "What's old Bill got his britches hot about this time?" the big man asked.

"I wouldn't know, sir," Ord said stiffly and moved on.

Bang-bang-bang roared the small Mexican cannon from across the river. *Pow-pow-pow!* The little balls only chipped dust from the thick adobe walls. Ord smiled.

He found the second man he sought, a lean man with a weathered face, leaning against a wall and chewing tobacco. This man wore a long, fringed, leather lounge jacket, and he carried a guitar slung beside his Rock Island rifle. He squinted up at Ord. "I know . . . I know," he muttered. "Willy Travis is in an uproar again. You reckon that colonel's commission the Congress up at Washington-on-the-Brazos give him swelled his head?"

Rather stiffly, Ord said, "Colonel, the commandant desires an officers' conference in the chapel, now." Ord was somewhat annoyed. He had not realized he would find these Americans so—distasteful. Hardly preferable to Mexicans, really. Not at all as he had imagined.

For an instant he wished he had chosen Drake and the Armada instead of this pack of ruffians—but no, he had never been able to stand seasickness. He couldn't have taken the Channel, not even for five minutes.

And there was no changing now. He had chosen this place and time carefully, at great expense—actually, at great risk, for the X-4-A had aborted twice, and he had had a hard time bringing her in. But it had got him here at last. And, because for a historian he had always been an impetuous and daring man, he grinned now, thinking of the glory that was to come. And he was a participant—much better than a ringside seat! Only he would have to be careful, at the last, to slip away.

John Ord knew very well how this coming battle had ended, back here in 1836.

He marched back to William Barrett Travis, clicked heels smartly. Travis' eyes glowed; he was the only senior officer here who loved military punctilio. "Sir, they are on the way."

"Thank you, Ord." Travis hesitated a moment. "Look, Ord. There will be a battle, as we know. I know so little about you. If something should happen to you, is there anyone to write? Across the water?"

Ord grinned. "No, sir. I'm afraid my ancestor wouldn't understand."

Travis shrugged. Who was he to say that Ord was crazy? In this day and age, any man with vision was looked on as mad. Sometimes, he felt closer to Ord than to the others.

The two officers Ord had summoned entered the chapel. The big man in the Mexican jacket tried to dominate the wood table at which they sat. He towered over the slender, nervous Travis, but the commandant, straight-backed and arrogant, did not give an inch. "Boys, you know Santa Anna has invested us. We've been fired on all day—" He seemed to be listening for something. *Wham!* Outside, a cannon split the dusk with flame and sound as it fired from the walls. "There is my answer!"

The man in the lounge coat shrugged. "What I want to know is what our orders are. What does old Sam say? Sam and me were in Congress once. Sam's got good sense; he can smell the way the wind's blowin'." He stopped speaking and hit his guitar a few licks. He winked across the table at the officer in the Mexican jacket who took out his knife. "Eh, Jim?"

"Right," Jim said. "Sam's a good man, although I don't think he ever met a payroll."

"General Houston's leaving it up to me," Travis told them.

"Well, that's that," Jim said unhappily. "So what you figurin' to do, Bill?"

Travis stood up in the weak, flickering candlelight, one hand on the polished hilt of his saber. The other two men winced, watching him. "Gentlemen, Houston's trying to pull his militia together while he falls back. You know Texas was woefully unprepared for a contest at arms. The general's idea is to draw Santa Anna as far into Texas as he can, then hit him when he's extended, at the right place and right time. But Houston needs more time—Santa Anna's moved faster than any of us anticipated. Unless we can stop the Mexican Army and take a little steam out of them, General Houston's in trouble."

Jim flicked the knife blade in and out. "Go on."

"This is where we come in, gentlemen. Santa Anna can't leave a force of one hundred eighty men in his rear. If we hold fast, he must attack us. But he has no siege equipment, not even large field cannon." Travis' eye gleamed. "Think of it, boys! He'll have to mount a frontal attack, against protected

American riflemen. Ord, couldn't your Englishers tell him a few things about that!"

"Whoa, now," Jim barked. "Billy, anybody tell you there's maybe four or five thousand Mexicaners comin'?"

"Let them come. Less will leave!"

But Jim, sour-faced, turned to the other man. "Davey? You got something to say?"

"Hell, yes. How do we get out, after we done pinned Santa Anna down? You thought of that, Billy boy?"

Travis shrugged. "There is an element of grave risk, of course. Ord, where's the document, the message you wrote up for me? Ah, thank you." Travis cleared his throat. "Here's what I'm sending on to General Houston." He read, " 'Commandancy of the Alamo, February 24, 1836' . . . are you sure of the date, Ord?"

"Oh, I'm sure of that," Ord said.

"Never mind—if you're wrong we can change it later. 'To the People of Texas and all Americans in the World. Fellow Freemen and Compatriots! I am besieged with a thousand or more Mexicans under Santa Anna. I have sustained a continual bombardment for many hours but have not lost a man. The enemy has demanded surrender at discretion, otherwise, the garrison is to be put to the sword, if taken. I have answered the demand with a cannon shot, and our flag still waves proudly over the walls. I shall never surrender or retreat. Then, I call on you in the name of liberty, of patriotism and everything dear to the American character—' " He paused, frowning. "This language seems pretty old-fashioned, Ord—"

"Oh, no, sir. That's exactly right," Ord murmured.

" '. . . To come to our aid with all dispatch. The enemy is receiving reinforcements daily and will no doubt increase to three or four thousand in four or five days. If this call is neglected, I am determined to sustain myself as long as possible and die like a soldier who never forgets what is due his honor or that of his homeland. VICTORY OR DEATH!' "

Travis stopped reading, looked up. "Wonderful! Wonderful!" Ord breathed. "The greatest words of defiance ever written in the English tongue—and so much more literate than that chap at Bastogne."

"You mean to send that?" Jim gasped.

The man called Davey was holding his head in his hands.

"You object, Colonel Bowie?" Travis asked icily.

"Oh, cut that 'colonel' stuff, Bill," Bowie said. "It's only a National Guard title, and I like 'Jim' better, even though I am a pretty important man. Damn right I have an objection! Why, that message is almost aggressive. You'd think we wanted to fight Santa Anna! You want us to be marked down as warmongers? It'll give us trouble when we get to the negotiation table—"

Travis' head turned. "Colonel Crockett?"

"What Jim says goes for me, too. And this: I'd change that part about all Americans, et cetera. You don't want anybody to think we think we're better than the Mexicans. After all, Americans are a minority in the world. Why not make it 'all men who love security'? That'd have worldwide appeal—".

"Oh, Crockett," Travis hissed.

Crockett stood up. "Don't use that tone of voice to me, Billy Travis! That piece of paper you got don't make you no better'n us. I ran for Congress twice, and won. I know what the people want—"

"What the people want doesn't mean a damn right now," Travis said harshly. "Don't you realize the tyrant is at the gates?"

Crockett rolled his eyes heavenward. "Never thought I'd hear a good American say that! Billy, you'll never run for office—"

Bowie held up a hand, cutting into Crockett's talk. "All right, Davey. Hold up. You ain't runnin' for Congress now. Bill, the main thing I don't like in your whole message is that part about victory or death. That's got to go. Don't ask us to sell that to the troops!"

Travis closed his eyes briefly. "Boys, listen. We don't have to tell the men about this. They don't need to know the real story until it's too late for them to get out. And then we shall cover ourselves with such glory that none of us shall ever be forgotten. Americans are the best fighters in the world when they are trapped. They teach this in the Foot School back on the Chatahoochee. And if we die, to die for one's country is sweet—"

"Hell with that," Crockett drawled. "I don't mind dyin', but not for these big landowners like Jim Bowie here. I just been thinkin'—I don't own nothing in Texas."

"I resent that," Bowie shouted. "You know very well I volunteered, after I sent my wife off to Acapulco to be with her family." With an effort, he calmed himself. "Look, Travis. I have some reputation as a fighting man—you know I lived through the gang wars back home. It's obvious this Alamo place is indefensible, even if we had a thousand men."

"But we must delay Santa Anna at all costs—"

Bowie took out a fine, dark Mexican cigar and whittled at it with his blade. Then he lit it, saying around it, "All right, let's all calm down. Nothing a group of good men can't settle around a table. Now listen. I got in with this revolution at first because I thought old Emperor Iturbide would listen to reason and lower taxes. But nothin's worked out, because hotheads like you, Travis, queered the deal. All this yammerin' about liberty! Mexico is a Republic, under an Emperor, not some kind of democracy, and we can't change that. Let's talk some sense before it's too late. We're all too old and too smart to be wavin' the flag like it's the Fourth of July. Sooner or later, we're goin' to have to sit down and talk with the Mexicans. And like Davey said, I own a million hectares, and I've always paid minimum wage, and my wife's folks are way up there in the Imperial Government of the Republic of Mexico. That means I got influence in all the votin' groups, includin' the American Immigrant, since I'm a minority group member myself. I think I can talk to Santa Anna, and even to old Iturbide. If we sign a treaty now with Santa Anna, acknowledge the law of the land, I think our lives and property rights will be respected—" He cocked an eye toward Crockett.

"Makes sense, Jim. That's the way we do it in Congress. Compromise, everybody happy. We never allowed ourselves to be led nowhere we didn't want to go, I can tell you! And Bill, you got to admit that we're in better bargaining position if we're out in the open than if old Santa Anna's got us penned up in this old Alamo."

"Ord," Travis said despairingly. "Ord, you understand. Help me! Make them listen!"

Ord moved into the candlelight, his lean face sweating. "Gentlemen, this is all wrong! It doesn't happen this way—"

Crocket sneered, "Who asked you, Ord? I'll bet you ain't even got a poll tax!"

Decisively, Bowie said, "We're free men, Travis, and we won't be led around like cattle. How about it, Davey? Think you could handle the rear guard, if we try to move out of here?"

"Hell, yes! Just so we're movin'!"

"O.K. Put it to a vote of the men outside. Do we stay, and

maybe get croaked, or do we fall back and conserve our strength until we need it? Take care of it, eh, Davey?"

Crockett picked up his guitar and went outside.

Travis roared, "This is insubordination! Treason!" He drew his saber, but Bowie took it from him and broke it in two. Then the big man pulled his knife.

"Stay back, Ord. The Alamo isn't worth the bones of a Britainer, either."

"Colonel Bowie, please," Ord cried. "You don't understand! You *must* defend the Alamo! This is the turning point in the winning of the west! If Houston is beaten, Texas will never join the Union! There will be no Mexican War. No California, no nation stretching from sea to shining sea! This is the Americans' manifest destiny. You are the hope of the future . . . you will save the world from Hitler, from Bolshevism—"

"Crazy as a hoot owl," Bowie said sadly. "Ord, you and Travis got to look at it both ways. We ain't all in the right in this war—we Americans got our faults, too."

"But you are free men," Ord whispered. "Vulgar, opinionated, brutal, but free! You are still better than the breed who kneels to tyranny—"

Crockett came in. "O.K., Jim."

"How'd it go?"

"Fifty-one percent for hightailin' it right now."

Bowie smiled. "That's a flat majority. Let's make tracks."

"Comin', Bill?" Crockett asked. "You're O.K., but you just don't know how to be one of the boys. You got to learn that no dog is better'n any other."

"No," Travis croaked hoarsely. "I stay. Stay or go, we shall all die like dogs, anyway. Boys, for the last time! Don't reveal our weakness to the enemy—"

"What weakness? We're stronger than them. Americans could whip the Mexicans any day, if we wanted to. But the thing to do is make 'em talk, not fight. So long, Bill."

The two big men stepped outside. In the night there was a sudden clatter of hoofs as the Texans mounted and rode. From across the river came a brief spatter of musket fire, then silence. In the dark, there had been no difficulty in breaking through the Mexican lines.

Inside the chapel, John Ord's mouth hung slackly. He muttered, "Am I insane? It didn't happen this way—it couldn't! The books can't be *that* wrong—"

In the candlelight, Travis hung his head. "We tried, John.

Perhaps it was a forlorn hope at best. Even if we had defeated Santa Anna, or delayed him, I do not think the Indian Nations would have let Houston get help from the United States."

Ord continued his dazed muttering, hardly hearing.

"We need a contiguous frontier with Texas," Travis continued slowly, just above a whisper. "But we Americans have never broken a treaty with the Indians, and pray God we never shall. *We* aren't like the Mexicans, always pushing, always grabbing off New Mexico, Arizona, California. *We* aren't colonial oppressors, thank God! No, it wouldn't have worked out, even if we American immigrants had secured our rights in Texas—" He lifted a short, heavy, percussion pistol in his hand and cocked it. "I hate to say it, but perhaps if we hadn't taken Paine and Jefferson so seriously—if we could only have paid lip service, and done what we really wanted to do, in our hearts . . . no matter. I won't live to see our final disgrace."

He put the pistol to his head and blew out his brains.

Ord was still gibbering when the Mexican cavalry stormed into the old mission, pulling down the flag and seizing him, dragging him before the resplendent little general in green and gold.

Since he was the only prisoner, Santa Anna questioned Ord carefully. When the sharp point of a bayonet had been thrust half an inch into his stomach, the Britainer seemed to come around. When he started speaking, and the Mexicans realized he was English, it went better with him. Ord was obviously mad, it seemed to Santa Anna, but since he spoke English and seemed educated, he could be useful. Santa Anna didn't mind the raving; he understood all about Napoleon's detention camps and what they had done to Britainers over there. In fact, Santa Anna was thinking of setting up a couple of those camps himself. When they had milked Ord dry, they threw him on a horse and took him along.

Thus John Ord had an excellent view of the battlefield when Santa Anna's cannon broke the American lines south of the Trinity. Unable to get his men across to safety, Sam Houston died leading the last, desperate charge against the Mexican regulars. After that, the American survivors were too tired to run from the cavalry that pinned them against the flooding river. Most of them died there. Santa Anna expressed complete indifference to what happened to the Texans' women and children.

Mexican soldiers found Jim Bowie hiding in a hut, wearing a plain linen tunic and pretending to be a civilian. They would not have discovered his identity had not some of the Texan women whom the cavalry had captured cried out, "Colonel Bowie—Colonel Bowie!" as he was led into the Mexican camp.

He was hauled before Santa Anna, and Ord was summoned to watch. "Well, Don Jaime," Santa Anna remarked, "you have been a foolish man. I promised your wife's uncle to send you to Acapulco safely, though of course your lands are forfeit. You understand we must have lands for the veterans' program when this campaign is over—" Santa Anna smiled then. "Besides, since Ord here has told me how instrumental you were in the abandonment of the Alamo, I think the Emperor will agree to mercy in your case. You know, Don Jaime, your compatriots had me worried back there. The Alamo might have been a tough nut to crack . . . *pues*, no matter."

And since Santa Anna had always been broad-minded, not objecting to light skin or immigrant background, he invited Bowie to dinner that night.

Santa Anna turned to Ord. "But if we could catch this rascally war criminal Crockett . . . however, I fear he has escaped us. He slipped over the river with a fake passport, and the Indians have interned him."

"*Sí Señor Presidente*," Ord said dully.

"Please, don't call me that," Santa Anna cried, looking around. "True, many of us officers have political ambitions, but Emperor Iturbide is old and vain. It could mean my head—"

Suddenly, Ord's head was erect, and the old, clear light was in his blue eyes. "Now I understand!" he shouted. "I thought Travis was raving back there, before he shot himself—and your talk of the Emperor! American respect for Indian rights! Jeffersonian form of government! Oh, those ponces who peddled me that X-4-A—the *track jumper!* I'm not back in my own past. I've jumped the time track—*I'm back in a screaming alternate!*"

"Please not so loud, *Señor* Ord." Santa Anna sighed. "Now, we must shoot a few more American officers, of course. I regret this, you understand, and I shall no doubt be much criticized in French Canada and Russia, where there are still civilized values. But we must establish the Republic of the Empire once and for all upon this continent, that aristocratic tyranny shall not perish from the earth. Of course, as an Englishman, you understand perfectly, Señor Ord."

"Of course, excellency," Ord said.

"There are soft hearts—soft heads, I say—in Mexico who cry for civil rights for the Americans. But I must make sure that Mexican dominance is never again threatened north of the Rio Grande."

"*Seguro*, excellency," Ord said, suddenly. If the bloody X-4-A *had* jumped the track, there was no getting back, none at all. He was stuck here. Ord's blue eyes narrowed. "After all, it . . . it is manifest destiny that the Latin peoples of North America meet at the center of the continent. Canada and Mexico shall share the Mississippi."

Santa Anna's dark eyes glowed. "You say what I have often thought. You are a man of vision, and much sense. You realize the *Indios* must go, whether they were here first or not. I think I will make you my secretary, with the rank of captain."

"*Gracias*, Excellency."

"Now, let us write my communiqué to the capital, *Capitán* Ord. We must describe how the American abandonment of the Alamo allowed me to press the traitor Houston so closely he had no chance to maneuver his men into the trap he sought. *Ay, Capitán*, it is a cardinal principle of the Anglo-Saxons, to get themselves into a trap from which they must fight their way out. This I never let them do, which is why I succeed where others fail. . . . You said something, *Capitán?*"

"*Sí* Excellency. I said, I shall title our communiqué: 'Remember the Alamo,' " Ord said, standing at attention.

"*Bueno!* You have a gift for words. Indeed, if ever we feel the *gringos* are too much for us, your words shall once again remind us of the truth!" Santa Anna smiled. "I think I shall make you a major. You have indeed coined a phrase which shall live in history forever!"

ONE WAY STREET

by Jerome Bixby

Jermone Bixby (1923–   ) is a writer who will always be remembered for one story—the terrific "It's a Good Life" (1953), which formed the basis for an excellent episode of The Twilight Zone. *However, he was a solid professional who wrote many other fine stories, which can be found in his collections* The Devil's Scrapbook *and* Space By the Tale *(both 1964). He also did good work as an editor and assistant editor of several science fiction magazines in the 1950s, including those published by Fiction House, Standard Publications, and Galaxy Publications. He has worked in Hollywood, the city of his birth, since the late 1950s, producing screenplays for the movie industry (he co-wrote* Fantastic Voyage, *1966) and for television, including four produced scripts for the* Star Trek *series.*

Pete Innes skidded his '49 Dodge coupé into a tree at fifty-five per, out along Northern Boulevard, one Monday morning. He was on his way to work in Manhattan from Greenhill, Long Island, where he had a ranch-type house, a wife, a dog named Prince, an eleven-year-old son . . . a life.

He started swearing as the car turned over. As the top crunched in, he was thinking, *Now why in hell should I black out for a second and sideswipe a tree? Going to die, damn it.*

A little academic—but you get that way when you unexpectedly see the scythe coming. Your brain works faster than your glands: you don't have time to feel much, you only think: your first impulse is a kind of interest.

Luckily the impact of the sideswipe flung Pete over on his face across the front seat: the car flipped, and the top smashed down, but Pete didn't get his head broken—it wasn't there.

The car turned over again: Pete rattled back and forth between the seat cushions and the crumpled top only a few inches away from his back. Metal howled; glass shattered, dispersing like water; a tire went *whop!* and then another. Pete's muscles wrenched agonizingly, particularly those in his back and neck.

The car lit upright and settled, rocking. Thousands of tiny squeakings for a few seconds. Silence.

Pete kept hearing all the noises, retaining them. He kicked until the left-hand door flew open. He inched himself backward toward it, and did all right until his shoulders reached the steering wheel, which had been shoved back a foot nearer the seat. He tried to turn and crawl past on his side; he couldn't turn; the squashed roof was too tight overhead. All he could do was let out his breath, pull in his shoulders, and squirm.

His legs emerged, waved in air; he bruised a shin on the running board. He screwed up his arms and shoved against the steering wheel, which was now about even with his chin. He went out the door, his coat up over his head. His feet found ground, then his knees. He was kneeling, his cheek against the cold metal of the sprung door. Hating the car, he shoved himself away from it, hard, with both hands. He went over backwards on grass and dirt. He lay on his back, and brought his hands up to his face and started to cry.

A screech of brakes; footsteps running. Someone knelt beside him. Two hands touched his wrists lightly, as if they wanted to draw his own hands away from his face but were afraid to.

"Are you okay, mister?" a voice said.

The hands got rough. Pete's hands were dragged away from his face. Then the voice sighed, and Pete felt a breath of tobacco across his face: "Lord, I thought your eyes were cut up."

Now Pete was shuddering—long shudders that started in his abdomen and ran up to shake his shoulders.

Another screech of brakes. More footsteps. A new voice said, "Man, how'd he get out of *that* one! He okay?"

The first voice said, "I think so. He's half nuts. Shaken up. Got the hell scared outa him . . . oh, I'm sorry, lady—I didn't see you there."

"I've had first aid," she said. "Move over. I'll feel him."

Pete found that funny. He began to laugh. Stopped. Hell with it.

There was a studying pause. A light woman's touch ran over

his head, his jaw, his neck. Down along his chest. Ran over again, a little harder. It tickled. Pete laughed.

He got a slap on the left cheek that rocked his head: a slap to bring him out of it.

Shock to hysteria to rage. He said ten filthy words, most of them present participles.

The woman said, "I think he's all right. Some ribs broken— bad to laugh."

Pete tried to sit up. He said another few words—gasped them, rather, clapping one hand to his side.

The woman said, "Get down."

She helped him do it. He felt a crunching in his side. Pain was starting. He took a look around at the faces, saw nothing, closed his eyes again and waited for things to happen. He wasn't his own problem, right now: he was theirs. Social action was underway: policemen would come, and an ambulance, and he would be taken care of. People were focused on him: it often takes disaster to do it, but that's when you're loneliest.

Sound of a motorcycle. Footsteps coming up, then going away at a run; the motorcycle blurted off. About that time Pete slipped into a pain-shot night.

The first thing that was wrong was the telephone in the hospital where he woke up about noon, the same day.

The nurse who was straightening his blanket said, "How are you feeling, Mr. Innes?"

He winced up at her. "Alive."

"Aches and pains?"

"They're lovely."

"It was a bad crash. The officers said the only thing that saved you was that you were pinned between the crumpled roof and the seat—you couldn't bounce around a lot. Except the steering wheel caught your ribs."

"Has my family been notified?"

"I came in to see if you were awake. Your wife's waiting outside."

Pete sighed. "It'll be nice to stay off the job for a while and romp with my kid . . . as if I could romp!"

The nurse paused at the door, smiling a little severely. "You know, it's no help to put your identification in code, or whatever it was."

Pete blinked.

"Your wallet told us your name, of course—but you have your address and telephone number wrong."

"I don't get you."

"The phone especially—the address was almost right; 1801 instead of 1811. But the thing you have down for your phone number does not make any sense. There's no such exchange. We had to check with information before we could locate your family."

"You're very pretty," Pete said slowly, "and evidently nuts."

"Thank you, and I'm not," she smiled. "You'd better get that straightened out."

"My identification," Pete said, "is in perfect order—"

But she was gone.

He lay there frowning.

The stuff he'd had in his pockets at the time of the crash was piled neatly on the table beside the bed. He reached over and picked up his wallet and leafed it open to his celluloid-covered card:

> Peter M. Innes
> 1801 South Oak Street
> Greenhill, Long Island
> New York
> Highview 6-4509J

It was absolutely correct.

The nurse had said it was wrong. Hadn't they *tried* it? The phone? She'd said there was no such exchange. There was a telephone on the table. He gave it a sour look as he put the wallet back beside it. Ordinary black French phone. Maybe a little more streamlined than most—

With a dial that went like this: A-123—B-234—C-345—D-456—E-567—and so on to J-000 . . . whatever that was.

He was staring at the phone and shaking his head when Mary came in.

Tears, of course. "Oh, thank God, thank God, thank God," she kept saying against his shoulder. The pressure of her against his side hurt, but he pressed her closer, thinking the same thing: *Thank God.*

Then she was saying, "Oh, darling, I'm sorry, I'm sorry—"

"For what?" he said.

"The argument." She pressed against his side. "You wanted to die. I just know that's why you had the accident!" He couldn't help gasping at the pressure. She made a shocked sound and pulled back: "Oh, darling, I was hurting you—"

"Loved it," he said.

Her dark eyes were filled with tears, and she did something she hadn't done in years. She bent her head so her hair fell over her face and she brushed the hair across his face, lightly. He inhaled with satisfaction.

"You're not mad, then?" she asked through her soft hair.

"Mad about what?"

"The argument."

He thought a moment, hand on the back of her neck. "What argument?"

The hair swished across his face delightedly. Then her nose was pressed under his ear, and something else happened that hadn't happened in years: she caught a bit of skin between her teeth and worried it with her tongue. His hair lifted.

"Then you're *not* angry anymore?" she whispered softly.

"I—" He gulped, feeling many things. "No, honey, I'm not mad. I—I've even sort of forgotten what we argued about."

"Oh, you *sweet*," she said.

With gentle force he removed the source of the disturbance, getting her to sit up. "This bed's too small for two," he said. "Besides, people like doctors keep wandering in. Cut it out, honey."

She got out a tissue and wiped tears away. She wasn't crying anymore—just dry-sobbing a little. She sat on the edge of the bed and held his hand. "You get well," she said.

"Not much to it. Just a couple of busted ribs and some bruises, they tell me. I can leave in a couple of days." He looked at her with a fondness he hadn't felt in some time: maybe the accident had been a good thing. Maybe it had struck away some unpleasantness—or indifference. Married for twelve years. Up and down. A kid. Getting on toward forty, both of them. She was still a darned attractive woman, and he wore his years better than most. Lately they'd been—well, just apart. But now she seemed to have taken on flame, and it was welcome warmth. Let it burn. He could feel response in himself; and that old fondness. Flicker, flicker, flame—

"It was an awful quarrel, wasn't it?" she said. "I've felt awful for days. But it was my damned old pride . . . if you thought I was fooling around with Phil Tarrant, I wasn't going to try to change your mind."

"Phil Tarrant," he said vaguely. "Phil Tarrant . . . do you mean Phil Terrance?"

She frowned. "Phil Tarrant. Our next-door neighbor." Then she smiled. "Our big, bald neighbor, who's just about as attractive to me as a water buffalo! Oh, Pete, how could you ever think I was having an affair with him? And I'm sorry I threw the picture at you—"

Pete Innes closed his eyes. His next-door neighbor was a big fellow named Phil Terrance. Phil Terrance had all his hair. He was a nice guy, happily married: Pete had never in his life said a word, or even thought a thought, about the possibility of an affair between Phil and Mary. *Never.* He knew damned well that Phil was the big, jovial type of guy that Mary found sexually unattractive. Besides, Mary wasn't the affairing kind: after twelve years he still had to employ the most delicate gambits or else meet a wall, and lately things had simply been *nicht.* Now, of course, Fate had struck a spark; the prognosis was good; maybe if he *had* suspected her of tramping, he would also have suspected that someone had done a fair job of velociting her. But he didn't suspect anything of the sort, and he'd certainly never accused her of it.

It would all straighten out.

"What picture?" he asked cautiously.

"Oh!" She bent and kissed him. "You just want to pretend you've forgotten all about it! It's *sweet!* But don't. Let's admit honestly that it happened, and *then* forget it. Now—I'm sorry."

"I—I'm sorry too," he said.

Indirection was in order.

"Lucky you didn't hit me," he said.

"Well—" she grinned a little shamefacedly. "I really didn't throw it to hit. But it certainly wrecked the finish on the piano!"

Piano. . . .

He *had* no piano. They'd been planning to buy one, for Pete Jr., but they hadn't yet.

It was too much.

"*What* piano?" he said, half-rising against pain. "We don't *have* one. Mary, what in blazes is going on? I don't remember you throwing any picture. I don't remember any argument. Phil Terrance is *not* bald. I've never accused you of fooling around with him. *What's going on?*"

*   *   *

The doctors said, "It's probably only temporary, Mr. Innes. Amnesia induced by shock."

Pete said patiently, "Doctor, I do not have amnesia. There is no blank spot in my memory. I remember everything right up to the moment of the crash."

"Well," said the doctor, smiling, "I wouldn't worry about it. Not exactly amnesia. You've just forgotten certain things, and gotten others a little mixed up."

Pete said, "Like hell I have."

"You wouldn't *know*, Mr. Innes. You wouldn't know if you had things mixed up. They would seem real to you, even if you were seeing pink dragons. But—well, after all—you have described some other sort of telephone, for example. What can I say, Mr. Innes? I am fifty-seven years old. Since I was a child, telephone dials have been numbered in this manner. They're that way all over the United States, I believe, and very possibly all over the world."

"They're not."

The doctor sighed. "You're a little confused from shock, that's all. I wonder if you'd mind talking with one of our staff psychologists—"

"I would."

"I've already taken the liberty of calling him."

"I resent that," Pete said coldly.

"You shouldn't."

"I'm as sane as you are."

"I'm sure you are. But he will be able to do a more expert job of convincing you that the things you imagine to be true, and the things you imagine not to be true, are simply as they are and must be accepted as such—because you *are* sane."

Pete reached for the telephone. He let his fingers think for him. He could make no sense out of the number system anyway. He dialed his office—not the number, but the finger hole sequence.

A voice said, "Yes?"

Pete said, "Reilly, Forsythe and Sprague?"

Pause: "Sorry, buddy, wrong number."

Pete tried again, letting his fingers do the aiming. He dialed his mother's place in the Bronx:

"Mom?"

"Not that I know of," a man's voice said dryly.

Pete slammed the phone down on the carriage so hard the bell tinged. He lay back and closed his eyes.

Mary said—she was crying a little again—"Oh, Pete, darling. . . ."

Pete compressed his lips.

"You'll be all right. . . ."

"I *am* all right."

And the whole world's wrong.

"Of course you're all right," the psychologist said. "You're not crazy."

"Don't use kid terms on me, doc," Pete said. "I took psych in college. I'm not afraid I'm 'crazy.' I can describe the condition you think I'm in just as resoundingly as you can. But I'm not *in* it."

"Then you didn't pay attention to a very important point in your psych course," the psychologist said. "It's the hardest thing in the world for even a trained person to apply to himself. You should know that a person who is illuded or hallucinated or subject to fantasies of any kind cannot be expected to—"

"So I'm—"

"—the validity of his beliefs—"

"—I'm not in a position to evaluate in terms of the real world," Pete said wearily. "*A priori* you're right, *ipso facto* I'm wrong."

"—needs outside assistance, don't you see?"

"*Caveat emptor.*"

The psychologist indicated the phone, as the doctor had done. "This is the real world. It exists. Evidence. As a lawyer you must appreciate evidence."

Pete Innes thought very deliberately and carefully for two, three, four, five minutes, while the psychologist waited, as psychologists do.

Then he said, "I suppose so. You *must* be right. I hope I sound sane. Phones have always been built that way. I have a piano. My wife threw a picture at me . . . what picture, honey?"

"The picture we took last summer of Pippy," Mary said.

Pete's lips tightened. "Pippy?"

"Our dog . . . our . . . don't you—remember?"

"I remember," he said. *Our dog Prince.*

"It should pass," said the psychologist. "Traumatic amnesia and fantasies. I would advise you strongly to see an analyst if it doesn't pass—you may not be able to recover all you've forgotten, but he should be able to—"

"Get out," Pete said.

"—and help you adjust." The psychologist rose. "I'll drop in later."

"Don't." Pete stiffened his body on the bed, wanting to leap and scream. "Get out, Mary."

"*Pete*—"

The psychologist said quietly. "Come, Mrs. Innes." He paused at the door. "You won't like this, Mr. Innes, but I'll naturally have to take precautions. In your state—"

"I understand," Pete said. "I accept. Have me watched. I don't care. I just don't want to talk anymore."

The psychologist went out. Mary started after him, nose buried in tissue.

Pete felt two tears start down his own cheeks. Suddenly his eyes filled. He yearned. He was terrified and cold. His back teeth gritted together. "Stay, Mary," he said.

They were close on the bed for a few minutes, she lying on his broken ribs and hurting them, he hugging her fiercely so it would hurt more. Pain was real.

She was crying silently, eyes and nose running—the way she cried when she was really miserable, not just being feminine. After a while she got up and went over to the window. The venetian blinds were down and slanted shut. "Maybe some sun will cheer us up," she said.

Up went the blinds.

Pete knew he was in the New York Hospital. On the tenth floor. Looking out the window he could see the Chrysler Building, downtown on 42nd Street, and beyond it, the Empire State Building, with a slender spiral atop it, like the Chrysler, instead of a never-used blimp mooring mast and TV tower surmounting, good old Channel 4.

He screamed. It all came out. A large intern was in the door and at his side, looking wary, before he had exhausted the breath. Mary fainted.

Two months later they let him go home.

He objected at first to what was virtually imprisonment, but they said, "Citizens' Protection Law, you know."

He didn't know. And he was a lawyer.

The psychiatrists were good. They worked hard. He understood that their fees were paid by the government—Citizens' Protection Law. Well, fine.

They made him socially acceptable. They showed him where and how he was wrong. They brought in proof by the armload—

books, photographs, films, actual documents and records of his own life containing mention of three jobs he couldn't rememeber even having held and numerous other interesting data, such as his former marriage to a girl named June Massey—

Once he had been engaged to a girl named Jane Mason.

They brought in the proof and talked to him about it.

They convinced him. They proved that the world he lived in was not the world he thought he knew. They proved that he was imagining. That he was occluded here, and was building dreamstuff of asynchronic data there. They proved that the Empire State Building had always had a spire; that the U. N. had resolved the Korea conflict two months after hostilities had commenced; that Prokofiev—always a favorite of Pete's—had not died in 1953 but was still alive, though ailing; that television was not yet commercially perfected; that Shakespeare had written no *Hamlet*—

He quoted from the play. They were amazed. They said, My God, you should write!

There were times when he thought he'd go crazy. Other times he was certain that he already was. There were still other times when it was all a diabolic plot—Pete Innes vs. the World.

Heady conceit. For a madman.

Pete wasn't, of course . . . just a whim that delighted him, and concerned the psychiatrists, at one stage in his progress.

There had been no Shelley. He quoted Shelley.

Keats, they said.

He quoted Keats.

My God, you should write!

Still, they adjusted him. Physical facts talked.

But he never ceased to recall the world he'd imagined. It remained as clear in every "remembered" detail as this one, the real one, was in physical fact.

They adjusted him.

After all, he was an intelligent man. The theory of what had happened to him was clear: the actuality of it, once presented authoritatively to him, was equally clear.

They adjusted him.

Now he knew what it must feel like to believe you are Napoleon. Long fall from the saddle.

Emotional acceptance came.

He believed.

*   *   *

Home was different. Well, he'd had to expect it to be.

Pippy was a cocker. *Prince had been a Collie.*

His house had five rooms. *Six.*

It was green. *Rust.*

There was a flower garden out back. *Vegetable garden.*

Pete Jr. was dark-haired. *Towhead.*

He wandered around, acquainting himself with his life. Some things were a lot different. There were shades of difference in others. Still others were identical, or so nearly so as to defy him.

His library . . . he went over it book by book, and came across his autographed copy of Bertrand Russell's *History of Western Philosophy*—the one he'd taken to Russell when the philosopher was in New York on a lecture tour back in '45.

He sat there, hugged it, cradled it, loved it. It was a remembered thing. Then he opened it.

He had *never* made marginal notes in that book.

But obviously he had.

Adjust.

That night Phil Terrance—Phil *Tarrant*—came over. Phil was bald. *Brown hair.* Pete found that he was evidently not quite so close to Phil as he'd been in his dream world. He mentioned the golf games they had played together.

They hadn't.

Undressing for bed, Pete said, "Where do you suppose I *got* that world, honey? The dream one. It's so—complete."

Mary tossed aside her slip and swayed a little toward him, her dark eyes inviting, warm, soft.

"Forget your dream world, Pete," she whispered. "This is real."

A much nicer, more open bit of enticing than he could remember Mary ever doing. He wondered what had triggered her, and thanked whatever it was. And she had a small mole on her stomach that he didn't remember.

They made the kind of vigorous, exhausting love they hadn't made in years . . . the years of his dream world, at any rate. Now his still-mending ribs made it both a little difficult and delightful. They laughed at the necessary concessions, and had fun. This was a sweeter Mary than dream Mary.

In the following days home from the office he spent a lot of time at the typewriter.

Doing?

He was writing a conspectus of the dream world. He was looking for identities, similarities, antitheses in the real world, and noting them. He was pouring out his incredible fantasy before it should vanish in years.

He used a two-column system:

DREAM WORLD	REAL WORLD
Jewish State: Israel	Sholom
FDR died in 1945	Same
Atomic power	Not yet
Stalin dead	Alive
Lautrec a dwarf	Normal

. . . and long pages of intense lawyer's analysis, drawing fine and significant distinctions, searching for historical bases for existing things and measuring them against "memories." The manuscript grew to several hundred pages. It could have gone on forever. It's perhaps easier to change a world than one's understanding of it.

Through this project, and the omnivorous reading it involved, he became closer to the real world. His analyst—he had consulted one, and now visited him twice a week—was thoroughly in favor of it. He learned. At first it was often shocking. Then only exciting. At last, enjoyable, nothing more.

Then it palled. Pete ceased writing. Six months had passed. He only read. More calmly, now. The need to discharge tension, and even a tiny lingering disbelief, had vanished.

There had been newspaper publicity, of course. At first just a little—then, as the sensational aspects of his case got out, a lot.

NEW YORK LAWYER
HAS DREAM WORLD
Sex, Science and Sociology on
Another Earth

The *Times* did a dignified interview. *Life* gave him four pages, *Time* a column, *Scientific American* a squib.

Adjusted. And far happier than he'd ever been in his life.

Then they came and tore it all to shreds.

The dry voice on the phone said, "Mr. Innes, we've read about your case in *Scientific American*."

"Yes?" said Pete, wondering what they were selling or buying—he'd already signed for several articles.

The voice hesitated. "I don't think this should be discussed over the phone. May we come and see you personally, at your convenience?"

"Who are you?"

"Forgive me—I—this is all rather extraordinary, Mr. Innes. Most extraordinary. My colleagues and I . . . allow me, I am Doctor Raymond van Husen. I—hello? Hello?"

Pete was staring across the room. At his bookcase. At the green-jacketed book entitled *The Coming Conquest of the Atom*, by Dr. Raymond van Husen, twice Nobel Prize winner. Van Husen, who in the dream world had figured so importantly in the Manhattan Project and Oak Ridge.

"Yes, Doctor," he said. "I've heard of you. What can I do for you?"

"What is important," said van Husen, "is what *we* may already have done to *you*, and what we may be able to do about it."

Pete clutched the phone so hard his knuckles crackled in his ear. "*Done to me?*"

"I—well, actually, *we* didn't do it to you. If our theory is correct . . . Mr. Innes, I think we had better come and see you."

"Tonight," Pete said harshly, standing alone between wavering realities. "Tonight."

Van Husen's gray goatee bobbed as he said, "Parallel worlds, Mr. Innes. Coexisting worlds. We believe that you are on the wrong one, simply on the wrong one."

Pete was sprawled in the big chair by the fireplace. Enrique Patiño, physicist, sat on the piano bench. Doctor Hazel Burgess, an attractive woman of fifty or so, was on the couch, sitting beside Mary.

Pete said, "Simply on the wrong one."

Mary said, "Pete . . . Pete, what are they saying?"

"They're saying I'm on the wrong world. Don't listen."

Mary bit the back of her hand.

Pete took a belt at the straight Scotch he held. "So your machine got out of whack," he said. "Somebody forgot to tighten a bolt, you say. It flipped on its mounting, you say. Instead of shooting its tight beam at the pretty target, it went through the side of the building, across Flushing Meadows, and walloped me before you got it under control. You say."

"Not *our* machine," said Hazel Burgess. "Our machine radiated at the real Peter Innes, you see."

"That's either stupid, or insulting," Pete said. "I think it's both, in fact. *I'm* Peter Innes." He took another belt.

"I'm sorry," Hazel Burgess said. "I meant that our machine radiated at the Peter Innes who belongs on this Earth. The machine on your Earth radiated at you." She stopped and bit her lip. "I *am* sorry. When we read about you . . . it was quite a shock to finally realize what must have happened—"

Pete stood up quietly and, without a break in his motion, flung his glass into the fireplace with every ounce of his strength. Scotch hissed on the burning logs. "Damn you," he said, "Damn you, one and all."

"Two Earths," van Husen said, looking at the blue alcohol flames. "Almost identical. Two almost identical experiments, aligned on the time continuum. Two almost identical mishaps. A transposition of Peter Innes. It must have happened that way. There is no other satisfactory explanation. Very likely identical results as well. The automobile accident—the hospitalization—the . . . m'm—" He looked at Mary, caught Pete's eyes full-blast and looked away, goatee bobbing.

"Don't be a damned old Dutchman, Raymond," Hazel Burgess said. "My God!"

"Please go," Pete whispered.

"Perhaps we can help you, Mr. Innes," Enrique Patiño said softly. His wrinkled face turned toward Mary. The look he gave her was old and Latin. "If you wish us to, that is."

Pete swayed on his feet.

Mary got up and half-ran into his arms. "Peter, I *don't* understand—"

Mary? Was it Mary?

"Our experiment," said van Husen, "was an attempt to—"

"God damn your experiment. Get out and leave us alone!"

"But, Mr. Innes, we may be able to reverse the effect and return you—"

At last tears came. They rushed. Sometimes a man has to cry like a baby—when the world gets as fearsome as a baby's. Or when there isn't any world.

"He's been drinking since you called," Mary said, holding him fiercely.

The scientists left. And they left a card:

*　　*　　*

GRADEN RESEARCH INSTITUTE
FLUSHING, N.Y. 27 F-E 395

He became a meaningless man. A wrongness. Earth beckoned. His own reality called: called in a giant voice that sounded
his nature like a taut voice, now that he knew.

He couldn't doubt.

Men of van Husen's caliber didn't speak loosely. They'd all
seemed pretty positive. And, of course, it explained everything.

Earth called.

At times he felt alone in the Universe. This Universe. Mary
lay warm beside him, holding him with body and mouth, and
this Universe was an icy microfilm between them that kept him
alone.

He became aware of a force. A tension grew in him, became
nearly intolerable. *He shouldn't be here.* Originating in the
farthest slow galaxies, transmitted to nearer ones, gaining am-
plification with every angry star, transmitted again and again,
strong with the hearts of novae and the rioting pulse of vari-
ables, a complex of forces seemed to be gathering—forces that
were trying to push him out of this Universe: as if in some
manner he were alien, a dissonance. Fact? Fancy? Had he
added one atom too many to the sum of this Universe? If so, he
might break the gears.

Pete Innes, Universe wrecker. Once or twice he watched red
sunsets, wondering if this might be the night of his nova.

No longer alone.

Pressure.

This Universe was too much with him.

The little things closed in:

Eroica	Napoleon Symphony
Democrats	Jeffersons
Trueorfalse?	Trueorfalse?

This Universe hated him. Resisted him. Struck at him. Whether
real or imaginary, the sensation grew to a torment and a terror.
It lashed at him from directions he could not defend against, or
even define. . . .

Unable to sleep, he would pace in darkness comparing his
now-situation with his then-situation.

Earth II—he thought of this world that way—was preferable

to him in many, many ways. He liked this job—he'd discovered that he was a partner in his firm—

But only one thing was important. The love and warmth at home . . . the new Mary . . .

He paced, and cringed, and thought, and cursed this Universe—and decided.

She cried when he said he must go back to his Earth.

He explained and explained. He wasn't her Pete. She wasn't his Mary. This wasn't his world. He could not remain here and stay sane.

"Oh, I love you," she wailed. "I won't let you do it."

"You'll get your own Pete back," he said heavily. "On my Earth he must be going through just about the same thing as I am here. The scientists will have contacted him. He'll be planning to return."

"I don't want any other Pete! I want *you!*"

That, he thought, *goes double,* and he went for a long and miserable walk. Nothing else to do.

He wondered if his counterpart, his *Doppelgänger,* was out walking too, feeling all the things he felt: the tearing need to get back to his own life situation, but with specific regrets. Perhaps he'd even found Mary *I* something comparable to the things Pete had found in Mary *II.* It was possible, in this intricate business of balances.

Also, he probably had a hating Universe on his back—

At any rate, there was no way out. Or rather, the *only* way was out.

And his double on Earth would be thinking the same thing, for whatever reasons. Identity. Or near identity.

He decided on one last week. Mary seemed reconciled. The reality of the situation, and its necessities, had at last become clear to her; or perhaps she had at last accepted it.

They spent that last week almost as lovers. They went out. Nightclubs, the theater. They had fun together. Their sexual encounters were spiced with a certain feeling of adventure, discovery. They had fallen in love for the second time, really, yet for the first time, really, and they made the most of it—she perhaps unconsciously trying to hold him, he enjoying for the last time the woman Mary *I* was not.

The day they drove to Graden Research Institute, he expected her to cry. But she didn't. She seemed to be thinking.

His tears? . . . They would come later, on lonely Earth. Best if she didn't know how much he cared.

* * *

The machine was bigger than he'd thought it would be. An enormous metal tube running off at a tangent from something very like a cyclotron. At the end of the tube was a metal ball about three feet in diameter, suspended on an equatorial axis. One round red glass eyelet peered out of the surface opposite the end of the tube—peered into a large, open-ended metal box, through which was strung an intricate webwork of wires.

"We wanted to send one atom—just one atom—into another dimension," Enrique Patiño said. "So, I'm almost certain, did our counterparts on your Earth. But we sent our Peter Innes instead. And they sent you to us." He pointed at the two desks that stood back to back across the room. They were heaped high with papers. "We have computed. This has taught us interesting things. It would appear that one atom—and, believe me, our beam would scarcely touch more than one at a time—one atom will insist upon taking the organic whole of which it is a part with it on its trip between dimensions."

"I wonder if I crashed my car, then," Pete mused, "or his. Where's the thin red line? Molecules mixing, the vapor that is me mixed with the vapor that is the car—"

"His, we believe. It would be impossible to say for certain. It is our belief, however, that the phenomenon of transposition-of-the-whole applies only to living matter and all objects within the effective range of its electromagnetic field—"

He talked on.

Pete looked at the machine.

Was another Pete Innes, on another Earth, looking at a machine right now?

He hoped so. And he hoped he was a good man. Mary *II* was a damned good woman.

"Where," he said, "do I get my ticket?"

"This way," called van Husen, from over by the metal ball. He'd been fussing with the round red eye.

"Shouldn't there be a fanfare?" Pete said sourly. "Reporters, cameras? Not that I'm in the mood."

"We—" Enrique Patiño paused. "Understand, Mr. Innes, we would like to delay your departure, at least for a short while, and question you about your Earth. We might have questioned you before, but we had no wish to invade the privacy of your rather peculiar domestic situation. We wanted you to come to us. Now . . . well, I'm afraid we will have to be satisfied with the observations of *our* Peter Innes. Our recent work indicates that it may be very dangerous for you to remain here. Dangerous for you—and for us."

"I've felt it too," Pete said. "Out of tune. I don't jitter right."

"We made our decision this morning. We were preparing to invite you when you came of your own accord."

"And if you'd invited me, and I said no, you'd have called out the Marines."

Patiño smiled an astonishly young smile. "Oh, yes. Actually, we doubt that your introduction into our Universe will affect it for many millions of years. The disruption would have to proceed to fantastically high levels before it would make itself felt. But as scientists, we cannot take the chance of letting you stay any longer. Your influence is theoretically cubed every sixty-one point oh-four-six-nine hours."

"I'm not the same as when I came," Pete said. "I've shed millions of molecules. I've incorporated others. I'm wearing different clothes."

"We must predict some sort of compensating mechanism, and hope we're right."

"Then maybe there's no problem . . . aside from the way I feel?"

Patiño sighed. "Perhaps. But we know so *little* about such things . . . which accounts for the lack of fanfare. After you've gone we will dismantle the machine. The less anyone knows about this line of research, the better. Perhaps, right now, we are being foolish. But perhaps we should be terrified."

"Well," Pete said a little nervously. 'When do we start?"

"Anytime."

"When will *they* start?"

"When we do . . . or vice versa. I believe that identity on that level can be relied on: we seem to be expressions of Universal laws . . ."

"*Now,*" snapped van Husen. "Let's not talk all day."

"If I could only take—a book or something," Pete said.

Patiño shook his head. He took Pete by an arm and stood him in front of the globe. The red glass eye pointed at Pete's forehead.

Pete had said his goodbyes to Mary. He didn't look at her now.

It happened very quickly.

Patiño lifted a hand in farewell.

Van Husen pressed a button somewhere behind the metal ball.

Mary cried. "*Pete—*"

Machinery whined to instant high pitch, drowning her cry.

Mary was in his arms.

The laboratory was about the same. So was the machine. The round red eye lost its brilliancy. The whining stopped.

Everybody just stood and breathed.

Holding Mary, Pete looked around and smiled. He said. "I hardly recognize you without your beard, Dr. van Husen."

Then he said to Mary. "I'm glad you did that. I couldn't ask you to."

Now she was crying. "I—I thought that if I did, then *she* would . . . or maybe *she* thought of it first—"

"You'll like *my* Pete Junior," he said softly. "And the Mary who just left here will be a good mother to yours."

The scientists were coming alive. Ten minutes of gleaming-eyed inquiry followed, after which Pete said that he and Mary would like to get along.

Van Husen trailed them out into the corridor. The other two, an identical Patiño and a somewhat less attractive Hazel Burgess, were busy dismantling the machine.

At the elevator door van Husen said, "You *will* cooperate with us, Mr. Innes?"

"With deepest gratitude," Pete said, and squeezed Mary's arm.

The elevator door opened. Inside was nothing but a steady blue light.

Van Husen said politely. "After you."

Pete said, after a moment, in a dead voice, "It's okay, darling—our elevators are different. Quite different."

Grimly he stepped off into empty blue space five stories above the ground, Mary at his side. Van Husen followed.

They floated on blue light toward the ground floor.

Pete thought: *The only thing to do when you're going down a one-way street to nowhere is pull over to the side: I'll pull over here, I guess: I won't tell Mary: I'll keep quiet, and the others will too.*

His eyes opened wide. *How many others?*

Down.

The ground floor.
We'll just have to see if it's millions of years or tomorrow. Maybe this one won't hate me.
It wasn't tomorrow. And it didn't.

About the Editors

Robert Adams lives in Seminole County, Florida. Like the characters in his books, he is partial to fencing and fancy swordplay, hunting and riding, good food and drink. At one time Robert could be found slaving over a hot forge, making a new sword or busily reconstructing a historically accurate military costume, but, unfortunately, he no longer has time for this as he's far too busy writing.

For more information about Robert Adams and his books, contact the National Horseclans Society, P.O. Box 1770, Apopka, FL 32704-1770.

Martin H. Greenberg has been called (in *The Science Fiction and Fantasy Book Review*) "the King of the Anthologists"; to which he replied, "It's good to be the King!" He has produced more than one hundred of them, usually in collaboration with a multitude of co-conspirators. He is a professor of regional analysis and political science at the University of Wisconsin-Green Bay.

Pamela Crippen Adams is living proof of the dangers of being around science fiction writers. Originally a fan, she now spends her time as an editor and anthologist. When not working at these tasks, she is kept busy by her two dogs and ten cats.